BLACK AS NIGHT

THE DARKWOOD TRILOGY
BOOK TWO

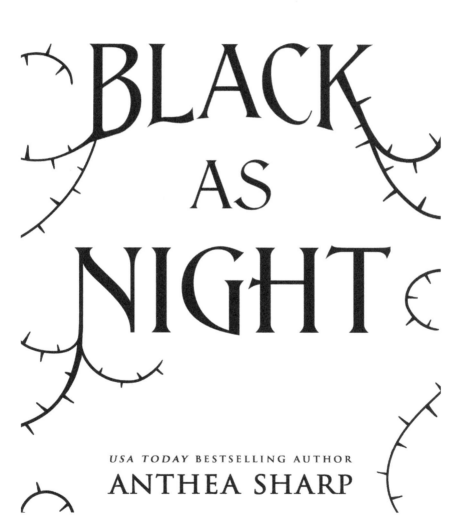

BLACK AS NIGHT

USA TODAY BESTSELLING AUTHOR
ANTHEA SHARP

Cover by Mulan Jiang. Map by Sarah Kellington. Professional editing by LHTemple and Editing720.

Fiddlehead Press
63 Via Pico Plaza #234
San Clemente, CA 92672

ISBN 9781680131468 (hardcover)

Subjects: Siblings - Young Adult Fiction / Fairy Tale & Folklore Adaptations - Young Adult Fiction / Royalty - Young Adult Fiction / Coming of Age Fantasy - Fiction

Visit www.antheasharp.com and join her newsletter for a FREE STORY, plus find out about upcoming releases and reader perks.

QUALITY CONTROL
We care about producing error-free books. If you discover a typo or formatting issue, please contact antheasharp@hotmail so that it may be corrected.

Don't miss the previous Darkwood-set books, ELFHAME, HAWTHORNE, and RAINE, available in print and ebook at all online booksellers.

DEDICATION

For all the sisters,
and especially for Sadie and Charlotte.

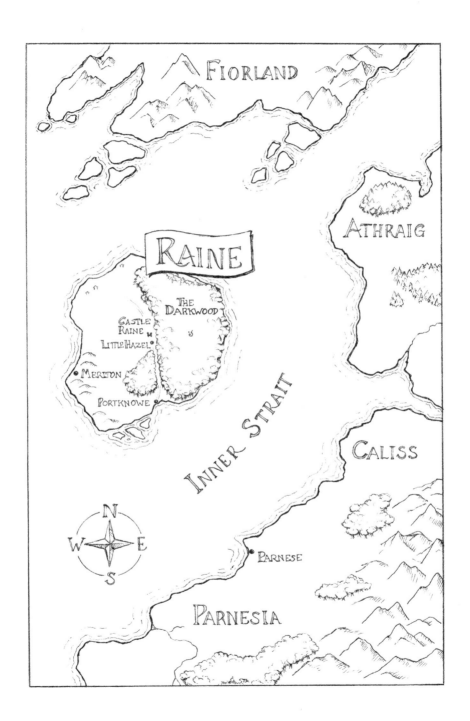

PART I

CHAPTER 1

The second time I traveled from the land of Parnesia to the shadowed forests of Raine, I was sixteen, and no longer a child. Instead of fearing the evergreen trees looming over the long road that ran from the town of Portknowe to the castle, I welcomed the sight. For the Darkwood was home to Thorne, whom I had not seen in months.

My heartbeat quickened at the thought of him, and I shot a guilty glance at the young man sitting across the coach from me. Prince Kian of Fiorland, with his golden hair and generous nature, was the complete opposite of quiet, dark-haired Thorne. And yet, despite my yearning for Thorne, I had to admit that Kian and I had grown close during our recent ordeals in Parnese.

Perhaps closer than was wise. The prince was supposedly meant for my stepsister, Neeve, who even now awaited us at Castle Raine, along with her father, the king.

Sensing my regard, Kian looked at me with a questioning smile.

"Are you ready to be home, Rose?" he asked.

"Yes," I said fervently.

While Castle Raine wasn't quite the home of my heart, it was far removed from Parnese and the threat of the red priests who'd tried to capture us there. Besides, I really had nowhere else to go.

"I'm glad to hear you say so," my mother said tartly from her place beside me on the velvet-upholstered bench. "Perhaps now you'll appreciate what it means to be a princess living in a castle, rather than a fugitive of little means, running desperately through the streets."

As ever, my mother knew just how to jab at me with her words. Only the presence of Kian, and the dour Sir Durum, captain of the king's guard, kept me from a rude reply. No matter what responses the wicked little voice inside of me whispered I should make...

That voice had grown quieter in recent months, however, and I was grateful. Perhaps due to my recent illness, or perhaps because I was growing older, it lacked the violent force that had spurred me into foolish acts in the past. I hoped it would fade away altogether.

And yet I also hoped it didn't. There was a certain wild zest in heeding its promptings toward recklessness.

The coach bumped oddly, and Sir Durum looked up, reaching for his sword. Then, with a crack, the vehicle listed sideways and came to an abrupt halt. I slid nearly on top of Mama, and Kian braced himself to keep from colliding with the captain.

Sir Durum was already opening the door. He sprang out, sword in hand, and Kian was quick to follow.

"What is it?" I called out the gaping door.

A faint drizzle slicked the bushes growing along the low bank, and the air was quiet and misty. It didn't appear that we'd been attacked, and I gently slid my own small dagger back into its sheath at my belt.

"Broken wheel, looks like," the captain said, displeasure clear in his gruff voice.

"Oh dear." Mama shook her head. "I hope we're not trapped here for the night."

I carefully moved to the other side of the coach, so I wouldn't have to remain squashed up against her. "Surely we're not that far from the castle. We've been traveling all day."

"It's an hour away," Sir Durum said, his voice muffled from where he'd bent to inspect the rear wheel.

The coachman joined him, and the two of them pushed at the wheel a bit, making the coach rock.

"We could walk," Kian proposed.

"Certainly not," Mama said. "It's raining. Besides, Rose is still far too weak."

I grimaced, wishing I could argue—but she was right. I was finally recovering from the sickness that had sapped my health for months, but what should be an hour's walk along the muddy road would take me twice that long. If not longer.

It was hard to tell, with the lid of clouds over us, but sundown couldn't be that far off. I glanced at the dark cedars lining the road. When night fell, we wouldn't be safe from the things that roamed the forest.

"Spoke's cracked," Sir Durum announced.

"Well, fix it and we can be on our way," Mama said, as if the captain of the guard were some simple cartman she could order about at will.

He straightened with a scowl. "It's not that simple. Your majesty," he added belatedly.

I knew he disliked my mother. After all, she'd abruptly married his liege, the King of Raine, three years ago, while the king was visiting Parnese—the very city we'd just fled. Their sudden wedding had come as a surprise to everyone. Myself included. Not that Mama had ever seen fit to let me know what she was thinking. She lived her life for herself, and no one else.

Certainly not for a troublesome daughter, as I'd been reminded throughout my entire existence.

Despite the rain, I clambered out of the coach, ignoring my mother's outstretched hand. I wished Thorne would appear from that shadowy wall of trees to rescue us, but it was late autumn, and quickly dimming into winter.

Thorne was gone by now—I knew it, though I hated the fact. Every fall he returned to Elfhame, the homeland of the Dark Elves, and didn't return until spring. Six long, dreary months would pass before I could hope to see him again.

The driver and Sir Durum began discussing the possibility of lashing stout branches on either side of the cracked spoke, the way one might splint a broken bone. I moved around to the back of the coach, which provided a little shelter from the rain, and Kian followed. Our boots squelched over the muddy ground. I let out a sigh, thinking of the dry climate of Parnesia.

"Don't worry," Kian said. "We'll be on our way soon."

"I know." At least, I hoped so.

"I wonder how Neeve is doing," he said.

I scanned his face, searching for a hint of fondness for my stepsister. "Did you miss her?"

A shadow of guilt, an echo of my own previous emotion, crossed his face, though the expression passed almost before I could see it.

"I just don't want her to get ahead of me in sword work," he said.

I let out a dry laugh. "I doubt that's possible. Are you fishing for compliments?"

"Are you giving me one?" He winked at me, and I felt my cheeks heat, suddenly too aware of how close together we were standing.

One more step, and I could be in his arms.

Oh, but this was no good.

Kian was fostering at Castle Raine in order to promote goodwill between the kingdom of Raine and his home country of Fiorland. The result of which, I'd been explicitly informed, was his expected marriage to Neeve.

Why? I railed inside. *Why does my stepsister get both Kian and Thorne, while I have no one?*

Because you don't deserve them, my spiteful voice suggested. I ignored it and clenched my teeth against the sour reminder that, as usual, I was on my own.

"Do you think we're safe from pursuit?" I glanced down the empty road behind us.

The thought of the red priests made a shiver run up my spine, and I drew my cloak more tightly about my shoulders.

"Their leader fell," Kian said. "The priests of the Twin Gods have other things to worry about, even if he's only wounded."

Warder Galtus Celcio would recover, I had no doubt. But the sorcerous red priests weren't welcome in Raine. I tried to tell myself that we were safe here, across the water. Besides, the island of Raine had allies no one else knew about—warriors who could wield magic unknown in the human world. Surely the Dark Elves would be able to repel the fire priests, if it came to that.

Which it wouldn't. I clung to the thought, to the belief that I was safe here. Even if it wasn't precisely true.

Faint lights bobbed in the depth of the forest, and I leaned forward, blinking. Was someone coming? *Thorne,* my heart insisted, though I knew it couldn't be.

"Do you see it?" I touched Kian's shoulder.

He followed my gaze, brows drawing together in a frown. "Too high for lanterns."

Glimglows, then—the mystical balls of radiance that had led me to the gateway located in the secret heart of the Darkwood. I began to move forward, and Kian caught my arm.

"Rose, what are you doing?" he asked roughly. "You know better than to follow glowing lights into the forest. Especially at dusk."

"But..." The argument died on my lips. The lights were gone.

And, if I was honest with myself, they hadn't been the golden color of glimglows, but a marshy greenish-blue. Wisps, the tales called such things, luring travelers to their doom.

"I wasn't going to," I lied.

Kian shook his head at me and released my arm. "Just because we've been gone doesn't mean the Darkwood suddenly turned safe in our absence."

He was right. In addition to the normal dangers of any wild woods, this one held all manner of magical threats. Poison-clawed drakes, sharp-mouthed boglins, nixies lurking in pools perfect for drowning unwary humans: I'd encountered them all and had no wish to repeat any of those experiences.

The stub of pinky on my left hand hurt. I rubbed it through my glove, wondering if the dampness was making the old injury ache. I was also reminded that I carried the forest's sigil—a leaf of binding inscribed on my inner arm. Not that it had done much to protect me. Rather the opposite, in fact.

"That should do," the coachman said, tying off the leather strapping he and Sir Durum had used to affix splints to the broken spoke. "We'll take it slow."

The bracken on either side of the road stirred, and for a moment I saw the outline of sticklike figures with sharp, serrated teeth.

"In you go," Sir Durum said, gesturing to me. "Be quick, the light's going."

I was well aware of the fact. Hastily, I gathered my skirts and, with Kian's assistance, climbed back into the coach. He followed, then Sir Durum came in, a bit gingerly, as if unsure the wheel would hold.

No rush of boglins rustled in at his heels, and I let out a quiet breath of relief. It seemed the Darkwood would let us pass without incident. This time.

The vehicle dipped as the coachman clambered up to his seat, and then we rocked into motion. The wheel gave an ominous creak. Mama let out a little gasp, hand going to her throat, but the repair seemed sufficient. We were on our way once more.

❧

SILVERY TWILIGHT HAD FADED into the charcoal of night by the time we finally reached Castle Raine. It had stopped raining, though mist veiled the air and gathered thickly in my lungs with every breath. Another stab of homesickness for the dry climate of Parnesia went through me—but despite my sun-warmed childhood memories, that place was no longer mine.

Torches mounted on either side of the castle gate sent wild shadows flickering across the stone walls as we passed, the teeth of the portcullis glinting darkly overhead. The coach clattered over the cobblestones in the front courtyard. At the sound of our arrival, a half-dozen servants filed out of the castle. They arrayed themselves along the steps, wet granite reflecting the thin flames of their lanterns.

We had arrived.

The coach rocked to a halt, the mended wheel creaking again. Though it had delayed our arrival, I hadn't minded. Part of me wanted to stay in the forest forever, away from the hard truths awaiting me at the castle. Away from Neeve's dark gaze, and the inescapable knowledge that I was, always, second best.

Kian, ever the courtier, jumped out to assist my mother from the vehicle. Sir Durum followed more stiffly, then turned and offered his hand to me.

"Thank you," I said, setting my gloved fingers in his.

It was a kind gesture on his part. While I wished I could step down from the coach without help, I was glad of his steadying grip. The smell of damp cedar wreathed around me. Beyond the castle walls, the evergreens of the Darkwood hushed, stirred by the night breeze.

At the top of the long set of steps, the doors leading into the great hall swung wide and the King of Raine strode through. My stepsister, Neeve, accompanied him, a pale, dark-haired shadow at his side. They descended to where we stood at the bottom of the stairs. A long rectangle of light cast from the open doors reached before them, giving the illusion of welcome.

"I'm glad you've returned safely, Arabelle," the king said, holding his hands out to my mother. "I was worried when I heard you'd braved the ocean storms to cross the Strait."

"It was time," my mother said simply, giving him a kiss on the cheek.

I sent her a sharp look. Had she not told her husband of our desperate flight from Parnese? Sir Durum grunted, low in his throat, and I knew the captain would fully inform the king of all that had transpired—no matter what soft illusion of the truth my mother preferred.

"Princess Neeve." Kian stepped forward, the lantern light glinting off his golden hair as he bowed to my stepsister. "It's good to see you after so many months. I trust you're well?"

"I am—and apparently better than Rose." Neeve glanced at me. "You look terrible."

I bared my teeth at her, secretly amused that her direct manner hadn't changed. "I'm glad to see you again, too."

Her mouth twitched, though with amusement or scorn, I couldn't quite tell. Neeve had always been skilled at hiding her emotions.

"Your rooms are ready," the king said, holding his arm out to my mother.

"Good—it was a tiring journey." She slipped her hand around his elbow and let him lead her into the castle.

Kian did the same for Neeve, which left me with Sir Durum. He grudgingly stuck his arm out in my direction. With a nod of thanks, I set one hand on his forearm and picked up my travel-worn skirts with the other. Silently, we followed the others into the clammy recesses of Castle Raine.

CHAPTER 2

At the landing leading to the family wing, Sir Durum abandoned me for his other duties, leaving me to trail behind Neeve and Kian. Exhaustion weighted my steps, though I did my best to keep pace with my stepsister and the prince. As we traversed the dim corridors, Kian brought his considerable charm to bear, and I saw Neeve smile at him—a rare expression indeed.

Jealousy flared in my chest, sharp and bright, but I ruthlessly tamped it down. No matter what feelings I might have for Kian, he must be my friend, and nothing more.

When we reached the heavy carved door of my suite, he stepped away from Neeve and turned to me, concern in his eyes.

"Will you be all right by yourself?" he asked.

"Why wouldn't she be?" Neeve's voice held a hint of impatience. "She's not a child any longer."

"Yes, but..." Kian trailed off, studying my face.

With a shock, I realized it would be the first time in months I'd go to bed without anyone close by. Not my mother, not Sir Durum, and especially not Kian, who'd helped care for me so gently during my long recovery. If not for him, I doubted I'd be standing there. Not on my own two feet, at any rate.

"I'll be fine," I said, mustering up a smile for his sake. "I can ring for Sorche if I need anything."

Assuming she was still my maid. Yet surely not that much had changed at the castle, though I'd been away over five months.

"Take care then, Rose." He lifted his hand as if to smooth my hair, then, with a glance at Neeve, checked the motion. "Good night."

I nodded and wearily pushed my door open. "Good night, you two."

No matter how witty and warm Kian could be, Neeve's icy demeanor wasn't so easily melted, I reminded myself. She was in no danger of rashly losing her heart to anyone. Unlike myself. Though whether it was Thorne or Kian I preferred, I could not say with any certainty.

I might as well try to decide whether I loved the moon better, or the sun. Both were equally out of reach, sailing across the sky far overhead and unconcerned with the yearnings of a mortal girl.

"I'll help you get ready," Neeve said, unexpectedly stepping forward. "Sleep well, Kian."

She left him standing there, blinking, and I couldn't help waggling my fingers at him as the door shut in his face.

A cheery fire burned in the small hearth of my sitting room, pushing away the chill of impending winter. I turned, glad to see my books and a few trinkets arrayed on the shelves: a dark river-polished stone the exact color of Thorne's eyes, a downy owl's feather I'd found in a thicket, a bronze music box I'd brought with me from Parnese the first time I came to Raine.

"Why is he so exhausting?" Neeve asked, as she went to take one of the chairs before the fire. "I don't know how you could have stood his company, day after day."

"It wasn't so bad," I said, sinking into the other chair and trying not to blush. Hopefully, she'd attribute the color in my cheeks to the sudden warmth of the flames.

"Oh, yes, you were sick for most of that time." She regarded me levelly, and once again I was struck by the pallor of her face, the redness of her lips. "How are you feeling now?"

"Tired," I admitted. "It took me longer to recover than anyone wanted."

"But the doctor you went to Parnese to see—they cured you. Didn't they?"

"I'm here now, aren't I?"

In truth, I didn't remember anything about that visit, or what the doctor had done. I'd been delirious for weeks, unable to walk, or even think. The early portion of our time in Parnese was a fever-smeared blur in my mind.

Neeve studied me, a faint line between her brows. "You don't look cured."

"It was a hard journey."

She tilted her head, mild sympathy in her eyes. Had our positions been reversed, I would've been burning with interest, questions sparking from my tongue.

Yet the fact that she didn't press me for information made it easier to tell her some of what had transpired: our sudden, desperate flight from our lodgings, dodging the red priests at the harbor, the smuggler who'd finally agreed to help us out of the city.

Of the stranger events that had befallen us, I did not speak.

Had the red-haired leader of the priests of the Twin Gods truly summoned a massive fireball and flung it at us as we escaped? And had I really been able to wrest control of that deadly blaze and plunge it beneath the waves? It seemed a fever dream.

And it was impossible. Both Thorne and Mistress Ainya, the herb-wife, had confirmed that I had not a shred of magical ability.

Not as Neeve did, inherited from the Dark Elf mother she'd never known. The power of the elves was something I could not understand. Nor acquire, no matter how much I might yearn to. Though in turn, she could not wield the sorcerous fire that a rare number of humans controlled.

I leaned back in my chair, knowing I would tell my stepsister about the encounter with the priests...eventually. Surprisingly, we kept few secrets from one another. Though the names I carried in my heart were none of her business.

"How was your summer?" I asked, hoping to steer the conversation to Thorne.

"Uninteresting."

I let out a short, annoyed breath. It seemed I'd have to remind Neeve how to conduct a proper conversation once again. She'd clearly lost the ability during my absence.

"Don't huff at me," she said. "Or have you forgotten that when you left, the creatures of the Darkwood were stirring?"

"I didn't forget." How could I, when I still bore the scars from the wicked-clawed drake that had attacked us? "Does that mean you didn't spend all your afternoons in the forest?"

She frowned slightly. "No. Thorne was much occupied in strengthening the magical barrier protecting the Darkwood. We scarcely had a moment for my lessons—though I did learn about the wards surrounding the forest."

"Well, I suppose that's good."

I tried to suppress the flare of joy her words ignited. If I had to be deprived of Thorne all summer, it eased my pain to know that Neeve had not seen much of him either.

She gave me a sour look, as if sensing my thoughts.

"What else did you do?" I asked hurriedly, trying to divert her.

Although Neeve suspected how I felt about Thorne, the subject was not one I wanted to discuss. The one time we'd spoken openly of it, we quarreled. Badly. That grudge had lasted far too long.

My stepsister lifted one shoulder in a half shrug and didn't answer.

"I suppose you went out riding," I said, filling in the details she hadn't bothered to furnish. "And weapons training?"

Two things I wasn't particularly fond of, though my horsemanship had improved over the years. Not to her level, of course. The only ability I possessed that surpassed Neeve's was my musical talent, and she'd abandoned that field of competition fairly quickly. Drat her prickly Dark Elf pride.

"I worked on my sword training, of course," she said. "And herbalism with Mistress Ainya. And the normal schooling, though

Miss Groves didn't cover a great deal of material. She didn't want you to fall too far behind."

"Kind of her," I said dryly.

We sat in companionable silence a moment, my thoughts blunted with exhaustion as the warmth of the fire pressed into my skin.

"I reread the book," Neeve said at last.

I glanced at her. There was no need to ask which book. She could only mean *Elfhame: A Studie of the Dark Elves and Their Wayes*, which I'd discovered hidden in the library last year. Knowledge of its existence was one of our deepest shared secrets.

"Did you learn anything new?" I asked.

Though I'd read the book before giving it to Neeve, I hadn't fully grasped it. The account of the Dark Elves' homeland had been written in an archaic form of our language, the history rich with strange details and stranger customs.

"Yes." Yearning tinged her voice, a mist of sorrow and resentment sheening her eyes.

She could never set foot there, in the enchanted land that was her birthright.

Had it been kind of me to give her the book, or cruel? Not for the first time, I wondered if laying that tome in her open hands had been a mistake.

❦

THE NEXT MORNING, my maid Sorche—who was only a few years older than myself—appeared at my bedside with a cup of tea and a hesitant smile. Dim light filtered through the thick velvet drapes covering the windows, giving the impression that the world was underwater. With a soft groan, I pulled the pillow over my head.

"Good day, Miss Rose," Sorche said in her gentle voice. "Will you be rising now? I understand Miss Groves is expecting to see you in the classroom today."

Slowly, I uncovered my face, blinking against the residue of sleep that hazed my brain.

"I suppose," I said. "Would you open the curtains?" If I wasn't allowed to sleep any longer, I'd best get on with the business of waking up.

Sorche set the tea on my bedside table and went to the windows. A moment later, the soft gray light of October in Raine filtered into the room. With a sigh, I sat up and began drinking my tea.

"Will you need help in dressing?" the maid asked.

I wanted to tell her no, that I was perfectly fine—but the effort it took for me to hold my cup steady was proof enough that the journey had taxed my already low stores of energy.

"Perhaps, just for today," I admitted.

Sorche bobbed a quick acknowledgment and went to my wardrobe. She folded open the doors, and it was strange to see the rows of gowns hanging there. Due to the hastiness of our departure from Raine, my choice of attire in Parnese had been limited to two gowns and the nightdress I'd been wearing when they bore me out of the castle.

Not that it had mattered, once we were in hiding. There had been nothing to dress *for*.

"This one?" Sorche asked, pulling out a slate-colored gown.

I nodded. Not the most flattering color—I preferred the brighter golds and reds—but it would do well enough. Especially since I wouldn't be meeting Thorne anytime soon, and Kian had seen me at my worst. Far too often.

"Heavens," Sorche said as she helped me into the dress, "how thin you are. I'm not sure I can fasten the back tightly enough."

"Do your best."

I regarded myself in the wardrobe's mirrored door. My maid was right: the gown hung off my frame as though it had been made for a bigger girl, the fabric lying in slack folds where once it had hugged my figure. My cheeks were hollow, shadows smudged beneath my eyes. Even my hair had lost some of its exuberant spring, the color faded to dim copper.

Neeve's assessment the night before had been right: I looked dreadful.

But I was recovering, little by little.

"Maybe a sash, to help hold it up?" Sorche asked, glancing down to where the skirts dragged on the floor.

I gave her a crooked smile. "Worth a try."

She looped a green scarf about my waist, hitching the gown up so I wouldn't trip. The fabric bloused around my middle, but it would serve.

"We're not setting any fashions," I said wryly. "But at least I won't break my neck going down the stairs. Thank you."

"I'm glad you're back, miss," Sorche said, gathering up my empty teacup as she prepared to depart.

"Me too." At least the castle provided shelter and companionship, and whatever vestiges of family I had.

Do I belong anywhere?

I thrust the question back into the gaping abyss it had emerged from. The ache running through me was from the lingering effects of my illness, I told myself. Surely it, too, would heal.

Or at least scab over.

My suite seemed very quiet after Sorche left, and I was glad that at least I had the run of the castle. I'd spent far too many recent weeks trapped in one small apartment in Parnese—even if I scarcely had the strength to walk from room to room. Here, I had the roam of the hallways, the classroom, the library, and perhaps even Master Fawkes' study. I wondered if the master bard had returned to Castle Raine yet for the season. Even if he had, though, I wasn't at all sure I'd have the energy to immediately resume my studies upon the harp.

A soft knock came at the door, and I went to open it, expecting Neeve.

"I'm almost ready," I said, then froze in the act of pulling the door wide. The dark-haired figure standing at my threshold wasn't my stepsister.

It was Thorne.

My pulse jolted, and I had to remind myself to breathe as I studied the lean planes of his face and sharp cheekbones, the quirk of his eyebrows, how one pointed ear showed through the silky black fall of his hair.

"What...what are you doing here?" I sent a hurried glance up and down the hall. "Did anyone see you? Come in."

I stumbled back, nearly tripping over my skirts.

Thorne stepped smoothly forward and caught my elbow. "Take care, Rose."

The sound of his voice swept through me, turning my limbs to honey. Without his steadying grip, I might have melted entirely to the floor. He swung the door closed behind us then guided me to one of the chairs before the hearth. I settled gratefully, struggling to control my careening emotions: overwhelming joy tempered by the acute awareness of my wretched state, along with shock that he was even in the castle at all.

"I wanted to see you," he said.

The words warmed me far more than any cup of tea ever could.

"I missed you terribly," I blurted, then dropped my gaze to my hands. *Never let Thorne know how desperately you care for him,* I scolded myself. Nothing but pain could come from such an admission.

"And I missed you." He reached over, gently lifting my chin with his cool fingers. "When you left, I wasn't certain you'd survive."

I met his gaze, unsure if I'd imagined the slight waver in his voice. His dark eyes, flecked with amber, were as mysterious as the still pools of the Darkwood.

"What about your duties? The Oracles? I thought you couldn't leave your homeland during the winter." The questions spilled from me like water from an overturned pitcher.

The corners of his mouth turned up in a fleeting smile. "As curious as ever, I see. That's a relief. As to your questions, I can depart Elfhame for a short time and cross through the gate, if the need is great enough."

Was I truly that important to him? My flare of joy at the thought was quickly extinguished by his next words.

"I'm here to speak with King Tobin," he continued. "The Oracles and I have a plan, but he needs to help prepare as well. Come next summer, we must ensure that the protections about the Darkwood are impenetrable."

"Why next summer?" I tried not to show my bitter disappointment. He hadn't come to Castle Raine to see me after all. With effort, I kept my breathing shallow, so that I wouldn't succumb to the hot tears building in my throat. So that I wouldn't drown in his scent of cedar and wild magic.

"The *nirwen* harvest is coming," he said. "It's essential we hold our secrets close, now more than ever."

I nodded. Had it already been nearly three years since I discovered the gateway hidden in the depths of the Darkwood? It felt like only yesterday—yet it also seemed I'd spent an eternity lost to illness.

"What about Kian?" I asked. "Will the Fiorlanders be allowed the knowledge of Raine's secrets?"

"Not yet." Thorne's voice held an edge.

"But what if he and Neeve—"

"They are young. Another three years isn't too long to wait before making any rash decisions."

"She's almost seventeen," I reminded him. "And Kian is a year older, oh most ancient of *Galadhirs*."

I couldn't help my tart words. Thorne, despite his responsibilities, was only a handful of years older than me and Neeve. Even if he wanted to pretend otherwise.

A hint of exasperation flashed across his sharp-planed face. "And yet I am so much wiser. Please, trust me. The balance between the worlds is precarious enough as it is. We don't need to add the Fiorland prince into the mix."

"Have you reminded Neeve of this?"

"She knows. The secrets of Elfhame will remain closely guarded." He stood. "I must go. The king is expecting me."

"Wait." I rose, then swayed as a wave of dizziness swirled my senses.

Thorne grasped my shoulders, and for a moment I felt the warmth of his breath against my cheek. Something flickered in his eyes, and I leaned forward, my chest suddenly filled with stars.

Then his expression shuttered and he took a half step back, letting go of me.

"Sit down before you fall down," he said shortly.

"But...when will I see you again?" I couldn't hide my plaintive tone.

"In the spring, as usual." His expression softened. "Don't worry—it will come soon enough."

"For you," I retorted, gripping the back of my chair for balance. "It's very unfair that time moves differently in your land."

"Yet we cannot change it." His lips tilted into a crooked smile. "Rest. Regain your strength. You do not look well, Rose."

I could feel a blush heating my cheeks. Of course Thorne would see me at my most dreadful.

A knock came at the door, and it swung open before I could answer, revealing Neeve standing at the threshold.

Her brows rose as she glanced from me to Thorne.

"Have you come to meet with my father?" she asked him.

"Yes." He straightened and strode to the door. "And I'm late. Look after your sister."

"Stepsister," Neeve murmured, but stood aside as he brushed past her.

He paused, briefly setting his hand on her upper arm. "Take care, the both of you. I'll see you in a few months."

She inclined her head. "Goodbye, Thorne."

Then he was gone, leaving a gaping emptiness behind him.

"Well." Neeve turned to face me. "I didn't expect to see him in your rooms."

"Me either," I admitted. "He said he was worried about me."

She gave a short nod. "It was unclear whether you'd ever return to Raine."

Meaning, I supposed, that they thought I might die. Not very comforting.

"Did *you* think I'd come back?" I asked.

The corners of her mouth twitched up in the faintest of smiles. "Of course. Now, are you coming to the classroom or not? The maids will be delivering our breakfast soon, and I'm hungry."

She didn't wait for me to answer but stepped back into the hallway. It was a rhetorical question, anyway. Where else did I have to go? There was no point in cooping myself up in my rooms, moping over the unfairness of life.

As we traversed the hallways, Neeve slowed her steps to match my pace. That, even more than her matter-of-fact confidence that I'd return to the castle, made my heart open a bit more.

And I'd seen Thorne! For all too short a time, but still—it was a memory that could sustain me until spring greened the grasses and coaxed the first flowers into bloom.

I tried not to hope that we'd encounter him as we went to the northwest turret. Our classroom was the opposite direction from the king's study and council room.

"Rose!" Miss Groves met us at the door and enfolded me in a warm embrace. "I'm so pleased you're back with us. My, you're as a fragile as a bird."

She stepped back and looked me up and down, and I regarded her in turn. Her grayish-brown hair and eyes were the same as ever, her forehead marked with a faint line of concern.

"If only I could fly like one," I said wryly.

"I'll have the kitchens send up extra sweet rolls tomorrow," Miss Groves said, returning to her desk. "Now, let's see how much you recall of the early philosophers of Turima."

"Not much," I admitted.

We'd just begun studying them when I fell ill. Something about how life was shadows and the truth lay beyond our grasp. I dredged up what I could remember from the murky waters of my brain. Truly, I hadn't much liked their views, and it was easy to forget things one didn't enjoy.

"Is Kian joining us today?" Neeve asked, going to her seat at the long table facing Miss Groves' desk.

"He's otherwise engaged this week," the teacher said. "He'll rejoin us soon."

A soft knock came at the door, and two maids stepped in, bearing our breakfast trays. I was happy to see that they'd brought boiled eggs, fried potatoes, slices of apple, and the large sweet rolls the cook was renowned for making.

It had taken some time for my appetite to return, but now that it was back, hunger prowled restlessly in my belly. The scent of warm cinnamon was intoxicating. I took a large bite of roll and washed it down with a swallow of tea before looking up at Miss Groves again.

"What's Kian doing, anyhow?" I already missed his constant, sunny presence.

"Meeting with the king and the Fiorland emissary. Jarl Eiric has been concerned about his prince's long absence. And after that, I understand Kian is eager to resume his advanced weapons training."

"That's not fair." Neeve set her fork down with a clank. "Why can't I miss school for a week? Sword work is important to me, too."

"You've spent plenty of time these past months in the practice arena," Miss Groves said. "And you know as well as I that our pace in the classroom has been slow, due to Rose's absence."

"You didn't need to wait," I said, shifting a little with guilt. "I mean, Neeve is the princess, not me. Her education shouldn't suffer because I was ill."

"It didn't," Neeve said. "Being a monarch involves more than just book learning."

Miss Groves leaned forward with an intent look. "That may be so... but the theories of governance put forth by Plavelli are well worth studying. Shall we begin? Page thirty-two. Follow along while you finish your breakfasts."

She nodded to the heavy tomes set at our places. With a sigh, and slightly sticky fingers, I opened the book.

After Plavelli, we moved to mathematics, then a discussion of how geography influenced trade. By the end, my stomach was growling again, and weariness settled on my shoulders like a leaden cloak. The maids finally came in with lunch, and Miss Groves declared the morning lessons at an end.

With a deep sigh, I stretched out my arms. My body felt tired and so did my brain, unused to the rigors of sitting and wrestling with scholarly thought for hours.

"Weapons practice after lunch," Neeve said, glancing at me.

Detecting the faint concern in her eyes, I gave her a weak smile. "Wonderful."

Though it wasn't, particularly.

If I had to move about, I'd far prefer a slow walk through the rain-shrouded gardens to clumsy knife attacks against straw dummies. I dreaded how much I'd probably unlearned during my illness.

In Parnese, Sir Durum had made no mention of attempting to resume my weapons training—sparing both of us that particular frustration. I was terrible at all forms of combat. Our prior lessons had brought him nearly to his wits' end. I'd proved hopeless with swords, useless with a bow, spear, mace...

The only thing I could brandish with any kind of competence was a dagger little bigger than a kitchen knife. I could throw it with deadly accuracy, but once it was gone, I was defenseless. The arms master had made it clear that skill with an assassin's blade was no substitute for proficiency with *real* weapons.

Still, the hearty lunch of stew and bread revived my flagging energy. I even kept up with Neeve as we went back to our rooms to change into our training clothes. Perhaps I wouldn't embarrass myself too badly during training. Besides, Sir Durum knew the extent of my illness. Surely the weapons master would take that into account and keep his expectations low.

CHAPTER 3

"Point your blade higher," Sir Durum said to me, his tone gruff. "Have you completely forgotten how to hold a knife?"

I adjusted my grip, ignoring the gritty perspiration on my forehead. All hope that the arms master would go easy on me had fled the moment I stepped into the sawdust-floored training arena. Sir Durum had directed Neeve to face off against Kian, then brusquely told me to practice lunging against one of the stationary targets.

I'd assumed a fighting stance and landed a few weak blows before he stopped me, shaking his head.

"We'll have to start from the beginning, I see. Wrap your thumb more tightly around the grip. Now, hold your center of gravity."

He pushed my shoulder, and I swayed but managed not to stumble out of my fighter's crouch. Already I could feel my legs starting to tremble from the strain of holding the position.

Across the arena, Neeve and Kian were nimbly dancing about one another, swords flashing. The musical clash of their blades provided a counterpoint to my rasping breaths. Both of them seemed as skilled as ever, and once more I despaired. Why did my body insist on being so clumsy?

"Aim for the ribs," Sir Durum said, pointing at the straw dummy before me. "Then angle the blade up."

I nodded and lunged forward once more, stabbing my knife into the vaguely human-shaped target. The blade stuck in the straw, and I grunted as I tried to push it upward.

The weapons master gave me a dour look. "Again."

After three more tries, each worse than the last, I glanced at him.

"Might I rest a moment?" I asked timidly.

He let out a grunt that I took as an affirmative. Slowly, I straightened. My limbs felt like limp rags, squeezed of all strength. I drew a shaky arm over my sweaty forehead.

"Be gentle with her," Kian called, sparing me a glance.

Neeve took his momentary distraction as an opportunity to dart forward, but he leaped back and parried her blow. I was glad to see they'd donned protective leather chest pieces and armguards. Their days of training with wooden practice swords were long past.

"I'm all right," I said, trying to deny the dizziness sweeping over me.

Sir Durum studied me a moment, expression impassive.

"Sit," he finally said, gesturing to one of the hay bales scattered around the edges of the arena.

I sheathed my blade, then wobbled over to the bale and sank down with a sigh. How long would it take me to regain the basic strength I seemed to have lost?

A rustle behind me made me sit up straight and glance over my shoulder. Mice? I couldn't believe Sir Durum would allow rodents in his training arena, although there were mice dwelling in the castle. Even a large, cold pile of stones was better than a muddy hole in the ground, I supposed.

The noise came again, and I peered into the shadows. Whatever it was sounded larger than a mouse. Sudden worry seized me; maybe a creature from the Darkwood had breached the walls. Thus far, my encounters with the denizens of the forest had not been pleasant, with the exception of the White Hart. Even the bear that saved me on my first journey to Castle Raine had been terrifying.

A pair of glowing eyes flashed from the darkness, and I let out a yelp of surprise. Not a loud one, but Neeve still heard it.

"Hold," she said to Kian, then looked over at me. "What is it?"

"Something's there." I gestured to the back wall. "Some sort of animal."

"It's just a cat," Neeve said.

"A cat?"

"Aye," Sir Durum said. "One of the kitchen cats whelped here over the summer. They've all left, except the runt."

I glanced into the shadows again. "The runt? What's its name?"

Sir Durum gave a dismissive shrug. "It's a runt. It doesn't have a name. Neeve, Kian, back to sparring—your attack-defend sequences need work."

Neeve raised an eyebrow at me, then pivoted back to Kian, blade flashing. Grinning, he met her assault, and I was forgotten. Sir Durum turned his attention to them, and I let out a breath of relief as his heavy gaze moved elsewhere.

Even though he knew how sick I'd been, the weight of his expectation was like a pile of stones upon my shoulders. Luckily, there was a distraction at hand.

I swiveled on the prickly straw, searching for a sign of the cat. Nothing moved in the shadows, but that didn't mean it wasn't there.

"Hello, kitten." I waggled my fingers. "You can come out."

During my childhood in Parnese, I'd adopted all manner of street creatures: cats, dogs, birds, squirrels, even lizards and snakes. My mother, however, had refused to harbor any of them—especially the reptiles—and so I'd had to be content with slipping treats to the dogs that slept in the alleyways and the cats sunning themselves on ledges, or sprinkling a handful of crumbs for the birds flocking the square beside the fountain.

Now, however, I had my own suite of rooms to use as I pleased. Even to keep a cat, provided the feline was inclined to let itself to be befriended.

"Kitkit," I coaxed. "Here, kitten."

A pair of yellow-green eyes blinked at me from the gap between the hay bale and the wall. Then, slowly, the cat emerged. Its fur was the color of smudged charcoal, and it moved with a strange, lurching gait.

As it rounded the bale, I saw why. Its left hind leg was missing. Involuntarily, I glanced at the stub of pinky on my left hand. Although losing a leg would be far worse than a mere finger, I felt as though we matched in some way.

"Were you born like that?" I asked the cat. "I wasn't—not that it matters. You seem to be getting along perfectly well."

The cat sat down just out of reach, blinked once, then began grooming itself. It was a female, and small, as Sir Durum had said. And clearly not inclined to being sociable. Well, I could work with that. I'd befriended Neeve, after all.

"Rose," Sir Durum called. "Back to your lunges."

I glanced at him and nodded. When I looked back, the cat was gone.

❧❧

FOR ONCE, I looked forward to weapons training, as it meant I could try to entice the cat out with bits of my leftover lunch. The next day she was nowhere to be seen, but the practice after that she accepted a morsel of cheese. I had to lay it on the ground first and pull away before she'd come near, but I hoped she'd eventually accept food from my hand.

"Why bother with a three-legged runt?" Neeve asked as we headed for the arena, giving a pointed glance to the napkin I'd folded around the few scraps of chicken I spared from my meal.

Because I'm lonely, I wanted to say. But my stepsister didn't understand that emotion, and I didn't want her to think me weak.

"It gives me something to do during my rest breaks. Watching you and Kian whack at each other is tiresome."

"You might learn something," she replied, a hint of frost in her tone, though she knew I was teasing.

"I'm as hopeless with weapons as you are with music."

"But only one of those things is useful," she countered.

Stung, I blinked at her. "Maybe in this backwater kingdom that's true. But culture is prized on the Continent."

She was silent a long moment, shadows moving over her expression.

"There's only one place I care about," she finally said. "And it isn't your precious Parnese."

It wasn't Raine, either, for all that she was destined to inherit the throne.

It was Elfhame. The land of her mother's people, the Dark Elves. And her birthright.

Sudden sympathy pricked my conscience. Maybe Neeve *did* know what it was to feel desperately alone. She simply hid it perfectly.

"Would you like to help me name the cat?" I asked.

"Not particularly," she said, striding forward.

Then again, maybe she was as cold and unfeeling as everyone thought. Still, I'd seen the pain in her eyes when she thought of Elfhame. I trotted a few steps to catch up with her.

"I don't suppose there's a Rainish word for three-legged?" I asked. "Tripod, trifoot..."

"Triskele," she said.

"Oh, that's perfect! Trisk for short."

"Just because you've decided on a name doesn't mean the creature will answer to it."

"I know. But names have power—you know that." And Thorne had warned us to be careful about such things within the Darkwood. "I mean, the hobnies didn't tell us their names, but you've called upon them all the same."

"Because they owe us. At least, some of them still do." She gave me a warning look as we rounded the corner leading to the training arena.

I nodded. Best if Kian didn't overhear. The Fiorlanders might be Raine's allies, but the secrets of the Darkwood were ours to protect.

As Neeve went to don her leather armor, I headed for my usual hay bale. Sir Durum would put me through my lunge practice soon enough, but I couldn't wait to try to lure the cat to come to me.

"Here, kitten," I called softly, unwrapping the bits of chicken. "Triskele."

I perched on the edge of the bale, ignoring the prick of straw through my trousers. Two yellow-green eyes blinked at me from the shadows. Clicking my tongue against my teeth, I held out a piece of chicken.

The cat moved forward, her body dipping up and down as she hopped on her back foot. She came close...but not close enough to take the morsel from my hand.

"Come now," I said.

Slowly, she leaned forward, sniffing the air. I held my breath, waiting. She was almost near enough—

"Rose!" Sir Durum barked.

I jumped, and the cat skittered back into the shadows. With a sigh, I set the chicken down and wiped my fingers on the corner of the napkin.

"Stop lollygagging," the weapons master continued. "Your enemies won't wait politely for you to be ready."

"Yes, sir," I said, rising.

I cast a regretful glance over my shoulder, loosened my knife in its sheath, and went to force my body through the knife-training moves. At least I was getting stronger, though no less clumsy.

After a brief set of warmups, Sir Durum nodded for me to attack the straw-filled dummy that was my usual opponent. I widened my stance, blew a breath out through my nose, and began.

Flex the knees. Adjust my grip on the knife handle. Lunge, striking out from the shoulder. I tried to settle into the rhythm of it, even as my legs burned with effort.

"Again," Sir Durum said as my blade went wide for the fifth time in a row. "Aim for the heart, not the belly."

I bit my lower lip in concentration and didn't tell him I *had* been aiming for the heart. In my peripheral vision, Neeve and Kian were a graceful swirl of movement as they darted forward and back, blades flashing.

I can play the harp, I reminded myself. Even if Neeve didn't think it a useful skill. And even though I hadn't actually touched the instrument in months.

Now that my strength was returning, however, I'd see if Master

Fawkes would resume my lessons. The bard was back in residence at the castle—I'd glimpsed him a time or two in the great hall, and he'd waved to me in passing.

"Concentrate," Sir Durum said, a resigned note in his voice as I struck the target in the arm.

"Sorry." I wiped the sweat off my forehead with the back of my sleeve and tried to rein in my restless thoughts.

After stabbing the dummy in the gut, the elbow, and then missing altogether, Sir Durum declared a rest break. He probably needed it as much as I did. I retreated to my hay bale, noting that the chicken was gone. So much for getting Trisk to eat from my hand.

I sat, gulped some water from my flask, and tried not to feel itchy from hay dust and sweat.

A soft, questioning chirp sounded beside me. Keeping my movements deliberate, I turned to see the gray cat watching me from the corner of the bale.

"Hello, Trisk," I said.

She meowed again and took a tentative, lurching step forward.

"I don't have any more chicken," I told her, lifting my hand as slowly as if I were dragging it through water. "I'll bring more tomorrow, I promise."

She blinked at me, then leaned forward and touched her nose to my fingertips. A heartbeat later, she was gone in a surprisingly graceful leap, back into the soft gray shadows that matched her fur.

If she, with only three legs, could be so deft, then I supposed I could strive to do better with my training. A maimed finger seemed a small thing—especially since it wasn't even on my dominant hand. I took another drink of water and stood, ready to tackle the dummy once more and show Sir Durum that I wasn't as hopeless as he thought.

CHAPTER 4

The next day dawned clear and unseasonably warm—one of those rare early-winter gifts that lured one into thinking that, just maybe, autumn had decided to return. As a result, instead of going to weapons training after class, Neeve, Kian, and I went out riding.

I spared a thought for Trisk but knew I needn't worry about feeding her—she knew how to fend for herself. Still, I was sorry I wouldn't get a chance to try coaxing her to me again. We were making such progress.

But the warm sunlight beckoned, as gold as Parnesian *francas*, and as full of promise. After lunch, Neeve and I donned our riding clothes and went to meet Kian at the stables.

He was waiting for us, the sun bright on his hair, smiling as if he hadn't a care in the world. His blue coat brought out the hue of his eyes, and I caught my breath, recalling how sweetly he'd cared for me during my long illness.

"Neeve, Rose—the loveliest ladies in all of Raine," he said, sweeping us a bow as we entered the stable yard. "I am the luckiest of men, to accompany you on this fair day."

Neeve, never one for courtly manners, let out a disdainful sniff. For my part, I shot Kian a warning glance. Flirting with Neeve was perfectly fine, but he wasn't supposed to include me in such things. Even if we were friends.

Are you? the little voice inside me asked.

Of course, I answered, ignoring the jab to my heart. Oh, trying to manage my feelings was like balancing on a tiny bridge over a rushing torrent. One wrong step and I'd plunge into the current and be swept away.

I just *wanted*, so much. Wanted to belong. Wanted to be loved for who I was.

A trio of grooms emerged from the stables, leading our mounts. Peerless, Neeve's black gelding, was as awe-inspiring as ever. The chestnut that Kian preferred tossed his head and snorted. But best of all was the sight of Sterling, the dapple-gray mare I'd graduated to riding the previous summer. While little Snowbell had been an adequate pony, riding Sterling was a revelation. Who knew that a canter could be so smooth? Or that rides didn't have to end with a collection of aches and bruises that lasted for days?

Of course, it had been months since I was in the saddle. The same was true for Kian, but he swung up with ease and looked annoyingly comfortable atop his horse.

"Milady, some assistance?" The groom cupped his hands for me to step into.

"Thank you." Much as I wished I could mount unaided, I knew when to accept help.

A little shove, and I was up, boots in the stirrups, saddle hard beneath me. Sterling bobbed her head up and down as the groom handed me the reins.

"Hello, love," I said softly, leaning forward and patting her neck. "Remember me?"

She let out a whuffle that I chose to take as an affirmative. Then Kian let out a whoop and led us out of the stable yard. The thud of hooves grew sharper as we crossed the cobbled courtyard in front of the castle. In the sunlight, Castle Raine was transformed, the gray stones washed pale, the slate roofs of the turrets reflecting the blue of the sky.

We passed under the shadow of the portcullis, and I let out a deep breath. It was good to be out. The breeze stirred the tops of the dark cedars and teased my unruly red curls to tickle my cheeks. I sent a longing glance at the forest, but we never rode within those shadowed depths.

The paths of the Darkwood were small and tangled, only suitable for traversing on foot. No one rode there—except once every three years, when Thorne opened an enchanted road deep into the heart of the forest. That was when the *nirwen*, the flower that was essential to the Dark Elves, bloomed. It was an important blossom for Raine, too, used in rare medicines and cosmetics.

Its golden, radiant petals only opened for one day, so speed was of the essence. Everyone in the castle, and most of the villagers of Little Hazel, went to harvest the flowers. They would make camp the night before the *nirwen* bloomed, then spend dawn until dusk plucking the enchanted blossoms.

As Thorne had reminded me, this coming summer was the next harvest. It was a mystical event, and I would have looked forward to it with anticipation—except that Neeve's uncle, the Nightshade Lord, had indicated an interest in me. That imperious Dark Elf lord had implied to Lord Raine that a future alliance might be made between the courts, and hinted that I would be an acceptable bride.

The memory made me shiver. Neeve was the one who wanted to live in the ever-night realm of Elfhame. Not me.

I'd been just fourteen last harvest, but in the intervening years I'd become a young woman. I didn't know how young the Dark Elves wed. Seventeen was too young, surely? I fervently hoped so.

But the harvest after that, I would turn twenty.

Suddenly, the seven months until the harvest seemed all too few. The opening of the gateway would be upon us in a heartbeat. I shivered. A shadow of foreboding passed over me, as though a flock of ravens had flown between me and the sun, blocking all warmth and light.

My delight in the day gone, I urged Sterling forward to where Neeve and Kian rode. The grasses edging the road were dead and brown, and the few deciduous trees in the Darkwood had lost the last of their leaves, rusty coins scattered from a careless purse. It was not summer. It wasn't even autumn any longer, and I felt the sharp bite of winter in the edge of the wind.

I remained out of sorts for the rest of the ride—and even more so when Kian suggested he and Neeve play chess when we returned. He and I had spent countless hours playing during my convalescence, and it felt like a betrayal.

"Don't be jealous, Rose," he said, reading my face, though there was a teasing note in his voice. "I just want to see if Neeve is half as good as she claims."

"I am," my stepsister said evenly. "The match won't take long, and then you can play someone more suited to your level. Like Rose."

"Kian is better than I am," I admitted. "He might surprise you."

"Like when I disarmed you yesterday in our training duel." He grinned at Neeve. "Never underestimate your opponent, princess."

One of her dark brows rose. "I won't make that mistake again, *prince*."

I was glad they could banter with one another, but the reminder that they were royalty, and I was not, stung. Even though they hadn't meant it to.

I was not noble enough on one hand, yet well enough connected to the King of Raine that I could be considered a match for a terrifying Dark Elf lord. I blew a breath out, and Sterling shifted beneath me, sensing my mood.

"I'll have the kitchen send up tea and pastries," Neeve said.

I shot her a look. Was my stepsister learning how to be a gracious hostess?

"You'll need something sweet to bolster your spirits after I roundly defeat you," she added.

Kian laughed. "Just when I thought you were learning to be kind, you go and spoil it."

"I don't need to be kind," Neeve said. "There are far too many accommodating people in the world as it is."

"No need to worry," I said. "You won't be accused of an overabundance of charm anytime soon."

My stepsister glanced at me, the barest edge of amusement on her lips. "Unkindness *is* my charm, Rose. I thought you knew that."

I couldn't help smiling at her. Neeve was well aware that most people thought her grim and uncaring—and that, most of the time, I was not one of them.

Nor was Kian, obviously.

It's good, I reminded myself. *They understand one another.*

Still, when we returned to the stables, I turned Sterling over to the groom and told Neeve I'd join her and Kian a bit later.

"I'm tired," I said, which was a convenient excuse. "I think I'll lie down for a short while."

"It will take Neeve an hour, at least, to defeat me," Kian said. "Maybe two. But once you're done with your nap, do come and watch."

Neeve just sniffed in response.

"Let me know when the tea arrives," I said. "I'll come cheer Kian on and sprinkle crumbs on the chessboard."

Leaving the two of them, I made for the side door into the castle, and the peace of my rooms. Maybe later I'd ask Sorche to draw a bath for me. Despite the unseasonably pleasant weather, I felt in dire need of some warmth and comfort.

I was nearly to my suite when I noticed the creature crouched in the hallway outside my rooms. Trisk! I slowed my steps, worried she would skitter away as I approached.

"Hello, kit," I said softly. "Did you come to find me?"

She regarded me with an unblinking gaze and let out a quiet meow that I took to be a yes. I was delighted that, so far, she didn't seem inclined to run off.

"I don't have any chicken, I'm afraid." I opened my door. "But I do have some bread and butter from lunch. You might like that." The butter, at any rate.

I stepped over the threshold and turned, holding the door open. Would she follow me in? One ear swiveled back as she stared into the sitting room, assessing it for danger.

"It's safe," I assured her. "And look, I'll prop the door open. You can leave at any time."

I pulled over a chair to hold the door, and when I looked back to the doorway, she was gone. Drat it. Frowning, I peeked into the hallway.

To my relief, Trisk hadn't gone far. She'd simply removed herself from the commotion, but was still watching me.

"All right," I told her. "I'll just put a piece of bread down for you, and you can decide."

I went to the table, where I kept a tin of cookies, a covered bowl of fruit, and whatever else I'd chosen to save from my lunch. In general, I preferred not to bother the kitchens with requests whenever I was feeling hungry. I'd grown up fending for myself, and still wasn't comfortable ordering servants about when I could do perfectly well on my own.

I broke off a small piece of the dark bread, slathered it with butter, and set it at the threshold. Then, trying not to hope too much, I retreated to one of the chairs beside the hearth. It would probably be best if I seemed uninterested, so I picked up the novel I'd been reading —a tale of a pair of adventurers lost at sea—and pretended to be engrossed.

In truth, I was surreptitiously watching the door. One minute passed, then two, with not a sign of whisker or paw. Perhaps Trisk was disdainful of butter, or I'd scared her away. I'd have to remember to keep a bit of dried meat in my rooms for next time.

If there was a next time.

Finally, when I'd all but given up hope, Trisk hopped to the doorway. She sniffed the bread while I peeked at her over the top of my book. After a moment she licked the butter, then kept going until the piece of bread was bare.

She nudged it with her nose, and then turned her attention to me.

"Come in, if you'd like." I leaned over and stretched out my hand.

As if only waiting for my invitation, she did, galumphing with her three-legged gait across the velvety green carpet. She paused just out of reach of my fingers and sat, curling her tail around her paws.

"I could scratch your head if you came a little closer," I said.

Trisk only blinked at me, then began grooming herself. At least she seemed comfortable in my presence, though she wasn't in any hurry to jump onto my lap.

With nothing else to do, I settled back in my chair and began to read in earnest. However, even the storm-wracked struggles of the hero and heroine couldn't keep my eyes from drifting closed. Half dreaming, I closed the book and set it aside. Perhaps a short nap...

Voices in the hall woke me—Neeve and Kian returning from the stables. Clearly I hadn't slept long. I started to stretch, then froze as I registered the warm weight of Trisk in my lap.

"Well, hello," I said softly, glancing down at her.

She didn't bother opening her eyes. Carefully, I stroked her back, and she began purring, a soft vibration felt more than heard. Her fur was as soft as moth wings against my fingers.

"Rose," Kian said, pausing in front of my open door. "Is everything well?"

Smiling, I looked over at him. "Indeed."

Neeve peered around his shoulder. "Oh. The cat."

I nodded, glad that their presence didn't seem to have disturbed Trisk. It seemed that once she'd made up her mind to trust me, very little disturbed her.

"I'm glad." Kian grinned at me, his blue eyes sparkling.

"I suppose you can bring it into my rooms, if you must," Neeve said. "Are you coming now?"

"No." I looked down at the slumbering cat occupying my lap. "I'll be along later. But if you would close the door?"

"Of course." Kian moved the chair, then gently shut the door, leaving me to continue napping, uninterrupted, with my new friend.

CHAPTER 5

As winter settled, cold and damp, over the castle, it became clear that Trisk had adopted me. Sometimes a day or two might pass without her presence, but at some point I'd hear a scratching at my door, accompanied by her soft meow, and I would let her in. Or she'd scramble into my lap as I rested during weapons training, looking for the tasty morsels I inevitably provided.

Sorche had raised her eyebrows the first time she found the cat cuddled up against my side in the morning. But after that, a little dish of cream always accompanied my morning cup of tea.

Watching Trisk move about was inspiring. She didn't seem bothered by the fact of her missing leg. In fact, she probably didn't even know that she ought to have four. Her front legs and chest were well muscled, and she used them to pull herself up: onto hay bales, chairs, the bed.

My rose-embroidered coverlet was becoming badly shredded on one side, but I didn't mind. Trisk's company was worth far more than a few ripped bedcovers.

She lurched as she hopped about, but on several occasions I'd seen her run in pursuit of prey—a mouse in the training arena, a moth careening down the hallway. When she did, her gait smoothed out, quick and even. Anyone watching would think she was a regular cat, possessed of four legs instead of three.

I resumed my harp lessons with Master Fawkes, though it took my fingers some time to regain their deftness over the strings. Weapons training proceeded without much improvement, though Sir Durum didn't seem to scowl at me quite so often.

When training finished, I'd often cozy myself before the fire in my rooms, Trisk in my lap, and read. Other times I'd join Neeve and Kian in her rooms and watch her beat him at chess. Once he was done complaining, I'd play him in turn, sometimes winning, sometimes losing. Trisk wasn't interested in accompanying me to Neeve's rooms, and knowing there was at least one creature who preferred my presence to my stepsister's eased my sore heart.

"The Yule Feast is coming up," Kian said one afternoon as we faced one another across the chessboard. "What shall we do for our performance?"

I frowned at him. "Must we all three do something together?"

"Don't sound so excited about the idea, Rose," he said, shaking his head. "Wouldn't it be more fun if we plan something together?"

"No," Neeve said from the window seat, where she'd retreated to look over her books on herbalism.

"Why not?" Kian glanced from her to me. "We could do a dramatic presentation, or another show of arms—"

"Not that," I said. "I almost killed you last time. And when Neeve and I tried to perform together, we nearly burned down the great hall."

"I did hear about that." Kian waggled his eyebrows. "You keep things exciting, Rose."

"It wasn't my fault," I protested, ignoring Neeve's glance.

My stepsister still insisted I'd somehow started the fire, though we both knew I had no magic of my own.

I moved my shoulders uncomfortably beneath my robe, the memory of what had happened in Parnese rising like an unsteady bubble in my mind. The more time passed, the hazier my recollections became. And yet...I *had* used the fire priest's invocation to somehow control the huge ball of flame the priest had hurtled toward us.

Hadn't I?

"What about a dance?" Kian asked. "Surely that won't be dangerous."

"There are no dances for three," I said sourly, throwing off my unease. "But I could play my harp while you and Neeve trip merrily about."

The king and Jarl Eiric would certainly approve of a show of harmony between the two royal offspring. Especially if I cast myself in a supporting role.

"That sounds tiresome," Neeve said. "Besides, I already have my performance planned."

"You do?" I shouldn't have been surprised. Neeve always went her own way, little caring what others thought. "What is it?"

She met my gaze, her stare as unblinking as Trisk's. For a long moment, I thought she wouldn't respond at all. Then she shrugged.

"You'll find out."

The last time she'd undertaken a secret performance, she'd dazzled the feasters with a display of horsemanship. I wondered what she might be planning now.

"Well, Rose, since Neeve has plotted her own course, shall the two of us pool our talents?" Kian grinned at me.

I wanted to say yes, though it would be most unwise. The ache of our cooling friendship had finally become bearable, and the last thing I needed was to stir the embers into flickering flame once more.

"What?" I asked tartly. "A display of chess playing? That would bore the entire court to tears while they waited."

"Not if I played him," Neeve said, a trace of humor in her tone.

Kian gave her a look. "One of these days, when you least expect it, I'll get the better of you."

She tilted her head and lifted a skeptical brow at him.

"Sir Durum isn't expecting us to do another fighting display, is he?" I asked.

"He's made no mention of it," Kian said.

"I'm not sure I have the stamina, at any rate." I blew out a breath. "You and Neeve could show off your sword work, though. That's always exciting."

"I told you, I'm doing something else," Neeve said. "The two of you can juggle knives or sing ballads or stand upon your heads. I don't care. Just leave me out of your schemes."

"Always so helpful." Kian looked back at the chessboard and moved his rook. "Check."

I skittered a pawn up to protect my king, trying to simultaneously think about strategy and the Yule Feast. No clever ideas came to me, just a sudden weariness that pulled at my limbs.

Before the feast arrived, however, there was another day we should mark.

"What about your birthday?" I asked Neeve. "Should we plan a special celebration?"

"Whatever for?" She blinked at me.

"In Parnese, seventeen is an important birthday marking the path to adulthood. Is that not true in Raine?"

"I don't know," she said. "I never paid it much heed. Before you came to the castle, I knew no one my own age."

Kian cleared his throat loudly, and Neeve sent him a glance. "Rose was here first. Besides, your seventeenth birthday has already passed."

"Oh." I glanced at Kian. "It did. I'm sorry. Would you like a party?"

"Men have no need of such things," he said in a superior tone.

My sympathy fled and I kicked him under the table. "You needn't be so smug. You're not that much older than Neeve and I."

"Old enough," he said, taking my pawn.

I gave him an evil smile and slid my queen forward. "Check."

Neeve sat forward and surveyed the chessboard, then gave a nod. "You've trapped him neatly, Rose. Well done."

"We could have a joint celebration," I said. "A small party—something just for us, before the Yule Feast descends."

Kian huffed out a breath and reached for his bishop, then reconsidered and pulled his hand away. With effort, I kept the disappointment from my face. I'd counted on him making the rash move. It was how Neeve always won against both of us. She was far too patient, setting her traps well in advance and waiting for us to stumble in.

"I have no desire for festivity," she said quietly.

I glanced into her shadowed eyes. Of course she didn't. It was easy to forget that her reserve hid a well of deep unhappiness. I knew well enough that it was difficult to celebrate anything when one's heart yearned to be elsewhere.

"We should have a party," Kian declared, in a reversal of his prior opinion. "Neeve, all you'll have to do is come and eat pastry. I'll arrange for the kitchens to provide us sweet wine, too."

Grinning, he hopped his knight up and over, blocking the threat to his king. Luckily, that put him right where I wanted him. I pretended to study the board, savoring the satisfying tingle of victory within my grasp.

"In three days, then," I said. "I'll host it after supper, in my rooms." Then, holding Kian's gaze, I slid my queen up and captured his knight.

"Rose wins," Neeve said, just as I said, "Checkmate."

"You two!" Kian raised his hands in an exasperated gesture. "Rose, you were just trying to distract me this whole time, weren't you?"

"Maybe." I gave him a sly smile. "But it worked."

UNLIKE MY OWN BIRTHDAYS, which I'd come to dread, the day of Neeve's birth dawned clear and cold. Shivering, I hopped out of bed and let Sorche help me dress, then sent a jealous glance at Trisk, who slept on, curled warmly in a fold of the coverlet.

"I wouldn't mind being a cat," I said as I fastened my boots.

"Aye, it's a good life," my maid said. "Until, of course, it isn't. Not all kits get to sleep in a princess's bed and drink cream for breakfast."

I reminded myself that I also got to sleep in that bed, and had a fresh cup of tea awaiting me by the hearth. Too bad Miss Groves hadn't seen fit to cancel classes, but then again, she seldom did for any reason.

So, rubbing sleep from my eyes, I joined Neeve when she rapped at my door, and together we headed for the turreted classroom. Kian strode up behind us as we turned down the hall—he'd been joining us every other morning for what he called his "gentleman's education."

"As opposed to your usual Fiorland savagery?" I'd teased the first time he used the phrase.

He'd simply shaken his head at me, and I let the matter drop.

"Rose," he said now as he approached. "I've been thinking on what we can do for the Midwinter Feast."

I shot him a glance. "I'm just going to play my harp again."

It was the safest choice, by far.

"That's dull," he said, blithely ignoring my glare. "And I don't feel like reciting more Fiorland poetry, which is all I can do by myself. I think we should perform a scene from one of Mirrion's plays."

We'd been studying Continental literature recently, and of course the great playwright was at the heart of our readings. My mind immediately flashed on the famous balcony scene between Julio and Romina. *No. No, no.* I stuffed all thoughts of romance with Kian away.

"Something bloody, I hope." Neeve sounded amused at the idea. "You could do the death scene from *Trevalyn the King*."

Kian looked over at her. "Are you sure you don't want to join us? You and Rose would make wonderfully wicked crones as you danced about your cauldron."

"Tempting," she said, not sounding tempted in the least. "But no."

Kian slanted me a smile. "Well, Rose, it's just us. What do you think?"

"I suppose a dramatic scene would do."

If we could find something without romantic overtones. Or sword-play. But Mirrion wrote plenty of murder and deception and stirring monologues. Maybe Miss Groves would have some recommendations.

We presented her with the idea at the beginning of class, as the kitchen maids arrived with our breakfast.

"A fine thought," the teacher said. Tilting her head, she regarded Kian and I from behind her desk. "Maybe something from *Summer Folly*."

"The scene where the man is enchanted with a goat's head!" I turned to Kian. "You'd be perfect for that. And I can be the tricky faerie."

He narrowed his eyes. "I prefer the murder in *Trevalyn*. You can be the dying king, exclaiming over my treachery."

"It would be best to keep a blade out of Rose's hands," Neeve said. "Just in case."

She didn't mention the near-accident from the year before. She didn't need to.

"I've got it." Miss Groves stood and reached for her massive volume of Mirrion's plays. "The siblings reunited, from *Thus it Goes*."

I was relieved she hadn't suggested the more obvious romantic pairings. Then again, she was no stranger to the undercurrents of Castle Raine. Everyone knew that Neeve and Kian were meant to wed. Eventually.

"I'll read the scene while you have your breakfast," Miss Groves said. "And you can decide if it suits."

It did, we agreed, though Kian was not entirely convinced we needed to put in the slap.

"Of course we do," I said with relish. "Famir deserves a good wallop from his sister."

"What if I played Fortuna, and you played the brother?" Kian batted his eyes at me and raised his voice an octave. "Oh, hast thou grown so unchivalrous that thou wouldst insult me so grievously?"

"It's not meant to be a farce," I said, ignoring Neeve's stifled smile. "I'm Fortuna and you're Famir, or I go back to my harp."

Kian grudgingly consented, and the matter was settled.

CHAPTER 6

That evening, as Neeve and I entered the tall-ceilinged dining room, an air of suppressed grimness greeted us. A handful of the king's advisors stood in a clump by the doorway, and Jarl Eiric was speaking in low tones to Kian in the far corner.

"What is it?" I whispered to Neeve, but she shook her head, clearly as uninformed as I.

Then Lord Raine strode in, my mother at his side, and we dipped into our formal curtseys of greeting. Neeve's not so low as mine, of course, as she was the king's daughter by blood.

The king paused before us. I shot him an apprehensive look as I rose, but his attention was focused on Neeve.

"We had hoped to celebrate this meal by marking your birthday," he said. "But unfortunately, an urgent matter has arisen. Know that we are thinking of you."

He handed her a silver-wrapped box.

"Thank you." Her pale, slim fingers closed over the present, and she slipped it in her pocket. "What is happening?"

Lord Raine glanced at his advisors, then back to Neeve. "A message arrived earlier today, from the Queen of the Athraig. Her eldest son would like to make an alliance. With you."

I sucked in a breath. A deep-seated enmity lay between the two countries. Why would the Athraig make overtures now?

"Is it a ploy?" Neeve asked, her tone far milder than mine would have been under the circumstances.

"Most assuredly. But one we must discuss this evening. The Athraig aren't known for their patience."

She nodded, her expression flat, then stepped back as her father proceeded to his place at the head of the table. As soon as he took his seat, everyone else went to their chairs: my mother at his right hand, Kian at his left. Neeve sat beside my mother, and I was next to her, facing Jarl Eiric.

Sir Durum settled beside the Fiorland advisor, his expression grim, while Master Fawkes, with a brief smile of greeting, took the empty chair to my right. The other council members ranged down the rest of the table.

As soon as the group was seated, servants moved forward to pour wine and water and deposit baskets of savory buns upon the table. The king cleared his throat, waiting until he had everyone's attention. It didn't take long.

"As you all know by now," he said, "Prince Rolf of the Athraig has formally offered for my daughter Neeve's hand."

"Presumptuous," Jarl Eiric said, with remarkable equanimity given that *his* prince was supposed to marry Neeve. "Usually, such things are approached with more delicacy. Why the sudden interest in Raine?"

The king's mouth firmed. "It might have to do with the incursions upon the Darkwood—or it might not. I've sent word to the *Galadhir*, to see if he can provide any further insights."

Thorne. My heart thumped loudly in my chest. But even if he came to the castle, I wouldn't see him. He'd be there on important business, not to make social calls. Even if he *had* stopped by my rooms the one time...

"We'll tell the Athraig no." Sir Durum made a fist upon the table.

"Of course," the king said. "But not right away. We must determine what their game is. The unrest in Parnesia might be making them nervous."

Sir Durum let out a snort. "The Athraig aren't nervous. They're predatory."

"Still, it's unusual that they've approached us for an alliance," the king said.

"If they are serious, then perhaps a different princess might do." Jarl Eiric sent a pointed look in my direction.

My stomach clenched. Even though I was only a princess by marriage and not by blood, it wasn't outside the realm of possibility that Lord Raine could consider offering me up to the Athraig. What would I do, if he decided to sacrifice me to save Neeve and his kingdom?

"Heavens, no," my mother said, her voice higher than usual. "You've told me enough times that it's unwise to bargain with the Athraig. They always take more than is offered. Besides, Rose is still a child."

I'll be seventeen next summer. I bit my tongue on the words. Now was not the time to draw attention to myself.

"Good thing the winter seas are too rough for travel," Master Fawkes said. "Otherwise, we might have to contend with a delegation of Athraig upon our doorstep, pressing the matter."

The king nodded. "Have you any insight for us, bard, as to why they would suggest such an alliance?"

Master Fawkes furrowed his already wrinkled brow. "As we know, there's trouble on the Continent. Perhaps worse than we've suspected. If the influence of the red priests continues to spread north, their power may well be making the Athraig uneasy, as you've suggested."

"But why ally with us?" Sir Durum asked. "Raine's navy, though fierce, is too small to mount an offense against another country, and we've no army at the ready. Bluntly speaking, if I were the Athraig, I'd be looking elsewhere."

"Unless they have conquest on their mind," Jarl Eiric said.

I shared an uneasy glance with Neeve. Our solid little world of Castle Raine suddenly seemed frighteningly exposed.

"No," the king said confidently. "The Athraig will never invade Raine. Not after they were so roundly defeated."

"That was centuries ago," Sir Durum pointed out.

"And yet the same outcome would hold true today." Lord Raine held his captain's gaze, an intent gleam in his eye.

I had read the secret history of Raine and knew what the king was trying to communicate. If there was an invasion, the warrior mages of Elfhame would come to our aid. Mortal armies were no match for their power.

Jarl Eiric glanced between the king and Sir Durum, a trace of a grimace on his thin lips. "I must remind you that the crown of Fiorland has a prior claim regarding interest in an alliance."

I slanted another look at Neeve, unsurprised to find her cheeks reddening with emotion. Knowing her, it was rage rather than embarrassment. Her next words confirmed my guess.

"I'm not some pawn that you can dispose of at will," she said to her father, her voice tight with anger.

"Of course you are," he replied, his tone implacable. "But don't worry—you won't be thrown to the Athraig. We'll put them off, at least for a time."

His gaze slipped to me, and I froze like a hare under the eyes of a hawk. If I didn't move, perhaps he would forget I existed. Unspent breath choked my throat and my eyes stung as I held them wide and unblinking.

The scrape of Kian shoving back his chair broke the tense moment.

"My lord..." Jarl Eiric rose, reaching out a hand, but Kian brushed him off and rounded the table.

Panic clawed through me. Surely he wasn't... He wouldn't...

When Kian reached Neeve's place, he went down on one knee and lifted his palms to her. Now my stepsister was the one to go as still as a stone.

I wasn't certain if I was relieved or devastated that he hadn't continued on to me. Not that I had any right to hope, no matter the strength of the connection between us.

"Lady Neeve Mallory," Kian said, his voice stronger than it had any right to be, "Princess of Raine and heir to the throne, would you do me the honor of—"

"Stop!" the king commanded, abruptly rising. "There will be no rash declarations or promises made here tonight. Stand up, Prince Kian, and resume your place."

He meant more than just Kian's chair, and everyone at the table knew it.

Kian hesitated, then slowly rose, his gaze locked with Neeve's.

"One day," he whispered, so low that I barely overheard. Then, his back very straight, he returned to his spot at the king's left hand and, with precise movements, sat.

Silence gripped the room, as if no one could believe that Kian had been on the verge of proposing to Neeve. I could scarcely credit it myself. My emotions roiled through me like a thunderstorm, heavy with the threat of rain. After dinner ended—if it *ever* ended—I'd give in to the lashing torrents of grief in the privacy of my own rooms.

Beside me, my stepsister trembled. It was nearly imperceptible, the movement of a strong sapling when the wind first touches the bark, but I felt it. Slowly, to avoid notice, I reached under the table and took her hand.

Her fingers closed over mine, so tightly that I was sure she was squeezing all the blood from my hand, but I didn't pull away. I darted a glance at Lord Raine's face, which was set in deep lines of displeasure, then over to Kian, who looked sulkier than I'd seen him in a long while. No one liked to be robbed of their grand gestures.

"Prince Kian," the king said, "I will see you and your advisor in my study after dinner."

Mutely, Kian nodded, and Jarl Eiric didn't seem inclined to argue. The council members at the foot of the table exchanged nervous glances.

My mother grabbed her glass of wine and took a somewhat desperate swallow. Then, with a smile pasted on her face, she turned to Master Fawkes.

"We shall trust the king to sort this business out," she said, too brightly. "But now, let us speak of more pleasant things. Tell us, bard, what amusements did you encounter during your travels this past summer?"

"Ah." Master Fawkes quickly cleared his throat. "I witnessed a troupe of acrobats from Caliss perform. Quite astounding. They balanced on impossibly thin wires and executed feats of agility the likes of which I'd never seen before."

"The Masque Caliss, yes?" The sharp edges of my mother's smile softened. "I've heard of them and their fabled acrobatics school."

"Assassin school, more like," Sir Durum put in. "I knew a fellow once, graduated from there. He showed me a thing or two."

Beside me, Neeve drew in a deep breath. Her grip on my hand eased, but she didn't let go until the servants had served the first course.

The rest of the meal passed in stilted conversation, steered along by my mother. She'd been a skilled hostess back in Parnese, and could keep even the most awkward gatherings from splintering upon the rocks of social failure.

It was one of the reasons King Tobin had married her, I supposed —for all that their courtship had been shockingly brief.

Finally, the dessert course was served: a plum cake topped with spun-sugar flowers in honor of Neeve's birthday. Even though I usually loved sweets, my appetite had long since fled. Neeve prodded at the cake with her fork, moving bits of it about on her plate.

After a few minutes of this, she glanced at the king.

"Your pardon, father," she said, "but might Rose and I be excused?"

I was careful to keep my gaze averted from Kian, though I'd been aware of his stony expression throughout the entire meal. His comments had been brief, even when my mother tried to draw him into the conversation that Sir Durum and Jarl Eiric were having about the balance points of certain weapons—maces versus spears and the like. Usually, he was happy to discuss such things. But not tonight.

The king nodded to Neeve. "Good evening, daughter. I hope the rest of your night is restful."

She rose, unsmiling, giving my sleeve a sharp tug so that I would follow. I made my curtsey to the king and the rest of the table, then together Neeve and I fled.

We both wanted to rush away, I thought, but kept our steps measured over the flagstones. I fancied I could feel Kian's hot gaze upon our backs. He wouldn't be joining us in my rooms for the birthday party we'd planned for Neeve. Certainly none of us were in the mood for a celebration any longer.

Once Neeve and I gained the safety of the hallway, my stepsister let out a deep breath that hitched midway, a telltale sign of the emotion she fought so hard to conceal.

"I thought that miserable meal would never end," she said. "What am I to do about Kian?"

I frowned, thinking. "Let's talk about it in my rooms."

All the servants of Castle Raine were loyal, of course—to the king. But there would already be gossip circulating about the events of the evening, and we didn't need to add more fuel to the fire.

Neeve gave a nod, and silently we traversed the stairs and hallways of the castle. The cold granite walls, lit intermittently by single candles flickering dimly in their sconces, matched my grim mood to perfection.

When we reached my sitting room, I poked up the fire and lit two more lamps to banish the shadows. Neeve gracefully sank into one of the paired chairs before the hearth and stared into the flames.

"It's not that bad," I said, trying to cheer us both as I settled across from her. "We all knew Kian would offer for you someday."

"Someday! Not now. Not for years, yet."

"Well." I didn't point out that she'd been deceiving herself if she thought that date was years in the future. "His fostering period ends the summer after next. Surely there would have been an understanding between the two of you by the time he left."

"I was planning to put him off. Say I must visit Fiorland, meet his parents before making any promises. I don't want to marry Kian. I barely even like him."

I tilted my head. "I think you don't want to marry at all. But Neeve —that's not a path you can take."

"It is," she insisted, though her voice was hollow. "Besides, perhaps there's...someone else."

Thorne. My heart twisted in my chest.

"Is a match with one of your own even possible?" My throat was tight. "Isn't there a treaty between the realms regarding whom you must marry?"

"I'm half human," she said, her words bitter. "Surely that must count for something."

A quiet knock came at my door, welcome distraction from the bubble of unhappiness rising in my chest. Of course Neeve and Thorne loved one another. Truly, I'd known it all along.

"Who is it?" I called.

"Sorche," the maid answered. "I've brought up the pastries you requested."

The sweets for the party. I'd sent word to the kitchens for them that morning. Now, it felt like a thousand years ago.

"Come in." I sent Neeve an apologetic glance. "It would be rude to send them back."

She said nothing as Sorche came in bearing a tray with a pot of spiced herbal tea, three cups, and a variety of sweets: turnovers with flaky crusts, small cakes dusted with sugar, candied fruits. And a wedge of the plum cake from dinner.

"Thank you," I said. "It looks wonderful. Please convey our appreciation to the kitchens."

Sorche set the tray on the low table, then bobbed a curtsey, hands folded in her apron. "Can I fetch you anything more?"

"We have everything we need," I told her. "Good night."

She let herself out, closing the door quietly behind her, and I turned back to my stepsister.

"I know you're not hungry," I said. "We can save the treats for breakfast—or a snack. But at least drink some tea."

"You needn't fuss over me," Neeve said.

I took that for an agreement and rose to pour us two cups. The third one was an uncomfortable reminder that Kian had been supposed to celebrate with us.

"Do you think he'll try again?" Neeve asked, taking her cup.

I knew she meant Kian asking for her hand. "Eventually. But not right away, certainly. Not until the king deems it time. It was a rash move."

"Because of the Athraig." Her lips twisted in distaste. "Did Kian think he was protecting me? Or simply claiming me for Fiorland?"

"Both, maybe? But he does care for you, Neeve."

She waved a hand in dismissal.

"Truly," I said. "The two of you are friends, at the very least."

"Friends." She said the word as though the taste of it was unfamiliar in her mouth. "This makes everything worse."

I sipped my tea, the smell of warm cloves wreathing my face.

"Nothing has changed," I pointed out. "I mean, yes, Kian acted hastily, but he didn't do anything wrong."

Like propose to *me*, for instance.

Neeve gave me an intent look, as if guessing the direction of my thoughts. "What if the king decides to throw you to the Athraig?"

Carefully, I set my teacup aside, then laced my fingers together to keep them from trembling. "Would he really do so?"

"Maybe. If I refused to wed Kian."

"He'd use me as leverage against you?" But of course he would. A king used whatever tool was to hand.

Especially unlooked-for stepdaughters. Four years ago, I had arrived with my mother, becoming another handy, yet ultimately disposable, pawn upon the board.

Neeve leaned forward and set one hand upon my knee. "I won't let that happen."

"Maybe you should," I said bitterly.

If Thorne and Neeve married, I didn't want to remain in Raine. And if they did not and she wed Kian as she was supposed to, everyone would be miserable: Kian, bound to someone who did not love him; Thorne, seeing the woman he'd guarded and cared for so long promised to another; and Neeve, who would no doubt find a way to do something awful. Like die in childbirth, as her mother had.

It was all dreadful, and I could see no solution. But my staying in Raine wasn't likely to make matters any better.

"There is another option," my stepsister said. "Elfhame."

"You can't go there, or the gate will close."

"Not me." A touch of impatience shaded her voice. "You recall how the Nightshade Lord looked at you last harvest."

I shivered at the memory. "I do."

"Then, if it comes to the point, you would have a countermove to propose to the king."

I didn't answer.

An alliance with the dreadful Athraig, or with a terrifying Dark Elf lord. Neither one was a fate I wished to contemplate. Yet it seemed I had no choice.

CHAPTER 7

Neeve left shortly thereafter, taking half the sweets with her. I was glad—neither of us had eaten much at supper, and she'd be hungry later, if she wasn't already. As soon as she was gone, I curled up in the chair again, nibbling on a candied fruit.

A soft thump came from the bedroom—the sound of a cat vacating the bed. A moment later, Trisk hopped into the sitting room. She regarded me with her unblinking gaze, and I patted my lap.

"Come up?" I suggested.

She made a soft mew and headed for the door, then settled beside it with an expectant air.

"Very well." I was a little put out that she was abandoning me. "Go stalk the halls if you must. But if I'm asleep when you want back in, I can't help you."

I licked sugar from my fingers and then went to let her out.

Once she'd gone, my rooms felt empty. Which was foolishness, I knew. *Nothing's changed,* I told myself, ignoring the little voice whispering that everything was wrong.

The Athraig poking their nose into Raine's affairs had disrupted the balance, and my position felt more precarious than ever. If only I were still thirteen years old, only concerned with befriending Neeve and discovering the secrets of the Darkwood.

Now I was nearly of marriageable age, and knew too much. The past unspooled behind me like a fallen ball of yarn escaping across the floor. One that could never be scooped up and tidily rewound.

I stared blankly into the guttering fire as my tea grew cold, unable to marshal any plans. I did not belong in Raine. Or Fiorland. Or Athraig. Or Elfhame.

The only place that had ever felt like home was Parnese—but that was lost to me. Not only had I no family there, but the priests of the Twin Gods had seized power, and we'd narrowly escaped being taken captive.

A soft knock at the door roused me from my grim thoughts. Had Neeve returned with some new plan?

When I opened the door, however, Kian stood there, leaning against the jamb. He gave me a crooked smile that didn't reach his eyes and lifted the half-empty bottle of sweet wine he carried.

"Did I miss the party?" he asked.

"You know very well you did," I replied tartly. "It's late."

"May I come in?" A flicker of despair shone in his blue eyes.

I blew out a breath and stepped back. "Very well. But you can't stay long. It's not proper for you to be in my rooms alone at this hour."

"I'm not alone." He stepped inside. "I'm with you."

"That's my point." I shut the door quietly behind him, noting his slightly unsteady steps as he made his way over to the hearth.

"Your fire's dying," he observed. "Want some wine? I said I'd bring a bottle."

"It looks rather more like half a bottle. Did you drink all of that yourself?" But I knew the answer. It swayed tipsily before me.

I took the bottle from his unresisting grasp and set it on the table. He didn't seem to notice that I neglected to pour either of us a glass.

"Neeve won't have me," he said forlornly. "I proposed, and she turned me down. I'm an utter failure."

"That's not true!" I stepped over to him and held his gaze. "You didn't even get the words out, if you recall. Lord Raine stopped you, and Neeve had nothing to do with that. Don't be angry with her."

"Rose." He swayed, and I took his shoulders to keep him from stumbling into the fireplace. "I should... I should ask..."

"You should sit down."

Instead he set his hands at my waist. Sudden, bright heat bloomed from where he held me. We were standing far too close.

"I should ask *you*," he said softly, then pulled me against him and dipped his head.

I hesitated a bare second, though I knew I ought to push him away. Kian was not meant for me—no matter his drunken ramblings. Or how much I wished to be special.

Then our lips met, and it was sweet wine and candied fruit and forbidden sparks of fire. It was yearning and despair, and a sudden, sharp sense of my own skin.

It was hard to keep steady over the roaring flame rushing through me, but I pulled back.

"You're not thinking clearly," I said. "Sit down."

I pushed him, rather ungently, into the nearest chair.

He fell back, letting go of me, then stared up with a wounded expression. "Even *you* won't have me? What a useless prince I am."

Frustrated—with him, with myself—I folded my arms. "Do you want King Tobin to banish both of us from the castle?"

"You could come with me, back to Fiorland," Kian said. "It would solve everything."

It was tempting...but only for a moment. Deep down, I knew he'd only kissed me because he was angry with Neeve and the king. Not because he loved me so deeply that he couldn't help himself.

I wanted overwhelming emotion—on both sides. And now that we'd come to this point, I had to admit that I wasn't so recklessly attached to Kian that I would risk everything to run away with him.

Deep affection, it turned out, wasn't the same as true love. No matter how much I wished otherwise.

Besides, there was one very important issue that Kian was unaware of. No matter what she might say, Neeve must marry a mortal prince, or else the doorway to Elfhame would close forever. If that mortal prince wasn't Kian, that left the Athraig—and an alliance there would ultimately spell doom for the kingdom of Raine.

And Elfhame as well, knowing the warlike Athraig's history. They liked nothing better to than to conquer their neighbors and appropriate their riches. What would they do, once they discovered that a gateway to a magical land lay within the Darkwood?

"I can't possible marry you," I said. "What would your parents say when you returned with the wrong bride? It would strain relations between the countries to the breaking point if you passed over Neeve in favor of her non-royal stepsister."

"It doesn't matter—and you're related to the throne of Parnese, anyway, through your mother."

I didn't point out that it must matter, if he felt it worth mentioning.

"Come, Rose," he continued, levering himself up out of the chair. "Don't you love me? I'd rather marry someone who does. Why should I stay here and watch Neeve not love me?"

His voice broke slightly on the last words, dousing the few embers of possibility I hadn't quite stamped out.

"Really." I narrowed my eyes. "So I'm second best? It seems you want to inflict the same fate on me you wish to avoid. Namely, marrying someone who doesn't love you."

"I do love you!" he protested.

I simply stared at him, knowing my expression was skeptical and not bothering to hide it. He'd accused me of being too easy to read. Well then, let him see how I truly felt.

"You care for me," I said, trying not to wince at the truth of it. "But that's not enough. If you really do love Neeve, why would you go away and leave her to the mercy of an Athraig alliance?"

"I tried to protect her," he said, with some heat. "It's not my fault the king wouldn't allow it."

"He won't allow it *yet*. By all the stars, have some patience. Neeve just turned seventeen today."

"Why do you have to be so reasonable?" He leaned over and swiped his bottle of sweet wine off the table, then drank directly from the mouth.

"Go get some sleep." I took him gently by the arm and steered him to the door.

"Wait." He looked down at me. "Are you absolutely sure? Let me kiss you one more time, to be certain."

"Kian—"

His lips closed over mine, warm and sweet.

A soft rap came at my door, and before I could move away from Kian, Neeve opened it.

"Rose, I was thinking—" She froze, staring at us as I hastily stepped back, out of the prince's embrace.

"It's not what it looks," I began.

"I don't care." Despite the flatness of her voice, hot color had risen in her cheeks.

"Neeve." Kian held out one hand. "You're the one I—"

She made a sharp, slashing movement of denial. "Don't say it. Don't profess *anything* for me. And you, Rose. You should be ashamed."

The heat on my face matched hers, I was sure. "You're right. I'm sorry. But I can explain."

Shaking her head, she backed away. "I can't stand to look at either of you right now." Her voice was choked.

Then she turned and fled down the hall, back to her rooms. Her door closed with a heavy thud, matching the despairing beat of my heart.

Catastrophe layered upon catastrophe.

"You've ruined everything." I glared at Kian, ignoring his stricken expression. "Go. Now."

He made no protest, only stepped over the threshold and shambled away, the opposite direction from Neeve's rooms. I watched until he'd turned the corner. Only then did I give way to the fiery prick of tears, the hot wash of grief in my chest.

Nothing, I feared, would ever be the same again.

CHAPTER 8

The Yule Feast came and went. I did not act out any dramatic scenes with Kian or provide background music for him and Neeve to dance to. Each of us performed alone: myself on the harp, Kian reciting a grim Fiorlander poem, and Neeve gifting herbal sachets to all the guests—which I guessed wasn't what she'd originally intended, but seemed to suffice.

Every time the three of us had to interact—at dinner, or during lessons or weapons practice—we were cold and formal with one another.

The denizens of Castle Raine noticed, of course, but most of the gossip concluded that Kian was angry with Neeve and her father for cutting his proposal short, I was upset with Kian for attempting to propose to my stepsister, and Neeve was unhappy with both of us because she guessed we were in love.

Which was close enough, in vague outline. My stepsister *did* think that Kian and I shared a closer bond than we actually did. Kian *was* angry with the king. And I... Well, I had lost every friend I had in the castle except for Trisk.

The dark, rainy days dragged, though I did my best to fill them with harp practice and reading and, whether I willed it or not, weapons training.

Almost imperceptibly, I regained my strength and balance. Sir Durum grunted approval more often when I stabbed at the straw dummies, though I noted that he watched Kian and Neeve spar with a troubled expression. Kian never laughed any more during their quick, bright flurries of blade work, and Neeve never gave him that small, smug smile when she bested him.

I was glad to face neither of them—at least not with weapons. But I missed our chess games and former camaraderie. Would we ever regain even a semblance of it? Neeve, I knew, could carry a grudge an interminably long time, and it seemed that Kian was no better.

As winter slowly inched into spring, Miss Groves set us to studying the history of the Athraig, including their many warlike incursions upon their neighbors—Raine included.

"I don't understand," Kian said at the conclusion of one of our lessons. He stabbed a finger at the book open on the table before him. "It says here that several hundred years ago the Athraig invaded Raine and tried to force an alliance. They even brought troops as far as the castle and took the king prisoner! How could their coup possibly have failed?"

"Raine is fortunate to have a fiercely loyal, well-trained castle guard," Miss Groves said while Neeve and I exchanged wary looks, united for once in our apprehension. "The soldiers of Raine were able to throw the invaders back, and our navy—which has always been strong, despite its small size—chased the Athraig from our shores."

"But it doesn't make sense." Aggrieved, Kian glanced down at the text. "How could the castle's soldiers, no matter how fierce, have routed the entire Athraig army? Especially once the enemy was inside the walls?"

I knew the answer, of course—Elfhame's warriors had come to Raine's aid. But magical allies emerging from the Darkwood were the stuff of fables, not history books.

"Accounts become muddled over time," Miss Groves said. "And surely you're aware, Prince Kian, that every castle has its secrets. Hidden entrances, ways to move about unseen within the walls. Such things must certainly have played a part. But more than that, we'll never know."

Kian frowned but, to my relief, seemed to accept the teacher's explanation. Instead, he turned to Neeve. "Does Castle Raine truly possess secret passages?"

She gave him an arch look. "Does the Fiorland castle?"

"I'll tell, if you will." The trace of a smile ghosted across his expression.

I held my breath, waiting for my stepsister's response. *Be kind,* I prayed. Or, if not kind, at least not cold. This was the first unthawing any of us had done, and I hoped it wasn't just a momentary crack in the ice.

The moment was broken by a strangled sound from Miss Groves, and the sound of glass shattering from the window behind us.

I stared at the teacher, who was oddly frozen in mid-gesture, a horrified expression upon her face. She looked like a statue instead of a living person. Fear squeezed my breath as a hissing noise came from the back of the room, along with the scrabble of claws over the flag-stone floor.

Neeve leaped up, drawing her sword. Kian was already out of his chair, blade in hand, staring at whatever had come through the window.

"What is that thing?" he asked, an edge of revulsion in his voice.

"Basilisk!" Neeve cried, glancing away. "Whatever you do, don't look directly at it. If you meet its eyes, you'll end up like Miss Groves."

Kian was already advancing, but he hesitated at Neeve's words and put his arm up to shield his face.

I unsheathed my knife and turned, heart pounding. Through slitted eyelids I could just make out an ugly, gray-scaled creature skulking behind the back table. It resembled one of the lizards that darted upon the sun-warmed walls of Parnese—if those lizards were hideously misshapen and the size of a large dog.

"How are we supposed to attack something we can't look at?" Kian asked.

"Distraction," Neeve said grimly. "I'll start."

She picked up her chair one-handed and began banging it against the side of the table, her face averted from the creature. I sidled back with the thought of flinging my knife at it. Provided it gave me any opening.

With a hiss, the basilisk darted toward Neeve.

"Over here!" Kian yelled, rushing forward with a sweep of his blade.

The creature pivoted with deadly speed, long red tongue flicking out. Kian turned his head aside, barely in time to avoid its gaze, and stumbled against one of the chairs, overturning it. The basilisk rushed at him, jaws wide.

Neeve screamed, a high-pitched, ferocious sound that made me blink. Lifting her sword, she hacked at the creature's tail. Unfortunately, its scale-covered hide seemed well armored. Recalling the drake Neeve and I had faced in the Darkwood, I held my knife by its point, ready to fling it at one of the basilisk's eyes. The only problem was that looking at it long enough to see its eye could prove deadly...

The creature turned to Neeve again, giving Kian a chance to swipe at it, which distracted it once more.

"Strike behind the head," Neeve said a bit breathlessly as she scrambled out of the way.

So far, they'd managed to keep out of reach of its sharp jaws and wickedly curved claws, but an unwary moment could be all our undoing. It was time for drastic measures. And flinging a small blade at the creature, hoping for a direct hit, was not going to do. But perhaps I had another weapon at my disposal...

Squeezing my eyes shut, I imagined summoning fire—a ball of flame to blind and distract the basilisk. Then, quietly, fiercely, I chanted the fire sorcerer's incantation.

"*Esfera to quera, firenda des almar.*" As I said the words, I *pulled* with all my might, forcing my desperation into the summons.

Brightness flashed against my eyelids, and Neeve let out a yelp.

I opened my eyes, then quickly shut them again at the sight of the basilisk scuttling toward me. I was trapped against the wall, with no escape.

Doom, doom, my heartbeat pounded in my ears.

My only hope was that my companions would be able to turn the creature aside.

Another sharp cry from Neeve and a grunt from Kian. The sound of flesh thudding to the floor, a blood-choked gurgle.

I couldn't bear to look.

"It's all right," Kian said after an endless moment, his breathing heavy from exertion. "Rose. You can open your eyes."

I did, then shuddered at the sight of the basilisk lying a mere pace in front of me. Two swords protruded from its neck. Sluggish trickles of dark red blood slithered to the floor from the wounds, slowing even as I watched.

The creature's lifeless eyes were sheened over, powerless. I gulped back the queasy aftereffects of panic.

"What happened?" I asked unsteadily.

"The basilisk attacked you," Kian said, "giving us a clear chance to strike."

"But..." I trailed off, conscious of Neeve's intense stare directed at me.

Warning and accusation shone in her dark eyes. I wanted to ask if I had somehow—impossibly—summoned fire. Or if she'd used her Dark Elf magic to send the basilisk toward me. But with Kian there, I could do neither. Not without risking too many secrets.

Neeve gave me one last, narrow-eyed glance, then set her booted foot on the basilisk's corpse and pulled her sword free. Without hesitation, she wiped the blood off on her skirts, and I grimaced.

"What about Miss Groves?" I looked to the front of the room, where the teacher still stood, frozen.

"She should recover shortly," Neeve said. "Once a basilisk dies, its prey are released from the gaze spell."

"How do you know so much about it?" Kian asked, cleaning off his own blade, then sending her an accusing look.

"There are tales of the creatures who roam the Darkwood," my stepsister said calmly. "I've lived here my whole life."

Well. Neither of us could argue with that.

"Ah," Miss Groves said, slumping against her desk. She blinked a moment, then pushed up her glasses. Her gaze went from the broken window admitting a waft of chilly, damp air to the corpse of the basilisk sprawled at our feet.

It looked smaller and less dangerous in death. But I knew it could have harmed—even killed—all of us, had we been a little unluckier.

"Oh," the teacher said. "I see." Her voice sounded hollow. "I'll inform the king right away and get some guards in to clean up this mess. Class is dismissed."

Belatedly, I realized I still held my naked dagger. I sheathed it, surprised to see my hands were shaking.

"Come," Neeve said, jerking her head toward the door. "Both of you. We'll go to my rooms."

I nodded, glad of her invitation. I'd no desire to be alone, and judging from Kian's set expression, neither did he. A brush with death did that—left one vulnerable and cold, wanting nothing more than to affirm that life went on.

When we reached her rooms, Neeve summoned a maid to fetch tea, and then poked up the sitting room fire.

"I'm going to change," she said, glancing down at the smears of blood on her skirt. "Pour out the tea when it comes, Rose."

She retreated into her bedroom, and I went to one of the chairs beside the hearth. Kian leaned his forearm against the mantel and let out a heavy breath.

"I'm glad we were all armed," he said.

He and Neeve, with Sir Durum's approval, made it a habit to always wear their swords, and I was immensely grateful for the fact.

"Not that my dagger was any help." I stared into the quickening flames in the hearth, thinking again of how close we'd come to disaster.

"You distracted it," he said. "That was essential."

"Why did it come after me at the end?" I gave him a keen look. "Do you know?"

He shook his head. "One minute it was chasing Neeve, then it pivoted and darted for you. Maybe it liked your hair."

I made a face at him, pretending amusement. The teasing was heavy-handed, but I appreciated his attempt at normalcy.

"Neeve was..." He stared into the fire a moment, then shook his head admiringly. "She was amazing. I don't think I could have killed the thing on my own."

"Neither of us could have," my stepsister said, emerging from her room wearing a dark blue dress and twisting her hair into a braid. "Thank you, Prince Kian. You are an exemplary swordsman yourself."

Her tone was sincere, without a trace of mockery.

"If all it takes is a vicious battle with a mythical creature to make you think kindlier of me, I would've arranged such a thing ages ago," he said, lips twisting into a wry smile.

One of her dark brows rose. "Oh, certainly. Do keep that in mind for next time."

They stared at one another a heartbeat too long, and I shifted uncomfortably in my chair. Then the maid knocked at the door to deliver our tea, and the intensity between my stepsister and the Fiorland prince faded, like stars at dawn.

Neeve poured us each a cup of tea, the particular spicy blend we all liked, and I breathed deeply of the steam. Finally, I was starting to warm up.

"How did the creature even get to the turret?" Kian asked. "The castle guards should have stopped it when it first breached the walls."

My stepsister settled in the other chair, hands wrapped about her cup. Though she appeared outwardly serene, I guessed she craved comfort as much as I.

"It's not the first time a basilisk has attacked," she said. "They used to menace the village every spring, according to the tales. As for how it got in—it climbed."

Kian folded his arms, his expression skeptical.

"Its hide was the same color as the granite," I pointed out. "And the guards didn't spot it, since they don't constantly scan every inch of the castle walls."

"They will now," he said grimly.

"There won't be more of the creatures." Neeve took a sip of her tea. "Basilisks are very territorial."

"That might be, but where was your so-called guardian of the woods?" Kian frowned. "Isn't this something he should have dealt with *before* it came out of the forest to menace us?"

He was right. A poisonous creature of the Darkwood should never have gotten so far into the castle. I exchanged a worried glance with Neeve.

"Surely there's a reason," I said.

"That reason nearly got us killed." Kian didn't sound mollified.

I couldn't blame him. It certainly *looked* like negligence on Thorne's part—even though I could think of several excuses.

It was still the tail end of winter in Raine, and the forest shouldn't be stirring quite yet. And, though Kian didn't know it, the *Galadhir* inhabited an entirely different world until spring. Even if Thorne could cross between the realms when needed, a sudden, unexpected attack on us would've caught him by surprise.

"I'm certain my father will take all precautions, and speak with the *Galadhir*," Neeve said with an air of finality. Clearly, she was done discussing the incident.

Kian regarded her a long moment, then drained his tea.

"Back to our earlier conversation, then," he said. "Castle Raine's secret passages."

It took me a moment to recall the discussion we'd been having before the basilisk attacked. I'd been so hopeful for a fragile truce. Coming through a traumatic event together, as we'd just done, seemed the perfect time to try to steer us onto solid footing. Provided my stepsister cooperated.

"I don't know of any," I said mildly. "But I'm certain Neeve does."

It was only a small lie—I'd crawled through the tunnel from the onion cellar to the edge of the Darkwood, but that was the only secret passage I was aware of.

"Well then." Kian smiled at my stepsister, the ghost of his charm returning. "Will you reveal all?"

I expected Neeve to brush him off, but instead she tilted her head and studied him. I'd no idea what she was looking for, but after several heartbeats, she seemed satisfied.

"I might tell you something," she said. "But you'll have to defeat me at chess first."

I let out a breath of relief and slumped back in my chair. Despite my apologies, and Kian's, it had been up to Neeve to forgive us. I was glad she'd at last decided to do so. Or at least take the first steps along that road.

"Agreed." The corners of Kian's mouth tilted up in a brief smile. "Though I warn you, I've been studying my strategy."

"As have I." She glanced at me. "Rose, you must keep watch over the board and make sure Kian doesn't cheat."

"You wound me," he said, lifting a hand to his heart in exaggerated pain. "I'll defeat you on my own merits."

"No doubt." Her tone was dry. "Eventually." It was clear she anticipated that day would arrive far, far in the future. If at all.

I couldn't help smiling at both of them. I didn't care who won, or when. As long as we were back to being friends, I was content.

Outside the window, the evergreens swayed in a soft wind. The clouds had lifted, no longer a pewter soup tureen upturned over the castle, but a softer silver hinting at a sun-filled sky beyond.

※

MY GUESSES about why Thorne hadn't dealt with the basilisk before it left the confines of the Darkwood were confirmed by Neeve as we went to the classroom a few days later. Apparently one of the wards protecting the forest had failed, and while he and the Oracles were restoring it, the basilisk had escaped.

She could speak frankly of Elfhame, since it was just the two of us walking the halls. Kian was off with the king, Sir Durum, and Jarl Eiric that morning, making a full review of the castle's protections.

"Don't you want to be there too?" I asked Neeve.

She waved a hand in dismissal. "My presence isn't necessary. They all have the best interests of the castle at heart."

"All of them? Even the jarl?" I couldn't shed my distrust of the Fiorland emissary.

Neeve nodded. "He might not show it, but he is a staunch ally of Raine."

I lifted my brows. That might be true—but only to the extent that such things aligned with Fiorland's interests.

"Besides," my stepsister added, "Kian will tell me if there's anything I need to know."

I gave her a look. "That's convenient of him."

"Kian and I agreed some time ago—before you went to Parnese, even—to inform one another of anything important, should one of us be absent during a meeting of the council or such."

"Oh." I couldn't help feeling a little stung. "One of those secret pacts between royalty, I suppose."

"Rose." Neeve halted before the door to the stairwell, her expression serious. "If you cared about such things as the running of castles, we would've included you."

I supposed I couldn't argue with that, but I still frowned at her. "You *would* tell me if I were the subject of some of those meetings, wouldn't you?"

"Of course." She held my gaze steadily, and I believed her.

Mollified, we continued up to the turret, where the window had been repaired, the blood scrubbed off the flagstones, and Miss Groves continued our lessons unperturbed.

Now that Neeve, Kian, and I were on speaking terms once more, spring seemed to arrive with all speed. I was happy that matters were mended between the three of us, although sometimes a residue of awkwardness coated our interactions. Occasionally, I caught Kian looking at me with a serious expression, and I couldn't help noticing that even as he watched me, Neeve watched him, something calculating in her eyes.

I resolved to ignore the undercurrents, however, and tried to be a cheerful arbiter of their chess games. To no one's surprise, Kian continued to lose.

"I *am* getting better," he pointed out as unseasonable sunshine slanted in through Neeve's sitting room window.

"Marginally," she said.

"It's true, though." I was in the window seat, letting the sun press warm hands on me and watching the Darkwood's cedars sway in the soft wind. "Sometimes Kian actually offers a challenge."

"Actually!" he said, mock offended. "I'd like to see you rise to that level, Rose. You could, if you cared to study strategy."

I turned my attention to them, lifting my shoulders in a shrug. "I'll leave the court machinations to the two of you."

"Ceding the field of battle entirely?" Neeve's expression was cool.

Heat rushed into my cheeks. I knew what she was saying.

"I never really had any soldiers on the field to begin with," I said, a touch defensively.

Kian gave me a look. It was impossible to miss what we were refer-ring to. *Don't say anything*, I thought at him.

"I think you undervalue your troops," Neeve said. Then, barely even glancing at the board, she swept her queen across to pin Kian's king. "Checkmate."

He made an exasperated sound and pushed up from his chair. "One day, Neeve, I'll surprise you."

"I don't doubt it. Shall we reset the board?"

"Play Rose instead. I'm going riding. It's too beautiful an afternoon to waste inside."

He didn't invite either of us to accompany him. Not that I particu-larly wanted to, but I could tell Neeve would've accepted—and then turned that look on me that meant she wanted me along.

Just as well. She and I hadn't had many moments since the fight with the basilisk, and I'd missed her, no matter how prickly she might be.

As soon as Kian was gone, I took the chair across the chess table from her. Idly, I picked up one of the white pawns and turned it about between my fingers.

"That day, with the basilisk," I began, then caught my lip between my teeth, unsure of how to continue.

Neeve simply watched me, as unhelpful as ever.

I blew out a breath and tried again. "Did I do magic?"

"You can't do magic." Her voice was flat.

"I know. But I thought—I hoped..." I set the chess piece down with a thump.

"I'm not sure what happened," she said, bending a bit. "I was begin-ning to summon foxfire to lure the basilisk away from Kian—I know it would have revealed my powers; you don't need to give me that look. But something had to be done."

"Yes." I leaned forward. "And then?"

Her mouth pressed into a line. "Then there was a flash of light, and the creature attacked you. That is all I know."

"Kian didn't seem to see anything unusual." I folded my arms.

"It is easy to overlook what you don't believe in." Her voice hardened and she slanted me a look. "It's overlooking the obvious that's more difficult."

I knew what she meant and let out a sigh. "Neeve, I'm sorry. While Kian and I were gone, we—"

She cut me off with a sharp gesture. "I never asked what passed between the two of you in Parnese—because I don't want to know."

I opened my mouth, closed it again. Opened it once more. "If you think that we—"

"I told you," she said fiercely, "I truly don't want to know. Anything."

Subdued, I stared at the chessboard. My nature, always, was to talk, to solve problems by speaking of them—although I had to admit that sometimes it only made matters worse. But ultimately, I believed that silence caused problems to fester, like wounds covered for too long. They needed light and air to heal.

Neeve, by contrast, preferred to keep her own counsel. We'd argued about it once, bitterly. I still didn't understand, but explained it to myself by imagining that she encased whatever troubles she might have the way an oyster smooths a grain of sand into a pearl. Perhaps she found it easier to live with the small, cool jewels of her problems nestled inside instead of trying to spit out the jagged pieces.

Despite the burning impulse to blurt out that Kian and I had been friends, and nothing more—no matter the evidence of that kiss—I bit my tongue.

That, of course, left us nothing to talk about. My stepsister had never been much of a conversationalist. Silence rippled from her, expanding to fill the room. I drew in a deep breath, surprised to find that I'd missed it. Missed those moments of undemanding, utter quiet between us.

I peeked over at her, hoping it meant she'd forgiven me, to find her head turned toward the window. She stared out at the Darkwood, yearning clear in the slant of her lips, the furrow marking her forehead.

"Summer's coming," she finally said, and looked back at me.

"Yes," I replied cautiously. Much as she didn't want to discuss Kian with me, I felt the same way about her and Thorne. "Will we be free to roam the forest?"

"I don't know." The softness about her eyes tightened. "I will speak with my father."

I didn't add that it was a harvest year. The knowledge pricked through me uncomfortably whenever I thought of the approaching summer. Neeve and I were both well aware that the entire castle would venture deep into the Darkwood after midsummer to pluck the bright, transient blossoms of the *nirwen*.

Although both of us had been very careful with Raine's secrets, I could see no way to conceal this event from the Fiorlanders. Unlike what had happened with me, I imagined that drugging Kian and Jarl Eiric would be a terrible diplomatic breach. And they were clever enough to figure out, as I had, that something was afoot.

Surely, though, Lord Raine had a plan. I must trust that Raine's secrets, and the mysteries of the Darkwood, would remain hidden. And that, despite the unaccountable clutch of apprehension in my chest, I would emerge from the harvest unscathed.

PART II

CHAPTER 9

New green leaves trembled on the birch trees scattered at the edge of the Darkwood as Neeve and I stepped outside the castle grounds. The stretch of meadow between the stone walls and the shadowed recesses of the forest was studded with small pink-and-white flowers, the dried grasses of winter nearly covered by the spiky green of fresh growth.

I pushed my cloak behind my shoulders and breathed deeply of the cedar-scented air. The day was cool, but not unreasonably so. And despite my fears that Lord Raine would prohibit us from setting foot outside the castle, the king had agreed to let Neeve and me go into the forest.

Not without argument—there had been a heated conversation at dinner three nights earlier, when the subject came up.

"Neeve, Rose," the king had said after the main course—venison in wine sauce—was served. "I've determined it's safe enough for you to resume your lessons with Mistress Ainya this summer."

Happiness flashed through me, and I'd clutched the linen napkin in my lap to keep from exclaiming aloud with joy.

"The herbwife?" Jarl Eiric asked, frowning. "Isn't her cottage located on the outskirts of the forest?"

"It is," Lord Raine replied.

Kian leaned forward, expression intent. "Surely you're not letting them go into the Darkwood? What if there's another basilisk?"

"The *Galadhir* assures me the forest has settled," the king said.

Jarl Eiric gave him a skeptical look. "And you're willing to risk the princesses' lives on the strength of those assurances?"

"I am." Lord Raine's voice was cool. "No one knows the forest better than Thorne Windrift. If he says it is safe, I believe him."

I slanted a quick look at Neeve, who wore her usual impassive expression. We both knew that Thorne was present in our world now, and able to act immediately if we were threatened. Besides, with the harvest upcoming, he and the Oracles would be more watchful than ever for dangers.

Beyond the usual small perils the Darkwood always contained, of course: aggressive boglins, sharp-toothed nixies lurking in the depths of pools, and the cross little hobnies who, while they didn't present a threat themselves, often seemed in need of assistance from larger dangers.

The forest contained more than just magical hazards. Wild boar and wolves roamed the woods, along with at least one bear, though I wasn't as afraid of that creature as perhaps I ought to be. The Darkwood would never be entirely without risk—but then, nothing was.

The prospect of seeing Thorne once more, of treading the cool, leafy paths, of studying herb lore with the wizened Mistress Ainya, buried any lingering worry I might have about entering the forest.

"Surely you won't let the girls go alone?" Kian asked, unwilling to let the matter drop. "They need a guard. Someone skilled with weapons, who can protect them."

It was obvious he meant himself.

Lord Raine gave Kian a quelling look. "Thorne possesses everything necessary to keep Neeve and Rose from harm."

"That fellow!" Disdain flashed across Kian's face. "He hardly seems strong enough to wield a blade, let alone face dire—"

"Do not question the *Galadhir's* abilities." The king's voice held a note of warning. "I've made my decision. Twice a week, the girls will take their customary lessons with the herbwife. And they are not in need of your escort, Prince Kian."

Kian folded his arms and leaned back with a stubborn expression, but thankfully stopped arguing.

"I'll wear my sword as always," Neeve said. "And Rose has her knife." As if that were any kind of adequate weapon.

The king nodded, and the matter was closed. Neeve and I were free to go into the Darkwood. Not every afternoon, as we were used to, but I'd forced myself to be content with two days a week. And now, here we were.

My steps quickened as we crossed the meadow, heading for the large cedar that marked our customary meeting place with Thorne. *Thorne.* Anticipation tightened my breath, prickled my skin.

"Wait." Neeve cast a glance over her shoulder, then stopped. "Oh, the nerve of him."

I paused, then turned to see Kian step through the rounded doorway in the castle wall behind us.

"What's he doing?" I whispered, though it was plain he was following us.

"Poking his nose where he shouldn't," Neeve replied, eyes narrowed.

"If we run, maybe we can lose him in the shadows of the forest." I poised myself to dash for the trees.

My stepsister made a sound of annoyance. "So he can fall headfirst into trouble, like you did the first time you followed me? That will only make matters worse."

Her tone implied that I'd certainly made things worse—and perhaps I had. Thorne had been forced to reveal his magic when he scattered the boglins attacking me, and because of that I'd had to swear a promise bound in blood that had nearly killed me.

"Kian's not going to just go back into the castle," I said glumly. "Do we have to turn back?"

Though I desperately wanted to see Thorne, would he even meet us beneath the trees if Kian insisted on coming along?

Neeve scowled and shook her head, waiting for the prince to reach us.

"What are you doing?" she demanded, at the same time Kian asked, "Where is your so-called escort?"

The two questions tangled in midair, and I let out a sigh. So much for the harmony between them.

"Thorne will meet us in the forest," I said, gesturing to the feather-limbed cedars, then caught my breath as the *Galadhir* stepped from the shadow of the trees—as tall and severely handsome as ever.

"You shouldn't leave the castle without a guard," Kian said stiffly.

"We're capable of crossing a stretch of meadow without coming to harm, I assure you." Neeve brushed her fingers over the pommel of her sword. "Your assistance is unnecessary. Good day, Prince Kian. You may leave us now."

He ignored her dismissal and merely folded his arms, watching as Thorne strode toward us. Drat it! This wasn't the warm reunion I'd anticipated.

"Prince." Thorne inclined his head to Kian. "Thank you for your presence, but I have matters well in hand."

"Nonetheless," Kian said stubbornly, "I'll accompany the ladies today."

"You can't," I blurted out, then held his gaze despite the embarrassment scrubbing my cheeks.

"Why not?" Kian frowned. "Is something the matter, Rose? You seem upset."

Mutely, I shook my head. I could scarcely explain the emotions clashing through me: my delight at seeing Thorne marred by Kian's interference, my foolish belief that things between Neeve and I would return to the way they'd been in our childhood, once we resumed our summers in the Darkwood.

They would never be the same. No matter how bitter the taste of that truth, I must swallow it. We were older now, and the world was not as simple a place as I'd once believed.

"Hello, Thorne," I said, turning to him. "It's good to see you."

A brief smile flitted across his face. "Rose. You seem much improved. I'm glad you're feeling better."

It was a sideways compliment, if it was even that, though it was true that I hadn't been at my best when last we spoke. Still, it wasn't the kind of romantic greeting I'd secretly been hoping for.

"Neeve." Thorne turned to my stepsister. "I trust all is well with you?"

Her mouth twitched, more grimace than smile. "Well enough. I'm looking forward to resuming my lessons in the Darkwood. Winter was long this year."

It had been, for all of us.

By *lessons*, I knew she was also referring to her tutorials in Dark Elf magic with Thorne. Though how she was planning to slip away for those was anyone's guess.

"Speaking of which," I said brightly, trying to dispel the awkward eddies swirling around us, "I'm sure Mistress Ainya is expecting us."

"She is." Thorne made no move to go, however. He met Kian's gaze and slowly lifted one eyebrow.

Kian set one hand on his sword and leaned forward, baring his teeth in a smile. Tension simmered in the air between them. It was clear neither of them were going to give way.

Neeve let out an impatient snort. "The two of you are ridiculous. Thorne, lead the way. Kian, bring up the rear. We're wasting time standing here." When neither man moved, Neeve pushed Thorne's shoulder. "Go."

"I do not want him at my back," Thorne said—softly, but loud enough for Kian to hear.

"Rose will keep him from doing anything foolish." Neeve prodded him again. "You're supposed to be allies, remember?"

With a severe expression, Thorne turned and led us toward the trees. Neeve followed, and I came behind her. Kian brought up the rear, a victorious light in his eyes.

I wondered what he'd do once Neeve and I were settled with Mistress Ainya. Challenge Thorne to a duel? Return, alone, to the castle? I shook my head at the thought. Thorne might not hold much affection for Kian, but he wouldn't let the prince stumble heedlessly into the Darkwood's dangers.

Even if he might be tempted to do so.

We made our way silently into the forest. The soft loam of the path cushioned our footsteps, and brown birds flitted overhead, chirping softly. Pale trillium flowers shone from the underbrush. The coiled heads of ferns nodded as we passed, waiting for the days to warm before unfurling their lacy fronds.

Despite the angry set of his shoulders, Thorne moved nimbly through his domain. Kian, on the other hand, grumbled loudly every time the underbrush snagged at his cloak or a protruding tree root made him stumble.

"Neeve," I said, knowing both our escorts would overhear, "the path seems more overgrown than usual, don't you think?"

It wasn't, of course. But not so long ago, I'd been in Kian's shoes, blundering into sudden spiderwebs and being poked by wayward branches while Neeve and Thorne passed tranquilly through the Darkwood.

Thorne made an annoyed sound and lifted his hand in a quick, twisting gesture. I didn't know if the forest had been responding to his mood, or if the Darkwood had taken an initial dislike to Kian, as it had to me. Whatever the case, the *Galadhir's* motion seemed to calm it, and Kian stopped having quite so much trouble following us through the trees.

Thinking of my own first experience in the woods, I idly rubbed my left arm. Kian had seen the mark there: a green leaf inscribed on the pale inner skin of my elbow. When he asked, I'd made some excuse about it being a Parnesian tattoo. In truth, it was the visible sign of the spell binding me to the Darkwood.

Even though Thorne had broken that binding, sometimes I fancied I felt the leaf tingling, the magic pressing against my skin like a strange itch.

Not since I'd come back from Parnese, though. Maybe traveling so far from the forest had severed the connection for good.

"How far is this cottage, anyway?" Kian asked sullenly from behind me. "You shouldn't be going so far from the castle."

"We're almost there." I nodded to a large, decaying stump crowned by a fresh sapling. "The path forks just ahead, and we go to the right."

"Where does the other way lead?"

I shrugged, trying for nonchalance. "It winds about in the forest.

Nowhere in particular, if I recall. By a stream and a big rock."

And a meadow where Neeve and I had once glimpsed the pale, shimmering beauty of the White Hart.

I wasn't sure if I wanted to protect Kian from the Darkwood, or the other way around. But the Fiorland prince shouldn't be poking about the forest. Not when Raine's deepest secrets were hidden within its depths.

As well as sharp-mouthed boglins waiting to bite. I couldn't quite tell, but some of the sticks previously snagging Kian's cloak had looked suspiciously like the nasty little creatures. I could only hope that Thorne had made it clear to the forest the prince was not to be attacked.

The path turned, the trees thinning to admit more light as we entered the birch-fringed edge of the woods. A small clearing opened before us, and at the far edge stood the *cailleach's* cottage. Fragrant smoke drifted from the chimney poking up from the thatched roof, and although it was early in the year, several bright blossoms dotted the herb garden framing the whitewashed walls.

Thorne led us to the low fence enclosing the garden and opened the gate. Before he could step through, however, the top half of Mistress Ainya's green-painted front door swung open and the herb-wife leaned out. Her wispy white hair stood out from her head like thistledown and her blue eyes were as sharp as ever.

"Wait," she called, an unexpected urgency in her voice. "Don't come in just yet. I have another caller."

Her gaze went to Kian, and she frowned, the expression deepening the creases in her face. A moment later she ducked back into her cottage, leaving us to stand in a confused bunch before the garden gate.

"What's going on?" Neeve turned to Thorne. "Who's visiting?"

His mouth tightened. "I do not know."

"Aren't you supposed to know everything that happens in the forest?" Kian asked, a mocking note in his voice.

I waved a shushing hand at him, but I shared his question. Who was in the cottage, and why hadn't Thorne known that Mistress Ainya had a visitor?

CHAPTER 10

An uncomfortable silence fell as we waited. Thorne didn't bother replying to Kian's taunting words, Neeve wasn't much of a conversationalist under any circumstances, and although I was full of questions, it didn't seem prudent to voice them.

A breeze stirred the plants in the garden, carrying the scent of fresh mint and lemon balm. And a hint of lavender, though the only place it grew in Raine was Mistress Ainya's herb patch.

We didn't have to wait overlong before the *cailleach's* door swung fully open, and her visitor stomped out, a scowl on his ugly face. He barely came up to Mistress Ainya's waist, and considering that she was quite small of stature, that made the little fellow tiny. Despite his size, however, he was fearsome, as I knew from my prior encounters with his kind.

This was a hobnie—the one Neeve and I had rescued from being trapped beneath a rock, judging by the grubby yellow hat jammed over his misshapen head. He traversed the garden path without looking at us, though I could hear him muttering curses as he drew close.

"Out of my way, you sluglike emanations," he said once he reached the gate, then glanced up at Thorne. "Yourself excluded, Windrift."

Thorne nodded gravely. "Are you well, Amharach?"

"Of course not!" The hobnie held out his right arm, displaying the linen bandage wrapped from elbow to shoulder. "You'd best do something about those poison-clawed harpies. Why, I'd have lost my arm if not for the *cailleach's* remedies. Tend to your duties, *Galadhir*. Less important things can wait."

He shot a disapproving glance at Neeve, then turned his baleful stare on me, wrinkling his nose as though he smelled something foul. Kian he ignored altogether. Then, clearly done with us, he stalked away into the forest without a backward glance.

"Come in." Mistress Ainya beckoned to us from her doorway.

"What was that?" Kian asked as we stepped through the gate. He sounded curious, but not as confounded as I'd been the first time I came upon one of the foul-tempered little creatures.

"A hobnie," Thorne said. "They dwell within the Darkwood."

"I'd gathered as much." Kian gave the *Galadhir* a critical look. "Those poison-clawed harpies don't sound particularly pleasant. Remind me again why it's safe for us to be roaming about your forest?"

"The harpies dwell on the far side of the Darkwood, by the eastern cliffs," Thorne replied tightly. "There is no need for alarm."

Kian's eyebrows went up, but at least he didn't press his argument. "What other peculiar beings live in the forest, I wonder? Besides yourself and that grumpy little fellow, I mean."

"Nothing that concerns you," Thorne said coolly, striding forward.

I glanced at Kian as we brushed past a silver-leafed sage bush. "You don't seem...unduly surprised by meeting a hobnie."

"Similar creatures dwell in Fiorland," he said. "*Vettir*, we call them. I met one, once, while out hunting with my brothers."

Neeve paused and gave him a long, appraising look that made me slightly uncomfortable. What thoughts were passing behind that dark gaze of hers?

"Greetings!" Mistress Ainya said as we arrived at her door. Her smile seemed a touch weary at the edges. "My apologies that my unexpected visitor kept me from welcoming you properly, but do come in. I'll put the kettle on."

"Thank you, but I must, as Amharach put it so inelegantly, tend to my duties." Thorne stepped back. "Prince Kian, I'll accompany your return to the castle first."

Kian folded his arms. "I don't need a nursemaid to take a simple walk through the forest. Besides, I think I'll stay here, on guard. Especially since you'll be so *busy* elsewhere."

"We don't need a guard," Neeve said curtly. "Go back with Thorne."

"I don't think so."

Mistress Ainya glanced between them, forehead furrowed. "Perhaps you ought to discuss matters over tea."

"Another time." Thorne made her a slight bow. Then, a hint of annoyance on his face, he turned to Kian. "If you insist on staying here, remain within the garden until the girls are ready to return."

Girls. I felt a flush warm my cheeks. Did Thorne really still think of us as children? He was not that much older than Neeve and I, after all.

Neeve, temper sparking in her eyes, raised one brow. "If you *boys* are done with your spat, we shouldn't keep Mistress Ainya from her hospitality."

I wanted to cheer her words, but settled for giving her an appreciative smile. I might dislike being the object of my stepsister's pointed words, but when they were deservedly turned elsewhere, I didn't mind in the least.

Thorne gave her a resigned look. "If I'm not here by the time you're ready to return to Castle Raine, go back yourselves—and keep the prince out of trouble."

Kian made an annoyed sound, but didn't say anything as Thorne turned toward the forest. I tried not to watch him stride away through the herb garden.

"Well then," Mistress Ainya said, a touch too brightly. "Let's go inside."

She led the way into her tidy cottage, the flagstones scrubbed as clean as I recalled, the bunches of dried herbs hanging from the ceiling perfuming the air. We took our places around the small table crowded with four chairs as the herbwife bustled about, swinging the kettle on its hook over the fire, strewing a handful of herbs into a stout brown teapot.

Some calming blend, I hoped, that would help ease the tensions swirling between us.

"What do your lessons here consist of?" Kian asked, as Mistress Ainya set out four earthenware mugs.

A silence followed his question.

"The properties of herbs and poultices, mostly," I answered, when it became clear that neither Neeve nor the herbwife were inclined to do so. "Medicinal, culinary, how to preserve and store them. Surely you have similar lorekeepers in Fiorland?"

"The *Kloka*, yes. Though I don't know that they particularly tend toward bandaging up strange little forest creatures." He gave Mistress Ainya a pointed glance.

"A healer's duties extend wherever necessary," she said mildly, swinging the kettle off the fire. "Now, Rose, I hear you were very ill. Are you feeling quite recovered?"

I squirmed a little under her assessing look. "Yes. At least, I think so. I feel much better."

The herbwife regarded me a moment longer, eyes bright in her wizened face, then poured boiling water into the teapot. The sweet smell of chamomile and mint filled the air. When she was finished, she set the kettle aside and came over to where I sat.

"Give me your hands," she said.

Obediently, I held them out, palms up. She grasped them, closed her eyes a moment, then frowned. Neeve leaned forward a little, curious. I wondered what she saw in Mistress Ainya's face.

"Hmm." Mistress Ainya opened her eyes. She released my right hand, but kept hold of the left. For a moment, the stub of my pinky ached. "What did the doctor do to cure you in Parnese?"

I shook my head. "I don't know—I was delirious at the time. But Kian was there."

"Were you?" The herbwife glanced to him.

"Not at the physician's, no," he said. "Rose's mother and Sir Durum took her, and when they returned, she started getting better. Slowly."

Mistress Ainya pressed her lips together in thought. "They transported Rose, ill as she was, to see the doctor? One might think a proper physician would come to his patient."

"Hers," I said. "The doctor was a woman, I think. From what my mother said."

Kian nodded his agreement, and Mistress Ainya released my hand, a troubled look upon her face.

"What is it?" Neeve asked in a low voice.

"I'm not certain." The herbwife slid a look at Kian. "But it's no matter. The tea's ready—and we may begin our lessons. Neeve, tell me the uses of mugwort."

We sipped our herbal tea and answered Mistress Ainya's questions, while Kian looked increasingly bored. Finally he slurped back the rest of his tea and pushed away from the table.

"I'm going outside," he said.

"Don't leave without us," Neeve said. Not because we craved his escort back to the castle, of course, but at least she wasn't foolish enough to say so.

"What will you do?" I asked him.

"Watch the bees. Practice my sword work."

"Don't practice too much," Neeve said.

Kian winked at her. "What, you don't want me getting better than you? I already am."

She gave him a sour look, and, with a laugh, Kian stepped out of the cottage.

"Rose," Mistress Ainya said, turning to me, "tell me the properties of milk thistle."

I thought a moment, trying to recall the pages of the herbal primer both Neeve and I studied. "It helps with an upset stomach and...ah yes, one can make a clarifying tonic with it."

"Indeed. And used in conjunction with sage, what type of benefits might one expect?"

Neeve tilted her head while I searched for an answer.

"Might one include nettle, as well?" she asked.

The herbwife nodded at her. "An excellent addition, yes."

I tried not to pout. "What are you talking about?" I felt like a child left out of an adult conversation.

Mistress Ainya held my gaze. "In combination, these herbs help clarify, as you said, but they also hold strong rebalancing and cleansing qualities." Her expression turned serious. "I think you ought to prepare a tincture and take it daily."

"Me?" I blinked at her. "Why?"

"I sense something amiss with you, Rose. Some imbalance or internal occlusion that an herbal tonic might help ease."

Well. I scarcely knew what to say to that. Resting my elbows on the table, I stared down into my mug of tea, letting the fragrant steam wreathe my face. I wanted to protest that I felt perfectly fine—but in truth, if I were completely honest with myself, I did not.

Haltingly, I searched for the words to explain my state of health. "I suppose you're right. In Parnese, I was too exhausted most of the time to notice, but it's been"—I did a quick calculation—"ten months now, and I still feel...hazy I suppose. Depleted. Do you really think a tonic will help?"

"In the proper dose—namely, not too much—it certainly won't hurt," Mistress Ainya said. "Why don't you finish your tea and get started with that, while I quiz Neeve on her other studies."

Those other studies being magical in nature, of course.

"Is that wise?" Neeve glanced out the window, to where Kian dodged and whirled, wielding his blade against an imaginary opponent.

"Theoretical conversation only," the herbwife said, then shook her head. "If your young man insists on accompanying you to the cottage regularly, I don't know quite how we'll manage."

"He's not my young man," my stepsister said, red blossoming on her cheeks—though whether from anger or embarrassment, I couldn't say.

Mistress Ainya pursed her mouth and didn't argue, and the two of them turned to a discussion of energy flows. I stood and went to the jars of herbs ranged along the workbench at the other side of the room, pulling out the nettle, milk thistle, and sage.

As I sifted and measured, my mind was preoccupied. With Kian so insistently watchful, how would Neeve manage to study her magic with

Mistress Ainya, let alone with Thorne? Was the prince truly as nonchalant about encountering the hobnie as he seemed? Would the herbal tonic I was currently preparing help me feel any better?

And, most concerning of all, what, precisely, was the matter with me?

CHAPTER 11

The pattern of our days was quickly set. Despite our arguments, Kian insisted on accompanying me and Neeve on our twice-weekly outings to Mistress Ainya's. Although Thorne met us at the edge of the Darkwood each time, he often left it to the three of us to make our way back to the castle afterward. He clearly disapproved of the Fiorland prince's presence, but just as clearly wasn't going to do anything about it except stare coldly at Kian every time their paths crossed.

I was convinced Neeve was managing to meet with Thorne to continue her lessons in Dark Elf magic. Though I didn't catch my step-sister slipping away, I suspected she was using the secret passage in the cellars that tunneled out to the forest. The one time I attempted to follow, however, Kian intercepted me. I was forced to deflect by saying I'd been looking for him, and would he like to play a game of chess?

Grinning, he agreed, and though our game was pleasant, I couldn't help being distracted by the thought of Neeve in the forest, and my own lost opportunities to see Thorne.

Neeve and Kian were another thing that made me uneasy. My step-sister had softened toward him once again, and it seemed that their friendship was back on even footing. But sometimes I caught her watching him with a look in her eyes that seemed quite removed from the warmth of affection.

She dismissed my attempt to speak to her about it, of course. Since the subject of Kian was still a sensitive topic between us, I let the matter drop—though my worries remained.

Dutifully, I drank my tonic every evening, in a dosage that Mistress Ainya had approved of. I thought perhaps it had a slight effect on my sense of sluggishness, but it was difficult to be certain. Spring folded into early summer, and my birthday loomed.

The day before I was to turn seventeen, Neeve stopped me as we exited the schoolroom.

"Thorne wants to speak with you," she said softly. "Today."

My heart leaped. "What? Where? Oh, I knew you were sneaking out!"

"Shh." My stepsister glanced up and down the hallway. "Leave the castle via the herb shed. He'll meet you."

"What about training?" Weapons practice was slated for the afternoon.

"I'll make your excuses to Sir Durum," Neeve said. "A stomachache, perhaps?"

I nodded. "I'll skip dinner, just to make it believable. Bring me some bread, though. And a bit of meat for Trisk."

By now, the cat was used to the leftovers I smuggled nightly up to my room. She was my most constant friend in the castle, and though she was quite capable of catching her own dinner, I liked spoiling her.

Despite the impatience burning through me at the thought of seeing Thorne, I waited to go meet him until Neeve departed her rooms for weapons training. She'd keep Kian from coming to look for me. If he discovered me skulking about the hallways, it would certainly put the lie to my supposed ill health.

Once the way was clear, I all but flew down the deserted corridors and out the side door of the castle. The air was damp from the morning's rain, and my skirts darkened as I passed through the trimmed shrubbery and roses just beginning to bud.

I rounded the sculpture of the dancing maiden and dashed to the slightly decrepit garden shed built up against Castle Raine's outer wall.

It seemed an ordinary outbuilding, unless one knew of the secret door that led through the walls, allowing a person to leave the castle unobserved. The musty dried-herb smell of the interior tickled my nose as I jiggled the hidden lever. It stuck for a moment, then gave way.

I burst out into the sward of meadow separating Castle Raine from the Darkwood. Somewhat to my disappointment, Thorne wasn't hovering there in wait—but of course he wouldn't be standing about in the open. In addition to his natural reticence, the *Galadhir* was most comfortable in the shadows of the forest he guarded.

Picking up my skirts, I ran through the cornflower-spotted grasses and arrived, slightly breathless, at the tall cedar that was our usual meeting point. Thorne strode forward from the shelter of its branches, smiling at me, and then I truly couldn't catch my breath. His dark eyes were filled with golden sparks.

"I've missed you—" I began, then cut off in shock as he kept coming and folded me into his embrace.

His arms were strong about me, and I leaned into the slim, sturdy length of him. I managed a single, perfect sigh before he stepped back, and I had to force my fingers to release his shirt, or risk clinging to him like a fool.

"Forgive me for presuming," he said, his smile going slightly crooked. "I've been worried about you."

"I don't mind." Heat flashed into my face at the truth of how very much I *didn't mind*. "Have you come to wish me a happy birthday?"

"In a way, yes—I wanted to speak with you about the pattern of calamities you seem to experience surrounding the date of your birth. Come, sit."

He led me to a downed log cushioned with moss, then waited for me to settle before sitting beside me. Close enough our sides nearly touched, I couldn't help noticing.

"I'm not sick on *every* birthday," I said, somewhat defensively.

"No—but in the time I've known you, you've fallen grievously ill twice. I intend there should not be a third."

"One of those was your fault," I reminded him. "And don't forget the nixie almost drowning me."

All trace of humor had gone from his expression. "I bear full responsibility for the harm done to you. Which is why I intend to safeguard you tonight. With your permission."

I stared at him a moment. "How, precisely, do you intend to do that?"

"As guardian of the forest, I have certain powers of protection that I can extend over you for a short time."

Without thinking, I rubbed my left elbow. "I don't particularly want another binding put on me."

"No—we both learned our lesson there. But the wards I intend to cast require my proximity to remain in effect. I'll need to keep watch from within your rooms. If you agree."

I swallowed, my throat suddenly dry. "You mean, while I sleep?"

Whatever would Sorche think if Thorne spent the night in my suite? Even if he passed the entire time slumped into one of the chairs in the sitting room, I was now of an age that such a thing would provoke a scandal. Even if nothing whatsoever happened.

Which it wouldn't, of course. Despite that quick embrace, I knew Thorne had no romantic inclinations toward me—and even if by some miracle he did, he was far too honorable to act on them.

As if he'd read my thoughts, one of his brows angled up. "I would remain invisible to all but your eyes, of course."

"Oh, yes. Of course. Well." I glanced down at my hands, idly moving my stubby pinky up and down. "If you think it's wise, I'm happy to agree."

The thought of Thorne in my rooms made my skin prickle—half with longing, half with mortification. What if I snored loudly? Or drooled in my sleep?

"Then it's settled. I'll arrive after dinner."

"I'm not going to the dining room tonight," I said. "My excuse to miss weapons training today was a stomachache."

The hint of a smile lifted the corner of his mouth. "Then look for me at dusk."

"I will." My heart thumped loudly beneath my ribs.

I supposed I'd spend the intervening hours trying to study or lose myself in the pages of the most recent adventure novel I'd chosen from the library—though at the moment I couldn't even recall the title.

Thorne nodded. Then his gaze went to the gray stone walls just visible through the screen of trees.

"You'd best return to the castle, before you're missed."

Not that anyone would be looking for me. Except, perhaps, the cat.

"This evening, then." Before I could say anything foolish, like *I can scarcely wait* or *how wonderful it will be to spend time in your company*, I turned and hurried back across the stretch of meadow.

The sky was overcast again, the low pewter clouds promising rain within the next few hours. Altogether, a fine afternoon to curl up beside the fire.

And wait.

A KNOCK SOUNDED at my door before dinner. I opened it to see Kian, slightly disheveled from weapons practice, a lock of hair stuck to his forehead with sweat.

"Neeve said you're not feeling well." He looked me up and down. "Will you be all right, Rose? I mean—it's almost your birthday, and I remember what happened last year, with your illness..."

The concern in his eyes was touching.

"We don't know if my birthday has anything to do with it," I said untruthfully. Thorne was right when he'd noted that I tended to fall ill right around that date.

But Kian was chivalrous, and it would be like him to make an impulsive offer to keep watch over me that night—which would certainly complicate matters, as Thorne was due to arrive at any moment.

"Still, maybe someone should—"

"I'll speak with Sorche about having someone nearby," I said. Of course, when I did so, I'd tell her it wasn't necessary, but Kian didn't need to know that. "I'll be well attended to, don't worry."

At least that much was true.

The concern in his eyes didn't lessen. "If you're sure. I don't really want to rush off to Parnese again to keep you from dying."

"Neither do I." My pulse stuttered at the memory of flames

consuming me from within. My fever had been so high that I was delirious for weeks. And I couldn't forget how tenderly Kian had cared for me during my long recovery.

"If you change your mind, tell me," he said, holding my gaze. "I don't like that you're already feeling ill."

Oh—I hadn't considered that Kian might fret when I'd come up with that ruse.

"I'm mostly recovered," I said brightly. "I've asked Neeve to bring me some bread and meat from dinner. I didn't feel quite up to a long, formal meal. But I'll be fine."

Movement at the end of the hall caught my eye. I glanced over, to see Thorne pause in the shadows.

"What is it?" Kian turned. "Is someone there? Neeve?"

"The cat, I think." It was obvious he couldn't see Thorne, who was fully visible to my eyes. "At any rate, don't worry about me. You should go wash up—you stink of sweat."

Kian didn't smell—at least not very much—but insulting him would help speed him on his way.

"You're becoming as gracious as Neeve," he said, shaking his head. "Very well. But tell me if you change your mind."

"I will." I smiled sweetly at him. "I promise."

I made to shut the door, though I kept it open a crack as Kian turned and strode down the hallway. He passed Thorne without a moment's hesitation, and was gone.

The *Galadhir* waited a few heartbeats, then made his soft-footed way to my door. I opened it and he slipped inside. Once the latch clicked down, I went to my sitting area and gestured for him to follow.

"Neeve will be coming up after supper," I said, settling in my favorite chair. "Will she be able to see you?"

"She will sense me," he replied. "It's better if I don't try to deceive her."

Of all the people in the castle, Neeve was the best at keeping secrets. I wasn't delighted with the idea that she would know Thorne planned to pass the night in my rooms, but there was no helping it. At least she wouldn't jump to conclusions. We both knew that Thorne was in love with her, not me.

On the heels of that thought, a quick knock came at my door. Without waiting for my reply, Neeve stepped in, bearing a tray.

"I brought you food—" She halted, blinking once at the sight of Thorne standing beside me. "You seem to be making a habit of entertaining gentlemen callers, Rose. Hello, Thorne."

Thorne nodded a greeting, then turned to me. "I did notice the prince buzzing about your doorway earlier."

"Again?" Neeve made a disgusted sound. "Don't tell me he's still angling for your affections, Rose."

Heat flashed into my face. "No."

Clearly my stepsister hadn't yet forgotten, or entirely forgiven, that kiss.

Thorne's expression darkened. "Are you saying he often visits you in the evenings?"

"He was just checking on me," I said. "You're not the only one who noticed I get sick around my birthday."

"Is that what Thorne's doing here?" Neeve asked, moving to set the tray on my small table. She tilted her head at him. "Do you think Rose's affliction is magical in nature?"

"I don't know what to think." He sounded frustrated. "Perhaps she's simply reactive, making ripples in fate the way a stone in a stream forces the water into new patterns."

"I'm rippling fate?" I disliked the notion of being some passive obstruction, though Mistress Ainya had implied as much in the past. "That sounds uncomfortable. What does the rock think as the water runs over it?"

"Rocks don't think anything," Neeve said, thrusting a half loaf of bread wrapped in a napkin at me. She took the other chair, leaving Thorne standing. "You've consulted the Oracles about Rose?"

"Not specifically. But in the course of our scrying, her image has appeared a number of times." A shadow moved across his expression. "She seems involved in the futures of both Raine and Elfhame."

He snagged the low stool I kept under the table and brought it over to the fire, perching upon it far more elegantly than I'd ever manage.

"Like the scrying Neeve and I both saw?" I asked.

That image was even now clear in my mind: Neeve and I facing one another, her with a glowing blue sword, me with flame at my fingertips. I shivered at the memory.

"Not precisely like your vision." Thorne closed his mouth, suddenly looking inscrutable.

"You won't tell me?" I tried not to sound peevish.

"It's better not to speak of such things," he said. "Eat your dinner."

"A hunk of bread is scarcely dinner," I grumbled, but tore off a bite. I had to admit that it tasted good—soft and fresh from the afternoon ovens.

"I brought an apple, too. And meat, as you requested." Neeve glanced about. "Where's the cat?"

"She comes and goes. Right now, she's gone. She doesn't much like company." I wondered if she'd appear later, or if Thorne's presence would keep her from my rooms all night. "How was dinner?"

Neeve's brows drew together in a dark-winged frown. "Jarl Eiric was on again about the Athraig threat. Now that the seas have calmed, he's worried they'll renew their efforts to force an alliance. The navy is alert and patrolling the coast, but there's still a danger."

"Did your father say anything more about"—I threw a glance at Thorne, then forged ahead—"your various marriage options?"

"He's implied to the Athraig that a match with Fiorland is already secured." Her tone was grim. "Though he's forbidden Kian to do anything about it, for now."

"You mean propose." Again. I took a bite of bread to distract myself.

"He must wait until after the *nirwen* harvest, at the very least," Thorne said.

"Don't you think our allies should know Raine's secrets?" I asked, chewing thoughtfully.

"Of course," Thorne answered. "But in due time. Once the betrothal's firmly settled, then the Fiorlanders will be privy to that knowledge."

That seemed backward to me—but then, I wasn't in charge of running a kingdom. I glanced at Neeve to see what she thought, but her expression was shuttered. Only her dark eyes betrayed the pain she felt.

"The jarl mentioned you again," she said, looking at me. "That perhaps the Athraig would settle for a lesser princess. A bone to throw them, to keep them from Raine's door."

My throat tightened and I could barely swallow the bread in my mouth. "I'm sure my mother objected."

"Not quite as strenuously as before, I'm afraid." Neeve's expression softened. "Don't worry. I won't let them bargain you away."

"Nor I." Thorne's voice was hard. "The scrying shows that your future lies here, not across the sea. If you marry anyone, it will be—"

He broke off, catching himself, and I stared at him, a bright jab of apprehension going through me.

"Who?" I asked urgently. "Who am I to marry?"

He shook his head, suddenly looking as young as Neeve and I. "I'm sorry. Forget I spoke of it."

"It's Nightshade, isn't it?" Neeve asked, her voice low.

"Surely not," I whispered, shivering at the thought of being bound to the forbidding Dark Elf lord.

Thorne looked miserable, but refused to answer.

"I won't do it," I said, a flame of rebellion kindling in my chest. "Nobody can make me say any vows against my will."

"The king can," Neeve warned me.

Not if I'm not here. I didn't voice the words aloud. Perhaps it was time to start laying plans of my own, to secure a future that, whatever Thorne might say, lay well beyond the shores of Raine.

CHAPTER 12

Neeve left shortly thereafter, and I wrapped away the bread and apple, my appetite gone. There was no sign of Trisk, but I set the morsels of meat in a small dish out in the hallway, just in case. Thorne watched me curiously, but didn't object.

"Now what?" I asked, after I'd washed my hands and tidied up the sitting area.

"I'll cast the wards about your bedroom," Thorne said. "And then you will sleep."

"What will you do?"

He gave me level look. "As I said—keep watch."

"What if you get tired?"

"The wards will wake me if anything goes amiss. But I don't intend to sleep."

"Do you have to be in my bedroom the whole time?" Embarrassed heat prickled up from the soles of my feet to the top of my head.

"Not if you don't want me to." He tilted his head. "Does such a thought make you uncomfortable?"

"No," I lied. "I just think I'll sleep better if you stay in here, by the fire."

"Then I will do so. Now, make whatever preparations you need, and when you're ready, call me to come in."

I nodded, trying to keep my expression serene, then lit the second lamp and carried it into the bedroom. I'd dismissed Sorche earlier, telling her that Neeve would help me prepare for bed that evening, but that meant I had to struggle with the laces of my gown alone. I managed, too proud to ask Thorne for help. It wouldn't be proper, at any rate. I might daydream of his embrace, but asking for his aid in undressing was too far outside the bounds.

I donned my most modest nightgown, braided my unruly red curls back, and hopped beneath the covers. Then, blankets drawn up to my chin, I called for Thorne.

He came in, the lamplight casting a sheen on his ebony hair and highlighting the pallor of his face. It was impossible to miss his uncanny resemblance to Neeve—their Dark Elf blood bound them together in ways I could never understand.

I sighed, and he gave me a concerned glance. "Are you well?"

"Yes. Oh, but I forgot my tonic." I sat up, covers still clenched about me, and nodded to the bottle of pale gold liquid on the nightstand.

He went to pick it up, then hesitated as his fingers wrapped about the glass.

"What's in your concoction?" he asked, holding it up.

I named the herbs, and he frowned slightly as he handed it to me.

"It's on Mistress Ainya's advice," I told him. "Everything in it is perfectly safe."

"I know." He gave me a thoughtful, slightly troubled look. "Does it seem to be helping?"

"Maybe? I'm not sure. But at any rate, I'm not feeling any *worse*."

I took a grimacing swallow of the tonic, wishing I'd added more honey, then stoppered the bottle and handed it back to him. He set it on my bedside table, where the lamplight sent golden reflections through the liquid.

"Make yourself comfortable," he said. "I'll set the wards."

"Can I watch?" Even if he said no, I'd peek. It wasn't every day magic was performed in my bedroom.

The memory of the one time I'd tried to summon flame tickled at me, and I resolutely shoved it back down. Despite the fact that nothing happened, I'd memorized the chant—though it hadn't done any good against the basilisk, either.

"Of course you may watch. Though I'm not sure it will be very interesting." He sent me a warning glance. "I'll be focusing on the casting and won't be able to answer any questions or explain what I'm doing."

I nodded my understanding and wrapped my arms around my updrawn knees. The shadows danced over his face, throwing his edged cheekbones into sharp relief. Then he spoke a soft word in elvish, and a glowing ball of blue fire sprang to life in his palm.

He flicked his fingers, and the globe floated up to hover at his shoulder. With soft footsteps he strode over to my curtain-draped windows and made a complex move with his hands, again speaking in the strange syllables of his own language.

Although I kept my eyes wide, I didn't see any particular result as he paced to each corner of my room and repeated his casting. Finally, he came to stand at the center, near the end of my bed. Raising his arms, he pivoted to face me.

"*Varna,*" he said, his dark eyes meeting mine.

I thought I saw a tracery of blue lines fold over my room, delicate as a spiderweb, but the impression was overtaken by a dart of pain midway up my left arm.

"Ow!" I shoved up the sleeve of my nightgown.

The leaf inscribed at the inside of my elbow was glowing. Even as I watched, the green pulse of light faded, the sharp prick subsiding to a dull itch.

Thorne was at my side in a moment. Gently taking my elbow, he bent over to study the sigil the Darkwood had set into my skin. His long hair brushed my forearm, and I trembled at the feel of it.

"Does your arm hurt?" he asked.

"It did for a moment—but now it more...buzzes." Like a bee was trapped on my skin, not angry, just confused.

"Hm." He brushed his thumb over the mark, and I tried not to hold my breath at his nearness. "The residue of the binding reacted to my wards, I think. And perhaps..." He shot a glance at the nearby bottle of herbal tonic. "Perhaps the herbs have contributed as well."

"Should I stop taking it?"

"I don't think you need to worry." He released my arm. "The interactions don't seem to be doing you any harm. If anything, they're adding a layer of protection, which is all to the good."

"Do you really think I need to worry about turning seventeen?" I pulled my sleeve back down.

He fixed me with a look, the sparks of amber in his eyes glinting. "Rose. You nearly died last year. We're taking no chances."

"All right." I pulled in a breath that turned into a yawn, and a faint smile stole across his expression.

"Rest. I'll be right here." He glanced toward my sitting room. "Or there, as the case may be."

I nodded, and he leaned over and blew out the lantern on my bedside table, then made his surefooted way through the darkened room. For a moment his slim, graceful form was silhouetted in the doorway. I heard soft rustlings as he moved one of the chairs and unfolded the blanket draped over the back.

Despite having Thorne in the next room, and the thrill of knowing I lay beneath a magical protection, slumber stole over me, easing me into the dark.

My dreams, however, were uneasy. I was dimly aware of tossing and turning in my sheets, damp with sweat, while the tracery of blue lines about my room flared. Words in Elvish, the feel of Thorne's presence, a sudden image of myself pushing back a wall of questing fire with my bare hands.

In the morning, I awoke surprised to find myself clearheaded, my room uncharred. Sunshine filtered in past the draperies, a single bar of light lying over the leaf-colored carpet.

With a deep breath, I slipped out of bed and went to open the curtains.

"Rose—you're awake?" Thorne peeked in from the sitting room.

Embarrassment flamed through me. I darted back to bed, pulling the covers around my shoulders like an awkward cloak.

"I am," I answered, rather belatedly. "Come in."

He did, and despite the faint smile hovering about his lips, he looked tired. His eyes were shadowed, and a line of worry marred his forehead.

"Did you sleep well?" he asked, coming to stand at my bedside.

"Mostly. But it seems you didn't. What happened in the night?"

His mouth tightened. "Something came questing—a sorcerous power made of flame that taxed my magic. Fortunately, in the end, I was able to repel it."

I wrapped my arms about myself, recalling the red priests of Parnese. "Did it...recognize you, or the magic of Elfhame?"

"I cannot say. I must speak with the Oracles and see if they have more insight."

"Will this strange power..." I dropped my voice, though we were alone in my bedroom. "Will it threaten the *nirwen* harvest?"

"A better question is whether it still threatens *you*, Rose. Why did it come seeking you on your birthday?"

"Perhaps it's my magical powers, looking for me?" It was a foolishly hopeful thought, but I couldn't help voicing it.

To my disappointment, he shook his head. "Powers rise from within—even among humans. Mistress Ainya and I have discussed the possibility at length, and we both are certain that whatever is attacking you on your birthdays, it is not some lost creature coming home to roost."

When he put it that way, I could see how absurd the notion was. Magic wasn't a stray puppy gone missing in the streets, whining from door to door in search of its owner.

"So, am I safe for another year?"

"I believe so." He lifted his head, as if listening. "Your maid will be in momentarily to attend you. I must go."

I didn't want him to leave—but I could hardly make him stay. Still, I reached out my hand to him. He took it, bending over it as if I were a queen, his fingers warm on mine.

When he straightened, I saw echoes of some strong emotion in his eyes and recalled our conversation the night before. And his accidental admission that fate had shown him whom I was to marry.

Pulse beating in my throat, I held his gaze.

"Thorne—"

"I will see you shortly," he said softly, then released my hand and turned away.

And with that he was gone, as quiet as a leaf falling in the forest, and I was left to face the rest of my seventeenth birthday alone.

Despite my melancholy mood, however, I was soon attended by Sorche, who brought my usual cup of hot tea and a buttery scone for my breakfast, then helped me dress in my new gold velvet gown. Trisk slipped in along with the maid and, purring loudly, happily settled in my lap as I sat before the fire.

I hadn't quite finished my tea when Neeve rapped upon my door. Sorche let her in, and she stepped into the sitting room, looking about as if seeking any traces of Thorne.

"Good morning," she said. "I'm glad to see you're still alive."

"So am I." I smiled at her. "Come, sit. Would you like tea, or something to eat?"

"I've already had my tea. And we should make for the classroom soon."

I let out a sigh. No reprieve from schoolwork, even on my birthday.

A moment later, Kian knocked and came in, expressing the same sentiments as Neeve about my continued health, although he did so more gracefully. He leaned one elbow on the mantel and grinned at me.

"Let's all go riding this afternoon," he said. "It's a glorious day."

"If Rose would like," Neeve said, for once deferring to me.

"Certainly." Though I didn't adore riding, as Neeve and Kian did, I'd become an adequate enough horsewoman to take some pleasure in it. Especially in the company of my friends.

Looking about my full sitting room, I had to admit that I couldn't wallow in the falsehood that I was alone and unloved.

Even if Thorne wasn't there.

"Oh, I nearly forgot," Sorche said, coming in from making up the bed in the other room. "Your mother desires to see you after lunch, Miss Rose."

"She does?" I blinked at the request.

For so long, I'd been nothing but an afterthought, a piece of baggage dragged along when my mother wed Lord Raine. At one time, the prospect of spending the afternoon with Mama would have filled me with happiness—but I was no longer that child eager for crumbs of her affection.

"Did she say what she wanted?" I asked.

"No, miss. Perhaps she wants to wish you a happy birthday?"

I thought it unlikely. But whatever the reason, it shouldn't take long. Mama was never one to linger in my company.

"We'll ride after I meet with her," I said to Neeve and Kian. "There should be plenty of time before dinner."

CHAPTER 13

That afternoon, I made my way to the east wing of the castle, where my mother's rooms lay. The door to her suite was carved with stags and delicate vines, the deer highlighted with gold leaf.

"Come in," Mama called when I knocked, her voice light and sweet.

With a fortifying breath, I opened the door and stepped into her parlor. My pinky stub ached as I crossed the threshold, and I absentmindedly rubbed it as I looked about. I'd never actually set foot in my mother's rooms, I realized with a pang.

Her lavishly appointed sitting area was easily twice the size of mine, and filled with brocade-upholstered chairs, little tables covered with crystal figurines, and a long settee overflowing with pillows. I had only a moment to notice that the back of the couch was draped with a large collection of gowns before my mother wrapped me in her perfumed embrace.

"Rose, my darling girl!" she said, as though she hadn't seen me in months. Perhaps she'd been afraid of the consequences of my birthday, too—though I doubted she'd admit as much.

She drew back quickly and waved at one of the ornately carved chairs drawn up beside the couch. "Sit—we have so much to talk about."

"We do?" I frowned and moved to the indicated seat.

"Well, of course." Mama perched across from me and clasped her hands. "You're of an age now when we must discuss womanly matters."

"I know about such things already," I reminded her, shifting uncomfortably. "We had this conversation when I turned twelve." Even though it had taken nearly a year after that for my body to begin the changes she'd described.

"Not *that* conversation." She let out a little laugh. "No, I mean how to present yourself in the best light, what creams and cosmetics to use, which gowns will show you off to advantage when suitors come to call."

She waved at the array of opulent dresses spread over the couch.

"Suitors?" My chest tightened. "I don't think it's the right time—"

"It's the perfect time. Now that Neeve is all but betrothed to the Fiorlander prince, we must make arrangements for you. A pity my Tobin didn't have any boys for you to wed here, but no doubt we can find you a prince somewhere."

"I don't want a prince, here or anywhere," I said hotly, beginning to stand.

"Sit." My mother's voice lost its sweetness, the light in her eyes hardening. "Rose, this is your destiny. You are of royal blood, by descent as well as marriage. Even if your connection to the Parnesian throne is distant, you are now a daughter of the King of Raine and will wed accordingly."

"And if I refuse?"

She blinked at me. "That is not an option. Really, Rose, what else would you do? Where would you go? You're not suited to a life on your own, out there in the world."

"I could learn to make my way," I said tightly. "I did well enough in Parnese, growing up."

"Parnese is too dangerous—anywhere in Parnesia or Caliss would put your life in danger. No, we must look further north for an alliance."

"I don't want—"

"Prince Kian has any number of brothers," she continued, ignoring my protest. "And there is always the Athraig."

"Why?" I cried. "Why now?"

My mother gently reached over and patted my hand. "Because you are now of marriageable age. And because..."

She glanced at the closed door, then back to me. A shadowed apprehension moved through her eyes, a fear I could not name.

"What is it?" I asked softly.

"I simply want you to be safe. Protected."

"I'm safe here," I said.

Her expression tightened, her smooth face showing the faintest trace of wrinkles about her eyes. "You are not. The king has suggested an alliance that I cannot countenance. The only way to avoid it is to make sure you are engaged elsewhere."

Apprehension shivered through me. "Do you mean the Night—"

She sliced her hand through the air, cutting me off. "We shall not speak of it. Suffice it to say that we must look outside the kingdom for your betrothal."

I glanced at the cream-colored carpet beneath my feet, misery and fear knotting in my chest while my thoughts whirled.

My fears concerning the Nightshade Lord had just been confirmed. Although my mother refused to speak openly of it, the dire fact that the King of Raine was considering marrying me off to that forbidding Dark Elf lord loomed between us.

But surely, despite Mama's insistence to the contrary, there was another way to avoid that fate other than binding myself to an unknown Fiorlander. Or worse, the Athraig prince.

I must leave Raine. And though my heart still yearned for the Parnese of my childhood, that golden city was no more. Where could I go? Once, I might have coaxed Thorne into letting me set foot in Elfhame, even though that was Neeve's dream more than my own.

But with the Nightshade Lord waiting just beyond that gateway, Elfhame was no more a refuge than Raine. Perhaps I could go to the lands south of Parnesia...

"You like Prince Kian well enough, I believe," Mama said. "Surely one of his brothers would suit. I think it the best option."

I did not, but there was no more point in arguing with her. I must buy time in order to lay my own plans, which meant pretending to agree.

"Will you invite one of them here?" I asked, swallowing back the lump in my throat.

Mama's face brightened and she gave me a smile. "I knew you'd see sense, my darling, once I explained things to you. Why don't you ask Prince Kian which of his brothers you ought to marry?"

Oh, that would be a terribly awkward conversation—and one I had no intention of having. Nonetheless, I gave her a meek nod. I couldn't recall the name of Kian's next-oldest brother, but I'd wheedle it from Neeve and give it to my mother.

"I'll speak to the king," Mama continued. "The sooner the better, I'd think. And now that the matter's settled, stand up. We must determine which of these gowns best brings out the color of your eyes."

"Will it take long?" I could hardly wait to escape her sweetly scented rooms. My head was beginning to ache, pulsing in time with my left hand. "I'm supposed to go riding this afternoon."

"This is far more important," she said. "After the gowns, we have cosmetics and jewelry to discuss. It will certainly fill the entire afternoon. I'll have the servants send up tea and pastries to sustain us."

Wonderful.

"Let me go tell Neeve and Kian I won't be joining them."

"No need." Mama waved her hand airily. "I'll have the maid inform them. Now, let us see about the gowns. Begin with the pale green."

I dutifully stood and held the green gown against me, which met with approval, then the lavender, which was immediately dismissed as making me look sallow. The pale rose one after that seemed to suit me very well, to Mama's evident surprise.

"With your hair, one wouldn't think so," she said. "No, no, leave the orange one be—I can already tell that color is an utter disaster for you."

For all her faults, my mother had an impeccable eye, and I took mental note of her choices. Not because I wanted to be princess of some foreign land someday, but because of Thorne. Even though I knew it was hopeless.

The food revived me somewhat, and we moved to the jewelry,

which was a bit more enjoyable—especially as Mama allowed me to eat and drink without fear of getting crumbs and tea stains on the expensive fabrics. To my surprise, my mother had a number of pieces that seemed, to my eye at least, to be the work of Dark Elf artisans.

"This is lovely," I said, picking up an elegant bracelet fashioned of twining silver vines that glimmered in the afternoon light. "I don't think I've ever seen you wear it."

She laughed and waved at the dressing table laden with a treasure trove of necklaces, bracelets, brooches, rings. "I've so many pieces, I truly can't keep track."

Her laughter had a hollow ring, however.

I set the bracelet down and turned to face her. "What do you know of Elfhame?"

It was a question I'd wanted to ask her ever since the summer three years ago, when I discovered the secret gateway between the worlds. By word and deed, my mother had indicated she was aware of the Dark Elves' existence, though she'd never openly said so.

I wanted her confidences—for her to treat me, if not as an equal, at least as a young woman and not a child. Instead, I received only a bland smile.

"I don't trouble myself with such things," she said. "Tobin runs his kingdom as he sees fit. I certainly don't involve myself in his business."

"Except when you plot behind his back to keep me from wedding a Dark Elf lord," I said tartly.

Her mouth firmed into a line, but she didn't rise to my bait.

"Clear the necklaces away," she said. "And sit there, in front of the mirror. It's time for the cosmetic enhancements. This cream here is most efficacious."

She picked up a small jar and uncapped the lid. The smell of summer wafted out: chamomile, sage, and...

"Is that *nirwen?*" I leaned forward, reaching for the jar, but she pulled it away.

"*Bellarmes,*" she said reprovingly, calling the mystical flower by its Continental name. "It aids in rejuvenation of the skin. Even at your young age, the restorative properties are not to be underestimated. Those circles under your eyes, for example."

They'd been caused by fragmented sleep and the edges of night-mares, not that I was going to confide as much to her. She kept the door to her world locked against me, and I would do the same in return.

As it ever had been.

"Are we done?" I asked, letting a bit of petulance slip into my voice. If she wanted to treat me as a child, I'd be happy to oblige.

"Patience," she said, dabbing her fingertips into the jar. "Close your eyes."

I did, submitting to the cool touch of her hands against my face. She smoothed a bit of the cream under my eyes and upon my forehead, then brushed something powdery on my eyelids.

"Part your lips a little," she said, and as soon as I did, she swiped something over my mouth, then my cheeks.

"You can open your eyes, you silly girl," she said after a moment.

I did, then stared, astonished, at the woman looking back at me from the mirror.

"Your hair is still unfortunate," Mama said. "Though I think it could be tamed into a slicked-back coiffure. But your face is comely enough, with the proper treatment."

I'd never thought of myself as beautiful. There was no need to measure appearance here in the forested kingdom of Raine. Neeve and I were as different as night and day, and I knew that due to her heritage and station she'd already won the affections of the two men I'd ever daydreamed over.

But my reflection stunned me. I looked like royalty, much as I hated to admit it. Whatever my mother had smudged above my eyes made my gaze smoky and mysterious. My cheeks glowed, my lips were enticing, and I looked a good deal more mature than newly turned seventeen.

I wished Thorne might see me in that moment.

"Well?" My mother arched her brows at me. "What do you think?"

"I..." I searched for the words. "I didn't realize such things could make so much difference in one's appearance."

She gave a satisfied nod. "You'll need to practice, of course. I'll see to it that an assortment of cosmetics is delivered to your room. However, take care with the *bellarmes* cream. It is to be used sparingly."

"Really?" I glanced at her. "It's in short supply even here, in Raine?"

Her gaze slid from mine. "The supply is not the issue. Now, hurry off—the dinner gong is about to sound."

I knew when I was being summarily dismissed. And when my questions were being avoided, as well. Was there something dangerous about using *nirwen*? I'd have to ask Neeve.

"Thank you, Mama," I said, rising from the dressing table. "It has been a most instructive afternoon."

"I'm so glad you enjoyed it, my dear." She smiled distractedly at me and escorted me to the door.

Enjoyed was far from the word I'd use, but I nodded and dipped her a curtsey all the same. She was the queen, and my mother, and she'd meant well in her own way.

As I trudged back to my rooms, I mulled over what I'd learned. None of it was pleasant, except for the slight satisfaction in discovering what colors suited me and that I could make myself look beautiful with some judiciously applied cosmetics. But that knowledge paled in comparison to the options Mama had arrayed for my future.

The distantly dangerous prospect of being married off to the Nightshade Lord had suddenly become a present peril. Especially as the *nirwen* harvest was only a few months away. Panic scraped the inside of my ribs at the thought, and I forced it back down.

I would not be forced to wed a severe and terrifying Dark Elf. My mother wouldn't let that happen.

And neither would I settle for one of Kian's brothers who, no matter how charming, would never be a substitute for what I'd lost.

An alliance with the Athraig prince sounded nearly as frightening as one with Nightshade, and equally fraught with political expectation. I was hemmed in by unhappy choices every way I turned.

Unless I were to run away, forever.

First Parnese was ripped from me, and now, when it finally felt like home, Raine.

The thought of leaving it made me want to sob—but it was the only way I could see to control my own destiny. And faced with the alternatives, I must take it.

But not yet, a part of me protested. *There's still time. They won't wed you off until after Neeve is married.*

Perhaps. Still, I would lay my plans. If I managed to take ship away from Raine at the onset of the late fall storms, I might be able to escape immediate pursuit. Where I'd go, I had no idea. Away, that was all.

Away, though my heart might break from it.

Away.

CHAPTER 14

Neeve came to collect me for dinner, as was our habit. When I stepped out of my room, she halted and blinked at me.

"What did you do to your face?"

"Do you like it?" I tipped my chin up to the light of the nearest hall sconce, not expecting any praise.

"You look strange."

"Says the oddest girl in the castle."

She sniffed at the mild—though true—insult. "Was it pleasant, spending time with your mother?"

"Not particularly." I kicked at my skirts as we headed down the hall. It wasn't terribly graceful or ladylike of me, but it was the only form my defiance could currently take. "She spent the afternoon darkly hinting that I'm about to be married off to any number of terrifying monarchs."

"It's not a future I'd wish on anyone," Neeve said, sympathy flashing from her dark eyes.

I nodded ruefully in return. At least she'd known all her life she must marry for political reasons. I was still accustoming myself to the idea.

Not that I'd actually let myself be used as a pawn. For the first time, I wondered if Neeve was as obedient to her fate as she appeared.

"But what choice do we have?" I asked, my voice echoing forlornly against the stone walls.

"None," my stepsister said, her expression grim.

We rounded the corner to find Kian awaiting us on the landing.

"Are you planning a murder?" he asked, laughing. "I don't think I've ever seen the both of you quite so dire." Then he bent forward, peering at me. "Rose—you look strange."

"Such a compliment," I said tartly.

"You're supposed to say she's beautiful," Neeve said.

"Well, she is, of course. As are you. Aren't all princesses, by their nature?" He offered her his arm.

Ignoring it, she stepped past him and began descending the stairs.

Kian shrugged and turned to me. "Might I escort you to dinner, Rose the Beauteous?"

"Don't let my mother hear you," I cautioned him, slipping my elbow through his.

"Is she so set on being the most beautiful woman in the castle?" He gave me a questioning look.

"No." I leaned closer and lowered my voice. "She may be vain, but it's not that. You aren't destined for me, remember?"

"So I'm not allowed to give you any compliments?" He shook his head. "All this scheming over betrothals is wearying."

"I completely agree. I'm ready to be done with princessing—at least for a little while."

Unfortunately, my wish was not to be granted.

Dinner went well enough, with even Jarl Eiric wishing me a happy birthday, but just before the dessert course, Lord Raine clapped his hands.

One of the footmen scurried over, bearing a polished wooden box the size of a large tome, and the king stood.

"Lady Rose," he said. "In recognition of your status here at Castle Raine, I have a gift for you."

It seemed a time for formality, so I rose and dipped him a curtsey.

"Thank you, your majesty," I said as the servant bearing my gift rounded the table.

When the man handed it to me, my heart sank. I could guess what was inside. I lifted the lid and forced a smile onto my face at the sight of the golden circlet nestled inside. Two years ago, I would have been delighted at the sight of a crown, no matter how simple. But now it represented a role I'd no wish to play.

I removed the crown from the box, the metal cool against my fingers. The workmanship was lovely, though not quite as exquisite as Dark Elf jewelry. The filigreed metal came to three small points at the front of the circlet, each one topped with a crystal-set rose.

"Wear it in good health," the king said.

"Go ahead," my mother urged, "put it on."

With the courtiers, the servants, and my family all watching me, I had no choice. I lifted the crown and placed it over my springy curls.

"You see?" My mother gave the king with a significant look.

He nodded in return, then commanded the servants to bring out the cake. And even though it was my favorite—almond cake with cherries baked in, topped with delicate sugar spirals—it tasted like dust in my mouth.

⚜

DESPITE THE FRAUGHT acknowledgement of my station, the next few weeks passed peacefully. The normalcy of weapons training, time in the classroom, and the twice-weekly visits to Mistress Ainya's wrapped me in a cocoon of safety.

I set aside my worry—and my tenuous plans to leave Raine. After the *nirwen* harvest, there would be time for me to sort out my future.

As the summer days lengthened, I watched Jarl Eiric and Kian to see if they showed any knowledge of the upcoming harvest. I noted that the king never made mention of the Dark Elves or Raine's most closely held secret. Namely, the hidden gateway in the center of the Darkwood.

Neeve grew more prickly as the weeks progressed, becoming short-tempered and terse—even beyond her usual.

One day, after a weapons practice that hadn't gone well for her, she stormed off, leaving me and Kian to finish racking the weapons and tending the targets.

"Whatever is the matter with her?" he asked as we stuffed straw back into a slashed-open dummy.

I thought for a moment, choosing my words with care.

"Neeve is a child of winter," I finally said. "This summer is rather warm, you must admit. I don't think she's been sleeping well."

He frowned. "It doesn't seem any hotter than usual."

"I think it's also...feminine moods." That last was a complete lie, but I knew that men sometimes complained about women suffering such things.

"Well then." Kian's expression cleared. "I hope she's over it soon. And I should tell her that summers in Fiorland are cooler than here. When we're marr—"

"Perhaps you should wait on that," I said hastily. "Until fall."

"I don't like it." He whacked the dummy with the flat of his hand, and more straw fell out. "This business of stringing the Athraig along with insinuations of alliances the king has no intention of keeping."

I scooped up the prickly handful of hay and gave it to him. He sounded confident, but I couldn't share that certainty. Oh, I knew Neeve was safe from the Athraig, but as for myself...

"Are you sure?" I asked.

"Of course." Kian glanced down at me. "Raine will never ally with the Athraig. Don't worry, Rose, you'll likely end up with—"

He cut himself off, shoved the straw back into the dummy, then headed for the door.

"Wait." I brushed bits of hay from my tunic and hurried after him. "You can't not tell me. What do you know?"

Kian had been attending council meetings with the king for some time—as had Neeve, though she was incredibly close-mouthed about it.

The tips of Kian's ears reddened. "My brother Jenson is going to be invited for a visit this fall. That's all I can tell you."

So, the plotting continued beneath the surface. I shouldn't have been surprised. Even though I'd resolved not to think of such things, the machinery of the kingdom turned, preparing to grind me to dust.

Thorne, my heart insisted, over and over. But what I wanted didn't matter.

"Well," Kian said after we'd walked silently up the stairs. "Aren't you going to ask me anything about Jenson?"

"No."

I had no desire to hear about Kian's brother. Not when everything about the Fiorlander would be the opposite of the slender, dark-haired *Galadhir.*

Perhaps that was for the best, I told myself. Perhaps I'd marry Kian's brother and go to Fiorland and live in the aching cold until all my emotions froze. Then I'd drop them, let them shatter, and never shed a tear for the Dark Elf I'd once loved.

I was a princess, after all, as the king and my mother had taken great pains to press upon me. And no matter what burdens I carried, they could never match the depth of Neeve's sorrow—exiled from her kin, denied the birthright of her blood. Ever outcast.

Yet the two of us shared one thing: our heart's desire lay always just out of reach.

CHAPTER 15

As the days approached midsummer, an air of suppressed excitement began to vibrate through the castle. Although I didn't know the exact date of the *nirwen* harvest, it was surely almost upon us.

Thorne stopped meeting us at the edge of the forest, letting Kian escort me and Neeve to Mistress Ainya's cottage. Although Kian was scornful of the *Galadhir's* apparent shirking of his duties, I knew that Thorne was gathering his energies for the great magic he must perform at the end of the harvest, namely, transporting all the denizens of the castle, plus the carts, horses, tents, camp goods, and bushels of glowing *nirwen* blossoms from the center of the Darkwood to the courtyard of Castle Raine in the blink of an eye.

After that, I wouldn't see him again—until spring, supposedly, but if I were really going to go through with my plan to run away, then probably never. The knowledge hung about my heart like iron chains, bowing my shoulders and sapping my joy.

Kian thought my mood had to do with the forced alliances hemming me in—and he didn't even know about Nightshade. In a misguided attempt to cheer me up, he prattled on about his brother. I had to hear about what a good hunter and dancer Jenson was, and how

all the maidens seemed to like his wavy blond hair and blue eyes—
though his hair was not as thick or his eyes as piercing as Kian's own,
of course—until one evening, heading back to our rooms after dinner, I
could take no more.

"Enough," I said, pleasantly but firmly. "I'm sure your brother is
eminently suitable in every way, but I think it's for the best if I make
my own determination as to his merits."

"But he—"

"Stop." My voice was sharper now. "If you don't stop talking about
Jenson, I'll kick you."

Kian glanced down at my footwear. "With your fearsome embroidered slippers?"

"If you need a stronger deterrent, then I promise to throw knives
at you during weapons practice. You can bat them out of the air with
your superior swordsmanship."

Neeve, walking ahead of us, let out an amused snort.

"I wouldn't mind a change of subject either," she said, glancing over
her shoulder. "How is your tonic-making going, Rose?"

"Slowly," I admitted. I was almost out of the restorative liquid.

Every time I went to Mistress Ainya's, I meant to make more, but
kept getting pulled away into other duties, or distracted by new
assignments.

Next time, I promised myself. I wasn't sure what the consequences
of running out might be, but it was probably better not to find out. If
the infusion truly were keeping any strange fevers at bay and strengthening my constitution, I'd do well to continue taking it.

As it turned out, however, I wasn't given the chance to distill more.
Later that night, Neeve rapped on my door. I let her in, and she went
right to the point.

"Pack your travel kit. The castle goes out tomorrow for the
harvest."

"Tomorrow?" My knees felt suddenly weak, and I reached back,
gripping the nearest chair for support.

She gave me an impatient look. "Don't look so frightened—I
promise that the Nightshade Lord isn't going to snap you up like a
hungry wolf."

I gave her a sharp look, wishing I could share her certainty. "How do you know?"

"For one thing, you're too young to marry by Dark Elf standards, according to the *Studie*."

"That's an ancient book," I countered. "Things could have changed over the centuries."

"And for another," she continued, ignoring my words, "my father has told me your betrothal won't be settled before mine is decided. Since matters between Raine and Fiorland haven't yet been confirmed, you're safe."

"Until the next harvest," I said. "But what about the Athraig?"

She went to take one of the chairs, and I settled across from her.

"It's a delicate dance," she said, "running a kingdom, balancing enemies and alliances. While my father has no intention of encouraging the Athraig, neither does he want to anger our old adversaries."

"So I'm still a pawn on the board?"

"We both are." She tilted her head, regarding me. Her eyes were very dark, her eyebrows slashes of black across her pale forehead. "I believe that during this harvest, the king plans to speak with Nightshade about the possibility of your betrothal."

I shivered at the thought. "Please, Neeve, don't let him barter me away."

Her mouth twisted. "I suffer the same fate."

I laced my fingers tightly together. "Then both of us will end up exiles—you in the human world, me in Elfhame. I wish we could change places."

"It is a great irony," she said, her voice as sharp as the edge of her sword. "But no matter what agreement is struck, neither of us will end up wedding the Athraig prince. I promise you that. And you'll have a reprieve until the next harvest. Who knows what may transpire before then?"

She meant my likely marriage to Kian's brother. Not that I was planning to take that course. I would leave Raine instead. And as much as I cared for Neeve, I wasn't yet ready to entrust her with my plans. After the harvest, perhaps.

"What time do we leave tomorrow?" I leaned forward, shifting my thoughts to what lay directly ahead instead of what might be.

"At first light. It's a long day's journey through the forest, even with the *Galadhir's* help."

"And what of the Fiorlanders?" I asked.

Some emotion flickered over her face, so quickly I couldn't name it. "They will be given the sleeping draught," she said. "Once I'm betrothed to Kian, they'll be privy to our secrets."

"Why not before?" I asked the questions that had been pricking me for some time. Neeve's argument seemed foolish to me. Here was the perfect opportunity to demonstrate to Kian and Jarl Eiric the truth of what lay in the center of the Darkwood.

"The problem is twofold," she said. "First, my father doesn't quite trust the jarl, for all that he's been dwelling in Castle Raine for years."

I nodded, as I shared that distrust. Jarl Eiric was a bit too smooth around the edges, and a bit too interested in the castle's defenses. I wondered if he'd encouraged Kian to ask about the secret passages. It wouldn't surprise me in the least.

"Second, until I'm officially betrothed to Kian"—Neeve grimaced slightly—"he isn't privy to Raine's greatest secrets."

"And why is the king waiting to announce that betrothal, again?" It all seemed very convoluted to me, despite my lessons in statecraft.

"Because, until the winter storms close the Strait, the Athraig might take it into their heads to attack Raine if we rebuff their overtures. As you know, their messages have hinted as much. Once that danger is past, then I will have to accept Prince Kian's suit."

"You needn't sound as though it's akin to being thrown in the dungeon," I said, affronted on Kian's behalf. "He's not so terrible as all that."

Neeve shot me a look. "Do you still yearn for him, then?"

"I never did!" I protested, though it wasn't *quite* true.

During our time in Parnese and right after, there had been a door open between Kian and me. A half-seen path to a different outcome... until we'd both retreated from it, constrained by duty and honor.

I tried not to sigh.

My stepsister lifted one brow, but didn't argue. Perhaps she knew where my true affections lay—she'd hinted as much—but the less we spoke of Thorne, the better. Especially as it seemed neither of us were destined to have him.

"I need to finish packing." She rose and shook out her skirts. "I'll see you in the morning. Be ready."

She accompanied her words with a pointed look, as we both knew I was not the earliest of risers.

"I will," I promised. "I'm sure Sorche will wake me in time."

⊙⊱⊰⊙

THE JOURNEY through the Darkwood the next day was far different than the one I'd taken three years earlier. That time, I'd followed the cart tracks through the forest until dark fell, unsure of my destination and starting at every shadow.

Now I rode cushioned in the back of a cart, along with Neeve.

"Why aren't we riding our horses?" I'd asked as we assembled in the dawn courtyard.

"Because every living being Thorne must transport back to the castle drains his energies," she'd told me. "The fewer mounts, the better."

So I'd clambered into the cart behind Neeve. Sorche and two other maids had followed, and we made ourselves as comfortable as we could with the rolled-up bedding and the cloth bags used to harvest the *nirwen* flowers.

The king had his own mount, I noted, but he was the only one not relegated to jostling about in the back of a cart.

As the sun cleared the shadow of the Darkwood, a dozen vehicles packed with passengers and supplies rattled out of the courtyard. We passed under the portcullis and quickly turned off the road. I was glad to leave the teeth-jarring cobblestones behind. As we entered the forest, the trees seemed to stand further apart, making a wide pathway where before there had only been a threading of game trails and narrow paths.

This was the *Galadhir's* magic, smoothing our passage, and I smiled at the thought of seeing Thorne at the end of the journey. Then sobered as I recalled the Nightshade Lord would be there too.

The processions did not stop for lunch. We passed bread and cheese around, and if anyone needed to leave the cart, they simply hopped out, then jumped back in again once their business was concluded. Neeve left our vehicle for quite a while, and I glimpsed her riding several carts back, for some reason. Perhaps she'd gotten tired and didn't want to catch up.

I walked for a time myself, watching the bright dart of birds through the trees and breathing deeply of the scent of cedar and loam. As always, the Darkwood had the power to soothe my senses and restore a much-needed feeling of calm. When I returned to our cart, Neeve was there. She made no mention of her long absence, and I decided not to ask.

The soft jolting motion made me sleepy, and I curled up against a bedroll, pulled my cloak over me, and took a nap. When I awoke, the sky overhead had shaded from blue to silver, the shadows between the trees deepened to velvet.

"Are we almost there?" I asked Neeve.

"Yes," she said, clearly feeling no need to elaborate.

Not long after, the cart rocked to a halt as the entire procession stopped. The tall evergreens grew more sparsely here, replaced by graceful, white-barked trees with silvery leaves that shimmered in the breeze. Beyond them, I glimpsed the clearing that lay at the heart of the Darkwood. Two rune-marked stones stood upright in the center of that meadow, marking what I knew was the doorway to Elfhame.

Sorche and her companions left the cart, and I glanced at Neeve. "Are we sharing a tent?"

"We are." She didn't sound terribly happy about it.

I bit my lip, recalling the sound of her bitter tears the night after the gateway had closed. Neeve preferred to keep her emotions hidden. She wouldn't like having a witness to her grief—but she knew I would say nothing.

So many secrets between us, spoken and unsaid, glimpsed and half guessed. I wondered if that was ever the way with sisters, or if Neeve and I were beyond the usual.

As we sat there, me with comforting words clogging my throat, Neeve with her usual severe expression, a trio of little sparks arrived to swoop and dance over our heads. They glowed softly, their radiance bright against the quickly fading light.

"Glimglows." I smiled and lifted my hands. "Hello, friends."

One of them descended to swirl about my wrist a moment, and I fancied they were greeting me. Perhaps they were the same ones who had guided me through the forest three years earlier. If so, I owed them a debt of gratitude.

Neeve glanced up, her face softening as the glimglows darted about us. I squinted, just able to make out the tiny figures with quick-blurred wings at the heart of each ball of light.

After a few more moments they darted away, and Neeve let out a low breath. Their flickering glow was now echoed by newly kindled cooking fires and lanterns hung on long poles. Tents had sprouted beneath the trees like mushrooms after a warm rain.

My stepsister grabbed a bedroll and her small bag. I did the same, then followed her to a midsized tent set beside the largest pavilion, which belonged to the king. We laid out our blankets side by side, and I pulled on my cloak against the evening chill.

"They'll have dinner for us by the campfires," Neeve said. "And then early to bed, so that we can begin the harvest first thing tomorrow."

I yawned at the thought. "And here I thought our usual schedule was dreadfully early."

Neeve simply shook her head at me then crawled out of the tent.

It was pleasant to eat our stew and bread beneath the trees. The flickering lights, along with the occasional darting glimglows, lent the entire camp a magical aspect. On the morrow, when the *nirwen* bloomed, it would become even more enchanted.

And, of course, the Dark Elves would join us for a farewell feast. I glanced about the camp, wondering if Thorne had already arrived.

As if my thoughts had summoned him, he strode from beneath the trees.

"Thorne!" I couldn't help smiling at him.

He smiled back, the firelight flickering warmly against his face as he came to join me and Neeve around the small campfire we'd claimed.

"Good evening, Rose," he said, nodding at me, and then my stepsister. "Neeve."

"Have you eaten?" I asked. "We could find you some stew, if you'd like."

"I'm well provided for, thank you."

Belatedly, I remembered the sweet water and bread he'd shared with me the previous harvest, when I snuck in and hid at the edges of the camp. At least this time I was better provisioned, with a bedroll and tent. But I spared a pang for the memory of sleeping on the mossy ground, Thorne's cloak over me.

That had been a simpler time, when I was blissfully unaware of the responsibilities awaiting me. The world had seemed full of adventure back then, but more recently the consequences of my actions weighed heavily upon my shoulders. Stay in Raine, or flee? Accept the courtship of a Fiorland prince, without ever telling Thorne how I felt?

I stared at him, feeling as though I were falling into the dark pools of his eyes. My breath felt jagged and hot in my lungs.

"Well." Neeve rose abruptly. "I'll leave you two to talk. Good night."

"Wait." I tore my gaze from Thorne, but my stepsister was already stepping outside the circle of light cast by the campfire. I set my palms on the cool mosses, ready to rise and go after her, but Thorne held out his hand.

"Let her go," he said softly. "The *nirwen* harvest is not an easy time for her. Nothing you can say or do will help ease her pain."

"It's not fair." I blew out an impatient breath.

"It's the way of the world. We cannot have what we want." His gaze met mine and held.

Sorrow and yearning moved in the darkness of his eyes, and I had to look away at the reminder of the depth of his emotions for Neeve.

"No," I said, my voice shaky. "We can't."

The fire popped, sending up a few wayward sparks. I watched them rise until they blended with the specks of fire in the sky and were gone.

CHAPTER 16

"Wake up." Neeve prodded my side, and I groaned, trying to roll away from her.

I fetched up against the clammy side of the tent and reluctantly opened my eyes. Wan light filtered through the fabric. The new day was at hand.

"A little more sleep," I pleaded, pulling her empty pillow over my face.

"No." She grabbed the pillow away. "I've already let you lie abed too long. Sit up, Rose. The monarchs are about to meet in the clearing, and you must be there."

Her words were a cold douse of water, bringing me fully awake. I sat, blinking, and pushed my hair out of my face. It smelled of wood smoke, and my mouth felt gritty.

"Here." Neeve thrust a bannock at me, and a mug of tea.

"Thank you," I said, belatedly realizing that she had, indeed, let me sleep past breakfast.

While I ate, trying not to shed crumbs all over my bedroll, she brushed my hair as best she could. When it was more or less tamed, she pulled it back from my face and fastened it with a green ribbon, then handed me the homespun dress I'd taken out of my pack the night before. There was no need to wear court finery for the harvest. Just for the formal feast afterward. I tried not to dwell on the thought.

I hurriedly changed out of my nightgown, let Neeve lace up the dress, then threw my blue cloak about my shoulders.

She ducked out of the tent, and I followed, my heart beating in my throat. The camp was mostly empty, tendrils of smoke drifting from banked fires, the memory of cooked meat hanging in the air.

"Hurry," Neeve said as I stumbled after her through the underbrush.

"I am," I replied crossly, yanking my skirts free of a briar bush, though in truth, I wasn't eager to reach the clearing.

While the sight of the assembled Dark Elves had amazed me last harvest, I couldn't escape the fact that the fearsome Nightshade Lord would be there—and this time I couldn't skulk behind the trees, unobserved.

We stepped into the meadow, the dewy grasses dampening the hem of my cloak. Neeve towed me along the path to where her father stood, facing the glowing upright stones that flanked the doorway to Elfhame. Beyond the portal, I glimpsed a gathering of elves standing in their own Darkwood. The trees there rose taller than the ones surrounding us, and their forest floor was carpeted with pale white flowers.

The Nightshade Lord strode through the gate, wearing a cloak the color of the midnight sky. His elegantly braided black hair flowed over his shoulders, blending into the shadowy fabric. As he emerged, he nodded at Lord Raine, then stood aside to let the rest of his people through.

It seemed I was beneath his notice for the moment, and I breathed easier, able to lose myself in the wonder of the assembling Dark Elves.

They wore clothing that was both practical yet elegant—silken fabrics wrapped and gathered about them, gems winking at their throats and wrists. Each of them carried a large bag or basket to harvest the *nirwen*.

A stack of baskets and picking bags at the edge of the meadow like-wise awaited the humans. Once the sun cleared the trees—which would be soon—the *nirwen* would open. Then everyone would set to plucking the flowers as quickly as possible. By nightfall the blossoms would fade, not to be seen again for another three years.

Well, three years in the mortal world, which was only a matter of months in Elfhame, according to Thorne.

The last Dark Elf stepped through the gate, and my heart squeezed to see that it was Thorne. He turned, and, with a gesture, the portal closed. It would reopen late that night, after the celebration feast, and the elves would return to their land, bearing their portion of the harvest.

The *Galadhir* took his place at the Nightshade Lord's left shoulder, his gaze flicking to me and Neeve, then away. He looked more somber than the occasion warranted, and my stomach clenched again with worry.

"Greeting, Nightshade," Lord Raine said, striding forward. "We meet again in peace and prosperity, for the benefit of both our peoples."

"I offer you greetings in return," the Dark Elf monarch said. "For another turning of the moons, let us be united in our purpose."

He clasped hands with the king. A breeze sprang up, riffling the cedar trees, and a half-dozen glimglows appeared, flitting and swirling over the gateway stones. The runes inscribed there sparked with light as the sun cleared the tops of the evergreens and slanted down into the clearing.

For a moment, the world held its breath.

Then radiance spread all around us as the *nirwen* blossoms opened, each five-petaled yellow flower glowing like a star. It was as though a lake of gold had been poured into the meadow, rippling out into the fringes of the forest surrounding it.

A cheer rose from Dark Elves and humans alike, and then a rush of motion as the harvest began. Later, there would be time for the formal greetings and presentations between the human and elvish courts—but while the flowers bloomed, there was no time to waste.

I was glad of the reprieve.

Neeve and I grabbed two baskets and picking bags, and I followed as she strode to the little dell beneath the trees where she'd discovered me during the last harvest.

"At least there are no stowaways this year," I said, sending my stepsister a cheerful smile.

She frowned at me and bent to her task. With a sigh, I did too, snapping the stems of the bright blossoms and tucking them into my bag. I'd forgotten how black Neeve's moods used to be—but now that she stood face to face with her old pain, it seemed her old habits had returned.

When Thorne joined us some time later, I glanced at him in relief.

"How do you think the harvest is going?" I asked, noting the pinched look about his eyes. "Is everything well?"

"Well enough." He gave me a strained smile. "Whatever happens tonight, remember that I will be by your side."

Neeve looked up sharply. "What do you mean, *Galadhir*? Is there something we should know?"

Thorne plucked a few more flowers before answering, and I noticed he'd led us even deeper into the forest.

"Nothing you didn't already suspect," he said softly. "The Nightshade Lord will declare his intent to offer for Rose next harvest."

I sucked in a breath, my heart giving a jagged thump. Beside me, Neeve nodded gravely.

"I won't say yes." I turned to my stepsister. "They can't make me wed him, can they?"

"No one will force you into anything against your will," Thorne said. "But there are good reasons to make the alliance."

"Such as?" I glanced down at the flower in my hands, belatedly realizing I was crushing the golden petals in my fist.

"I don't think Rose should be allowed to go to Elfhame while I'm trapped on this side of the gate," Neeve said, an edge in her voice.

"Your situation is part of the reason," Thorne said, giving her a sympathetic look. "You are the only anchor point for the gateway at the moment, Neeve—which puts both our realms in a precarious situation."

"And you're just now coming to this conclusion?" she asked bitterly.

"There weren't any other options. Before Lord Raine returned from Parnese with a new bride, there was talk of him wedding a Dark Elf lady. But obviously that came to nothing."

A fierce light kindled in Neeve's eyes. "Are you saying that if my father hadn't married Rose's mother, he would've taken another wife from among the Dark Elves—thus freeing me to go to Elfhame?"

"It was an unlikely possibility, at best," Thorne said. "The king loved your mother, in his own way. Marrying another Dark Elf would have exacerbated his sorrow, not eased it."

"But it would have made my life bearable!" Red spots bloomed on Neeve's pale cheeks, and her eyes were alight with anger. She whirled, her gaze locking with mine. "I hate that you came and ruined everything. I hate you, Rose."

I blinked, stunned at the force of her spiteful words. Cold lodged between my ribs, and I held my hand out to her, but she'd already turned away, stalking out of the light-washed glade.

She hurried beneath the trees, a shadow blending with the darker shadows of the forest, and I moved to follow her.

"Wait." Thorne set his hand on my arm. "Give her time."

He was right. Neeve's temper would take time to fade. Reluctantly, I turned back to the harvest, my heart wounded. I cared for Neeve, thought of her as my sister, and her declaration of hatred had struck me like an arrow to the heart.

"She didn't mean it," Thorne said, as if reading my thoughts. "Her grief weighs upon her."

"I didn't ask for my mother to marry the king," I said, finding an ember of my own temper. "It's hardly my fault."

"But you're safe to blame." Thorne slipped a comforting arm around my shoulders. "Neeve cannot rail against her father, or her uncle, the Nightshade Lord. But she knows that you understand. And will forgive her."

"Maybe." I stared into the darkness beneath the trees.

"In time," he said. "I'm sorry, Rose."

I sighed and let myself lean against him. The scent of herbs and loam tickled my nose, and I couldn't tell whether it was coming from him or from the forest surrounding us. Probably both.

"Do you really think I could help keep the doorway between our worlds open if I were to marry the Nightshade Lord?" I glanced up at him, my curiosity rising despite the awful possibility.

He stiffened and dropped his arm. "It's quite possible. Now that you are almost of marrying age, the Oracles have been assessing the chances."

Thank heavens I was still too young, or it seemed the Dark Elf monarch would've swooped me up in his talons this very harvest.

"My mother is opposed to such a match," I said quietly. "I believe there are...other options being discussed."

"I'm aware of them," he said unhappily. "Rose—whatever happens..."

He paused, staring at the nearby trees. The silence stretched between us.

"Yes?" I finally asked.

He shook himself and gave me a quick glance. "Nothing. We need to get back to harvesting."

With that, he turned away from me and resumed picking *nirwen*, leaving me heartsore and confused amid a sea of shining flowers.

CHAPTER 17

T horne and I plucked glowing blossoms until our bags were filled, then returned to camp to empty them and partake of a brief lunch. I looked for Neeve, and finally glimpsed her at the far side of the encampment. When she caught sight of me, she turned abruptly away.

Three years until the next harvest, I thought while I chewed my bread and cheese. Neeve would be married by then. Although perhaps she'd find a way to put Kian off, just in case the Oracles' mad plan to make me the gateway anchor worked.

Of course, I'd be long gone at that point.

Which would leave my stepsister trapped until she produced a child of her own. At that point, she'd be able to go into Elfhame. Provided the babe didn't kill her at childbirth, as had happened with her own mother.

I sighed heavily and took a long swallow of water from my drinking flask. There were no good answers—for any of us.

But there were still plenty of *nirwen* flowers to harvest.

"Back into the forest?" I asked Thorne as we finished up our meal.

"For a short while," he said. "Then the both of us should make ready for the evening court."

A rebellious part of me wanted to appear before the king and Dark Elf lord with twigs in my hair and smears of green on my homespun skirts. But Sorche had insisted on packing my gold velvet gown for the occasion. And the gold circlet Lord Raine had given me for my birthday, which was clearly now a requirement of my wardrobe during formal occasions.

Thorne and I moved away from the clearing and back into a different part of the forest. I noted that the place we'd picked earlier was beginning to replenish its blossoms, though not as quickly as before.

"Has anyone ever picked all the *nirwen*?" I asked.

He shook his head. "Some must be left to make seeds for the next harvest."

"It seems to me that if there are seeds, then the plant must be able to be cultivated."

"Alas—many have tried, both in your world and my own. Even though *nirwen* has been coaxed to grow from seed in a few rare instances, it never blooms. There is a magic about the gateway that is essential to its flowering."

"Do you really believe the legend, that a mortal woman's tears for her Dark Elf lover created the flowers?"

Thorne shrugged and avoided my gaze. "I did as a child, certainly. It's a pretty tale, and as good an explanation as any."

Despite the fact it seemed rather far-fetched, I liked the story. Maybe because a part of me insisted that if Thorne loved me, my own tears of desperation at the gateway separating us would be enough to perform miracles too.

We plucked flowers until my back ached and my fingers were sore. At last, as the afternoon sun slanted warmly through the forest, Thorne declared we were done.

"Finally." I stretched, then shifted my bulging picking sack and grabbed my overflowing basket.

The camp glowed with the abundance of *nirwen* gathered at the margins. Containers of gold blooms lined the side of the meadow, too, waiting for the Dark Elves to transport them back to their realm after the feast.

First, though, I had a court presentation to get through.

I took my leave of Thorne, my heart twisting at the fact that, after tomorrow, I wouldn't see him again until the following spring.

If ever... my little voice whispered. Ignoring it, I squared my shoulders and went to the tent I shared with Neeve.

As I lifted the flap to duck inside, she thrust herself past me with a haughty look.

"Neeve," I said. "Wait. Please."

She paused and glanced back over her shoulder at me. "I have nothing to say to you."

Despite her expression, something flickered in her eyes—regret, perhaps?

"But—"

"Be quiet, Rose." Her mouth tightened. "One day, you'll understand."

Understand what? I wanted to ask, but she swept away, her dark red cloak swirling behind her. Glumly I entered the tent, to find Sorche waiting, comb in hand.

⚜

WHEN SORCHE finally pronounced me ready, I stepped out of the tent to find that dusk lay over the clearing. The last shining flowers of *nirwen* had furled closed, their magical blooms gone until the next harvest.

When, according to Thorne, I was possibly going to be wed to the Nightshade Lord.

Never, my little voice said, and for once, I wholeheartedly agreed.

Gathering my courage, I strode toward the platform that had been erected in the clearing, where two empty thrones awaited their rulers. Lord Raine's was a small one I'd seen in the castle's throne room—sturdy wood with gilt accents and a green velvet cushion. The Nightshade Lord's was a fantastical twisting of silvery branches cradling a pillow of pale silk. The magical blue lights of the Dark Elves bobbed overhead, interspersed with human lanterns and torches. The sparks of glimglows chased each other across the clearing. In the eastern sky, just over the rough silhouette of the trees, the first star winked into view.

A semicircle of Dark Elves and humans were gathered before the dais. I joined them, spotting Neeve standing with a group of elvish courtiers. The King of Raine and the Nightshade Lord strode together onto the platform and took their seats.

I'd hoped that Thorne would join me, but he stood, mouth set, to the left of the Nightshade Lord. The *Galadhir's* dark gaze flicked to me unerringly, then to the necklace I wore. It was the pendant he'd given me for my fourteenth birthday—which I wore most days, though usually I kept it hidden beneath my bodice.

Tonight, though, I proudly displayed the blue-and-silver jewelry. We were among the Dark Elves, after all. To my surprise, Thorne's eyes widened and he gave me a stricken look, then glanced away again before I could even muster a smile for him.

No matter. I didn't much feel like smiling in any case. And why he should be bothered that I wore the jewelry he'd given me, I'd no idea.

The two rulers greeted one another, then addressed the crowd with words of welcome, rejoicing that another harvest had been successfully concluded.

"And where is my niece?" the Nightshade Lord asked, glancing about the gathering.

"Here, my lord." Neeve stepped forward and made him a graceful obeisance.

She wore a gown of misty green, and the torchlight sparked off the gemmed circlet set over her night-black hair. It was more ornate than my crown, I was glad to see. I'd kept the hood of my cloak up, in fact, hiding my own circlet.

I had little desire to be a princess, now more than ever.

"You look well, Neeve," the Nightshade Lord said. "Join me at the feast, and I will seat you at my right hand, as befits your rank."

"Thank you, Uncle." Scarlet rose in her cheeks and she shot her father a triumphant look.

"Excellent," the king said mildly. "The bond between our realms can only benefit from being strengthened. Thank you, Neeve."

Clearly dismissed, she stepped back to her place, chin held high.

"Indeed." The Nightshade Lord leaned forward, expression intent. "Which brings us to the next matter."

"So it does," the king said, and I held my breath. "Rose, come forward."

Pulse racing, I took three paces forward and halted before the stage. Unsure of the protocol when facing two rulers of equal stature, I dropped into my best curtsey, directing it halfway between the two thrones.

"Take down your hood," the Nightshade Lord said. "I would gaze upon your unshadowed features."

With trembling hands I pushed my cloak's hood away from my face, then stood, trying not to feel like a beast being appraised for auction.

"She's no beauty," the Dark Elf ruler remarked to the king. "Especially with that hair. But she'll do well enough."

Thorne leaned over his lord's shoulder. "An agreement, of course, depends on whether the Oracles determine if Rose can serve as an anchor," he murmured, so softly that I barely heard his words.

"Even if they do not," the Nightshade Lord replied, "it might be a good idea to make another alliance in the human world, binding us closer to Raine. It is not always Nightshade that coordinates the harvest, *Galadhir*, in case you've forgotten."

"I have not," Thorne said tersely, straightening.

The Nightshade Lord's gaze hadn't left my face. And despite his dismissal of my looks, there was a heat in his dark eyes that made me shiver.

"Then we are agreed," he said, finally moving his attention from me back to Lord Raine. "At the next harvest, we shall make a formal alliance, sealed with a wedding between myself and your stepdaughter."

The crowd shifted and murmured, and I could feel the weight of their gazes upon my back. I wanted to wail out my denial. Instead, I bit the side of my cheek and forced myself to remain silent.

Three years is a long time, I reminded myself. And I'd be well away by then, though my heart might break from it.

"Unless circumstances change," the king said, as if overhearing my thoughts.

The Nightshade Lord's dark brows drew together. "See that they do not."

"Hm." Lord Raine stood. "I believe our business here is now concluded. Are you ready to begin the feasting, elf lord?"

"Indeed I am, mortal king." The Nightshade Lord rose, then spread his hands wide and addressed the gathering. "Another harvest is complete! Let us celebrate with food and drink, merriment and music!"

The crowd sent up a cheer, my fate forgotten in the prospect of the feast ahead. A jaunty tune struck up from the musicians seated at the edge of the clearing. I glanced over, unsurprised to see Master Fawkes, though I hadn't noted him among the caravan from the castle. He was joined by a Dark Elf lady playing a round, many-stringed instrument, and a slender youth with a silver flute.

With a quick gesture, the Nightshade Lord summoned his magic. Tables appeared throughout the clearing, laden with food and illuminated with flickering bowls of blue fire. The two granite stones in the center of the clearing glowed softly, and the human-set lanterns gleamed with a warm and steady light.

Overhead, the stars shone, uncaring who or what assembled beneath the spark-spattered dome of sky.

The assembled mortals and elves gravitated to the tables and selected their places while servants circulated: humans bearing jugs of honey mead from the castle's cellars, elves with ewers of water that I knew tasted sweet, with a refreshing effervescence.

Out of habit, I started to join Neeve, then checked myself. We were at odds—again—and even if we weren't, she had been invited to dine with the Nightshade Lord. I'd no desire to place myself in such close proximity to the Dark Elf monarch, and instead took a few steps back toward the edge of the clearing.

"Running away?"

The question made me turn, though I'd already recognized Thorne's voice.

"I'm not in a celebratory mood," I said.

"Nor am I. Yet why go hungry? We needn't sit in the middle of things."

"Is that an invitation to dinner?" Despite the circumstances, my mood lightened.

"It seems to be," he said gravely, though there was a spark of amusement in his eyes. "What about that suitably shadowed table there, at the edge of the clearing?"

He nodded, and I followed his gaze, barely able to make out the shape of a small table tucked beneath overhanging cedar boughs.

"Perfect," I declared.

As we made our way over, Thorne snagged a ewer of water from one of the servers. By the faint blue light hovering above the little table, I saw there were only two chairs.

"Did you plan this?" I gave him a suspicious look as he pulled one of the chairs out for me.

He gave me a crooked smile. "I knew you wouldn't be in the mood for festivities."

I sat, then squinted at him. It was difficult to make out his expression in the dimness.

"We both know my reason," I said, "but why aren't you full of good cheer tonight?"

He poured us each a glass of water, then sat. A few platters of food awaited—fowl spiced with fruits, slices of strange pale melon, oatcakes and bread. Suddenly hungry, I filled the silvery disc of the plate set before me.

"If you'll recall," Thorne said, "the harvest isn't over for me. Tomorrow morning I must send all of you back to Castle Raine, then reopen the gate for my own passage home. Neither of those are simple magics."

"Why don't the Dark Elves wait, then? If they spent the night, then you could go back to Elfhame with them when the Nightshade Lord opens the gateway."

He lifted one shoulder. "As *Galadhir*, it's expected that I can make my way between worlds as I choose. To do otherwise, or ask for special favors, is to show weakness."

"They should make an exception." I waved my fork at him. "You'll have just performed a mighty enchantment, after all."

"My liege doesn't see it that way." Thorne let out a breath and took a drink of water. "Truly, Rose, I have enough power to fulfill all my duties. Don't worry."

"I'll stop worrying if you have some dinner." I gave him a pointed look. "I notice you haven't taken a single bite. Even mighty mages need sustenance."

He shook his head at me, but dutifully lifted his fork and began to eat. I lifted my glass and sipped the clear, sparkling water. We had nothing like it in the mortal world.

Beyond the fringe of branches screening our table, the clearing looked like something from a storybook. Music drifted from where Master Fawkes and his companions still played, though the lute strummed more softly, and the youth on the flute had changed over to a blackwood whistle.

The mood was both happy and sad, and I felt it deeply in my own heart. Life was marvelous and terrifying, momentous and filled with utter boredom.

I looked to where Neeve sat beside the Nightshade Lord. They seemed to be deep in conversation, and I wondered what they were discussing. Was Neeve asking questions, informed by the Dark Elf *Studie* I'd given her? Whatever she was saying, her uncle looked grave.

Neeve held up one hand, palm cupped to the sky, as if asking a question. After a moment the Nightshade Lord nodded, though his consent seemed reluctant. I wondered if they were discussing me—then belatedly recalled that my stepsister and I were, once again, enemies.

I let out a sigh, and Thorne followed my gaze.

"Don't worry about Neeve," he said softly. "She didn't mean her harsh words to you."

Part of her had—but it was too beautiful a night to ruin it with more argument.

"I'll miss you," I said, turning to look into his eyes.

"I will miss you as well," he replied. Bright flecks of gold moved through his dark gaze, and the forest quieted.

Then a chime sounded through the clearing, a shimmering silver sound, and Thorne looked away.

"The feast is ending."

"I know." I quickly jumped up from my chair, recalling that, in mere moments, the Nightshade Lord would wave his hand and dismiss the feasting tables. And chairs. I didn't fancy sprawling awkwardly to the ground when my seat vanished.

Thorne smiled at me, though his expression was tinged with melancholy. "Take a moment, if you like. This particular table isn't under Nightshade's dominion."

"Oh." I glanced at our little bower tucked within the trees. "You summoned it?"

"I knew you'd need a refuge after the events of the day."

My heart gave a pang at how well he knew me. "Thank you."

Slowly, I sat back down to finish my last piece of melon. Thorne was ever aiding me—and for the first time it occurred to me to ask if I might help him in return.

"I know I'm just a mortal girl," I said, "but is there anything at all I can do while you're in Elfhame?"

He tilted his head at me. "Such as?"

"I don't know." I frowned in thought. "Watch for strange incursions in the forest? Or help Neeve with setting protections—though I know I don't have any magic—or..." I ended with a shrug, belatedly recalling that I'd intended to leave Raine that very winter.

Which meant this was the last chance I'd ever have to be alone with Thorne.

"I'm finished." I stood again, abruptly, and waited for him to vanish our table and chairs.

Out in the clearing, the feasting tables were disappearing. The Dark Elves began gathering up their portion of the *nirwen* harvest and forming a long line leading to the gateway stones.

Thorne rose and waved his hand, and our sheltered dining area was gone as if it had never existed. He began to stride out to join his kin, but I grabbed his arm and pulled him back toward me.

"Wait," I said, then slipped my arms around his lean waist and kissed him.

Tried to kiss him, that was. He stared at me, then jerked his head to the side, so that my lips landed on his cheek instead of his mouth.

"Rose. What are you doing?"

I could feel his heart beating very fast. My own pulse raced, but despite the hot embarrassment rushing through me, I didn't let him go. His hands rested on my shoulders, and he didn't pull away either, even though he'd avoided my kiss.

"I thought it was obvious," I said, my breath hitching. "Don't you care for me?"

He turned his face back to mine. "I do. Very deeply. From the moment you set foot in the Darkwood, you have been under my protection."

The sting of tears pricked my eyes. I didn't want him to think of me as his responsibility, his ward. I had to tell him how I felt.

"Thorne, I—"

"Shh." He bent and pressed a kiss against the top of my head.

A pair of glimglows darted beneath the branches and circled us, then flew out into the clearing.

"We must go," he said, his voice tired. "The Nightshade Lord is about to open the gateway back to Elfhame, and I cannot be absent."

I dropped my arms, and he stepped back from me, then turned and strode into the clearing.

Goodbye, Thorne. Misery ached through me. I knew I'd see him on the morrow, but I'd lost my last chance to tell him how deeply I loved him. That, no matter what happened or where our futures took us, he would carry a part of my heart with him. Always.

But the moment had gone, and I refused to cry.

Still, the torches smeared in my tear-blurred vision as I went to watch the Dark Elves return to their magical land.

The line of elves reached from the forest's edge to the center of the clearing, stopping where the Nightshade Lord stood before the two upright stones. Each elf bore a large basket of *nirwen*, their strange, severe faces illuminated by the soft radiance of the flowers. As I slowly made my way from beneath the cedar, a faint breeze ruffled my hair, then died down to stillness.

Slowly, the Nightshade Lord raised his hands. They were outlined in blue light, and I shivered to see the force of his power.

"Farewell, Raine," he said. "We shall meet again in three of your mortal years. Until then, tend well to your charges, and keep the promises you have made."

"I will, Nightshade," the king said. "As you will do in turn."

The monarchs tilted their heads toward one another in a measured goodbye. I glanced about the clearing but couldn't make out Neeve among the cloaked figures. The king stepped back to where the rest of the humans stood, watching.

The Nightshade Lord, his long, dark hair crackling with blue sparks, turned to face the space between the two stones. He called out one of the liquid runes of the Dark Elves, and blue light flashed, as searing as lightning.

When that brilliance faded, the doorway to Elfhame shimmered between the runed granite. A half-dozen glimglows swooped over the stones from the mortal side, then darted through the portal to flit among the huge-trunked trees in the Dark Elf realm.

Flowers grew beyond the gate, their blooms glowing with soft violet light, and a swirl of warm air breathed out, scented with herbs I could not name. A crescent moon hung in the velvety sky, suspended amid unfamiliar constellations.

Strange yearning moved through me at the sight of Elfhame. If I wished, in three years I could step through that doorway and dwell among the Dark Elves. It was a terrifying, yet wondrous, thought.

You could stay close to Thorne, my treacherous heart said.

But at what cost? Marriage to the Nightshade Lord was too high a price. And even if I chose to pay it, only misery could follow. No—my path lay elsewhere, away from Raine and its bittersweet secrets.

The Dark Elves filed between the stones, one by one disappearing from the mortal world until only the Nightshade Lord remained. He glanced up at the mortal sky, then turned and strode through the gate. The light between the stones dimmed.

I caught my breath, a premonition shivering through me, and started toward the center of the clearing.

"*Edro!*" someone cried, and the gateway flickered back into life.

A red-cloaked figure darted from the crowd of watching humans, pulling another person with them.

Neeve.

And even before the hood fell from the second figure's head, revealing his golden hair, I knew who it was.

"Stop them!" Lord Raine called, but it was already too late.

Between one heartbeat and the next, Neeve passed through the gateway to Elfhame—taking Prince Kian of Fiorland with her.

CHAPTER 18

"N o!" the king cried.

The doorway to the other world closed with the sound of metal cracking against granite. The glowing runes on the standing stones went dark, like a lamp suddenly extinguished.

I had reached the knot of people beside him—which included Thorne—and drew up, heart racing.

"*Galadhir.*" Lord Raine turned to Thorne, his expression thunderous. "You must fetch my daughter back. Immediately."

"Your majesty, I cannot leave your people stranded within the Darkwood." Thorne's words were measured, though I heard the edge of panic in his voice. "As soon as I send you all back to the castle, then I'll go after Neeve. But surely the Nightshade Lord will expel her from Elfhame."

Recalling what I'd glimpsed of my stepsister's conversation with her uncle, I had my doubts. Besides, Neeve would fight with everything she had to remain in the world of the Dark Elves. Finally, she'd achieved her life's dream, and she wasn't one to let such a thing go so easily.

The king shook his head. "We can travel back the way we came."

"The forest will not open for you," Thorne said. "Your journey to Castle Raine will take days, and the *nirwen* will lose its potency."

"My lord," said one of the king's advisors, "we don't have enough supplies for more than a day's travel."

"Then the *Galadhir* will have to send us all back to the castle tonight." Lord Raine's expression was as hard as stone. "I refuse to let my daughter remain in Elfhame a moment longer than necessary. The gateway will open, will it not, even though Neeve has stepped through it?"

"Yes," Thorne said with a hint of relief. "Since she took the Fiorland prince with her, the terms of the *geas* still hold. The door is not shut forever."

Someone with royal Dark Elf blood had to remain on the human side of the portal, I recalled. Or royal human blood in Elfhame. And since Neeve apparently didn't count as human to whatever magic kept track of such things, that meant Kian was now the anchor between the worlds.

Much that had been perplexing me suddenly fell into place: Neeve's sudden absences, the sly way she'd watched Kian, even her fight with me.

She must have been planning her defection for some time. She'd smuggled Kian along, somehow, and I wondered what she'd told him. I was fairly certain he hadn't known until the very end what was actually happening.

And now Neeve and Kian were in Elfhame, likely with the grudging consent of the Nightshade Lord. But why would the monarch agree? I couldn't fathom it.

"Pack up the camp!" the king called. "Make ready to depart as soon as possible."

The people around us swirled away, and a moment later I was left with the king and Thorne in the center of the dark clearing.

"Take me with you," I said to Thorne, a plan forming in my mind even as I spoke. "I must go into Elfhame."

"What folly is this?" Lord Raine scowled at me. "Two wayward children passing through the gateway is unacceptable. We hardly need to add another."

"Please, my lord." I turned to him with a beseeching look. "Neeve and I are close. She will listen to me."

Despite our recent fight, which I now suspected she'd engineered in order to keep me at a distance. Though it hadn't been completely without cause.

"It's imperative we retrieve both Neeve and the Fiorland prince from Elfhame," Thorne said urgently. "Especially the prince. It will be difficult enough to put off Jarl Eiric, but if Kian's brother arrives later this year to discover the prince is still missing..."

"Having been spirited away into a realm our allies had no idea existed—it could be seen as an act of war," the king finished grimly.

I shivered at the implications as I realized the cause of Thorne's alarm. According to him, time moved at a slower pace in Elfhame. A few days with the Dark Elves would equate to months in the human world.

My mind whirled with thoughts: Neeve, Kian, kingdoms and alliances in ruin, gateways closed forever.

My own place in the web of fate.

The terrifying Dark Elf lord who awaited on the other side of the gate. Stepping through that portal would seal my fate—I felt it in my bones.

But I'd asked Thorne earlier that night if I might aid him. Now the path lay directly beneath my feet—if I had the courage to take it. I dug my fingernails into my palms and willed my voice to steadiness.

"My lord," I said to the king, "if the Oracles are correct, and my presence in Elfhame can serve to keep the doorway open between the worlds, then I must go there. Even if Neeve won't return, I can..." I paused, swallowing back my utter fear. "I can go through the gateway and take the prince's place."

The lines bracketing Lord Raine's mouth deepened as he frowned at me. But he didn't immediately dismiss the idea. I heard Thorne suck in a breath, but I kept my attention on the king. If he agreed, then the *Galadhir* would have to obey.

"It seems that circumstances are forcing our hand," Lord Raine finally said. "I would have liked to see what the intervening years brought before formally sending you between the worlds, Rose. Yet now I have no choice. Ah, your mother will have my head."

"Tell her..." With effort, I kept my voice from trembling. "When you return to the castle, give her my love, and tell her not to worry."

Which, considering my mother's nature, wasn't too great a concern. She would be fretful, of course, but would eventually convince herself that sending me into Elfhame had been her preferred choice all along. And who knew? I was still too young to marry the Nightshade Lord. Perhaps I could find a way to untangle everything.

"Rose." Thorne gripped my shoulder and turned me to face him. A wild, frantic light shone in his eyes. "Don't make this choice. Please. I would do much to keep you from sacrificing yourself in such a manner."

"I must go—and who knows?" I tried to smile at him, with little success. "Perhaps the Oracles will deem me unsuitable after all, and Neeve will see reason, and we'll all return in a matter of hours."

Though it seemed unlikely.

"Your majesty." Thorne shifted his gaze to the king. "You can't let her go. She's just a child—"

"I am not," I said fiercely, even as Lord Raine shook his head.

"She is old enough to make this choice," he said. "When you return to Elfhame, *Galadhir*, you will take Rose with you. I command it."

Thorne's expression twisted, but he couldn't disobey a direct order from the King of Raine—even if he answered to a different monarch.

I swayed slightly, my relief quickly swamped by a wave of panic.

What had I done?

Fate had crashed over me like a wave, sweeping me out to sea. But I could make no other choice. And whatever dark future awaited me in Elfhame, at least Thorne would be there. I clung to that thought like a drowning sailor to the wreckage of their ship.

"Go make ready," the king said to me. "Raine thanks you for your bravery."

I dipped him a curtsey, threw an apologetic glance at Thorne, then fled the clearing.

The camp was already half dismantled. All the tents had come down and were being folded away, the cooking fires extinguished, people's bedrolls and the glowing baskets of *nirwen* loaded into the carts. I found Sorche near our former campsite, carrying my small sack of belongings. With a sudden jolt, I once again realized I had no more of the tonic Mistress Ainya had bade me drink daily. Surely, though, it wouldn't matter. I hoped.

"There you are," Sorche said, her expression growing lighter. "For a moment I thought we'd lost you, too."

A pang moved through me as I thought of the people I might never see again. Sorche, who'd served me so kindly. Miss Groves, my patient teacher, and Master Fawkes, who'd guided me on the harp. Mistress Ainya, who, despite my utter failure with magic, had declared fate had some purpose for me. Now, I supposed, she would know what that purpose was.

And, though I tried to ignore it, I felt a hot stab of grief that I wouldn't have a chance to say goodbye to Mama. Despite the gulf that lay between us, she was still my mother. Once, she had been the center of my universe.

I gave Sorche a serious look. "I'm afraid you're going to lose me after all. I'm to follow Neeve and try to bring her back." No point in explaining the rest of the plan in the likely event that my stepsister would refuse.

I lifted my fingers to the circlet on my head, considering removing it and giving it to Sorche for safekeeping. No—I was stepping into Elfhame as a princess of Raine, and the king would expect me to wear it.

"Going into the realm of the Dark Elves?" Sorche's eyes widened. "Oh, miss, how dreadful! And how very brave of you. Will you rescue the prince, too?"

"I intend to, yes."

"Oh, but that's romantic—the stuff of tales, it is. Your love driving you to follow him into that strange, magical world. Surely he'll marry you after that."

I'd forgotten that the castle gossips believed Kian and I were desperately in love. Our time in Parnese seemed like forever ago now.

"It's not love for Kian," I said. "It is my duty, as Neeve's sister."

The maid nodded, but I could tell she still believed I was going after Kian. And in a way, she was right—not about the prince, but about my motives.

Love *was* impelling me to act.

My love for Thorne, though we could never be together. My love for Neeve, the prickly stepsister whom I'd come to care for so deeply. My love for my adopted kingdom of Raine, and my great fondness for Kian—all of these had spurred my decision.

"Here." Sorche held out my belongings. "I suppose you'll need a change of clothing and your comb, at the very least."

"Thank you." I took the bag, then stepped forward to embrace her. "You've always been so kind to me."

"Well." A flustered blush rose on her cheeks. "For all that I'm not much older than you, you were a lost little thing when you first arrived. It was the least I could do."

A lost little thing? My brows rose, but I made no comment. I supposed I'd spent a fair amount of time drifting about the castle halls and losing myself in books during those early days. Certainly my own mother had cast me adrift, and Neeve had been difficult to get to know, to put it mildly. But no matter how lost I was at first, I'd certainly found my footing over time.

While Sorche and I had been talking, the final preparations to return to Castle Raine swirled around us. Now, the denizens of the castle were ready to depart. Carts creaking, steps somber, we made our way back to the clearing. The stars overhead were a scattering of diamond dust, the few lanterns accentuating the forbidding darkness of the forest as it sighed softly at the edges of the meadow.

Thorne waited beside the stones, his expression taut. The king stood next to him.

"My people," Lord Raine said when everyone was gathered. "Thank you for making such haste, so that the *Galadhir* may return to his land and bring our princess back home."

Those around me murmured in agreement, but my mouth twisted. Neeve *was* home, according to all her dreams—the home of her heart, where the Dark Elves dwelled.

"Additionally, the Lady Rose will be aiding him. Please, show your thanks for her bravery in service to our kingdom." He beckoned me forward.

With heavy steps, I went to take my place by the stones. People patted my arms and shoulders as I passed, a few bowed and curtseyed, and whispers of *good luck*, *be safe*, *bring our princess home* followed me.

I nodded to the well-wishers, trying to keep my face serene, despite the fear scraping my ribs with every breath.

Thorne glanced at me as I came to stand beside him, then quickly away.

"Is everyone ready?" he asked the king.

Lord Raine surveyed the gathering a moment, then turned to Thorne. "Take care of all your charges, *Galadhir*, and see that no harm comes to them."

Thorne set his clenched fist over his heart. "I swear it."

"Then we shall go. Ready yourselves," the king called to his people. "Hold thoughts of the castle close."

He moved to one of the *nirwen*-laden carts, where a groom held the reins of his horse, then nodded at Thorne.

The *Galadhir* drew in a deep breath, then raised his hands and spoke the incantation that would fold the forest and take the castle's inhabitants to the very edge of the Darkwood.

Blue light rippled from his fingers, then over the meadow like a wave. When it cleared, the people were gone, the horses, the carts, the king, Sorche.

I swallowed, then looked at Thorne. My pulse beat in the silence like a trapped moth striving for the moon.

"Rose." He took my hand. "I have seen visions...this act of yours has far-reaching consequences. It's not too late to change your mind."

"It is." I gave him a strained smile, my heart twisting at the desperation in his eyes.

Perhaps he cared for me a small bit, after all—but it was too late for second chances. Fate had spoken, and this was the only choice I could make.

Thorne squeezed his eyes shut. When he opened them, his expression was full of grim determination.

"So be it. Hold fast."

Breathless, I dipped my head in assent and clung to his fingers as he gestured with his free hand.

"*Edro,*" he said forcefully.

The runes on the gateway stones flared to life, the air between shimmering to reveal the mysterious land beyond.

Thorne glanced at me, then, hands clasped tightly together, we stepped through the doorway between the realms.

PART III

CHAPTER 19

P ain flared at my elbow as we crossed the threshold between
worlds, and I clenched my teeth together to keep from crying
out. Then the enormity of where I was spread out before me,
washing over my senses, and my momentary discomfort was forgotten.

Elfhame.

I stared at the huge evergreens rising around us. They grew three
times taller than those of the Darkwood, their feathery tops nearly
brushing the stars. Those stars were flecks of silver in a deep purple
sky. There was no moon, but the land was filled with soft radiance.

Nodding, bell-like flowers beneath the trees glowed as if their
petals were lit from within by tiny candles. Violet blossoms scattered
on the nearby bushes gave off a quiet light. Sensing our presence, a trio
of glimglows came to dance and weave, bright sparks above our heads.

Thorne released my hand and conjured a ball of blue flame. He sent
it to hover behind our shoulders, where it cast our shadows before us
over the soft carpet of moss. Looking closely, I saw that even the
mosses were spangled with tiny flecks of light.

"It's beautiful," I said, my voice low with wonder. "Are we still in
the Darkwood?"

"On this side of the gateway, the forest is called the Erynvorn. And it contains dangers aplenty, as well as beauty."

"Oh, I've no doubt." I shivered slightly, thinking of the dire creatures I'd encountered in the mortal world. Bears and wolves, of course, but poison-clawed drakes and deadly basilisks, too. "Are there hobnies here?"

He shook his head, the motion barely discernable in the dim light. "The Darkwood shares many things with the Erynvorn, but there are certain creatures of mortal legend that remain on your side of the gateway. The hobnies are one such."

I wondered what else was. The nixie who had nearly drowned me? The White Hart, whom Neeve and I had glimpsed one lazy summer afternoon?

I turned, searching the hushed and radiant forest for any signs of habitation. "Where is the Nightshade Court?"

"Not close." Thorne let out a weary breath. "Just as Castle Raine lies some distance from the gateway in your realm, so too do our courts."

The courts of Elfhame. I'd read about them in the book I'd found in the castle library. There were seven courts, as I recalled, each one named after a slightly toxic plant or flower. "I take it Nightshade is one of the closer courts?"

"Along with Hawthorne, and Rowan further to the north."

"How will we get to the Nightshade Court? Are we walking? How long will it take?"

"Peace, Rose. Give me a few moments to recover."

I bit my lip—which reminded me of the pain I'd felt as we crossed between the worlds. Carefully, I pulled back the left sleeve of my golden gown. The leaf inscribed at my inner elbow was a constant reminder of the magical binding Thorne had performed upon me the first year I came to Raine.

A binding that had unexpected consequences, and that apparently was *still* behaving in odd ways. For the leaf tattoo had changed, growing a long, curling tendril that spiraled halfway down my forearm. Tiny leaves studded that new vine, and my stomach clutched at the sight.

"Look." I held out my arm to Thorne.

Frowning slightly, he cradled my elbow between his cool hands and inspected the new markings.

"Does it hurt?" he asked.

"It did when we came through the gateway," I admitted.

He glanced up at me. "Why didn't you say anything?"

"The pain passed—and then we were here." I glanced at the magnificent forest. "I was distracted."

"Hm." He looked back at my arm, then slowly traced the new vine with his finger.

The feel of his touch made me tremble. A sensation of heat—not burning, but sweet as honey—raced over my skin, and my breath hitched.

"Painful?" he asked, halting.

"No." I pulled my arm from his grasp, unable to admit to him how he made my senses reel. "What does it mean?"

His mouth tightened and he regarded me for a long moment. "I don't know. But clearly your presence in Elfhame triggered the change. Just as the Darkwood marked you on that side of the gateway, the Erynvorn has marked you here. But the Oracles will be able to tell you more. I plan to send for them as soon as we reach Nightshade."

Nightshade. I shivered at the reminder of the Dark Elf lord who dwelt there.

Hastily, I shoved the thought away and concentrated on Thorne's plans to summon the mysterious Oracles. How many were there? How long would they take to arrive? What if they decided I was a satisfactory anchor to replace Kian—or what if they deemed me unsuitable? Questions raced through me like a leaping river, but I dammed them up.

Although patience had never been one of my strengths, I'd learned over the years to bide. At least for a short while. I would learn the answers in time—or press for them when I could wait no longer.

Thorne took his water flask from the pocket of his cloak and drank deeply before handing it to me. The water tingled against my lips, sweet and melancholy over my tongue.

When I finished, he tucked the flask away and drew in a deep breath. "I'll use my magic to transport us to the Nightshade Court."

I gave him a concerned look, my eyes finally adjusted enough to the lack of light that I could see the lines of weariness on his forehead. "Is that how you normally do it?"

"No. When I return, a warrior comes to meet me with an extra mount—but there are now two of us. Also, I'm not due back in Elfhame for another several turns, and time is of the essence."

"Are you... Is your power recovered enough?"

I recalled the time Neeve had overused her magic and was unable to draw upon it at a moment of need. I'd hate for that to happen to Thorne.

"It will do," he said, a grim note in his voice. "Speak with Neeve as soon as we arrive. She must change her mind and return with the Fiorland prince to the mortal world, before too much damage is done."

I wondered what Kian was making of all this. I'd known about the Dark Elves and the gateway, and yet Elfhame still was overwhelming in its mystery and magic. How would the Fiorlander feel after being unexpectedly transported so far from the normalcy of the human world?

I supposed I'd soon find out.

Thorne took my hand again and called out the spell to speed us magically across the forest. Blue light wreathed us—

And then his hand was wrenched from my grasp, and I was falling through blackness. I flailed, barely able to feel my limbs, and screamed his name, though no sound emitted from my mouth.

A heartbeat later, I landed in a patch of bushes with enough force to knock the breath from my lungs. I lay there a long moment, stunned, the smell of plant sap sharp in my nostrils, the stars watching mercilessly overhead.

"Thorne?" Slowly, I levered myself up to sitting and glanced about.

The enormous evergreens encircled me. Nothing moved among the black columns of their trunks. I blinked and widened my eyes, trying to see more clearly. It seemed darker, and I realized that the glowing flowers scattered through the forest had furled closed, taking their radiance with them.

"Is anyone here?" My voice was a thin thread stitched through the air.

No answer came, confirming the dire truth of what I already suspected: I was lost in the middle of the Dark Elves' forest, presumably dropped when Thorne's magic failed.

Failed, despite his assurances to the contrary. I took a wavering breath. Then, pulling my cloak tighter about me, I stood.

He'll find me, I reassured myself.

But to do that, Thorne would need to use his magic—which seemed to have been drained by his recent exertions. Even the *Galadhir* wasn't all-powerful.

If he'd made it to the Nightshade Court, then he'd mount a search party for me. And if he hadn't, then surely he must be somewhere near. I turned in a slow circle. Part of me wanted to set out to look for him immediately—but I had no idea where he might be. And bumbling about in the darkening forest calling Thorne's name was surely not the wisest course.

Better to find a safe place to spend the night. In the morning, if this strange, dim land even had such a thing, Thorne would find me. And if he did not, perhaps I'd have some better inkling of which direction to go.

The beginnings of panic shivered up my spine, but I forced it back down. I could survive for a few days, as long as I could find water. And didn't get attacked or eaten by some dreadful creature of the forest. At least I had my knife, which Sir Durum insisted I carry at all times—even when wearing my court gowns—just in case anything were to happen.

It turned out he'd been right, though I suspected he'd been thinking more along the lines of sudden attacks on Castle Raine, not me becoming unexpectedly lost in an enchanted wood.

I also had my small bag containing the serviceable dress I'd worn for the harvest, a change of stockings, my comb, and an empty flask. I couldn't remember whether I'd tucked any provisions into the bag, but sadly, I suspected not.

A wave of tiredness washed over me. It had been a very long day—starting with the dawn awakening, working hard to harvest *nirwen*, the feast, Neeve's unexpected escape from the mortal world with Kian, my subsequent decision to follow... I yawned. It was no wonder weariness tugged at me, weighing down my thoughts.

I must find a safe place to rest.

Sleeping on the ground underneath a bush felt too exposed. I glanced thoughtfully at the huge trees surrounding me. Sheltering for the night in the crook of a wide branch, not too high up, seemed a better option, provided I could find an evergreen with low enough branches that I could clamber into it. Most of the trunks rose cleanly for several times my height before branching out.

Finally, after a bit of stumbling about and tripping over half-seen rocks and shrubs, I found a cedar tree that would suit. The first branch lay slightly higher than I could reach, but I was able to throw my cloak up and loop it around the branch.

It wasn't a graceful ascent, but after tumbling down twice, I managed to clamber into the tree. My hands were scraped, my dress smeared with moss and crumbling bark, but at last I straddled the branch triumphantly.

My glee was short-lived, however, once I realized I'd need to go higher to find a wide enough place to sleep. With a sigh, I swiped my hair out of my face, stuffed my cloak into my bag, and kept climbing. At least the branches offered more hand and footholds, and midway up the huge trunk I found a satisfactory place to rest.

Two branches emerged from the trunk, one a little higher than the other, creating a hollow filled with cedar needles. I cut a stick from the feathery branch and stirred the needles to make sure I was the only one bedding down there for the night.

No birds or small creatures took flight. Satisfied, I wrapped my cloak around me and settled into the hollow. I pulled the circlet from my head and hung it on a nearby branch. It shone softly, a reminder of everything I had left behind.

On the morrow, I'd tuck it away in my bag of clothing, but for now I intended to use the bag for a pillow. It was already lumpy from my water flask, but I was too tired to do more than prod the flask to the side, away from my cheek.

Don't fall out of the tree, I reminded myself as, despite the strangeness of my situation, sleep descended.

I woke several times, rousing at every strange noise: the creak of branches rubbing together, the rustle of something moving through the underbrush below. Finally, the slim crescent of an unfamiliar moon poked into the sky, just visible through the screen of branches. Birds chirped, waking around me—which was enough to send me at last into deep slumber.

⚜

THE MOON HAD TRAVELED some way up the purple sky when I woke again. Thirst dried my mouth, and I felt awake enough to navigate my descent. I collected my crown, then slung my bag over my shoulder, tied back my cloak, and left my little nest with a murmured thanks.

Once on the forest floor, I was glad to see that the glowing flowers had reopened. Their soft radiance, plus the filtered moonlight coming through the trees, was enough to let me navigate without stubbing my toes or tripping over fallen branches.

But which way to go?

I turned first to the right, then the left, straining my ears for the sound of running water. Nothing—just the hush of the wind in the high branches overhead. I swallowed uncertainly, but the forest seemed a little less dense directly ahead of me, so I set out.

I passed bushes laden with red berries, and pale mushrooms springing up from the loam, but though my stomach was tight with hunger, I wasn't going to risk eating anything I didn't know was safe. Which, sadly, was everything around me.

Though I supposed I could chew on the bitter tips of cedar branches as a last resort.

I walked for what felt like a long time, in a dreamy state punctuated only by waves of thirst. Finally, I glimpsed something bright ahead and hurried forward—only to discover with disappointment that what I'd taken for a glint of water was only a pale slab of mica-flecked granite.

With a sigh, I drew my cloak around me and perched upon the

stone for a short rest. Maybe I should pick a spot in the forest and wait there for Thorne—but truly, I *must* find water, and I'd no idea how long it would take for the *Galadhir* to locate me.

Something moved in the shadowy depths of the forest, too low to the ground to be Thorne, and moving on four legs, not two. I scrambled to my feet and drew my knife, pulse racing. A rank odor drifted to my nose, and I wondered if I should flee, or if that would only make me more tempting as prey.

The creature moved closer, snorting and snuffling. A boar, I thought, catching a glimpse of a curved tusk, a glint of its red eye. I tightened my grip on my knife, wishing I'd shown an aptitude for any other weapon.

Quickly, I surveyed the surrounding trees, thinking I might be able to climb one to escape if the boar attacked. But here, as in so much of the forest, the branches were higher than my head. Maybe I could back away, quietly and stealthily enough that it wouldn't notice me, and then make my escape to another part of the forest.

I sheathed my blade and slowly began putting distance between myself and the creature, stepping carefully over the moss-covered ground. My heart pounded so loudly in my ears that I was certain it would give me away, but the boar seemed not to notice my presence.

Until I trod on a stick, which broke with a sharp crack. I froze, teeth clenched to hold back my panic.

The boar halted, head raised, and scented the air. It turned to face me, beady eyes glowing with a reddish light. My breath seized in my lungs. Could I somehow frighten it away? Wave my cloak over my head to make it seem I was a bigger creature?

For a long moment, the boar didn't move. Then, as if making up its mind, it started trotting toward me. It didn't seem a friendly approach.

Taking the edges of my cloak in my hands, I raised my arms.

"Go away!" I shouted, flapping the material.

The boar shied a few steps, then kept coming. So much for that plan. Pulse racing, I drew my knife again. Perhaps I could fling it into the beast's eye—but Sir Durum had always said that a fighter who threw their weapon away was asking for defeat. If I didn't score a direct, fatal hit, I'd be completely defenseless.

I spared a momentary thought for the pair of slim throwing knives back in my room at Castle Raine. I'd left them behind, thinking the *nirwen* harvest would be safe. If only I'd known...

The boar charged, and I darted back, throwing myself behind the nearest tree trunk. The creature came close enough to tear a rent in my cloak with its tusk. If it gored me, I had no doubt I'd bleed to death beneath the huge trees of the Erynvorn.

Keeping myself pressed close against the nubbled bark of the evergreen, I sidled around until the massive trunk was between me and the boar.

My pulse was a waterfall of fear thundering through me, my fingers clenched tightly around the handle of my knife. I strained my ears, trying to determine which side the creature would choose to attack from. It would come at me, from one direction or the other, but perhaps I could evade it until it grew tired of chasing me around and around in a deadly game of seeker's prey.

A rustle from my right.

I flung myself to the left, the bark scraping against my cheek. Just in time. The boar rushed past, snorting.

Then, far more quickly than I'd given it credit for, it pivoted and charged again.

I threw my knife, missed, and tried to dodge around the tree once more. *Too slow,* my thoughts screamed, as I braced myself for the pierce of that sharp and deadly tusk.

Blinding silver light arced across my vision. I blinked as the majestic antlered form of a white stag landed gracefully between me and the boar. It lowered its head, scooped up the boar, and tossed it into the underbrush.

A squeal, a rustle. I watched the bushes warily. The boar emerged, red eyes bright, snorting with rage. I dug my fingers into the bark behind me and braced for another attack.

The stag pawed the ground and snorted in warning, and after a brief hesitation, the boar turned and fled into the shadows.

I slumped against the tree, my whole body trembling.

"Thank you," I managed to say to the great, glimmering creature standing before me.

The White Hart.

Neeve and I had glimpsed the enchanted beast once, in the Dark-wood. While it had been an inspiring sight in the mortal world, here in the depths of the Erynvorn it seemed three times as magical. Its antlers spread majestically and its hide glowed like the moon.

It made no response to my thanks, other than to regard me silently. By the light of its pale coat I could see where my knife had fallen on the dark mosses. Keeping a wary eye on the magical deer, I crept from the shelter of the tree trunk and retrieved my blade.

As soon as the knife was in my hand, I sheathed it. I wanted to offer no threat to the White Hart, who could no doubt dispatch me as easily as it had dealt with the boar.

"Now what?" I asked softly.

The White Hart let out a soft snort, then bounded into the velvet shadows beneath the trees, the air shimmering in its wake. My heart contracted, from the pain of its beauty—and its withdrawal.

It didn't go far, however, but halted and looked back at me, as if expecting me to follow.

"Do I come with you?" I asked, knowing it wouldn't answer.

Still unsteady from the aftermath of my exertions to avoid the boar, I moved toward it. If I were not meant to come along, the White Hart could leave me easily enough.

The stag turned and slowly began walking ahead of me through the forest. The glow from its hide painted the trunks and limned the branches overhead, giving the illusion that we were moving through a tunnel of light.

I increased my stride, but no matter how quickly I went, the White Hart remained an equal number of paces ahead. So much for my half-formed hope that I might ride upon its enchanted back. Although the magical creature was aiding me, clearly I didn't merit *that* much help.

Still, I was overwhelmingly grateful for the stag's presence—not only as it had driven the wild boar away but because it was leading me *somewhere.*

To Thorne, I desperately hoped.

Despite our easy pace, I began to tire. I felt lightheaded from thirst. The shining hide of the stag blurred in my vision as my steps faltered.

Think of something pleasant, I told myself. Something to distract my mind and keep myself moving forward.

Though I'd gladly dwell on thoughts of Thorne, those would only remind me that I was currently lost in the Erynvorn. Instead, I turned my mind to memories of Parnese. I smiled, recalling the warm paving stones in the streets reflecting the heat of the sun, the smell of orange trees in blossom—so sweet you could almost taste their fruit upon the air.

The market squares where vendors sold spices and silks. The splash of bright water in the fountains, where one could perch on the edge and hold a cupped hand beneath a nymph or a porpoise pouring liquid down, and drink—

No, I mustn't think about my thirst.

I thought of the winding streets, the coolness of the small alleyways, shaded by several stories of dwellings overhead. If one headed up toward the palace, the winking blue sea spread out below, the waves dancing...but no, now I was thinking of water again.

And hearing it, too.

I shook my head and blinked, trying to clear the illusion, only to realize that, *yes,* I did hear the gurgle of flowing water. Belatedly, I realized the White Hart had halted on the bank of a stream cutting through the forest. As I watched, it lowered its head and drank.

"Thank you," I gasped, rushing forward to kneel beside that cool, blessed water.

Heedless of the mud beneath my knees, I scooped up mouthful after mouthful, until my face was glazed with moisture, the front of my dress darkened where water had run down off my chin.

Finally, I sank back on my heels and heaved a deep sigh. Already my mind felt clearer.

While I'd been drinking, the stag had leaped to the opposite bank. It still watched me, its gaze deep and fathomless.

"Again, thank you," I told it. "Do you know where I might find the *Galadhir?*"

It bobbed its head, then turned and bounded downstream, far

faster than I could hope to follow. In a matter of heartbeats, it was gone—swallowed up by the dark reaches of the woods.

I dropped my hands, which I'd unconsciously lifted to reach after it, but it seemed clear I was not meant to journey further in the White Hart's company. The burble of the stream was my companion now, and my guide.

Rummaging in my bag, I retrieved my water flask and filled it. To my delight, I also discovered a bit of food tucked in a napkin beneath my spare dress: a wizened piece of fruit and a hunk of bread—dried out, the crust hardened, but I didn't care. With a glad sigh, I moved away from the muddy stream bank and ate a breakfast that tasted far more delicious than it would've under any other circumstances.

Much restored after my meal, I refilled my flask, then set out in the direction the White Hart had gone. I suspected I wouldn't see that enchanted creature again. It had saved me, twice over, and given me a path.

The rest was up to me.

CHAPTER 20

The strange light of the forest gave my journey along the stream bank a dreamy feel. Sometimes I was forced to push through stands of dense willows, my boots damp from the boggy ground. Other times I had to detour around huge boulders and clamber down rock-rimmed ravines while the water surged below.

Through it all, the stream hummed and gurgled. Even when I lost sight of the silvery thread of water, I could follow the sound, and it made me feel less alone.

I marked my progress by the crescent moon swinging across the sky. When it passed its zenith and began to slide down the other side, I stopped to take a longer rest than the short breaks I'd been allowing myself.

At least I had enough to drink, though hunger was gnawing at my belly again. I settled beneath a hemlock tree near the water and folded my arms about my knees. Absently, I noted that my gold velvet gown was in dreadful condition. The skirt was torn in several places, sap and dirt ground into the fabric, the embroidery unravelling along one arm and across the bodice.

It would never serve as a fashionable court dress again.

Of course, I might never see the inside of a castle again. The Erynvorn seemed to stretch endlessly around me. Despite following the stream, I didn't seem any closer to the edge of the forest, or any sign of habitation.

But the moon had not yet set. I decided I would walk until it was nearly down, then find another tree to spend the night in. Whatever came after that, I refused to speculate.

With a sigh, I heaved myself to standing and kept going. My feet were sore, and my stomach growled, tired of only water, but at least I wasn't being chased through the forest by a feral boar.

The trees around me thinned, the stream bank flattening. From the corner of my eye, I glimpsed strange ripples in the stream, seeming to keep pace with me instead of flowing with the current. Whenever I turned my head to look at them, they disappeared. Warily, I walked as far from the edge of the water as possible.

The stream widened and slowed, making a lazy ford. Mint and cress grew thickly along the verges, scenting the air. I plucked some of the mint, sniffed it once again to be sure, turned the square stem between my fingers, then popped a leaf in my mouth to chew on. At least it would give my belly the illusion I was eating something.

The ripples in the stream reappeared—three of them, standing up higher and higher as I watched. I set my hand to the knife at my belt and backed away, recalling the nixie that had tried to drown me in the Darkwood.

The three waves leaped out of the edge of the stream, somehow turning to ripples of mud and silt. They rolled about, taking on form and substance, as though shaped by some force from within. The transformation seemed more strange than frightening, even when the mud began to look humanlike, arms and legs growing from the torsos, rounded heads perched on top.

One of the evolving creatures reached into the stream with wavering fingers made of trailing sand and plucked out two shiny rocks. It set them into its face, then turned to look at me.

Its features sharpened—growing a nose, lips, chin. It grabbed a clump of cress and draped it atop its head to create a semblance of long, curling green hair. A sheening skirt of mud formed about its legs.

It was a maiden, made of the silt of the streambed, of mud and magic. I wondered how sentient it might be.

Nervously I nodded at the being. "Hello."

The mud maiden dipped her head in return, her mouth moving, but no sound came out. Her two companions were still adorning themselves, one choosing a clump of grass for hair, the other a spiky halo of cedar needles. Their dresses, likewise, were made of whatever material was to hand. The first maiden had stuck ferns about her waist, while wet leaves and mint flowers adorned the other two.

"Can you speak?" I asked, raising my hands in question.

The first maiden mimicked me, holding up sticky hands made of silt, her mouth moving silently. I heard laughter, high-pitched and barely audible, as her companions linked hands about her, dancing in a circle.

Distracted, my imitator whirled with them, her vegetal hair flying, casting out a skein of droplets. They seemed as blithe as the stream itself.

Suddenly, the mud maidens halted, turning to face the forest behind me. With another rill of half-heard laughter, they leaped back into the stream, their bodies dissolving. The wavy strand of cress floated lazily down the current, accompanied by a single flower.

Why had they gone so quickly? Pulse pounding, I turned to peer beneath the trees.

Lights shone beneath the dark branches, and for a moment my heart leaped, thinking they were torches. I'd been found! Then I realized that no torch or lantern light would dip and dart in such a manner. They were glimglows.

And something was following them, moving noisily through the underbrush. Thorne would never stride so loudly through the forest, and I edged back toward the stream. On one hand, I trusted the glimglows, who had guided me in the past.

But on the other—what were they leading toward me?

The rustling grew closer, and a half-dozen glimglows darted from beneath the trees to dance above my head.

Followed by the rough-furred figure of an enormous bear.

Run! my senses screamed.

No, I argued, while my body trembled, begging for flight.

The bear halted as soon as it cleared the trees. It gave me a look from dark eyes set back behind a long, wet-tipped nose. Then, as if sensing my panic, it slowly lay down.

I hovered, mouth dry with fear, beside the stream. Flee or stay?

Clearly, the bear wasn't planning to eat me. Or even do me harm—unless it was trying to lull me into believing it was safe. But the presence of the glimglows inclined me to trust it, however much one might trust a wild creature of the woods.

The White Hart had led me true, I reminded myself. Why not a dark-furred bear with golden sparks in its eyes? And, unlike the mud maidens, I thought I glimpsed more than animal intelligence in the depths of its gaze.

"Can you...understand me?" I asked hesitantly.

Deliberately, the bear bobbed its head up and down. I let out a deep breath, trying to expel some of my fear. The creature watched me patiently, even as the glimglows darted between us, beckoning me to approach.

"Do you know where I can find the *Galadhir?*" The question trembled through me. If only I could reach Thorne, all would be well.

The bear let out a snort, then nodded again as the glimglows somersaulted over its broad back.

Very well. It seemed I must trust the creature.

"Let me refill my flask," I told it. "And then I'll follow you."

It laid its head down across its broad paws, which I took as agreement. Unwilling to turn my back on the bear, I sidled to the water's edge and dipped my flask, letting the silvery current gurgle over my hands. The mud maidens seemed long gone—another oddity of the Erynvorn I would likely never see again.

I tucked the filled water container into my bag and plucked another stem of mint to chew upon.

Then, with shaking steps, I walked toward the bear. To my relief, it lay quietly, watching me approach. I halted a few paces away.

"Well—go ahead," I said. "I'll follow you."

It blinked at me, then rolled onto its side, clearly not going anywhere.

"This is no time to take a nap," I said, my trepidation giving way to annoyance. "I'm ready to go. Take me to the *Galadhir*."

It snorted again and rolled back onto its belly, then nodded twice at me. The glimglows swirled over its broad shoulders, then settled into the fur, making a bright circle. It took me a moment to understand, and when I did, I took a step back.

"Ride you? I don't think—"

The bear roared. Not a tremendously loud sound, but forceful enough to let me know my disagreement wasn't an option.

I swallowed and stood my ground. "Don't yell at me. How do I know you aren't going to carry me off somewhere and eat me?"

It blinked at me, with a slow deliberate gaze that reminded me it could leap up and devour me at any moment. The glimglows rose from its back, swirling in what looked suspiciously like amusement.

"Are you sure I can't just walk behind you?" I asked.

The bear shook its head and gave a low, impatient growl, as if I'd wasted too much time in arguing. I blinked at the huge, dark trees, and realized that the pale light of Elfhame was dimming. The stream faded to pewter, the sky to indigo overhead. The moon must be setting.

"Very well." I forced myself forward, though it wasn't the easiest thing to walk right up to a bear.

I was glad to find that it smelled only slightly musky, with a hint of herbs, though maybe that was the mint I still clutched in my hand. The glimglows darted encouragingly about me as I set my hand to the bear's side. Its fur was rough on top, but softer beneath. It turned its head to watch me.

"I don't want to hurt you," I said. What if I jabbed it accidentally with a knee or elbow as I clambered onto its back? Would it instinctively take a bite out of me?

It huffed softly in reassurance—or what I hoped was reassurance. And really, what choice did I have?

I stuck the mint in the inner pocket of my bedraggled cloak and made sure the bag slung over my shoulder was secure, the knife at my belt firm in its sheath. Then I took two handfuls of the bear's fur and hoisted myself onto its broad back. Kilting up my skirts, I straddled it.

Unladylike, and a bit awkward, but there was no one to see me and take offense.

"I'm ready," I said, keeping my hands buried in the thick black fur. It appeared I was destined to ride a magical creature of the Erynvorn after all, even if it wasn't the graceful White Hart.

With a lurch, the bear stood. It paused for a moment, but when I didn't immediately fall off, it began walking. The lilt of the stream faded behind us as my unlikely mount headed into the deep shadows beneath the evergreens.

Riding the bear reminded me a little of Snowbell, the poor pony who had suffered along with me as I reluctantly learned how to ride. I was about the same distance from the ground, but there the resemblance ended.

Where Snowbell's gait had rattled my teeth, the bear padded along smoothly. Its broad back, even without a saddle, was cushioned enough that I felt safe. Perhaps I could've ridden sideways, if I'd wanted.

The bear was warm, too, and surefooted as it moved through the forest. Gradually, it increased its pace until it was loping along. Smoother than a canter, I was rocked back and forth while the glimglows swooped on either side.

Perhaps I dozed, for one moment it seemed we traveled beneath the spreading cedar branches, and the next we were at the top of a grassy hill, a thousand unfamiliar stars sprinkled overhead. Some distance away, a palace stood, a graceful expanse of white stone, with towers rising at either end. It was surrounded by ornate gardens and a high wall.

To our left, I made out a road leading toward a gate in that encircling wall. Were we nearly at the Nightshade Court? I rather desperately hoped so.

The bear headed down the hill, and I lost sight of the castle for a time. We paralleled the road, but my mount seemed unwilling to run upon it, choosing instead to skirt through groves of pale-barked saplings and meadows dotted with faintly glowing purple flowers.

Finally, a few paces from the smooth white walls rising about the palace, the bear veered onto the road, halting at the ornate metal gates barring the way. It roared, and to my surprise, the gates sprang open.

"Halt!" a guard stationed on the far side of the wall cried, confusion creasing his stern elven features, but the bear charged past, heading directly for the palace.

I wondered, with misplaced hilarity, if it would insist on carrying me all the way into the throne room, and what the monarchs there might think to see a grubby human girl arrive perched on the back of a bear.

More glimglows joined our small escort as we rushed past the gardens, until nearly two dozen of them glimmered above our heads. As we neared the palace, I saw curved crystalline bowls of blue fire mounted beside curved doorways running the length of the building, but we seemed to be headed for the widest arch that denoted the main entrance.

Two guards stood there, at the top of a shallow set of stairs. One held a spear, the other had two swords belted at her waist, but neither drew their weapons or seemed unduly worried that a large bear was hurtling toward them.

The bear halted at the base of the steps, our glimglow escort scattering like golden sparks around us. I wasn't sure whether to dismount, but the bear bucked slightly, as though it was considering shrugging me off. I slung my legs together and slid down its side, clutching a fistful of fur as I landed to keep my balance.

The warrior with the spear bowed, the intricate braids in his long silver hair swinging forward with the motion.

"Welcome," he said. "We've been waiting for you."

"You have?" I blinked, weariness and confusion tangling my thoughts. "Is this the Nightshade Court?"

"Indeed. And you are Lady Rose of the mortal world, are you not?" he asked.

"Well, yes."

"Then enter," his companion said, stepping forward. "I will escort you to your sister."

I turned to the bear who had borne me so steadily through the forest. It watched me, gold lights flickering in the depths of its dark eyes.

"Thank you." I bobbed a curtsey, little caring what the elves might think to see me bowing to a wild creature of the woods. This was no ordinary bear, after all. "I owe you a debt of gratitude."

Indeed, the bear had almost certainly saved my life.

The creature brought its face close to mine and snuffled. Its warm breath stirred the curls that had worked themselves into a red frizz about my face.

"Come along," the sword-bearing warrior said, gesturing to the palace door.

I mounted the shallow steps and, with a last look over my shoulder at the bear, the glimglows sparkling against the dark, the hushed gardens beyond, stepped into the Nightshade Court.

CHAPTER 21

I stared about me in amazement as the warrior led me through graceful corridors broken at regular intervals by arched doors. Whenever one hallway intersected another, the ceiling soared overhead, decorated with carvings of leaves and vines. Crystal bowls holding flickering blue flame, smaller than the ones I'd seen outside, shed soft radiance over the white stone walls and polished floor.

It was the exact opposite of Castle Raine. I'd grown used to those shadowy, cold corridors, the uncompromising walls of hewn granite, but they'd never felt welcoming. Not like these open and graceful halls.

We passed a large room where a fountain played, and another that seemed to be a dining hall of some kind, elegant tables and chairs arrayed within. My escort led me by several Dark Elf courtiers, who regarded me with faintly horrified looks as we passed. They were all garbed in flowing silks the color of tourmaline, or clouds at sunset. Elaborate jewels winked from their necks and wrists and even their hair.

I couldn't tell if they disdained humans in general, or if my bedraggled condition was the cause. Possibly both—although the elves at the harvest, while haughty in bearing, hadn't seemed scornful of mortals. The two races intermarried, after all, at the highest levels.

For the first time, I wondered if regular Dark Elves ever wed humans. There were a few myths along those lines, as I recalled. And a passage in the *Studie* had mentioned an ancient prophecy uniting elves and humans in a marriage to save both kingdoms.

Prophecy made me think of the Oracles, and of Thorne.

"Is the *Galadhir* here at the palace?" I asked my guide.

She gave me a bemused look. "Yes."

"Can I see him?"

Her brows rose, dark arches of surprise on her pale forehead. "I believe he is currently recovering. His wellspring is dangerously depleted from overuse. Which is why he was unable to—"

"Rose!"

I turned at the familiar voice and saw Kian striding toward me down the hall. His jaunty smile was nearly my undoing. Tears pricking my eyes, I flew forward to meet him, suddenly wanting nothing more than the comforting feel of his arms around me amid all this strangeness.

He held me close a moment, then stepped back. I was reluctant to let him go, but I reminded myself I wasn't a child, needing to cling to him for safety. Frowning, he looked me up and down.

"That Thorne fellow certainly didn't take very good care of you! You're a proper mess. Did he at least feed you on your journey?"

I was unwilling to explain that I'd gotten lost in the forest, with almost no food, and had to be rescued by wild beasts. Kian already disliked Thorne. Why make things worse, especially as we were all trapped together in the Nightshade Court?

"I am hungry," I admitted.

"And grubby. Go clean up and I'll see about getting some food to your room."

"Do you know where it is?" I glanced from him to my escort, who stood patiently watching our exchange.

"Of course I do—you're right next to Neeve. I'll stop by the kitchens and be there soon."

He turned back the way he'd come and strode down the hall, the lights casting blue reflections over his golden hair. It was only then that I realized he was garbed in Dark Elf fashion: an ornately embroidered, tunic-like wrap over velvety leggings that looked both comfortable and elegant. I was glad to note that at least he wore his own boots. He seemed so at ease that I wondered what Neeve had told him about Elfhame. And what she'd withheld.

"Lady?" My guard gestured. "Your room is waiting."

And I was standing in the hall, gawking. I shook myself, then let my escort lead me onward.

One more corridor crossing, and she drew up at an arched doorway midway down a smaller hall. I quickly counted the doors on either side —two on the left, three on the right—so that I would know which was mine in the future. Of course, finding this particular hallway again was going to be a challenge.

"Your sister is here," the warrior said, pointing to the door on the right. "And this is your room."

She opened the door, then stood aside for me to enter. I took one step into the dark, then turned back to look at her.

"Um. Is there a candle I might light?"

She blew a quick breath from her nose, then called a word into the room. Instantly, three bowls of blue flame sprang to life. Wonderful— the lights were controlled by magic, which I did not possess. I supposed I'd have to ask Neeve to turn them on and off for me. Another reminder that she belonged in this world and that I, most emphatically, did not.

"There is a water alcove there," the Dark Elf said, nodding to the right side of the room. "And a sleeping alcove straight ahead. I will inform your sister you've arrived."

With that, she shut the door, leaving me alone to inspect my new surroundings.

The water alcove turned out to be a room for bathing and taking care of other such needs. A small basin carved of the same white stone as the wall had a small, fountainlike stream of water emerging above it and cascading down, to drain away. There was a much larger, empty basin set on the floor.

I'd probably need magic to take a bath, too, I thought sourly. The Nightshade Court was turning out to be equal parts wonder and frustration.

And somewhere in its depths, a fearsome Dark Elf lord waited...
But surely Neeve would make the right choice, and soon enough we'd
all be back in Raine. I tried to force myself to believe the cheerful lie.

I splashed some of the running water over my face and arms, then
washed as best I could using a sweet-scented bowl of what seemed to
be liquid soap. I dried off using an absurdly fluffy white towel that was
warm to the touch, and seemed to dry again the moment I hung it
back on its hook. As I left the area, I glimpsed my reflection in a gilt
mirror mounted across from the basin.

I paused at the sight. No wonder Kian had laughed at me! I looked
like I'd been rolling through the forest instead of simply traveling
through it. In addition to my poor, abused gown, my hair looked like it
had captured half the cedar needles it had met, along with a wayward
strand of cress and some bits of lichen. Grimacing, I pulled out the
worst of it, then went to explore the rest of the room.

The sleeping alcove was, despite its name, more of a room than a
cupboard. The opening between it and the main room could be closed
off with a heavy azure curtain embroidered with stars, and the wide
bed had room enough to walk on either side. The head was pushed up
against the far wall, where two narrow, arched windows let in dim light.

I skirted the small nightstand beside the bed, noting an empty
crystal bowl that could only be lit by Dark Elf power, and knelt on the
pillows, trying to see what was outside.

More gardens, I thought, squinting at the dark shapes of what
might be hedges. Or flower bushes. A short distance beyond, the white
wall rose, pale under the starlight. And that was all, except the sweep
of sky overhead, filled with inscrutable stars.

I sighed and went back to the main room, which held a small couch
and two comfortable chairs, all upholstered in rich blue tapestry. The
couch boasted a scattering of colorful pillows in jewel tones—ruby,
emerald, amethyst—and a cloud-soft blanket the color of mist. The
interior of the Nightshade Court was comfortably warm, and I pulled
off my cloak, laying it over the back of one of the chairs.

Between the couch and chairs sat a low table made of light wood. A
massive, empty armoire and a row of shelves with nothing upon them
took up the far wall.

I pulled open my small bag, which I'd deposited on the table when I entered, and sorted through the few belongings I'd brought from the mortal world.

My crown, seeming no worse for being stuffed in a sack and hauled through the Erynvorn. My water flask—which had saved me. The linen napkin, a little stained, that had been wrapped around the dried fruit and hunk of bread. My comb, carved of a hard, dark wood that grew in the far south, beyond Parnesia.

Finally, I pulled out my change of underthings and stockings, and the simple brown dress I'd worn to harvest *nirwen* in. I shook it, then held it out for inspection. The skirts were dirty at the hem, and the bodice had a splotch where I'd dropped an overripe berry during our harvest lunch and hadn't noticed until it was smushed into the fabric.

Overall, though, it was in much better condition than my battered gold velvet. I could wash the hem and scrub the berry stain out. Not to mention comb the cedar needles and bits of bark from my hair.

Dress over one arm, comb in hand, I headed back to the water alcove.

It took some time to get the dress presentable, and a dismaying amount of dirty water flowed away before I was satisfied. I laid the damp garment over the large basin so the hem could drip inside, then went to work on my hair.

A bath would have been lovely, but once I got clean I didn't want to don my gold gown again, and it would take some time for the other dress to dry. At least I was able to tame my hair, twisting it back into a bun to keep it out of my face.

I headed back to the couch, eyeing my cloak. It, too, could use some attention, though being made of a dark blue fabric, it didn't show the dirt quite as badly.

A knock came at my door, and I heard Neeve say my name.

I hurried over, emotions mixing in my chest. I'd be glad to see her, but angry, too. This entire situation, after all, was her fault.

"Are you there?" Neeve called.

I lifted the silver latch and pulled the arched wooden door open.

"Where else would I be?" I asked sharply. Apparently, anger was winning.

My mood wasn't soothed by the sight of my stepsister looking every inch the Dark Elf lady. She was wrapped in a dress the color of leaves after a spring rain, and rubies sparkled in her intricately braided hair. The pendant Thorne had given her shone upon her chest. I belatedly recalled I'd tucked mine under my dress when we started through the Erynvorn, to keep it safe.

It would seem childish to yank it out that very moment, though I had to battle the urge to do so. Still, I lifted my hand and fingered the chain where it hung about my neck, reassured that at least I had a bit of Dark Elf finery of my own.

Neeve stared at me silently, taking in my ruined gown with a quick flick of her eyes. Her mouth tightened, and for a bare moment she looked remorseful.

"I see your journey through the Erynvorn wasn't a simple one," she said.

"No thanks to you," I replied hotly. "What were you *thinking*, running through the gate and dragging Kian with you? I can't believe you'd do this to all of us."

Scarlet spots bloomed on her cheeks, and she lifted her chin, her remorse gone. "I'm not going to stand out here in the hallway and explain myself. Either invite me in, or I'll go."

Although I was tempted to slam the door in her face, I stepped back with exaggerated politeness and waved her into my room. I did shut the door with a bit more force than was necessary, however.

"Well?" I folded my arms and faced my stepsister, who had gracefully seated herself on the couch.

"I could not lose my chance to come to Elfhame," she said, as though I shouldn't be angry with her for it. "And I brought Kian so the gate wouldn't permanently close."

"That's not an excuse! What does he think about the fact that you used him for your own purposes? Did you even tell him in advance what was going to happen?"

"Of course I did," she said, though her gaze slid away from mine. "And he thinks it a fine adventure."

"What Kian thinks and what the reality of the situation is are two completely different—" I broke off as a knock came at the door.

I was sorely tempted to ignore whoever was out there. Neeve and I had far more we needed to say to one another—though I had the feeling I'd be doing most of the talking.

"I can hear you in there," Kian called, his voice muffled by the thick wood. "I brought food."

That decided it. And he deserved to be a part of the conversation. All three of us were equally affected by Neeve's rash decision, though in different ways.

Kian grinned at me as I let him in, lifting the tray of food he carried. My eyes widened at the assortment of plates and bowls, some stacked three layers high.

"I wasn't sure what you'd like—some of the things they eat here are very odd," he said. "So I brought a selection. Whatever you don't eat, I will. Hello, Neeve. I'm not surprised you're here."

He set the tray down on the low table, then took a seat on the couch beside my stepsister.

"We have a great deal to discuss," I said, not liking the fact that Kian seemed closely allied with my stepsister.

I hoped that would change, once he fully understood the gravity of her actions.

"Certainly, we'll talk," he said, lifting a round pastry of some kind and holding it out to me. "But try a honey cake first. Maybe it will sweeten your mood before you scold us."

"You deserve more than just a scolding." Anger coiled tightly in my belly again. "Or at least Neeve does. Do you even know where you are?"

Since I was holding the cake, I took a bite and tried not to sigh at how delicious it tasted. Although Kian had called it a honey cake, it was only a little sweet, flavorful with roasted grain and a piquant spice that reminded me of cinnamon.

"In Elfhame, the land of the Dark Elves." He shook his head in wonder. "I never would have thought such a magical realm existed outside of legends and fables."

"You weren't supposed to know about it." I glared at Neeve. "Raine's secrets aren't a trifling matter."

Unruffled, she looked calmly back. "Kian and I have reached an understanding. As prospective king and co-regent of Raine, he's entitled to know everything. I merely told him about Elfhame a bit earlier than my father would have desired—but Kian would've learned the truth of our kingdom soon enough."

I blinked, swallowing the last of the honey cake along with the information that Neeve had, apparently, agreed to marry Kian.

"And what did the Nightshade Lord think when you darted through the doorway on his heels?" I asked. "I'm surprised he didn't throw you back out immediately."

Neeve's lips curved in a secretive smile. "When I explained things to my uncle at the feast, he agreed that Kian and I could visit the Nightshade Court."

I narrowed my eyes. "I'd wager he meant the next harvest, though. Not this one."

"Once we passed through the gateway, it didn't much matter," she said, lifting one shoulder in a delicate shrug. "Try the melon—it's quite refreshing."

I didn't want to do anything that my traitorous stepsister suggested, but Kian nodded and handed me a slice of the pearly green fruit. Unfortunately, it was every bit as refreshing as Neeve had said.

"So, you see," Kian said. "We might have acted a bit hastily, but there's no harm done."

"No harm done?" I nearly choked on my bite of melon. "I nearly died in the forest, and Thorne recklessly depleted his powers. For that matter, I must go see how he's faring. The two of you can leave now."

I stood, scolding myself for not seeking out Thorne immediately. Instead, I'd gawked at my room and wasted time arguing with Neeve and Kian. Of course, I had no idea how to find the *Galadhir*, but I could screw up my nerve enough to ask any Dark Elf I might see.

"Sit down," Neeve said. "Before I knocked on your door, I was checking on Thorne."

I didn't sit. "Then you can take me there."

She gave me a look tinged with exasperation. "He is fast asleep, Rose—in a deep, healing rest that you'd be unwise to rouse him from. If you even could."

I curled my fingers into fists. "I want to see him."

"You will, once he recovers. And once you have something adequate to wear."

"I've another gown, drying," I said defensively.

"Surely you've seen how the Dark Elves dress," Kian said. "We're odd enough here without you going about looking like a scullery maid."

I flashed a look at him, cheeks warming. "Is it so important to you, what the Dark Elves think?"

"I believe you were schooled in diplomacy, Rose. Don't you recall it's courteous to adopt the customs of a foreign people when you're in their land?" Despite his words, he looked a little sheepish, and picked up a honey cake to cover the fact.

"I've plenty of clothing you may borrow," Neeve said. "My uncle has spared no expense when it comes to my wardrobe. Of course, he'll provide you with anything you ask for."

She gave me a significant look and I knew what she was implying. Nor had I forgotten the Nightshade Lord's interest in me. Deflated, I sank back down into my chair.

"We can't stay long enough for me to dress up and play Dark Elf lady." I frowned at my stepsister. "It's essential we go back to the human world immediately."

"We can't," Neeve said flatly. "The only one with enough power to open the gate between worlds when it's not harvest time is the *Galadhir*. And he can only do that once his wellspring has regenerated."

I stared at her, mouth going dry. "But can't the Nightshade Lord... I mean, what use is it to have a doorway between worlds if no one can open it?"

Neeve shook her head, the gems woven through her hair winking scarlet. "It would be far worse if the gateway were easy to open. What if every curious woodcutter who stumbled into the center of the Darkwood ended up in Elfhame, or every disobedient Dark Elf child who ran away into the Erynvorn then crossed over to the mortal realm?"

"Then there wouldn't be nearly so many secrets," I shot back.

"It's best if kingdoms hold such things close," Kian said, waving his honey cake at me. "I don't blame Neeve for not revealing state secrets."

He'd watched our interchange with a faintly amused look on his face, but now I turned on him.

"This is serious, Kian. The longer we stay here, the more trouble brews in Raine."

"Then we can go back after a week or two." He smiled at me. "I don't know why you're so worried—unless you think the Nightshade Lord will pay you too much attention. But you won't be of age for nearly another year, and I understand the Dark Elves are quite strict about such things."

My heart squeezed with dismay, his words confirming my growing suspicion that Neeve had neglected to mention a crucial consequence of spending time in Elfhame.

I turned to my stepsister accusingly. "You didn't tell him."

"I knew you would," she replied.

"You didn't even know I was coming!"

She raised one brow. "Didn't I? There was a very strong chance you'd convince Thorne to bring you through the gate. I'm not at all surprised you succeeded."

I scowled at her, thinking of our endless games of chess and how often she'd beaten both me and Kian. "We're not some pawns that you can shove about at will."

"Tell me *what*?" Kian leaned forward, looking from Neeve to me. "Why do I get the feeling there's something more serious going on?"

"Because there is." I turned to him. "What my stepsister neglected to mention was that time moves differently here in the land of the Dark Elves."

He gave me a questioning look. "How can such a thing be? Are you certain?"

"Thorne told us so—it's part of why he let me come with him. Because a week here, as you put it, equates to months in the human world. You can't be gone that long, much less kidnapped into a secret realm that Raine hasn't told their closest allies about."

Finally, Kian grew serious. He leaned back, arms folded, and I let him work out the implications for himself. Especially after ribbing me on matters of diplomacy, he was clever enough to see what his unexpected, prolonged absence would mean.

"What will the king tell Jarl Eiric?" he asked.

"The truth," Neeve said. "He would have learned it soon enough."

Kian's mouth firmed into a grim line. "He won't believe it. If you hadn't noticed, my advisor is a suspicious man. He'll think you took me into the Darkwood and had me murdered for some nefarious purpose —especially if, as you say, a few weeks have already gone by in the handful of days we've been here and Lord Raine can't produce evidence of my continued good health."

"But Neeve and I are gone as well," I said. "Won't he have to consider that the king might be telling the truth?"

"Maybe. Or perhaps he'll conclude that some terrible accident befell the three of us in the forest, and everyone is covering it up."

"A suspicious fellow indeed," Neeve murmured. "Still, he is one man, alone at Castle Raine. What can he do but bide?"

"Oh, he won't stay in Raine," Kian said, his voice hard. "He'll wait a month, maybe a bit longer, then head back to Fiorland. There, he'll alert my father to my unexplained disappearance and prevent my brother from coming to Castle Raine. And then, well—hopefully we'll have returned at that point."

That point most likely being hostilities between the two kingdoms. I shivered at the thought.

"Rose is right." Kian turned to Neeve. "We have to go back to the human world as soon as possible."

A sorrowful light in her eyes, Neeve nodded. "And yet we can do nothing until the *Galadhir* is recovered."

"Can't your uncle do anything?" It seemed to me that a Dark Elf lord ought to have enough power to force the gate open, though clearly I knew little of how such things worked in Elfhame.

"We can ask him," she said.

I shook my head violently, sending a wayward red curl swinging across my cheek. "I'll keep my distance, thank you."

During the course of our conversation, I'd realized that the longer we stayed with the Dark Elves, the more quickly my birthday approached. If we tarried too long, I'd be old enough to marry the

Nightshade Lord, and I most definitely did *not* want to remind him, or anyone, of that fact.

Neeve frowned at me. "Don't be childish. The three of us must plead our case together. But it's getting late, and most of the court is abed already. We can make further plans on the morrow."

"And get Rose presentable," Kian said, only half in jest.

I made a face at him, but that reminded me that I needed my step-sister's help.

"Neeve, how do you summon the lights?" I asked. "And the bath, for that matter?"

I didn't want to slip between the sheets in my currently grubby condition, and splashing water on myself from the sink would only do so much.

"You need a talisman," Kian said, pulling a softly glowing object from his pocket and holding it out in his cupped palm.

I leaned over to inspect it. It was a faceted white crystal, longer than it was wide, and pointed at one end. I sent Neeve a questioning glance.

"It's a small repository of power," she said. "The Dark Elves use it for young children who haven't yet mastered their wellsprings. With it, you'll be able to call and dismiss the foxfire."

She spoke a word and waved her hand, and the room was plunged into darkness—except for the softly glowing crystal in Kian's hand and the faint light filtering through the arched windows in the sleeping alcove.

Kian smiled, a quick flash of teeth, and held his talisman up.

"*Calya,*" he said.

The blue flames sprang again from their crystal bowls. Wide-eyed, I glanced from them to the prince.

Magic.

Granted, it was bestowed by an object, but still. It was what I'd yearned for all my life. If the circumstances weren't so dire, I would have let myself fall in love with Elfhame on the spot.

"That's amazing," I said. "Where can I get one?"

"From the magic tutor," Neeve said. "Meanwhile, I'll help you. Do you want your bath now?"

I nodded, and she rose and went to the water alcove. A moment later, I heard the splash of water falling into the large basin.

Kian stood too and pulled me out of my chair to give me a sideways embrace. "Finish your dinner, and sleep well, Rose. We'll untangle all of this soon. Don't worry."

I did worry, though. Our situation grew more precarious with every passing hour.

CHAPTER 22

Despite the fears coiling about me, I slept heavily. Enough food in my belly, a warm bath, and the general exhaustion caused by fleeing through the Erynvorn combined to pull me into a vast and shimmering sea of slumber.

I woke once, confused, to see golden moonlight falling across my bedcovers. A quick glance out the window showed a large full moon in the sky, in addition to the smaller crescent that had accompanied my journey through the forest.

With a sigh, I fell back asleep.

Insistent knocking on my door roused me. Groggily, I pushed the covers back and sat up.

"Rose?" Kian's voice. "Are you still alive in there?"

"I'm coming," I called, getting to my feet. At least there was enough moonlight filtering through the windows that I wouldn't stumble blindly into the walls.

I glanced down at the sleeping dress Neeve had fetched for me after my bath. It was a gossamer thing, very comfortable, but embarrassed heat prickled through me at the thought of Kian seeing me in such attire. As I crossed the darkened main room, I grabbed the soft blanket draped over the couch and wrapped it around myself. It wasn't as long as my cloak, but it would do.

I opened the door, blinking, to see both Kian and Neeve standing there, once again garbed in Dark Elf finery. Today my stepsister wore scarlet, which brought out the pallor of her face and the redness of her lips, and an assortment of dark purple gems around her throat and wrists that glittered dangerously. Kian wore a gold-embroidered tunic of deep blue over dark leggings and, as usual, his sword strapped at his side.

Impatient light sparked in my stepsister's eyes, but Kian offered me his usual easy smile.

"More food." He hefted the tray he carried. "This is getting to be a habit."

"One I don't mind." I stepped back so they could enter.

Neeve spoke the word that conjured light, then continued into the room, going to settle on the couch.

"We'll take our evening meal in the dining hall, though," she said. "You can't hide in your room forever, Rose."

I folded my arms. "Can't I try?"

"No. Now, eat something, and we'll get you properly attired to pay our respects to the Nightshade Lord."

Wonderful.

Despite my apprehension, I was able to eat heartily of the delicious, if unfamiliar, Dark Elf food. In addition to the honey cakes, melon, and pale, creamy cheese I'd had the night before, Kian's tray held savory pastries with spicy filling, and some kind of fried tuber. He'd also brought a glazed pitcher full of the sparkling water the Dark Elves preferred.

Neeve nibbled at a few of the round red fruits I'd tried earlier, and Kian was happy to consume whatever I didn't finish. When we were done eating, he scooped up the tray.

"I'll leave you two to get ready," he said. "I'll come back in, hmm, three turns?"

"Turns?" I stared at him.

He held up a tiny crystal sphere fastened to his belt by a silver cord. I leaned forward, seeing that it was divided in two: one chamber empty, the other filled with something that looked like shiny black sand.

"It's like an hourglass," he said, flipping it so that the sand began to trickle from the full side into the empty.

"But doesn't it get jostled when you move about?" I asked.

"No," Neeve said, taking out her own little sphere and starting it as well.

Of course not. Magic would see to that.

"How do the elves keep track of the hours?" I asked. "I mean, they must partition their days out somehow."

Kian shrugged at me. "They think of time more fluidly here, it seems. There are the moons, which go at different rates across the sky, and turns, which are always the same measure, though obviously not standardized to an external mark."

"And here at court, there are chimes to mark certain events," my stepsister said. "Receiving hours in the throne room, mealtimes, and the like."

"Oh." I nodded.

I'd heard them twice, soft peals that sounded more like a struck wineglass than bells ringing. At the time they'd just seemed a magical part of the Nightshade Court. Of course the walls would occasionally give off random chiming sounds.

"Have fun." Kian waggled his eyebrows at me, then slipped out the door.

"I've picked out some clothing for you," Neeve said, once he was gone. "Help me bring it all over from my room. Oh, and I brought you this."

She held out one of the glowing crystal talismans like Kian had.

I took it from her hand, the surface cool beneath my fingers. "How do I use it?"

"To dismiss the lights, say *gwath*. And to summon them again, the word is *calya*."

Gwath and *calya*. I tested the shape of the sounds in my mouth. "Can I try it?"

She nodded, and I held up the crystal.

"*Gwath*," I said. The blue flames in their bowls flickered, but didn't go out.

Was I so very unmagical, then, that I couldn't even make use of the simplest magic? The thought pulled my shoulders down.

Neeve shook her head. "Don't draw the syllable out so. Try again— like a command. As though you *mean* to extinguish the light."

At least there was no trace of pity in her eyes. Perhaps she knew I couldn't have borne her sympathy at my failure. I pulled in a breath and said the word once more, shortening and sharpening it, *meaning* it.

This time, the balls of blue fire snuffed out immediately.

"I did it!" I grinned exultantly at Neeve, now a shadowed shape on the couch. "I performed magic!" Even if it was a small thing any Dark Elf child could master.

"Well done."

I thought I heard the trace of a smile in her voice, but it was impossible to see her expression in the dimness. Very well. What was the word for light again? *Calya.* Heeding my earlier failure, I focused on my desire for light, then spoke the word.

As if I had the power of an elf, the balls of blue radiance popped into existence again—one on the table, one on the top of the shelves, one mounted on the wall near the door. And even, to my surprise, smaller flames on the nightstand and in the water alcove.

"Good." Neeve nodded at me. "Though you might want to put out the smaller ones, to conserve the talisman."

I glanced at the glowing crystal. "How long does it last?"

"I don't know—though I think the power can be refilled if necessary."

"Like a wellspring?" I frowned as a thought occurred to me. "If the Dark Elves can put magic into objects like this, why don't they store power to help with larger spells, or to replenish their wellsprings?"

"I asked the same thing when Kian was given his talisman," she said. "Apparently only a small amount of power can be housed in a crystal."

"Yes, but have they *tried*—"

"You can ask the tutor later." Neeve held up her hand. "But for now, we need to go fetch your clothing. Although maybe you should put on your dress before stepping into the hall."

She was right. I slipped into the water alcove to don my brown dress, which was only slightly damp. Compared with her silken finery, I looked like a drab sparrow—but that would change soon, I reminded myself.

I extinguished the lights, then followed her out the door, down the short stretch of corridor, and into her room. Stepping through the arched opening, I saw that her space was a mirror image of mine. But unlike my austere shelves and empty armoire, Neeve's room was lushly decorated.

Shimmering tapestries adorned the walls, depicting moonlit gardens filled with strange flowers. Her shelves held trays filled with a sparkling array of jewelry, and the open armoire doors revealed dozens of colorful silken gowns hung inside.

More clothing was piled on one of the chairs, including belts and scarves and delicately woven shawls. I peeked into the sleeping alcove and saw a lush, ivy-like plant draped along one wall, with yet another tapestry across from it. The sills of her arched windows held an assortment of crystals and polished stones, and her water alcove was likewise festooned with plants and trinkets.

Clearly, as the niece of the Nightshade Lord, Neeve warranted a certain level of consideration that I, as a mere mortal, did not.

"Don't worry," Neeve said, catching sight of my expression. "Once my uncle makes his favor toward you known, you'll start receiving dozens of small gifts."

"I don't want the gifts. Or the favor." Especially not that.

She gave me a keen-eyed look. "Now that you're here, you can't escape it."

"Is this what you wanted?" I turned on her, suddenly furious. "To trap me in Elfhame so that you'd be free to stay here, no matter what happened?"

Blinking, she took a step back. "No."

"Then what?"

Color washed her pale cheeks, and she looked away. "I wanted to see Elfhame, and bringing Kian with me was the only way. But I thought that you and Thorne would be on our heels, and that my uncle would banish us all back to the mortal world after only a day or two."

"It didn't turn out that way, though, did it?" I folded my arms and glared at her. "I do wish you'd stop pushing me toward the Nightshade Lord."

"Honestly, Rose, I'm working on your behalf." She met my gaze. "When you and Thorne arrived at the gates, my uncle wanted you brought before him immediately. I begged him to wait."

"And what?" I made an impatient gesture. "You've earned me a day, nothing more."

"A day closer to Thorne's recovery," she retorted. "As soon as he's restored, we can go back through the gateway."

"So this was just a little jaunt? A selfish sightseeing tour?"

She had the grace to look abashed.

"A little," she admitted. "But it was the only chance I'd ever have to see this world."

"That's not true. You could have brought Kian over as soon as you were wed. *Without* spilling Raine's secrets prematurely."

Again, her gaze slid evasively from mine. "I thought you might want to see Elfhame too."

"If the king forces me to wed the Nightshade Lord, I'll see more than enough of it." In fact, I'd probably never be able to leave again.

"He won't." Neeve sounded sincere. "Without your consent, such a binding could never take place. My father is simply shifting all the pieces about to see what emerges."

Much like Neeve was doing, I thought sourly.

"So you wagered I'd come as your unwilling guest, gawk about, and then what? Go back to Raine and meekly wed Kian's brother?"

"I don't know," she said, in a rare admission. "I can't read the future. Perhaps the Oracles will answer your questions."

"Are they here?" I glanced about her room, though of course they weren't ensconced on Neeve's couch or any such thing.

"No. I understand Thorne sent for them."

"He's better?" I half turned toward the door. "I want to see him."

My stepsister shook her head. "As I understand, he summoned them before he collapsed."

"Collapsed?" I stared at her, my heart squeezing with worry. "If you won't take me, I'll find my own way."

"If you'll stop wasting time in argument, we can get you dressed. Make haste, and we'll be able to stop by the healer's enclave on the way to the throne room."

The throne room? I brushed away the shiver that went through me at the thought of meeting the Nightshade Lord before all his glittering court.

"That dress, then." I pointed at random to the pile of garments on the chair.

She gave me look tinged with exasperation. "Rose."

"Honestly—I don't care. Pick something." Despite myself, though, I gave the bright-hued silks a closer look. "The green one." It was the color of summer leaves, deep without veering into darkness.

Neeve plucked it from the pile, and I was surprised to see it wasn't a gown—not the way we thought of such things in the human world. The fabric had openings here and there, presumably for a person's head and arms, but I couldn't make much sense of it.

I skimmed out of my drab brown dress, and Neeve popped the silk over my head.

"Put your arm through here— No, *here*. Higher."

"You don't make a very good lady's maid," I said crossly as my elbows tangled in the fabric.

Finally, I got myself sorted out, though the garment hung loosely and gaped across my chest. I glanced at Neeve in her sublime scarlet.

"Why does yours fit and mine doesn't?" I asked. We weren't shaped that differently, after all.

"Patience."

She took up a scarf that seemed woven of cobwebs, it was so delicate, and wrapped it about my waist, letting it drape on one side. Then she pulled and folded, somehow forming the dress to my body.

"How does it stay fastened?" I asked, craning to see how she was tucking in the bodice.

"Lady Sillweth showed me," Neeve said. "It's not difficult."

My brows rose. I was certain that, if I tried to do it, my whole gown would fall off the moment I attempted to curtsey to the Night-shade Lord.

"As long as it holds," I said. "Are we done?"

Normally I would have enjoyed the soft fabric against my skin, the comfort of movement the strange garment afforded me. But more than anything, my thoughts were fixed on Thorne.

"Jewelry," Neeve said, moving to her shelves.

"I have this." I held up the gold and sapphire pendant Thorne had given me—nearly a twin to her own silver and ruby one.

"For a court appearance, you need more." Neeve returned, her hands full of sapphires and emeralds, which resolved into a choker, a bracelet that wrapped twice about my wrist, and several jeweled hairpins.

"My hair." I lifted one hand to the curly mess. "Can't I wear a hood or something?"

"We'll braid it back," she said, her deft fingers already going to work.

"You know the pins won't stay."

She gave me a sideways look and didn't argue, only finished off the braid and stuck an assortment of twinkling jewels through it.

"Did you bring your crown when you came through the doorway?" she asked when she was finished.

"Yes." I was reluctant to admit it, for that meant appearing as a princess before the Dark Elves. But the Nightshade Lord had already made his interest known at the harvest gathering, so there was little help for it.

"Go put it on, while I braid my hair," Neeve said, though I thought her dark tresses looked perfect. "Then we'll visit Thorne."

I ducked back into my room, polished a smudge off the golden circlet with a corner of the bedcovers, then plopped the crown on my head. In the hallway, Neeve frowned at me and adjusted the crown forward. It felt heavy on my forehead, pressing with the weight of expectation.

"What about Kian?" I asked as I followed her down the hall. "Wasn't he going to meet us?"

"He'll guess where we've gone."

I paid careful attention as we threaded through the polished corri-dors of the Nightshade Court, counting the turnings on my fingers. Fortunately, it wasn't too complicated a path. I felt certain I could find my way there from my room again, and wouldn't have to beg Neeve to be my guide.

Halfway down a wide hall, Neeve turned through an arched door-way. A large space lay beyond, with a fountain splashing in the center. Several beds were ranged against the far wall beneath the usual arched windows of the Nightshade Court.

Two of the beds were occupied, but I had eyes only for Thorne, who lay in the one farthest from the door. His dark hair spilled over his pillow, his skin was nearly as pale as the sheets, and his eyes were closed, shadows smudged like bruises beneath.

"Lady Neeve." A tall woman rose from a table by the door to greet us. Her silver hair was looped in coils about her ears, her gray eyes weary with the weight of years. "This must be your sister, Lady Rose."

I opened my mouth to argue that we weren't full-blooded sisters, but Neeve shot me a warning look, and I subsided.

"Greetings, Mistress Almareth," Neeve said. "How fares the *Galadhir*?"

The Dark Elf woman's serious expression grew even more somber. "He sleeps heavily."

"Is that a bad thing?" I looked over at Thorne's motionless form, then back to the woman I presumed was the healer.

"Sometimes..." She hesitated a moment, as if unsure what to tell these strangers to her world. "If a wellspring is too deeply depleted, the patient becomes lost in the shadowland and never wakes."

Fear sent a dart through my heart, and I traded an anxious look with Neeve. If Thorne never woke, we were trapped here until the next harvest—and the consequences for Raine were dire.

"There is no need for alarm," the healer said, though I heard her unspoken *yet*. "If the *Galadhir* still slumbers after the next moonrise, then we will attempt to wake him by various means."

"Can I go near him?" I asked.

"Certainly." The corners of the healer's eyes crinkled, though she didn't smile openly. "His weariness is not some illness you can contract.

In fact, you should talk to him. Sometimes hearing familiar voices helps sleepers emerge."

"Go say hello," Neeve said to me, showing a surprising amount of tact in realizing I might want a private moment with Thorne. "I have a few questions for Mistress Almareth."

I nodded and quickly went to Thorne's bedside, my emotions twisting with anguish to see him lying so silent and still.

"I'm here," I said softly, resting my hand on his shoulder. Even through the blanket I could feel the lean strength of him. "I didn't get lost in the forest or eaten by wolves. We're all here, at Nightshade, and safe. But Thorne—"

My voice broke, and I had to take a quick breath to master myself. I glanced at Neeve, deep in conversation with the Dark Elf healer, then looked back at the man who had stolen my heart.

"Come back to us," I whispered. "I love you."

He didn't stir, except for his slow, even breaths. His eyelashes were soot-black, the line of his mouth soft in sleep. He looked exhausted and vulnerable, reminding me that he was only a handful of years older than I. When he pulled the mantle of *Galadhir* about himself, it set a distance between us that, in sleep, disappeared.

"There you are," Kian said from the doorway. "Aren't we supposed to be attending the Nightshade Lord?"

I let out a sigh and moved away from Thorne's bedside.

"How is he?" Kian asked as I rejoined Neeve beside the fountain.

I shook my head, and Neeve said, "Slowly improving." Which might or might not have been true.

"Come on, then." Kian set one hand to his sword, then looked me up and down. "You're pretty enough for the court now, I'd say."

Not *too* pretty, I hoped. Though with my darker skin and wild curls, I knew I was different enough from the Dark Elves to cause comment no matter how nicely I cleaned up.

We bade farewell to the healer, and then Kian and Neeve whisked me down more hallways. They grew wider and more ornate, the wall sconces carved like flowers, the motifs of trailing vines scrolling overhead, until we came to a place where several corridors converged in a high-ceilinged anteroom.

The far wall had double doors folded back from a tall archway, and through it I glimpsed a large room alive with the bright silks and winking jewels adorning the members of the Nightshade Court.

At the far end of the room stood a raised circular dais, and upon it a throne carved of dark purple stone, the exact shade of nightshade blossoms. The Nightshade Lord sat upon that throne, chin in one hand, a slightly bored expression on his severe features. Then he caught sight of us as we stepped into the room, and his gaze sharpened.

He smiled, then, with an edge that made me shiver.

CHAPTER 23

I followed Neeve, with Kian at our heels, through the glittering throng of the Nightshade Court. The courtiers whispered, but I couldn't catch their words. I could guess at them, though—how strange the mortal girl looked, and how dismaying that their ruler was considering making a match with her.

That wouldn't happen, though—not if I had any say in the matter.

The crowd parted, opening a path to the dais across the subtly patterned stone floor. I thought we were treading over more vines, a silver inlay twining across the white marble, but I had little attention for the flooring. My focus was on the Dark Elf lord watching us approach. His pointed crown glinted atop his head, though he was dressed in dark silks that seemed no more opulent than the garments of his courtiers.

When she reached the throne, Neeve made him a graceful curtsey.

"Greetings, Niece," the Nightshade Lord said. "Will you do me the favor of making the formal introduction to our newest visitor here before the Nightshade Court?"

"Certainly, my lord," Neeve said calmly.

I felt as though my throat was full of butterflies as my stepsister drew me forward to stand beside her.

"Lord Mornithalarion Shadrift, ruler of the Nightshade Court," she said, "I am pleased to present to you Princess Rosaline Valrois, daughter of the current Queen of Raine, cousin to the rulers of Parnese, and my sister."

Surprised, I glanced at her. Here, in front of the whole court, she was claiming me as her kin by blood, not just a relative by marriage. I was also slightly amazed that she knew my full name. She'd never seemed to pay that much attention—but then again, she was the daughter of royalty. And I knew better than most the secrets that she kept shuttered behind those dark eyes.

I dropped into a low curtsey, concentrating on keeping my balance. Despite the food and night's rest, I still felt a trifle unsteady.

"Welcome, Princess Rosaline," the Nightshade Lord said as I stood. "I hope you find our court pleasant, and your room comfortable."

"I do, my lord," I said. "Thank you for your hospitality."

And for not throwing out the wayward humans who kept appearing on his doorstep, though I supposed he really had little choice in the matter. We were Neeve's companions, after all.

"It is my hope that you will feel at home here," the ruler said, one eyebrow tilting up, so that no one could mistake his meaning.

I firmed my mouth and made no reply. Though my room was nice enough, I had no intention of remaining at the Nightshade Court any longer than was necessary—and certainly not of calling it home.

"I would like to become better acquainted with you and your mortal friends," the Dark Elf said, turning his attention back to Neeve. "Attend me at the fourth chime for a private dinner in my rooms." His dark gaze swept over me, then went to Kian. "All three of you."

"It would be our pleasure," Neeve said, then sent me a look.

"Certainly, my lord," I managed, and Kian made the Nightshade Lord a courtly bow.

The ruler nodded, then waved his hand in dismissal. Following Neeve's example, I curtseyed again and took two steps back from the throne. Already the courtiers were parting around us like water around a stone, eager for the Nightshade Lord's attention. We were gently pushed back toward the doorway as they surged forward, and I didn't mind it one bit.

"Well." Kian gave me an encouraging smile. "That wasn't so bad, was it?"

Neeve sent him a look tinged with exasperation. "Our audience with Nightshade is hardly over, if you hadn't noticed."

Unrepentant, he grinned at her. "But we've cleared the first fence. Dinner will be easier, without all these court trappings."

I couldn't agree with him. The formality of the throne room was preferable to a more intimate setting, in my opinion, but this wasn't the time or place to argue about it.

Now that the interview was over, I was able to take in a bit more of my surroundings, and noticed the musicians tucked against the far wall. They played so softly that the music blended into the ambiance, barely discernable, like the faint gold glow emanating from the walls and the ever-present blue fires dancing in their crystal bowls.

Now that I was aware of it, however, I could appreciate the delicate thread of melody. I recognized the musicians, too—the tall Dark Elf lady and the flute-playing youth who'd joined Master Fawkes at the harvest feast.

At least not everything at the Nightshade Court was bewildering and strange.

Only most of it.

"What next?" I asked Neeve in a low voice. "Are we obliged to stay here?"

She turned to me with a slight frown. "Only if you want to."

"What Neeve means is that she would like to mingle with the Dark Elf courtiers," Kian said. "But I'm ready to go, if you are."

I nodded quickly, then glanced at the dais. "As long as the Nightshade Lord doesn't mind."

"Since he'll have us in his clutches later, I don't imagine he will," Kian said dryly.

"He means you no ill," Neeve said.

"That's easy for you to say," I retorted. "You're not the one in danger of being married off to him."

"Don't worry." Kian held up his fist. "I'll defend you with my life, if it comes to that."

I couldn't tell if he was playing the dramatic princeling or not. I hoped not.

"We just need Thorne to wake up," I said. "I'm sure he'll be able to help us sort everything out."

"Perhaps," Neeve said coolly. "And perhaps not."

KIAN and I ended up slipping out to the gardens—though it wasn't as if we were sneaking about the Nightshade Court. Guards watched us constantly, and I noticed that an armed Dark Elf was never far away, no matter if we were traversing the halls or strolling between the moonlit hedges.

"What do you think of it?" Kian asked, waving his hand at the softly illuminated garden, though I knew he meant Elfhame in general.

"It's a beautiful land," I said. "And the court is lovely. But I miss the sun."

"As do I." He grinned at me, his smile a flash of white in the starlight. "We'll be back in our own world soon, though, so I've decided to enjoy as much of this as I can."

"Will we, though?" I gave him a worried look. "What if Thorne doesn't recover? What if the Nightshade Lord decides that I..." I swallowed, unable to finish the sentence.

Kian halted beside a bush covered with pale, trumpet-shaped flowers that gave off an intoxicating scent.

"I meant it before." One hand went to his sword. "I'll defend you to the death before you have to marry some Dark Elf. Even if he's the ruler of a court."

"Shh." I glanced about. Talking about killing the Nightshade Lord didn't strike me as the safest of topics, even if there was no one directly in earshot. "Surely it won't come to that."

Please—let it not come to that.

"Still. You have better options, Rose."

Stung, I stared at him. "My entire life isn't about who I'm going to marry. Maybe it will be no one." And so there.

"Maybe." He shrugged, then gave me a lopsided grin. "My brother's very nice, though. Almost as handsome and wonderful as I am."

He ducked the swat I aimed at his head and danced a few paces back.

"Then maybe Neeve should marry *him* instead," I said with a touch of spite.

"No." He grew serious again. "We have an understanding."

"About that." I folded my arms. "What did you do, hold her at sword's point until she agreed to marry you?"

"Of course not." He gave me an affronted look. "She asked me if I were serious in my intentions toward her. I told her I was, and then she gave me one of those haughty looks, held out her hand, and said that if that were the case, I might as well ask so that she could say yes."

I could envision it all too clearly.

"So, you did," I said. "You asked Neeve to marry you."

"Or she asked me...but that was the plan all along, wasn't it? We all know why I was fostered at Castle Raine."

I gave him a long look. The silence stretched out between us for three heartbeats, and then he looked away.

"You know I'm very fond of you, Rose," he said softly.

"I know." I fought to keep my voice light. He was fond of me—but he was going to marry Neeve. As he was meant to.

It was only that, for a brief time, I'd felt that Kian and I were fated —that I belonged somewhere, at last, and that place was at his side. But we'd already left that path behind, I reminded myself. Indeed, we were far better off as friends.

"Do you even love Neeve?" I asked.

To his credit, he didn't jump in with empty assurances. Instead, he frowned slightly, his gaze focusing inward.

"I think I do, though it's not the heart-wrenching emotion the poets describe—at least not for me."

"Then what is it?" I peered closely at him.

"Attraction, though she's hardly let me kiss her." He gave a rueful laugh and shook his head. "Intense admiration, certainly. The sense that we'll make a formidable team. I respect her a great deal—and I think that is a good foundation to go on."

Despite myself, I nodded. "Does she feel the same? After all, she dragged you into Elfhame for her own reasons."

"But she told me clearly what they were beforehand," he said. "Once I knew, I agreed to come anyway. I've always wanted to see a magical world, after all. Haven't you?"

"Well, yes." I sighed and looked up at the small moon gliding serenely across the purple-hued sky.

A pale moth rose from the nearby flowering bush, spots on its wings like dark eyes. It fluttered a moment, then drifted quietly away until I lost sight of it among the hedges.

I closed my eyes a moment, shutting out the lush, shadowy gardens filled with glowing blossoms and heady fragrance. It was enchanted and wondrous, and I missed Castle Raine with a sudden, unexpected wrench.

"I'm sorry," Kian said softly.

"Don't be." I opened my eyes. "I think you and Neeve will do very well together. When is the wedding to be?"

"Next summer, after she's eighteen. Plenty of time before then— nearly two years."

"If Thorne doesn't wake up soon, it might be summer again before we manage to escape Elfhame," I reminded him.

"So you've said." He gave me a steady look. "Don't worry. Everything will sort itself out."

I folded my arms and drew in a deep breath of the dark, perfumed air, wishing I shared his optimism. Hoping that Thorne would wake soon and take us all home.

CHAPTER 24

Although I thought I looked quite presentable, Neeve insisted I pick another dress for our dinner with the Nightshade Lord. I stood, somewhat sullenly, before the pile of colorful silks still laid over her chair. In our haste to visit Thorne earlier, we hadn't yet transferred the garments to my room.

"Everyone will notice if you wear the same thing," my stepsister said. "Have you forgotten all your court etiquette lessons?"

"Of course not."

I wanted to argue that I didn't care what the court thought—but I bit my tongue on the words. Even if I preferred not to curry favor with the Dark Elves, Kian's previous reminder that we were their guests still rang in my ears. Besides, it was important to Neeve.

"What about that one?" I pointed to a length of sky blue. A sky that only appeared in the mortal world.

Neeve shook her head. "I was thinking this one."

She held up a shimmering garment, the cloth appearing silver in one direction, but purple if held the other way. It was gorgeous, but I frowned at it.

"I don't particularly want to wear Nightshade's colors."

My stepsister lowered her arms and gave me a narrow-eyed look. "Would it really be so horrible to be queen of a Dark Elf court?"

"If I have to marry a terrifying lord to do so, yes! Don't push me into the role you wish for yourself."

She grimaced. "That's a disgusting implication. I'm hardly going to marry my own uncle."

"But you'll foist him on me? And you know I didn't mean it that way." I softened my voice. "I only meant you've been dreaming of being a Dark Elf lady your entire life, and now you're here, at the Nightshade Court. But that's not my dream. I don't want to marry anyone, let alone a dreadful Dark Elf."

Her brows rose slightly, dark slashes against her pale skin. "Are you certain about that?"

My thoughts went to Thorne, lying unconscious, and a blush warmed my cheeks. But he didn't love me. No, his heart belonged to Neeve. I caught my breath at the realization of the devastating news awaiting him when he woke.

"How will you tell Thorne that you and Kian are going to be married?" I asked.

She blinked once. "The *Galadhir* understands duty. He will not like it overmuch, but he will accept it."

"Duty?" I couldn't keep the edge from my voice. "Are you only wedding Kian out of obligation? He deserves more than that."

Her gaze hardened. "You and Kian are too similar, Rose. You'd be desperately unhappy together."

"I don't mean *me*." I slashed my hand through the air. "Yes, I love Kian, but more like a brother now, and I already told you I don't plan on marrying anyone. I meant that a loveless marriage is a grim fate— for both of you."

"It won't be loveless," she said quietly, something flashing through her eyes. "Not all of us give our hearts as recklessly as you do, Rose."

"I'm not reckless," I said, though her words held a grain of truth. "Do you mean—"

"And I'm not pushing you at the Nightshade Lord, whatever you might think." She tossed the silvery purple dress back on the pile.

"Pick whatever garment you wish, but do it quickly. And help me carry all these to your room. Fourth chime rings in less than a turn."

I sighed, knowing I wouldn't be able to pry any more confessions out of her. She'd already revealed too much—or at least I could tell she thought so, by the hard set of her mouth.

"Very well." I picked up the discarded dress, half in apology, half because it was beautiful. "I'm going to need to borrow some more jewelry, too."

"Of course." Her expression softened, and I knew we were back on even footing. At least until our next argument.

❧

I WAS glad that Neeve and I weren't at odds as we were ushered through the door of the Nightshade Lord's private dining chamber. Elfhame was strange enough without adding to the tensions by quarrelling with my stepsister. Despite our spats, though, I knew that, if we had to, we'd staunchly defend one another with word and with weapon.

As would Kian, of course, whom I noted wore his sword everywhere in the Nightshade Court. Including to a private dinner with its ruler. To her credit, Neeve did too. It was just that her blade was more easily concealed in the folds of her skirts.

The dark-haired warrior who'd come to fetch us took up her position beside the arched doorway and motioned us forward.

"Welcome," the Nightshade Lord said, rising from his place at a table set for four. "Thank you for joining me."

As if we had any choice. I hung back, letting Neeve go first.

The room was small and elegant, with a high, arched ceiling that rose to a point above the table. The outer wall bore a large window flanked by two smaller ones. I glimpsed the tip of the moon just setting behind low hills in the dimly lit landscape.

Glimmering tapestries adorned the white walls, their floral designs woven with silver and violet threads that caught the light from multiple foxfire sconces mounted about the room. A softer, golden light emanated from two blossom-shaped torchiers set close to the table.

"Come, sit." The Nightshade Lord pulled out the chair on his right for Neeve, then continued around the table.

"Princess Rosaline, if you will," he said, scooting out the next chair and nodding at me.

"Just Rose, please," I said, hurriedly taking a seat.

It didn't escape my notice that he'd placed me directly across from him. At least I'd have Neeve on one side and Kian on the other. I briefly considered displaying poor table manners—but that would be rude, and would certainly earn me a kick under the table from my step-sister. Besides, the Nightshade Lord was clever enough to see through my transparent schemes.

Still, I wasn't planning on making myself especially charming.

Kian nudged his sword out of the way and took the last seat, to the ruler's left and facing Neeve. A small dish of blue flame at the center of the table illuminated the silver-chased crystal goblets set before us, each one half-full of a darkly purple liquid.

"Elderberry wine," the Nightshade Lord said, nodding to the goblets. "I thought you might like to sample the preferred drink of my court. This is an especially fine vintage, reserved for special occasions."

He didn't glance at me, but I shifted uncomfortably on the cushioned chair.

"I understand it is a mortal custom to drink a toast," he continued, lifting his goblet and then casting an expectant look around the table. "Join me?"

Neeve picked up her wine, and Kian and I were quick to do the same.

"To new alliances," the Nightshade Lord said, this time meeting my eyes.

I hurriedly dropped my gaze, but not before I saw a quicksilver look pass between Neeve and Kian. Perhaps there was hope for them after all.

But there was none for me.

I wetted my lips with the dark liquid, which had a pleasing, flowery aroma and was far less bitter than the few wines I'd sampled back in the human world.

"A fine vintage indeed," Kian said. "Until now, I thought the best wine I'd ever drink in my life was to be found in Parnesia."

"Elfhame has much to recommend it," the Nightshade Lord said, then turned to Neeve. "Tell me, what do you think of our land? Is it everything you'd hoped?"

"Yes," Neeve said softly. "Thank you for allowing us to visit. It's a wondrous place."

"I'm pleased you think so." The ruler gave her a faint smile. "You are always welcome at my court."

I frowned, thinking unhappily of all the complications lurking behind that simple statement. Would the gateway remain open, or would it close forever if Neeve chose to stay in Elfhame? Would Thorne recover? If Neeve agreed to leave, would Kian be willing to cross between the worlds at harvest time and lose three mortal years while he dallied for a handful of months with the Dark Elves?

"Lord Kian, what do you think of my court?" the Dark Elf lord asked.

"Your warriors are impressive," Kian responded. "And seem very well trained. Do you often war among the courts here?"

The lord let out a short laugh. "Spoken like a true warrior. No—we are on guard against our old enemy, the Void, and the strange, twisted things that sometimes emerge from the Erynvorn. And any other threats from beyond our borders."

Those last being humans, I guessed. Which made sense. If the Athraig, for example, ever learned of Elfhame, they would love nothing more than to invade and plunder it for their own gain.

"What is the Void?" Kian asked.

"A malevolent force that wanders between the worlds. We defeated it generations ago—chased it from our realm—but we remain wary."

Neeve's eyes widened, and we shared a quick look. Was this mysterious Void the source of the subtle attack on the Darkwood? But surely, if that were the case, Thorne and the Oracles would know how to nullify it, which thus far hadn't happened. They'd protected the forest, yes, but according to Thorne, the threat wasn't gone—just turned aside.

"Should we watch out for this Void in the human world?" Kian asked, echoing my thoughts.

The Nightshade Lord shook his head, sending one of his intricate black braids swinging. "Elfhame lies in the path between the human land and the outer realms where the Void wanders. To reach your world, it would first have to lay waste to ours."

I pulled in a relieved breath. Not that I wanted any such thing to befall the Dark Elves, but I was glad to know that the mortal world was protected from some evil power wandering around outside the realms. Whatever that actually meant.

"Enough of this grim talk," the ruler said, shifting his attention to me. "What do you think of Elfhame, Lady Rose?"

"It's...magical beyond words."

I knew it was poor praise, but I couldn't admit the truth.

The land of the Dark Elves was enchanted and entrancing—a place rightly celebrated in fable and song, rich with mystery and the magic I'd craved my whole life. But if I acknowledged the dangerous beauty of the Nightshade Court, I'd have to admit that, though old by human standards, the lord of that court had a certain terrible charm.

I shook myself, trying to dislodge such thoughts from my head. No matter what the Nightshade Lord's intentions might be, I would not marry him.

If I envisioned myself with any Dark Elf, it was Thorne, whom I'd loved since the day he first saved me in the Darkwood. I lifted my hand to the pendant at my throat, the golden vines set with tiny blue gems, like drops of dew. It didn't match the garnets and amethysts the color of ripe blackberries that Neeve had produced for me to wear, but I didn't care. Nothing so trivial as a clash of colors would make me remove Thorne's gift.

The ruler's eyes narrowed slightly. "I see you're wearing one of Mirdan's pieces. Those are hard to come by, as his work is much in demand. Where did you get it?"

"The *Galadhir* gave it to me," I admitted, hoping it didn't mean trouble for Thorne. "He gave Neeve one, too."

"For our fourteenth birthdays," Neeve said, lifting her own silver and ruby pendant from her chest.

"Yours I understand," her uncle said. "Thorne Windrift is charged with protecting and serving you. But why extend such consideration to a mortal girl?"

I bit my tongue on the reminder that he himself had expressed an interest in me. That was better left unsaid until such evasions were no longer possible.

And hopefully, we'd be long gone from Elfhame by that point.

"Thorne is kind," I said. "He's always treated me as Neeve's sister."

Reflexively, I rubbed at my left elbow where the leaf tattoo was inscribed. I'd kept a close watch on it since coming to Elfhame, but other than that first transformation when crossing through the gate, it hadn't changed.

The soft peal of fourth chime rang, and the Nightshade Lord glanced at the three of us.

"Are you ready to dine?" he asked.

We all nodded, and he held out his arms, palms up. "Push your goblets toward the middle of the table and keep your hands in your laps. I've arranged for our meal to be delivered by magical means this evening."

I didn't ask what would happen if one of my hands got in the way of our dinner's enchanted arrival. My fingers sliced off by a plate, perhaps. I hurriedly clasped my hands beneath the table.

"*Nemata*," the Dark Elf lord said.

Instantly, a small silver bowl and crystalline plate appeared at each of our places. Steam wreathed up from the bowl, which contained a jade-colored soup smelling of herbs and onion. My plate held a flaky pastry like the ones Kian had brought to my room, a thick slab of grilled meat, cooked grain studded with dried fruit, and long spears of some unfamiliar dark green vegetable.

It all looked and smelled delicious, and I hoped my stomach wouldn't growl too loudly in anticipation.

"Enjoy," our host said with a nod.

"It looks wonderful." Kian reached for his utensils, which were wrapped in a square of linen-like cloth.

I did the same and discovered there was no spoon. Covertly, I looked at Neeve. Lips curving with mild amusement, she picked up her bowl and took a delicate sip of the contents.

It was easier to concentrate on eating than trying to make conversation, and my hunger had roared forth the moment the food arrived. I tried not to slurp my soup or lick the pastry crumbs from my fingers, but I was halfway through my meal in what felt like a matter of moments.

"You have a fine appetite, Lady Rose," the Nightshade Lord said.

Flushing, I glanced down at my half-empty plate.

"I didn't have anything to eat while I was lost in the Erynvorn," I said, by way of excuse.

"Indeed." The ruler's expression hardened. "For all your praise of the *Galadhir*, he failed in his duties to bring you safely across the worlds."

I couldn't help leaping to Thorne's defense. "Yet here I am, unharmed."

"While he lies useless in the healer's enclave." The Nightshade Lord's mouth twisted. "I might have chosen a better guardian than my cousin, had I known."

"Thorne is your cousin?" I stared at him. Did that mean the *Galadhir* and Neeve were related?

"Distantly." The lord gave an airy wave of his hand. "Perhaps, when the Oracles arrive, they will be able to rouse him."

"Will they be here soon?" Neeve asked, then took a sip of her wine.

"On the morrow," the Nightshade Lord said. "I'll expect you to attend the welcome ceremony."

"Of course." Neeve dipped her head, her dark hair falling in a silky curtain across her white cheek.

"That goes for all of you." The Dark Elf's gaze touched on Kian, then landed on me. "I'm particularly curious to know their opinion regarding you, Lady Rose."

A cold clutch of fear squeezed my ribs. There it was, all but spoken. The Oracles would determine whether I'd make a suitable anchor for the gateway. And then?

Please wake up, Thorne. Please. Without the *Galadhir*, I had no way to escape back into the mortal world.

"What time will that welcome be, Uncle?" Neeve asked, diverting his penetrating, dark gaze from me.

As soon as the Nightshade Lord turned to her, I took a gulp of wine. Kian shot me a sympathetic look.

"Sometime before moonset," the lord said. "Listen for the double chime. A turn after it sounds, the court will gather in the throne room."

Neeve nodded, then dabbed her mouth with her napkin. "This was a most delicious meal. Thank you."

I was surprised to see that, unlike in the human world, she hadn't needed to be prodded to eat her vegetables. Of course, it stood to reason that anything in the Dark Realm would be to her taste.

The ruler glanced at our empty plates and bowls. "I'm glad you enjoyed it. There is one more course, however."

Without needing to be told, we all put our hands in our laps.

The Nightshade Lord made a gesture, speaking a few words in elvish. The plates and bowls disappeared, replaced by round silver dishes with upturned edges. They looked empty, and when I leaned forward to check, the lord let out a soft chuckle.

"Patience, my lady."

I sat up straight, disliking that form of address—though I supposed it might be only politeness. But with the Nightshade Lord, everything seemed intentional.

He held his hands up toward the ceiling and murmured again. Light glowed over our heads, and I glanced up to see a four-petaled flower the size of a large platter floating above the table. A spray of golden stamens rose above the cream-colored petals, shading to rich brown at the edges.

A twist of our host's wrist, and the petals detached, each one floating down to land in one of our silver dishes. Once there, they transformed into a creamy substance that looked a little like custard. The golden stamens followed, descending to drizzle a honeylike syrup over the custard. Finally, a puff of dark pollen drifted, dusting a last bit of sweetness over the contents of the bowls.

Despite myself, I was enthralled by the display.

"What is it?" Kian picked up the spoon that had appeared beside the bowl and gave the dessert a gentle poke.

"We call it *voreniquesse*," the Nightshade Lord said. "It is rarely served, so I encourage you to savor each bite."

He sounded a touch weary, and I guessed that conjuring such a spectacle had used more than a little of his power.

I picked up my spoon and took a cautious bite, then nearly moaned aloud at the experience. It wasn't the flavor—though the rich, caramel-like syrup and slightly bittersweet dust melded wonderfully with the creamy custard. *Custard* was a misnomer, however. The petals had turned to something rich and cold that melted as I held it in my mouth.

"What *is* this?" Neeve asked, a note of wonder in her voice as she scooped up a second spoonful. "How did you make it so cold?"

Her uncle looked at her, the trace of a smile lifting the corners of his mouth. "A lady of the Moonflower Court invented the dish years ago, using a combination of ice-calling and sweetness runes. It's a foolish waste of power, some might argue, but it has its uses. Sometimes a bit of frivolity is all to the good." He looked at me, his dark eyes intent. "What do you think?"

He was asking about more than just the extraordinary illusion and its delicious results. I pulled in a breath, weighing how to answer without giving him undue encouragement. Part of me was impressed that he'd gone to such trouble, but clearly he'd done it for that very reason—to bedazzle his human guests, and myself in particular.

Unfortunately, it had worked.

"I've never tasted anything so marvelous," I finally said, with complete honesty. "Truly, the Nightshade Court is full of wonders." I hoped that was vague enough to suffice.

He nodded and leaned back in his chair, and I felt the tightness about my ribs ease.

The rest of the meal passed uneventfully. We finished our *voreniquesse*, and I resisted the urge to lick the bowl. I doubted I'd taste anything quite so amazing ever again. Perhaps due to spending some of his power to impress us, the Nightshade Lord's manner wasn't quite as sharp, and he let us depart without too much more innuendo directed at me.

Except for when we took our leave. He escorted us to the door, then swept up my hand and bowed over it, his dark eyes intent on mine. He did not do the same to Neeve.

I nodded to him, then pulled my fingers from his grasp and quickly followed Kian over the threshold.

"Well," Kian said as we trailed the dark-haired warrior back to our rooms, "that didn't go too badly."

I couldn't agree. My heart was still beating fast, like a rabbit's after the hawk soared overhead. I'd escaped those sharp talons—for now.

Neeve looked at me, as though she could sense my reaction. "Are you well, Rose?"

"Well enough," I said shortly, though as we walked the graceful hallways of the Nightshade Court, I realized my head was a little fuzzy from elderberry wine.

"Don't worry," my stepsister said quietly.

I frowned. What kind of deep game was Neeve playing? Half the time she seemed to support her uncle's not-yet-finalized plans for me, and then she'd turn around full of sympathy and seem to be all in favor of us departing Elfhame immediately.

I stared at her, but as usual, her serene expression gave nothing away.

"The Oracles are coming tomorrow," Kian said, oblivious to the undercurrents, or perhaps tipsy enough not to care. "That should be interesting."

"Indeed," Neeve said, unsmiling, her gaze never leaving mine.

CHAPTER 25

I t seemed we'd lingered over dinner longer than I'd thought. The corridors of the Nightshade Court were dim and quiet, with no courtiers going about their business. We left Kian at his rooms, and then the guard escorted me and Neeve to our doors and departed with a bow of farewell.

"Good night," I said to my stepsister as I went into my room, though it was neither night nor particularly good.

I still felt unsteady from the wine, and cold fear trickled through me at the thought of the Oracles' arrival. I had no doubt they planned to test me in some way, to see if I could serve as an anchor point for the gateway between the worlds.

Would their evaluation hurt? And even more worrisome, what if they determined I was, indeed, a suitable anchor?

I shivered. If only Thorne would wake. Surely he'd be able to help us navigate out of this maze.

Thorne.

I could visit him that very moment. The corridors were deserted, and I was certain I could recall how to get back to the healer's enclave. Besides, no one had told me I couldn't visit him, no matter the hour.

He'd be asleep anyway, so it wasn't as if I'd be disturbing him. But for my own peace of mind—and yearning heart—I must go.

I slipped out of my room, shutting the door silently behind me, then tiptoed past Neeve's room. I held my breath until I'd turned the corner, but continued to keep my footsteps as quiet as possible. Skulking through the court reminded me of my half-forgotten skull-duggery lessons in Parnese. Lessons I'd put to good use when I first arrived in Raine and followed my new stepsister into the forest.

How much had changed since that fateful afternoon.

I'd met Thorne that day, but I never would have guessed that sneaking after Neeve would lead to being swept away into the magical land of the Dark Elves, with the fate of kingdoms hanging in the balance.

One more turn brought me to the wide hallway outside the healer's enclave. I paused at the door, which was closed. But not locked, as I discovered when I pushed the latch down.

It swung open soundlessly. I peeked into the room to see if, despite the late hour, the healer was still at her post.

The chair behind the table was empty, the space dim and quiet. Even the fountain had stilled for the night, the basin mirroring the single lit sconce mounted on the wall. Reassured, I stepped inside and closed the door behind me.

Thorne's bed was the only one occupied, and he lay as unmoving as before. I forced away the hot grief tightening my throat and went to stand beside him. It was difficult to tell in the low light, but he looked as pale and drawn as before, his cheeks hollow, a faint line between his eyes.

"I'm here," I said quietly, reaching out to smooth my thumb over his forehead.

I wished I could erase the lines of weariness from his face with my touch. I slid my hand down to cup his face, my fingers coasting over the sharp line of his cheekbone. His skin was cool, and I leaned forward, suddenly worried that he wasn't breathing.

After a tense moment he exhaled, a brush of air feathering past my cheek.

Startled, I realized our lips were nearly touching. And there was no one to see if I dipped my head and kissed him.

Foolish, I told myself, even as I bent forward and brushed his mouth with mine.

My heart leaped, even though the kiss was one-sided. For a moment I pressed my lips more firmly against his, wishing that he was awake, that his arms would encircle me and he'd kiss me back and tell me...

Tell me what?

That we have no future together, my little voice said, robbing the moment of its joy.

"Thorne," I whispered, pulling back enough so I could gaze at his face.

A lock of my hair, escaped from its braid, fell down to brush against his cheek. And astonishingly, he stirred. Only the faintest of movements, but even as I watched, his eyelids flickered, as though attempting to open.

"Wake up," I said softly. "I know you can. I...I need you."

With a nearly inaudible moan, he opened his eyes. They were nearly black, the golden lights in their depths all but quenched. He looked at me in confusion, then, very slowly, smiled.

"Rose," he whispered. "You found me."

A blue glow winked on above his bed, and I glanced up. Did he conjure it, or was it some signal to the healer? Another light blinked on in the room beyond, outlining the doorway of what must be the healer's quarters.

"I must go," I told him, cupping his cheek one last time. "I'm so glad you're awake."

He didn't answer, but watched me as I whisked back to the door and pulled it open.

Just in time—I glimpsed the healer hurrying to Thorne's bed even as I silently shut the door behind me.

For a trembling moment I leaned against the cool white wall, tears of gratitude stinging my eyes. Thorne was awake at last. I hadn't lost him to an eternal sleep in the shadowland. Surely now everything would be all right.

THE NEXT DAY, facing the prospect of meeting the Oracles, I wasn't quite as optimistic.

Neeve woke me with an insistent rap on my door, and entered with a tray of food when I sleepily admitted her.

"Thorne's awake," she said, with a rare smile. "The healer just sent word."

I didn't tell her I already knew—and that perhaps I'd helped pull him from his deep slumber. Or maybe not. Already my stolen kiss felt like something out of a dream.

"That's good news!" I feigned surprise. "Can we visit him?"

I wondered how much of my night visit he'd remember, or if he even knew that I'd kissed him. Likely not. Nor would I ever tell, but carry that secret with me always, an ember in my heart.

"If you hurry." Neeve flicked her gaze over my disheveled hair and hastily donned dress—a dark blue one we'd finally brought over the previous day, along with a half-dozen others, so that I might have a rudimentary wardrobe.

"Of course," I said, already gnawing on a slice of melon.

I finished demolishing the contents of the tray, then brushed the crumbs from my skirt and washed my hands. Neeve braided my hair back and helped adjust the fit of my dress.

"Tie the belt a little higher," she advised as I attempted to tug the fabric about me. "And fold the neckline in."

I tried to do as she suggested, but after a moment she blew out an annoyed breath and took over, her nimble fingers transforming the unruly cloth into a gown worthy of a lady.

"I don't know how you do it," I said, glancing quickly at my reflection in the armoire's mirror. "Human clothing is much more understandable."

"But less comfortable, you have to admit."

It was true. Plus, the Dark Elf gowns and tunics could accommodate any number of body shapes, instead of being tailored to an individual. Perhaps I could bring a dress or two back with me when I returned to Raine... *If* I returned to Raine.

"Come along," Neeve said, heading for the door. "Don't you want to see Thorne?"

"Of course I do." I pushed my braid behind my shoulder and hastened after her.

The healer admitted us, her expression far more tranquil than the last time we'd visited. She nodded to the corner where Thorne lay, then resumed her place behind the table, allowing us a measure of privacy.

I was glad to see that Thorne was sitting, propped against the pillows with a tray of food in his lap. As Neeve and I approached, he looked up and gave us a tired smile.

"There you are," he said.

"Thorne." Neeve rushed forward.

He pushed his tray aside and folded her into a slightly awkward embrace. I glanced aside, my heart hurting anew when I thought of the news Neeve had yet to share, and how her betrothal would wound him.

After a moment, Neeve stood back, and Thorne held out one arm to me.

"Don't I merit a greeting?" he asked, his smile tilting wryly.

I kept my pace measured, despite the urge to fling myself at him, and only briefly leaned into his embrace. If I allowed myself to linger, I knew I would cling to him fiercely, and that would never do.

"I'm glad you're awake," I said.

"And I'm glad you're safe." He met my gaze, held it. I was pleased to see that the sparks in his eyes had brightened, though his face was still gaunt. "Rose—I'm so sorry. I failed you when my strength gave out, leaving you in mortal danger in the Erynvorn."

In some ways, my journey through the Dark Elves' magical forest felt like forever ago. Enchanted beasts, strange creatures, the lush mystery of the enormous trees—it was the stuff of dreams, not memories.

"I survived and made it safely here." I took his hand in mine and squeezed it. "It wasn't your fault."

His expression sobered further. "It was, and I can never forgive myself for thinking that my wellspring was strong enough for the task. That was the height of arrogance."

"Well, I forgive you." It was true—all my anger at him for abandoning me had fled the moment I saw him lying so pale and still in the healer's enclave. "And it seems to me that you performed several heroic acts of power in a row—transporting an entire castle's worth of people and horses and supplies through the Darkwood, then turning around and leaping through the gate between worlds, with me in tow. No wonder your wellspring gave out."

"Nonetheless." Regret haunted his expression. "I nearly lost you."

"Well, thanks to a tall tree, the White Hart, and an enchanted bear, I managed," I said, then glanced at Neeve as she gave a faint snort. "What?"

"Thorne was the bear," she said. "How have you not guessed that before?"

"What?" I blinked at her, the pieces slowly fitting into place as my confusion turned to anger. "More secrets you didn't bother sharing with me?"

I glared at her. I'd thought we were done with all that—but no. Neeve would always be too closed-mouthed for anyone's good but her own.

"I thought you knew." She lifted one shoulder in an apologetic shrug.

"No." I looked back at Thorne, who wouldn't meet my eyes. "Is that true? Can you really turn into a bear?"

He blew out a breath. "It is one of the powers granted to the *Galadhir*."

"Can all Dark Elves transform into beasts?" I glanced at Neeve, half expecting her to suddenly take to the air, screeching in the form of a feral hawk or some such.

She looked back at me, a hint of dry amusement in her expression, as if she could guess my thoughts.

"I am the only one," Thorne said. "And then, only in times of great need."

"So the White Hart..."

"Is neither elf nor human, but a creature of magic and prophecy. It can pass freely between the worlds, and even the Oracles don't fully understand its role in the web of fate."

"A bear." I firmed my mouth, thinking hard. "The first time I set foot in the Darkwood, it felt like the forest was trying to strangle me. A bear appeared that day and saved me—was that you?"

He nodded slowly. "Something about you triggered the Darkwood's wards. It perceived a threat where there was only a girl."

For a moment, the stub of my pinky ached. I rubbed at it, frowning. "The nixie tried to drown me that once, too. Why does the Darkwood think I'm a danger?"

"Perhaps because you are here, now, and you're not supposed to be." Thorne shook his head wearily. "But the binding between the three of us and the forest calmed it."

"You've rescued me twice now, as a bear," I said softly. I owed Thorne a life debt I could never repay.

"Four times, at least," Neeve said. "Don't forget the hobnie and the hawk. Or the wolves."

I shivered. I'd all but blocked out the memory of fleeing for the safety of Castle Raine's walls, the dire howling of the wolves just behind us. And the snarling of a bear as it attacked our pursuers.

"Why didn't you tell me in the Erynvorn?" I stared at Thorne.

"I used the dregs of my wellspring to transform," he said quietly. "There was no more power to turn back to my true form and try to explain. I had to trust you'd understand, and come with me."

I nodded slowly. Truly, it seemed like something out of an enchanted story—except in the tales, Thorne would turn out to be a prince.

"Are you royalty?" I asked, unsure of whether I truly wanted to know.

"I am of the Nightshade rulers' bloodline," he said. "But I am not an heir."

"Being *Galadhir* is greater than that," Neeve said. "The courts should treat you better than they do."

He gave her a pointed look. "And how do you think I'm treated? I assure you, I'm given all the respect I'm owed."

I glanced about the room—the row of empty beds, the quietly splashing fountain.

"This is a place infused with healing power," Thorne said. "If he were injured, even the Nightshade Lord would recuperate here."

As if the mention of recovery had summoned her, the Dark Elf healer came to join us at Thorne's bedside.

"Enough talk," she said gently. "*Galadhir*, finish your meal. Ladies, thank you for your visit."

I looked at Thorne a moment, wondering if he recalled anything of my clandestine visit. He only gazed levelly back.

"Lady Rose," the healer said, frowning as she regarded me a moment, "I have a request, though it might seem strange. Might I see your hand?"

She nodded to my left hand and the stub of my pinky. It had stopped aching, and I wondered what had drawn her attention to the site of my long-ago accident.

"She won't hurt you," Neeve said quietly as I hesitated.

"I know," I said hastily, though I knew no such thing. Inhaling, I held out my damaged hand.

Mistress Almareth gently cradled it between her palms, then looked at me, her pale eyes searching. "Does it pain you?"

"Almost never."

With mild surprise, I realized it was true—the constant ache I'd carried ever since coming to Raine had faded during the last year. Perhaps, in addition to curing the life-threatening fever that had swept through me, the mysterious doctor in Parnese had done something to fix my hand. I'd only experience a few pangs now and then, instead of the bone-deep pain I was used to.

"Hmm." She folded her fingers over mine and closed her eyes.

I felt a tickling along the side of my palm, moving up my pinky, and then—

"Ouch!" I pulled my hand from hers at the sharp sting and held my palm up before my face, half expecting to see blood. There was nothing.

"Forgive me." The healer's gaze was full of distress. "It was never my intent to cause you discomfort."

Discomfort? It had been rather more than that, but I bit my tongue on the hot words.

"What did you discover?" Thorne leaned forward, looking intently at Mistress Almareth.

"I..." Distress marred her smooth brow. "I cannot say. Something is there, but it is elusive, like a dark fish in the shadows of a pond. It slipped away before I could begin to name it."

"What about this?" I pushed up my sleeve and held out my arm, displaying the leaf and whorls of vines inscribed upon my skin.

"It changed." Neeve bent closer to see, the ends of her dark braids tickling my elbow.

"When we came through the gateway." I lowered my arm and looked at the healer. "What does it mean?"

Her frown deepened, and she looked at Thorne. "What binding did you put upon this girl, *Galadhir*?"

He slowly shook his head. "Nothing of ill intent. Only a rune that would prevent her from speaking aloud the secrets of the Darkwood."

"Which didn't work," Neeve muttered.

"Oh, it worked." I gave her a look. "All too well, as I recall, and with painful consequences."

"I presume you removed the binding?" the healer asked Thorne.

"Immediately. But Rose has always had a"—he looked at me—"a complicated relationship with the forest. The Oracles have confirmed that her fate intersects with ours in some way they cannot quite see. Only that she is important to the Darkwood. And to Nightshade."

Oh. I stared at him, thoughts spinning. Everything leading to this point felt suddenly less like coincidence. Was I, in fact, fated to wed the Nightshade Lord? A terrifying thought.

"*Important to* does not always have a positive connotation," Mistress Almareth said. "You and I both know the Oracles often speak in riddles."

He gave her a weary nod. "One can only hope they will be clearer today."

I blinked at the reminder that those mysterious visitors were about to arrive—though given the current conversation, I wasn't excited at the prospect of *too* much clarity. If they decreed that my destiny was to remain in Elfhame, what would I do?

"We must prepare for their arrival," Neeve said, "and let Thorne rest."

"How long until you're recovered?" I asked him, noting with dismay that he'd leaned wearily back against the pillows. Clearly our visit had taxed his strength.

"Soon," he said, which was no answer at all.

I looked to the healer, whose mouth had firmed.

"Whatever you might hope for, *Galadhir*," she said to him, "it will take a brightmoon, at least."

He gave a quick shake of his head. "Every day that Prince Kian remains within our realm, the danger to Raine grows. As soon as my wellspring regains enough power, I must send him back."

And Neeve too, I presumed. Otherwise, the gate between the worlds would seal permanently closed. It was a foolish arrangement, I thought privately. Look how it had hurt Neeve her whole life. But perhaps the terms of the gateway had been set in a different time, when the ties between humans and Dark Elves were stronger.

"Draining your wellspring again could prove fatal," the healer warned. "Is your life so unimportant to you that you would risk it for a mortal kingdom?"

"Yes," he said simply, then closed his eyes. His lashes were smudges of soot against his pale skin.

Neeve jerked her head at me in a clear signal to go.

"We'll be back later," I said, brushing my hand over Thorne's arm.

Without opening his eyes, he nodded, and my heart twisted at the sight of him lying there so exhausted.

"How long is a brightmoon?" I asked Neeve as we left the healer's enclave.

"In this world, or the human one?"

"Both, I suppose."

"Three palemoons here." She gave me a grim look. "Nearly three months in Raine."

I'd guessed as much, and my spirits sank even lower as I numbly trailed her back to our rooms. Unless the Oracles presented some solution—or opened the gate themselves, which Thorne seemed to think only he could do—then the future loomed as dark as an endless night, without even a scattering of stars to light the way.

CHAPTER 26

That afternoon, after a luncheon tray delivered by a quiet Dark Elf, I stared at the colorful silks hanging in my wardrobe. Neeve had unstintingly shared her supply of gowns with me, but I couldn't find anything that seemed appropriate for a life-altering meeting with the Oracles.

Everything seemed too bright, the fabrics too sumptuous, the scarves and belts too cheerfully embroidered. All except the silvery purple, but I'd already worn that to dinner with the Nightshade Lord.

A knock came at my door, and I went to open it, expecting Neeve. Instead, a Dark Elf youth stood there, garbed in the deep purple that denoted his status as a court servant.

"Lady Rose," he said, bowing and holding out the cloth-wrapped parcel he carried, "the Nightshade Lord sends this gift, with his regards."

I took the package, curious and a little apprehensive. "Please give him my thanks."

"I shall." The boy bowed again, then turned and hurried back down the hallway, off to perform some other errand for his ruler.

I closed the door and set the gift on the low table in front of the couch. For a moment I eyed it warily—but I'd already guessed from the feel of the parcel what it contained. Fabric, mostly. Given the circumstances, it was probably a dress the Dark Elf lord thought I should wear to meet with the Oracles.

Since I was having no luck with that on my own, I sighed and unfolded the cloth wrapping.

Silk as smooth as water met my touch, the color of twilight spilling into night. Slowly, I lifted the gown, which seemed to be in several parts. A pale lavender underdress without sleeves, then a gauzy length of smoke-hued fabric so fine that I almost thought it would dissolve like mist under my fingers.

There were a pair of trailing sleeves that appeared to fasten mid-arm and then flutter gracefully to the ground, the colors shading from moonlight to deepest violet, and a flowing cloak to match. Unlike most of the garments in my wardrobe, the underdress had a neckline elaborately decorated with swirls of gold where tiny clear crystals winked. The same gold and crystals edged the sleeves.

At the bottom of the parcel, beneath the gown, lay a golden belt, a necklace to match, and two bracelets.

It was a gown fit for a queen, and my pulse raced as I stared at it. Clearly, the Nightshade Lord wanted me to wear it to meet the Oracles.

But I would not.

I wasn't a pawn, or a princess, or a Dark Elf queen.

I was just me, Rose, a human girl who didn't belong anywhere. And despite my yearning to have a home, I wouldn't give up everything I was to obtain it.

Even though the gown was beautiful, it was a manacle, a promise of a life I could not, would not, envision for myself.

Slowly, I folded the gorgeous silks and closed the fabric wrapper over them, then set the parcel in the bottom of the wardrobe. Then, with a wry laugh at myself for my own folly, I took out the brown homespun dress I'd brought from the mortal world.

It was clean, if not fashionable. I donned it, then undid the braid taming the wild curls of my red hair, letting them spill down over my shoulders. My only concession to the adornments the Nightshade Court favored was the pendant Thorne had given me, which I wore openly. The delicate goldwork and tiny sapphires looked even more fragile against the coarse fabric of my dress.

I fastened my leather belt about my waist, settling the sheathed dagger at my hip. Whatever the Oracles might think of me, no matter how much the court might laugh, I was ready.

The double chime heralding the Oracles' arrival sounded as I was splashing water on my face. I dried my cheeks with the impossibly fluffy towel, then went to face Neeve.

She opened her door a moment after I knocked, then blinked at me, dismay flashing over her expression.

"Didn't you hear the chimes?" she asked.

"I did."

Her gaze dropped to the toes of my scuffed boots then slowly rose to my unruly brush of hair.

"I believe the Nightshade Lord will find your appearance an insult to his court." Though her voice was mild, her eyes were hard. "Can I persuade you to wear something else?"

"No." I shook my head, relieved that she didn't seem completely furious with me. She was stone, not ice. "I'm not going to pretend I'm something I'm not."

"At least wear your circlet?"

"Neeve." I narrowed my eyes at her. "You're the Princess of Raine, not me."

"Dressing like a castle servant isn't going to help you escape the Oracles' notice. Or change their minds about your place in the weave of fate."

I shrugged. "If the Nightshade Lord wants to make a match, then he'd best know what he's getting."

"This won't dissuade him." She waved a hand at my appearance. "It will only turn the court's opinion further against you. Why do you have to make things more difficult?"

"I don't care what the court thinks!"

Her eyes narrowed and she reached for me. "Come in, at least, and stop shouting your unpopular opinions for all to hear."

I scowled at her but let her draw me into her room.

She, of course, looked every inch the Dark Elf lady. Her green silk gown was overlaid with a silver tracery that looked like cobwebs, a single clear stone set in the middle of each web like a drop of dew. Emeralds wrapped in silver adorned her throat and fingers, and the same jewels were woven into her dark hair. She even had a new crown made of filigreed silver, where more of the green gems winked.

"I'm sorry I can't be what you want me to," I said. "I know you hope to stay in Elfhame, but at what cost?"

She glanced down, but not before I glimpsed the anguish in her eyes.

"I don't know," she said softly, her voice hoarse. "I just want what's best for us, Rose. For all of us."

I folded my arms. "And when those things are in direct conflict, then what? I suffer and you benefit?"

She jerked her head up, red spots blooming on her cheeks. "Or maybe the opposite. Why do you always think you're the one who must pay the price? Perhaps you get to live your dream while others remain miserable."

She was so clearly distressed that my anger melted into reluctant sympathy.

"There has to be a way out. For you, and me, and Kian, and even Thorne."

Her gaze was steady on mine. "You're breaking his heart, you know."

"*I* am?" I shook my head in disbelief. "You haven't even told him yet that you're going to marry Kian."

"He knows—we have spoken of it." She balled her hands, then slowly unfurled them, finger by finger. "But we don't have time to argue. We're expected in the throne room."

"Then let's go." I stared at her, daring her to keep trying to change my mind about my choice of clothing.

Lips set in a firm line, she only glanced at me, then away, and led me out of her room.

We didn't speak as we made our way through the pale halls of the Nightshade Court. I knew we made a comical sight: a regal Dark Elf princess garbed in silks and jewels and a ruddy mortal girl in rough homespun. Yet I was satisfied.

My confidence seeped away, however, when we stepped into the throne room. Starting with the astonished looks of the guards outside the door and continuing with the wave of whispers and shocked glances sent our way, I felt my courage crumble.

But I'd known this would be the reception I'd get when I chose to defy court etiquette. Steeling myself, I lifted my chin and strode resolutely toward where the Nightshade Lord sat upon his throne.

Kian had preceded us, and stood waiting off to one side of the dais. My steps faltered when I realized Thorne was beside him. The *Galadhir* was very pale, shadows in the hollows of his cheeks, but his expression was determined. When he saw me, the hint of a smile sparked in his eyes.

"He's not supposed to be out of bed, is he?" I asked Neeve in a whisper.

Frowning, she shook her head.

My concern for Thorne was eclipsed, however, when I glanced at the Nightshade Lord. His severe, elegant face seemed carved of marble, and his eyes, when they met mine, were icy with displeasure.

But whatever the consequences, I'd made my choice. Even if it meant weathering the storm of a ruler's rage.

That didn't mean my heart didn't tremble, my throat going dry with apprehension as I made my curtsey before the throne.

"Lady Rose," the Nightshade Lord said, his voice hard, "did you not receive my gift?"

"I did, my lord. And I thank you for your consideration."

"Yet you stand before me garbed in rags, an insult to me and my court." The anger in his voice was biting.

From the corner of my eye, I saw Thorne take a step forward. Kian set a restraining hand on his arm.

Despite the stone of fear in my throat, I forced my voice to steadiness. "I'm a human girl. I don't belong here, and it seems foolish to pretend otherwise."

"You could have a place at my court." His voice softened, but was no less dangerous. "Don't pretend you're blind to my interest, human girl." The last two words were heavy with scorn.

"Uncle." Neeve moved to stand shoulder to shoulder with me.

"Rose makes her own path. She always has, and even the power of the Nightshade Court cannot sway her."

"But can the power of prophecy?" a low, melodious voice asked from behind us.

The court swayed, turning like a field of tall grass pushed by the wind. I pivoted, along with Neeve, to see three white-veiled figures standing at the doorway to the throne room.

The Oracles had arrived.

And it didn't seem wise to stand directly in their path. Neeve and I exchanged a quick look, then backed away to join Kian and Thorne.

On the dais, the Nightshade Lord rose from his throne and extended his hands in greeting. "Oracles, welcome to my court. Nightshade is overwhelmingly pleased that you have answered our call."

"We answer the call of fate," the middle Oracle said, stepping forward. "Not of rulers."

The other two followed, flanking their leader as they moved up the wide aisle the courtiers made for them. I watched closely, but couldn't make out their features behind the gauzy veils, nor determine if they were male or female. They were mysterious figures, carriers of prophecy, garbed head to toe in shimmering white robes that seemed to deflect my gaze even as I stared at them.

Halting at the foot of the dais, the trio dipped their heads, but made no formal bows to the Nightshade Lord.

"We have come," the leader said, "because this court, at this time, is the center of a maelstrom."

The courtiers whispered, and their ruler raised his hand. "And yet," he said, "no storm seems to be upon us."

The Oracles stood motionless for a moment, then turned as one to where we stood—the interlopers to their world, and myself in particular. I imagined I could feel their gazes, heavy upon us, even through the opacity of their veils.

"Thornelithiel Windrift, *Galadhir* of the forest," the right-hand Oracle said. Their voice was a little higher than their leader's, but still genderless. "Do you see the tumult you have caused in the current of fate?"

"Only when it tosses me about," Thorne said. "I can't control the tide."

"Nor should you," the lead Oracle said. "But you, of everyone here, at least know what sea we travel."

"I glimpse it," he said hollowly. "The fate of two worlds hangs in the balance."

I sucked in a breath and glanced at him. Two worlds? Suddenly, our presence in the Nightshade Court wasn't a simple matter of Neeve bending the rules and me coming to fetch her back to Raine, but something far weightier.

"What have you done?" my stepsister asked softly, looking from Thorne to me.

I shook my head, and Thorne only stared gravely back at her, silent.

"And you, Princess Neeve Mallory of Raine," the left-hand Oracle said, leaning forward. "Will you answer for your actions?"

Her cheeks very pale, her lips very red, Neeve lifted her chin. "I will. I always do."

Hidden by the folds of her dress, I saw that her hands were tightly clenched. Surreptitiously, Kian leaned closer to her, his arm brushing hers in silent support.

"Prince Kian of Fiorland," the lead Oracle said, their tone lighter than it had been when speaking to the Nightshade Lord. "What do you think of our land, and the secrets that brought you here?"

"I think the world holds more mystery than most of us imagine," he said soberly. "I'm lucky to have seen a small part of it."

The Oracle nodded, as if in approval, then stepped forward until they were directly in front of me.

"Lady Rosaline Valrois, sometimes princess, sometimes fugitive, bearer of bindings and hidden truths—will you, too, accept the price and consequence of your choices?"

I stared at the white-cloaked figure a moment, my thoughts whirling. What did that even mean?

"I don't suppose I can say no," I finally said, giving up on untangling the implications of their words.

"One can always say *no*," the Oracle said, and I almost thought I heard a smile in their voice. "What matters most is saying *yes*."

I shifted uncomfortably. "I'm not going to just agree without knowing what I'm saying yes to."

The conversation was making my head swim. I was conscious of Thorne's gaze on me, but my attention was fixed on the Oracle.

"Oh, you will know," they said, their voice suddenly deeper and more resonant. "You will not be able to escape that knowledge."

Before I could sort my scattered confusion into actual questions, the Oracle stepped away, returning to stand with their companions in front of the Nightshade Lord's dais.

"We will retire now," they said—and it was truly all of them this time, speaking in unison.

"Your chambers are ready." The lord beckoned to one of his court servants. "Naithal will take you. I hope, after a sufficient rest, we will be able to speak further. Until then, please enjoy the hospitality of the Nightshade Court. There will be a feast later in your honor, of course."

The Oracles nodded as one, then followed their guide out of the throne room. The moment they stepped over the threshold, the room began buzzing with low conversation, like a nest of wasps readying themselves to emerge and sting everyone in their way.

The Oracles had stirred that hive and swirled my emotions into a hopeless tangle. Say yes, say no, ride the waves of fate?

As usual, I had no answers.

CHAPTER 27

"You can't wear that ridiculous dress to the feast, you know," Neeve said to me as we returned to our rooms.

Once the Oracles had departed the throne room, we'd extricated ourselves as quickly as possible. Although the Nightshade Lord seemed displeased to let us go, he nodded his permission, and Neeve, Kian, Thorne, and I had made a hasty retreat.

"I know," I said defensively, twitching my homespun skirt. "I just wanted to make a point."

"You certainly accomplished that." Her tone was dry.

I wished I could go visit Thorne, who'd gone back to the healer's enclave, but he clearly needed his uninterrupted rest. Kian had headed for the gardens, frowning, one hand on his sword. I guessed he was going to practice his solo blade work, as I'd often seen him do in the training arena at Castle Raine.

For a moment the remembered scent of sawdust and straw tickled my nose, and a pang went through me. What would Trisk think of my absence? Would the cat remember me when I returned?

If I returned...

"What do you think the Oracles meant, with their talk of choices and consequences?" I asked Neeve.

She shook her head, the gems in her hair winking with the motion. "They speak in riddles. I don't think we're supposed to understand."

I grimaced. I hated secrets. Including oblique declarations that left more hidden than revealed.

"Will we ever figure out what they're referring to?"

"Only after it's too late," my stepsister said grimly, pausing as we reached my door.

"Come in," I said, "but let me light the foxfire."

Even though I knew my power was borrowed from the talisman, it still gave me a thrill to speak the elvish rune and see blue flames spring to life.

Once we were inside, Neeve went to my couch and sat, her expression troubled. I took the chair beside her, snagging the cozy blanket and draping it over me. I wasn't cold, but I craved the comfort.

"I fear for Thorne," she said. "He insists on overtaxing himself."

"If you saw visions of the destruction of two worlds, you'd probably do the same." I hugged the blanket closer. "I wish he'd share his burdens with us."

"He is the *Galadhir*," Neeve said tightly. "He bears his sorrows alone."

"It's not right."

Privately, I vowed to sneak off and visit him again later. Not to scold him, though I would dearly love to do so, but to offer whatever support I could. I hadn't forgotten the haunted look in his eyes when he'd spoken with the Oracles and admitted to catching glimpses of our fate.

My stepsister lifted one shoulder. "Responsibility isn't always wisdom—but Thorne treads his own path."

I pressed my lips together, wishing things were different. Wishing for a future that could never be.

"Well," I said after a moment, "at least the Oracles seemed to like Kian."

The corner of Neeve's mouth twitched with dry amusement. "He is so perfectly earnest—how could they not?"

It was true. Kian viewed the world openly, with far less suspicion than either me or Neeve. She, of course, was the most guarded person

I'd ever met. Perhaps that was part of the bond I sensed between them. She and Kian were opposites, reflecting back to one another what life might be, if seen in a different light, from a different angle.

"I'll come help you dress, a few turns before fourth chime," she said.

I narrowed my eyes at her. "Making sure I don't wear my torn gold gown?"

Sadly, the velvet was beyond repair, but I had brought so few things from the human world that I refused to toss it away.

She gave me a look of mild exasperation. "To fix your hair and lend you some jewelry. And help with belting and such, if you need it."

We both knew I would.

"Very well." My tone was grudging, and I tried to follow it with a smile. "Thank you."

She nodded and stood, then paused partway to the door. "Rose..."

"What?" I asked when it seemed she wouldn't continue.

Neeve met my gaze. "Don't work yourself into a temper trying to puzzle out what the Oracles meant. This is not something you can answer for yourself."

"That's arrogant of you," I replied, stung.

She blew out a breath. "That's exactly what I mean. Perhaps you should join Kian in the gardens and go over your dagger moves."

"Why, so I can attack the Nightshade Lord if he tries to propose?" I folded my arms, our earlier camaraderie gone. "Goodbye, Neeve."

Her mouth tightened, but she simply shook her head at me and slipped out the door.

I stood there, aggravation moving like sand across my skin. I despised it when my stepsister put on superior airs. Bad enough that she had taken to the Nightshade Court like a flower to sun—or a mushroom to damp, I amended uncharitably. But she didn't have to treat me like a child into the bargain.

Jealousy is such a warm emotion, my little voice said. *Hold to it a bit longer.*

"Quiet," I told it.

I pulled in a deep breath, eyes closed, and tried to slow my spinning thoughts. We were all doing our best under trying circumstances.

Even if it felt like holding back the oncoming night with nothing more than a single flickering candle.

❧

As promised, Neeve returned to help me prepare for the feast. She didn't argue over my choice of garment, a subdued sage-green silk, and didn't even try to insist I wear my circlet, though her own crown was perched proudly atop her head.

Instead, she wove jewels in my hair, alternating tourmalines of green and gold. I refused all the necklaces she suggested, proudly pulling out the pendent Thorne had given me and letting it adorn my neck alone.

Kian, dressed in a midnight-blue tunic embroidered with silver, came to fetch us when the fourth chime rang. He grinned when he saw me, and shot a look at Neeve, who was resplendent in a rich scarlet gown that shaded to black at the edges.

"Did you have to tie Rose down to get her to wear something acceptable?" he asked.

"Of course she didn't," I said archly. "I'm not a complete fool."

"Some might argue the point," Neeve said in an undertone, but her eyes were warm, so I didn't take offense. Much.

We navigated our way through the graceful corridors, joining a steady stream of richly garbed courtiers making their way to the feast. I found it interesting that, unlike the protocols of the mortal world, we were allowed to wander freely about the court. Had we been foreign guests at Castle Raine, the king would have assigned a servant, and most likely several guards, to escort us about.

Not that the warriors of Nightshade weren't watching us. They were just subtle about it.

Perhaps the ruler felt we were no threat. Neeve was his niece, after all, and Kian and I had no magic.

We entered the formal dining hall of the Nightshade Court, which I'd glimpsed when I first arrived. It looked completely different now, however—the walls replaced by trees made of shimmering silver and gold, the tables spread about in bowers where clusters of glowing flowers shed both light and a delicate fragrance into the air. Neeve led us forward, and I tried not to gawk at the pale fountains running with dark wine, the spheres of foxfire floating lazily overhead. Even the marble floor had been transformed to a lush carpet of emerald moss.

"You're staring," Neeve said quietly, to both me and Kian.

I closed my mouth, which hadn't been hanging open *too* much. I hoped. "We're not really outside, are we?"

"It's an illusion," my stepsister confirmed.

"A most impressive one." Kian's voice was soft with wonder.

"I'm glad you think so," came a darkly amused voice behind us.

I whirled to see the Nightshade Lord standing there, though he hadn't been a moment before. Had he disguised himself as a tree so he could spy on his guests? It was an amusing, if unlikely, thought.

There was nothing amusing, however, about the regal tilt of his head or the understated opulence of his deep purple robes. They draped from his shoulders like folded wings, open in the front to reveal a tunic and leggings the color of pearls tumbled by the ocean tide.

He looked every inch the imposing king, and it was impossible to contain my apprehension. What did the Oracles think of his interest in me? What private words did they speak to the ruler of the Nightshade court?

"Come," he said, gesturing. "Your places are ready."

He led us to a table located at the base of an enormous, glowing sycamore tree. Fanciful lanterns hung from the branches, and flecks of light drifted down like golden leaves, disappearing when they touched the table.

As we approached, I was surprised to the see the white shine of the Oracles' robes. The trio had clearly arrived without fanfare and were already seated along one side of the table, which I noted was set for eight.

"Well met, again," the middle Oracle said as Neeve and I curtseyed and Kian made a formal bow.

The Nightshade Lord seated Neeve and Kian across from the Oracles, then went to the foot of the table and held out an ivy-twined chair.

"Lady Rose," he said.

I didn't want to sit facing him once again—but it would be childish to refuse. And the presence of the veiled Oracles robbed the heat from my rebellious thoughts. I glanced at the empty chair to my left.

"The *Galadhir* will be joining us," the ruler said, his tone cool.

I couldn't determine if the Nightshade Lord was displeased that Thorne was coming, or just annoyed that he was, apparently, late to dinner.

I sat, and the ruler pushed my chair in then rounded the table to take his own seat. He waved his hand, and the silver-chased goblets I recalled from our previous meal magically appeared at our places.

This time, however, I resolved to drink sparingly of the sweet wine. I needed a clear head to even attempt to navigate the waters of the Nightshade Court, and the Oracles' presence made everything that much more confusing.

The feast started without ceremony. Some courtiers had already seated themselves at tables nestled within the illusory forest and were eating and drinking, while others gathered in small groups, engaged in quiet conversation and not seeming inclined to begin their meal.

There were no servants, just magic. And music, I noted, flute and harp drifting through the air, joined by the silvery ring of finger cymbals. I looked, but I couldn't spot the musicians. Maybe the ruler had enchanted them to look like trees, too, I thought wryly.

Despite the elaborate dishes that kept appearing at the table—fish poached in a creamy sauce, crispy golden tubers with a piquant dipping sauce, greens sprinkled with fruits and nuts—I had little appetite. The Nightshade Lord conversed with Neeve, who was seated at his right hand. Beside her, Kian put in a word or two, but the empty chair separating us made conversation difficult.

The Oracles said nothing, merely lifted their utensils beneath their veils to eat. I watched them closely, to see if I could catch a glimpse of their features, but none of them obliged me by picking up a goblet and shifting their face coverings aside.

I wondered if they removed their voluminous robes in private, or if they always went concealed, even from one another.

At last, midway through the interminable meal, Thorne arrived. He still looked wan, but not nearly as exhausted as he had earlier. Clearly the healing was working, and I smiled at him as he slipped into the chair beside mine.

"Hello," I said. "I'm glad to see you." I pushed a nearby plate of honey cakes and the remainder of the fish toward him.

"Rose." He regarded me seriously. "You ought to know—"

"*Galadhir*," the Nightshade Lord said from the head of the table. "A tardy entrance, but I am pleased you managed to make one. The Oracles have important news."

He gestured, murmuring in elvish, and a curious quiet fell over our table. I sent Thorne a questioning look.

"Rune of containment," he said softly. "Only those of us at this table will be able to hear what is about to be spoken."

I swallowed. That didn't bode well.

"We thank you for taking precautions," the middle Oracle said, setting aside their utensils. "While a feast of welcome is not, perhaps, the best time to share our news, the findings from our most recent divinations are of urgent importance."

The Nightshade Lord nodded gravely. "Please, tell us what you have discovered."

"Dire portents indeed."

Veiled heads moving as one, the trio of Oracles looked across the table. Not, as I'd feared, at me. No, those mysterious, implacable gazes were focused directly upon Neeve.

CHAPTER 28

Wide-eyed, I stared from the Oracles to my stepsister. She had gone very still, her face as pale as moonlight.

"What is it?" Kian demanded roughly. I couldn't quite tell from where I sat, but I thought he'd taken Neeve's hand beneath the table.

"Neeve Mallory, Princess of Raine and daughter of Lady Tandenneth Shadrift, you should never have set foot in Elfhame." The Oracles spoke in unison, their voices echoing eerily. "The Dark Elf illness that is your heritage has lodged in your blood. Returning to the mortal world at this time will prove fatal."

My stepsister seemed carved of ice, her eyes huge, dark pools in her face.

Thorne pulled in a sharp breath and leaned forward, his gaze fixed on Neeve.

Oh, Neeve, what have you done? My pulse raced, even as the dreadful consequences of her actions whirled through my brain.

"How..." I cleared my throat, my tongue clumsy in my mouth. "If Neeve can't go back to our world, how will the gateway remain open?"

"It will not," Thorne said quietly. Hopelessly.

"That's ridiculous," Kian said, his voice strained. "Are you saying that Neeve is now trapped here, in Elfhame?"

The middle Oracle nodded, the strange magic binding the trio together gone for the moment. "Unless the healers can subdue the sickness in her blood, for Neeve to cross between the worlds is to court death."

"And the only way for the gate to remain open is if I stay in here?" Kian asked.

"Kian, no." Neeve turned to him, her expression stricken. "I can't allow you to make that sacrifice."

He gave her a crooked smile. "It won't be that terrible. And you're here too, after all."

My stepsister's expression softened, and for a moment I saw strong emotion shining in her eyes. Then she shook her head. "But what of the fate of our kingdoms? It would turn our countries from allies to enemies if you mysteriously disappeared from Castle Raine, never to return."

"That is not all we have to impart." The Oracles, uncannily chained together again, turned their opaque gazes to me.

Now I was the dove pinned by the hawk, about to be torn in two by the sharp talons of prophecy. I could scarcely breathe beneath the weight of their attention.

"Rosaline Valrois," they intoned, "claimed sister of Neeve and princess by distant blood, tied to the forest with a binding oath, we have determined that you will make a suitable anchor point."

Their words were steel in my heart.

Slowly, Thorne turned to look at me, horror in his eyes.

"This is my fault," he whispered.

"Then Neeve and I can stay here," Kian said, "and Rose can go back in our stead."

The Nightshade Lord let out a sharp, unamused laugh. "That is not what the Oracles mean, young prince."

No, it was not. Cold to the bone, I looked at the forbidding Dark Elf lord and forced myself to explain. "They mean that I could stay here to keep the gate open, and *you* could go back, Kian."

"Provided you were wed to a Dark Elf of royal lineage," the middle Oracle clarified.

The Nightshade Lord's gaze met mine, and even though the length of the table lay between us, I shivered. Fate cast a dreadful shadow over me, and I couldn't see how to escape it.

"That seems the best choice," the ruler said slowly, his dark eyes intent. "The Fiorland prince can return to the mortal world and avert the brewing war, and Neeve will remain here, giving the healers and Oracles the opportunity to try to stem her sickness."

"The brewing war?" Kian gave the ruler an appalled look. "What do you mean?"

I closed my eyes briefly. Disaster layered upon disaster. All my worst fears were coming true.

"Is Fiorland invading Raine?" Neeve asked grimly.

"They are gathering their army," Thorne said, the weight of a thousand years in his voice. "Jarl Eiric took word of the prince's disappearance to his king and queen, and they are acting accordingly."

Neeve rounded on Thorne, anger sparking in her eyes. "Why didn't you tell us?"

"We only just discovered it. I can—with great effort—scry between the worlds, but am currently too weak to do so without the Oracles' aid."

"Then I'll go back," Neeve said. "We will *all* go back to the mortal world. Immediately."

"And if you expire the moment you step through the gateway, it will close and the harvest portal will come to an end," the Nightshade Lord said, his expression stormy. "I cannot allow you to do such a thing, for it would mean the slow death of our realm into the bargain. Without access to the *nirwen* flower, Dark Elves will perish."

I knotted my hands in my lap. Death and destruction on all sides. I felt cold inside, like I'd swallowed icy darkness and it was eclipsing my entire being.

There was only one way through this appalling tangle. Only one way to save Neeve and Kian. And Raine. And Elfhame.

Even though it meant sacrificing myself.

Slowly, I got to my feet, ignoring Thorne's outstretched hand, Neeve's stricken look.

"Lord Mornithalarion Shadrift," I said to the fearsome ruler of the Nightshade Court, forcing my voice to steadiness, "if you so desire it, I will agree to marry you."

CHAPTER 29

Neeve gasped, and Thorne stood up with such force that it knocked his chair to the ground.

"Rose, no," he said tightly.

"It's the only way." I couldn't bear to look at him or my heart would shatter right there on the spot.

"She's too young." Thorne raised his voice for the whole table to hear. "Rose isn't yet eighteen. Under our laws, she cannot speak any binding oaths until then."

"*Galadhir.*" The Nightshade Lord stood and leaned forward, bracing his hands on the table. "You take your duties of protection too far. We both know that time is racing by in the mortal world. Surely her birthday is nigh."

Was it? The flicker of hope Thorne had given me faltered and died.

I knew that the days and months moved differently between the realms—indeed, I'd reminded Kian of the fact earlier. How long had I been in Elfhame? Surely it wasn't summer already. It couldn't be.

I swallowed and glanced at Thorne. "What season is it in Raine?"

"Spring," he said miserably. "By next moonrise, late spring. The one after that, early summer."

And my birthday. I squeezed my eyes closed, but I could still feel the Nightshade Lord's heavy gaze upon me.

"Then we will set the wedding for two palemoons hence," he said. "*Galadhir*, I trust that timeline will suffice."

Numbly, I looked at Thorne, who nodded at his ruler and avoided my eyes.

"You can't do this," Kian said to me.

"I must." I swallowed, trying to stay calm. Trying not to show the abyss that had opened beneath my feet.

All my worst fears had come true. The premonitions that had lurked in the shadows now leaped forth to devour me. I'd been right—the *nirwen* harvest had changed the course of my life, forever.

I would marry the Nightshade Lord, who even now watched me implacably, his dark eyes cold, the sharp, elegant planes of his face not that different from Thorne's. Perhaps I could—just barely—contemplate wedding the Dark Elf lord because he reminded me of the *Galadhir*, though admittedly a much more frightening version.

And of Neeve, as well. I'd come to love her as my own sister, where once I'd feared we'd become bitter enemies.

As if hearing my thoughts, she stood and rounded the table, coming to stand beside me.

"Rose—I am so very sorry," she said, taking my hand. For once, her skin was warmer than mine.

I stared mutely back. Nothing could be done to change the inevitable, or unwind the events that had led us all here.

"Don't worry." She leaned forward, dropping her voice to a low whisper. "All is not lost."

But, of course, it was.

"I believe our feast is nearly ended," the Nightshade Lord said, waving his hand.

The strange muffling effect surrounding our table dissipated. Once more I heard the soft strains of music, the murmured conversation and occasional laughter of the Nightshade Court.

Elfhame was an enchanted land, I reminded myself, gazing at the gold and silver trees, the radiant flowers. I'd always wanted to live surrounded by magic.

Be careful what you wish for, my little voice said spitefully.

"Nightshade Court," the ruler said, his voice ringing out over the gathering. The courtiers stilled, turning their gazes to our table. "Once again, we welcome the Oracles. And I have an announcement to make."

He held his hand out to me, commanding me to join him. Though my heart was leaden, I squeezed Neeve's fingers, then let go and walked the length of the table to stand at the Nightshade Lord's side. Whispers of speculation moved through the court like the wind rustling dry grasses.

"We are pleased to announce our engagement to Princess Rose," the Dark Elf lord said, setting one hand on my shoulder. I felt the prick of sharp, claw-like fingernails through the fabric of my dress, and tried not to shudder. "The ceremony will take place in two palemoons."

Another wave of murmurs swept the gathering. The nearest courtiers looked at me, and I was relieved to see only disdain and not outright hatred in their expressions.

"Congratulations, my lord," a voice called, and as if it were a signal, the rest of the court chimed in with their felicitations.

I bowed my head in acknowledgement, conscious of the Nightshade Lord's grip. The Oracles nodded, veils moving in an unseen breeze. Neeve had gone to stand with Thorne, their fingers laced together, while Kian gave me a grim look, his eyes shadowed.

This was not a path I could ever have imagined when I first followed my stepsister into the shadows of the Darkwood. But it was now the one I must walk—as bravely as I could.

THE NEXT DAY—ALTHOUGH there was no such thing in Elfhame— passed in a blur. After the feast, I'd gone to bed numb inside, my thoughts echoing hollowly inside my skull.

I woke in the dark, a cold reminder that it would *always* be dark. I would never see the sun again. The stub of my pinky ached ferociously, and the vine etched on my arm felt inflamed, though it looked perfectly normal.

This is what you wanted, my little voice whispered.

No—it wasn't.

But it was what I'd chosen.

Neeve brought me a tray of food, and I ate it, tasting nothing. We sat in silence for a long time, and I was grateful for her company, though I, uncharacteristically, had very little to say.

"Rose." She regarded me gravely, and I noticed that she'd woven no gems into her hair that morning, and her dress was very somber. "I've spoken with the healers. They've assured me that—with enough *nirwen* essence and magical healing—eventually they'll be able to control the Dark Elf sickness in my blood. Once they do, I'll go through the gateway and marry Kian. We'll come back here, and you can return to Raine."

"But I'll already be wed to the Nightshade Lord." I slowly shook my head at her. "And you can't ask Kian to give up the mortal world."

"*You* have," she said simply.

"I had to. Besides, years could pass in our world before you're healed enough to go back. Are you going to make Kian wait for decades?"

Anguish moved across her face, a dark shadow over water. I was not the only one whose heart was breaking. Sympathy edged through me, like a crack of light creeping beneath a door.

"At least we'll be together." I reached over and set my hand atop hers. "We can remind each other what the sun looks like."

"You'll be able to see it every harvest." There was a melancholy twist to her lips. "Until I'm healed, I can't cross over."

Misery descended like a mist, wrapping both of us in its clammy embrace. I sighed, and Neeve squeezed my hand.

"I'm sorry," she said. "If I had it to do again, I never would have dragged Kian into Elfhame with me."

"But you still would have come?" I gave her an intent look.

Her teeth caught the edge of her blood-red lower lip. I'd never seen my stepsister so unsure of herself.

"I don't know," she finally said. "I don't know anything, Rose."

"Except that I'm to be married tomorrow." I pulled my hand from hers and wrapped my arms around myself.

"I'll be at your side," she said. "And Kian will, and Thorne. You're not alone."

I closed my eyes and nodded. Perhaps some kind of life here could be salvaged, with Neeve's help. And Thorne's.

She left soon thereafter for another round of healing, and I crawled back into bed. At least when I was asleep, my thoughts weren't scraping the inside of my head raw.

Kian was the next to visit. I groggily opened the door, and he stepped inside. Like Neeve, he'd also brought food, and though I wasn't hungry, I thanked him.

"Don't worry," he said, setting the tray of honey cakes down, then flopping into one of the chairs beside the couch. "I'll go stop the war, explain everything, and then make Thorne open the gateway for me to return. I'll be back before you know it. Then I'll stay here, and you can return to Raine."

It was a simple plan—and completely doomed to failure, even if Thorne was suddenly rejuvenated enough to open the door between the worlds multiple times in a row. Besides, as I'd told Neeve, anything of the sort would be too late.

"I don't imagine my new husband would approve of that idea," I said wearily.

"I'll make him." Kian's hand brushed the sword at his side.

"Dark Elves are *magic*. Don't you understand what that means? Challenging the Nightshade Lord would only end with you losing. Badly."

He frowned, mouth tightening. "If I had help, though—"

"Stop. We are not going to stage a coup of the Nightshade Court. Even if Neeve is of ruling blood, I don't imagine the other Dark Elves would just sit idly by while humans took over one of their courts."

"Your *Galadhir* would lend his support," Kian continued, as if he hadn't heard me.

"I doubt it. And he's not my *Galadhir*."

"Oh, Rose, sometimes you're so oblivious." He shook his head. "Thorne would do anything for you."

"He would do anything for Neeve. I just happen to be along."

Kian waved his hand at me. "Believe what you like."

"I shall. Did you just come to pick a fight with me?" At least I was finally awake.

"Did it work?" He gave me a wry smile. "You have some color back in your cheeks, at any rate. Now, eat something."

To make him happy, I picked up a honey cake and nibbled it. Still, he needed to understand that humans were no match for the power of the Dark Elves.

"Do you remember when we were studying the Athraig," I said, "and you noted how strange it was that their invading army had been defeated by just the castle guard?"

"Yesss." He drew the word out. "And no matter what Miss Groves said, I know that their victory didn't come about because of Castle Raine's secret passages."

"Of course not. The Dark Elves arrived from the depths of the forest and routed the enemy. Not only that, they changed the Athraig's memories of what happened. No one outside Raine can know of Elfhame's existence."

Kian's expression grew serious. "What do you mean, changed their memories? Can the Dark Elves truly meddle about in our minds?"

I shivered, recalling the long-ago first time I'd met Thorne in the Darkwood. Neeve had encouraged him to erase the knowledge of his existence from my thoughts. Could he have done so? Would everything have come out differently if he had?

I gave Kian a long look. "Only when their very existence is threatened—or so I've been told."

"Don't let the Nightshade Lord muck about in your memories," he said, eyes narrowed.

"There's no need. I've consented to marry him of my own free will."

He grimaced. "There has to be another way."

"There's not." Once again I was faced with inevitability of my choice.

The Prince of Fiorland must be returned to the mortal world at all costs, to keep his country and Raine from being plunged into war. Yet the gateway must remain open, and Neeve could no longer set foot in the human world.

I was the only one who could keep the realms in balance.

CHAPTER 30

After Kian left, I curled up on the couch, pulled the blanket around my shoulders, and finished the honey cakes. I'd no idea what time it was, and I didn't care. The hours would march forward whether I was aware of them or not, ultimately delivering me to stand before the Nightshade Lord on the morrow.

What then? I assumed someone would coach me through whatever oaths the Dark Elf marriage ceremony required. As soon as that was done, the Oracles would help Thorne open the gateway and they'd send Kian through. And my life lived in darkness would begin in earnest.

I sat there staring at the blue glow of the foxfire for a long time, until a knock at the door roused me from my heavy thoughts.

I went to open it, expecting Neeve again, then took a step back when I saw Thorne at the threshold.

"May I come in?" he asked after a heartbeat.

"Of course." I gestured him to the sitting area. "I'd offer you a honey cake, but I ate all of them."

"Good. You need to keep up your strength." His strained smile didn't reach his eyes.

I returned to the couch and tucked the blanket over my lap. Vaguely, I knew that my hair was a tangle, and the dress I'd thrown on when Neeve visited hung in loose folds. I hadn't felt like folding it about me properly, and my stepsister wisely hadn't offered to help.

Thorne had seen me at my worst: petulant, and bloodied, and exhausted. In the face of my impending marriage, my vanity didn't seem very important. The lessons I'd learned that long-ago afternoon in my mother's rooms—how to apply cosmetics, which colors suited me—would matter at some point. Very shortly, in fact. But not today.

For now, I was just Rose. Not a princess, or even a court lady. Just a human girl who had made a terrifying choice. Tears pricked my eyes, and I turned my head away from Thorne.

"Rose." His voice was soft, and a moment later I felt him settle beside me on the couch.

He slipped his arm around my shoulders, and with a wavering sigh I leaned against him. Tears trickled down my cheeks, and I impatiently brushed them away.

"Shh," he said, his breath warm against the top of my head. "It's all right."

"It's not, though."

He didn't try to argue with me, though I half wished he would. I took a deep breath, tasting cedar and a hint of wildness, then turned to face him. Slowly, he let his arm slip from my shoulders.

"Tomorrow..." I met his gold-flecked eyes and swallowed back the remainder of my tears. "What happens at the ceremony?"

His lips twisted unhappily. "Oaths will be spoken, binding you to the Nightshade Lord. And to Elfhame."

"What of this?" I pushed up my left sleeve, and we both stared at the leaf patterns on my arm. "I'm bound to the forest, too. And Neeve. And...you."

My heart yearned toward him, like a flower seeking the light. Doomed to wither away.

He shook his head, his features drawn. "The promises you make tomorrow will take precedence over anything else. But it's not too late for you to escape."

"What do you mean?" I stared at him. "I can't go back to Raine, even if you're strong enough to open the gateway."

"I wish you would." His voice was solemn. "If you agreed to step back into the human world, I'd open that door for you this instant."

My heart twisted at the anguish I glimpsed in his eyes. Surely he blamed himself for our predicament—but there was no going back.

"You can't let the gateway close and your people perish," I said. "This is the only option."

"Perhaps not." He took my hands in his. "You could leave Nightshade, but remain in Elfhame."

For a moment my heart leaped at the thought, until reality shoved my hopes back down.

"And what? Live like a wild creature in the Erynvorn?" I shook my head. "That didn't go so well last time."

"I'd care for you." He pressed my hands. "Please, Rose, consider it."

"It won't work." Though I wished quite desperately that it would. "The Oracles said I must be married to the Nightshade Lord to serve as an anchor. And Kian can't stay here—we both know that."

Thorne closed his eyes briefly. The exhausted shadows beneath his eyes had faded, and the planes of his face were less hollow, his cheek-bones no longer sharp as blades. He was recovering, and I was glad, for it meant that the moment I was wed, he could send Kian back to the mortal world to avert the looming war.

We sat a moment, saying nothing. I was far too conscious of Thorne's fingers tightly clasped over mine, like a drowning man holding to the side of a boat. Wishing that things had not turned out the way they had.

I understood, but there was no fighting the tide. The only way through was to surrender.

"You can still help me, though," I said.

He gave me a searching look. "How?"

"After I am wed to Lord Mornithalarion—" I stumbled only a little over his name, then paused to pull in a steadying breath. "Whenever you can, spend time with me. Tell me how the seasons pass in Raine. Bring news of my mother, of Kian. Remind me how the sun feels against your face. Help me bear this exile."

He winced, his grip on my hands tightening. "I will. I'll do everything I can to aid you. And Neeve."

Neeve. Always Neeve.

"Maybe she won't marry Kian," I said bitterly, pulling my hands from his. "Now that she's trapped in Elfhame, everything has changed."

Brows drawing together, he stared at me as if he didn't understand my meaning.

I scowled at him. "Or is the *Galadhir* forbidden to wed?"

"No," he said slowly, his eyes dark with emotion. "But I will never marry. The woman I love is promised to another."

"There are better ways to live than wallowing in your sorrow," I said sharply, aware the words applied to both of us. "I'm sure if you spoke to Neeve—"

"Stop." He held up his hand. "I cannot discuss this with you, Rose. I'm sorry. For everything."

The misery in his voice erased my momentary anger. Impulsively, I leaned forward and embraced him. His arms went around me tightly, fiercely, holding me against him as though I were cherished.

I drank in the feel of him, the utter, heartbreaking sweetness that would be forever out of my reach.

"I forgive you," I said softly. "Everything."

He drew back, searching my eyes for the truth. He must have seen it, for his expression eased. "Thank you."

Leaning forward, he pressed his lips against my forehead. That kiss felt like a star against my skin, bright and impossible, burning into my memory. Into my heart.

"I will stand at your side tomorrow," he said. "You are strong enough for this, Rose. Be brave."

I blinked and lifted my chin. He didn't know how much his words meant to me.

"I will," I said softly.

I'd endured pain in the past, and terror. Surely wedding the Nightshade Lord wasn't the most awful thing I'd ever suffer. No matter how dire it seemed in that moment.

Thorne nodded, then stood. I wanted to cling to him, but I let him go. Just like the human world—sunshine, the familiar moon, my mother, and everyone I'd come to care for at Castle Raine.

I let them all go.

CHAPTER 31

Despite my assurances to Thorne, I didn't feel particularly brave when I awoke the next day. Faint moonlight filtered through the windows, and I lay there staring at the arched shadows on the wall until I felt able to rise. The sooner I faced what was to come, the sooner it would be over.

I sat and scooped up the softly glowing talisman I kept at the bedside.

"*Calya,*" I said, summoning foxfire.

Searing blue light flared from the crystal, all but blinding me. I shielded my eyes with one hand—and the talisman shattered.

The room was plunged into dimness again. I sat, shaking, my palm bleeding from where a shard had cut me. The remains of the broken talisman littered the covers, sparkling like broken ice in the moonlight.

My pulse raced in alarm. What had just happened? Had the Nightshade Court turned against me to keep me from wedding its lord? Was it even safe for me to venture out of bed, let alone go about the palace?

"Rose!" Neeve burst into my room, her hair half braided. "Are you all right? Where are you?"

"In here," I called, my voice unsteady.

She summoned light from the sconces without any problem, then hurried to the sleeping alcove.

"Careful." I nodded at the crystalline pieces littering my covers. "My talisman exploded."

"Exploded?" She glanced from the glittering shards to me. "I felt a surge of power...But, you're bleeding!"

"Only a little." I glanced at my palm, the thin trail of blood creeping toward my wrist. The stub of my pinky throbbed in pain, though as far as I could tell, it hadn't been injured.

"We must get you to the healers," she said, bundling the covers around the pieces of the broken talisman and then pulling them off my bed. "Go wash your hand."

Now that my cozy nest wasn't so cozy, it was easy to leave it. I rose and went to rinse the blood from my palm. Over the splash of water in the basin I heard a quick rap on the door, then voices.

I emerged from the water alcove to find the usual two warriors, one with silver hair, one with black, facing Neeve. Their stern gazes moved to me, and I couldn't tell if they were there to make sure I was unharmed or to accuse me of some treachery.

"Lady Rose," the silver-haired warrior said. "Are you well?"

"Yes," I said cautiously, suddenly aware I was wearing only a nightgown.

The door flew open, and Thorne rushed in, his face drawn with concern. Seeing me standing there, he halted abruptly and closed his eyes a moment, as though offering up a prayer.

"*Galadhir*." The dark-haired warrior turned to him. "What do you know of the strange power that just moved through the court?"

Thorne gave her an intent look. "It was similar to the force that has been testing the edges of the Darkwood. And yet the gateway is closed. There is no way mortal magic can reach into Elfhame."

"Unless someone has brought it here." The warrior's hand fell to one of the swords belted at her waist, and she gave me a hard look. "Lady Rose, what enchantments are you conjuring?"

"Nothing!" I wrapped my arms about me. "I only tried to summon foxfire, and the talisman shattered."

Neeve scooped up the soft blanket from the couch and came to drape it over my shoulders, then glared at the warriors.

"My sister is not a threat," she said coldly, with an imperious lift of her chin. "Now, leave us. I'm taking her to the healers."

The two warriors exchanged a glance, but Neeve in an icy temper was a force to be reckoned with.

"I'll accompany them," Thorne said. "You may tell Lord Mornithalarion that everything is under control."

"If you say so." The silver-haired warrior nodded grimly. "We leave it to you, *Galadhir*."

Thorne dipped his head in return, and the two warriors departed, though the dark-haired one threw me a suspicious look as they left.

As soon as they were gone, I turned to Thorne. "What do they think I've done?"

"I don't know." He crossed the room and took my injured left hand, giving it a careful inspection. "The cut's not too bad, but Neeve is right, it needs tending."

"Can't you make any guesses at what's happening?" With a grimace, I pulled my hand from his grasp. "If I can't even summon foxfire or use a talisman, I'll be little better than a child here, needing a constant nursemaid."

"I'll—" Neeve began, but I waved her to silence.

"I know you will—you both will." Angry tears clogged my throat. "But this is not how I imagined my life."

None of it was, of course, but at least I thought I'd have magic at my fingertips. Even if the power was only borrowed.

"Rose, be strong." Thorne put his hands on my shoulders. A strange, hopeful light shone in his eyes. "Remember that you're here for a reason, beyond anything we can guess."

"To marry the Nightshade Lord," I said bitterly.

"Perhaps." He stared deeply into my eyes. "Or perhaps fate has something else in store."

I felt like I was falling, his touch the only thing keeping me upright. It was all too much. My thoughts spun dizzily in my head.

"Fates or no," Neeve said, bringing me back to ground, "Rose is still bleeding."

Thorne released me. I swayed, but Neeve caught my arm.

"Turn around," she said to Thorne. "I'll help Rose dress, and then we can go."

With the barest softening of his expression, he did as she asked. Neeve towed me to my wardrobe and pulled out a dark red scarf.

"Hold out your hand," she commanded. "There's no point in leaving drops of blood in your wake."

For some reason, the thought made me smile dreamily. "A trail of rubies."

She frowned at me as she bound up my palm, which had indeed begun to bleed more freely. "You haven't lost nearly enough blood to be acting lightheaded."

She turned back to the dresses, selecting one in soft blue. I let go of the blanket cloaking me, then sucked in a breath at the sight of the tattoo on the inside of my left arm. It was sparkling, the green tendrils glowing, the inscribed leaf glittering as though dusted with crystals.

"Thorne," Neeve said urgently when she caught sight of it. "Come here."

He whirled around and was at my side in a moment.

"What does it mean?" I asked unsteadily. I felt as though I'd had too much elderberry wine, my senses strangely muddled.

"Is there any pain?" He gently traced the vines with one finger, and my knees buckled.

Thorne caught me, sweeping me off my feet and carrying me to the couch. He settled me gently, apology glinting in his dark eyes.

"I didn't mean to hurt you," he said softly, while Neeve draped the blanket over me once more.

"You didn't." I stared at him, belatedly realizing I held his tunic in a tight grip. Finger by finger, I made myself release him. "Nothing hurts."

Not even the thought of wedding the Nightshade Lord. Dimly, I knew that something was wrong. But somehow, I couldn't bring myself to care.

A double chime rang through the air, and Neeve pulled in a quick, anxious breath. She flipped the tiny glass at her waist, then glanced at me. "We only have two turns to prepare you, Rose. Not enough time to get you to the healers and dressed for the ceremony."

"I have some small healing ability," Thorne said. "Enough to stanch the bleeding."

"Do it," Neeve said. She turned back to my wardrobe and began flipping through the gowns.

"The queen dress," I said, as Thorne unbound my hand. "In the package, at the bottom."

Though I'd declined to wear the lavish gown for the feast, it seemed appropriate to don it for my upcoming marriage.

Thorne cradled my hand between his, and then it *did* hurt. Not the gash on my palm, which was still oozing blood, but my pinky, which pulsed in time to my heartbeat. *Pain, pain,* it flashed.

He spoke a few soft words in elvish and the bleeding stopped, the cut scabbing over as though it were hours old.

"What is happening to me?" I asked, staring up at him. "I feel strange."

He pressed his lips together and shook his head, fear and faith warring in his expression. "I can only guess that the imminent arrival of your eighteenth birthday in the mortal world is having some repercussions here."

"How is that possible?" Neeve arrived beside me, her arms full of twilight-shaded silk.

"I've no idea." He stood and, without her asking, turned his back once more.

My stepsister coaxed me to my feet, and a few minutes later I was garbed in the opulent gown the Nightshade Lord had given me. The violet-edged sleeves swooped to the ground like wings, and the folds of the dress felt as light as gossamer webs.

"You can look," Neeve said to Thorne, who had stood patiently facing the door while I dressed.

He turned, his eyes widening when he saw me.

"My hair's not done yet," I said hastily. "And there will be jewels—"

"You look every inch a queen," he said, his voice hushed. "Whatever happens today, know that you're worthy of this role, Rosaline Valrois."

I breathed in and stood a bit straighter. Perhaps what I'd taken for sheer surprise in his expression had been a touch of admiration, after all.

"Speaking of your hair," Neeve said, brushing a hand over my riotous curls, "where is your crown?"

"In the very back of the wardrobe," I confessed, though I didn't admit I'd flung it there in a fit of pique, hoping never to see it again.

She went to dig it out, and Thorne gave me a serious look. "Has anyone told you about the ceremony?"

"Who would have?" I asked, an edge in my voice. "Certainly Kian and Neeve know nothing about it."

"I know a little," Neeve said, her voice muffled by the gowns.

Thorne's brows rose, but he wisely made no argument.

"The wedding will take place in the throne room," he said. "Usually, the rulers of the court preside, but in this case the Oracles will stand as witness and hear your oaths."

I nodded, my mouth suddenly dry with apprehension. Whatever giddy mood had taken hold of me earlier faded like dewdrops on a summer's day.

"You will exchange rings—don't worry, I'm sure Lord Mornithalarion has procured one for you to give him. The main thing is to clasp one another's wrists and speak the Rune of Binding together. I'll demonstrate. Hold out your hands."

I did. My pinky ached, but at least the pain had subsided. The cut on my palm had faded to a thin welt. Thorne set his hands at my wrists, and I felt a delicate prick against my skin.

"Thorne," I said softly, "do you have claws?"

He gave me a crooked smile and held up his hand, then flexed his fingers. Pointed tips appeared from beneath his ordinary nails, and I stared at him. Another secret of the Dark Elves, and one I'd never guessed at.

"I don't," Neeve said, emerging disgruntled from the closet. It seemed she'd found my circlet, as well as the belt and necklace that matched my gown.

"Human blood is stronger than the Dark Elves' in such things," Thorne said. "But our magic breeds true."

"I suppose I should be grateful for that," Neeve said ungratefully, setting the circlet atop my head.

She began braiding my hair, her nimble fingers smoothing the flyaway strands, and I turned back to Thorne.

"How do you pronounce the Rune of Binding?" I prayed it wouldn't be difficult to say.

"*Gwedhyocuilvorn*," he replied, dashing my hopes.

I could just imagine myself standing there before the implacable gazes of the Oracles and the Nightshade Lord, stumbling over repeated tries to speak the Rune of Binding while the Nightshade Court tittered at my mistakes.

"Don't despair," Thorne said, clasping my hands. "We'll take it one sound at a time."

"I'll be back in a moment," Neeve said, twisting a last braid up around my circlet. "I'm going to fetch some jewels to weave into Rose's hair."

While she was gone, Thorne led me syllable by syllable through the word. Half the time I managed to pronounce it, or at least not mangle it too terribly. I could only hope that it would take a mere two tries during the ceremony to speak the rune. Much as I didn't want to marry the Nightshade Lord, the consequences of failing to do so were too dire to contemplate.

My stepsister returned, bearing not only a box of smoke-colored amethysts but an armful of white and purple flowers.

"One turn until the ceremony," she said tightly.

"I'll be ready," I said, my gaze meeting hers. I had to be.

CHAPTER 32

Neeve beside me, Thorne and Kian just behind, I paused before the arched doorway of the throne room of the Nightshade Court. I'd walk into that room as a human girl of no particular importance, and I'd come out as the Nightshade Lady.

It was an unfathomable thought, and for a moment my feet felt leaden, incapable of taking another step. My left arm was beginning to itch, and the stub of my pinky still throbbed in time with my heartbeat. All I wanted was to turn and flee from the fate that crouched ahead, waiting to devour me—not walk directly into its jaws.

Then Neeve touched my shoulder in support, and my paralysis was broken.

As we stepped into the room, a long chime sounded. The courtiers, arrayed in their glittering jewels and sumptuous silks, turned to look at me, their gazes implacable in their sharp-featured faces. Blue foxfire glowed from the wall sconces, but most of the illumination came from overhead, where the golden illusion of a huge *nirwen* flower hung over the court.

Heart pounding, I looked up at it, then over at Neeve. She met my gaze and nodded slowly. The flower was the exact one we'd seen in the scrying she'd cast—a radiant five-petaled flower, scribed with light.

I'd thought it a symbol, a sign of the importance of the gateway between the worlds. Yet here it was, down to every detail, confirming that I'd been on this path all along. Honestly, I didn't like the knowledge one bit—the notion that fate was driving me along like a horse harnessed to an invisible carriage.

What about the rest of the vision? my little voice asked. *You know—the part where you and Neeve are facing one another in a magical battle?*

I gave a shake of my head and shoved the words away. Neeve was my sister, and my friend, and I refused to imagine fighting her with deadly intent.

"The Nightshade Bride, Lady Rosaline Valrois," a violet-liveried elf announced from the doorway. "Accompanied by Princess Neeve Shadrift Mallory of Raine, Prince Kian Leifson of Fiorland, and Lord Thornelithiel Windrift, *Galadhir* of the Erynvorn and Darkwood."

Lord Thornelithiel? I nearly shot a glance over my shoulder at Thorne.

"We are seldom so formal here in the outer courts," he said quietly from behind me, as if sensing my surprise. "Only on rare occasions of state."

I supposed the ruler's marriage certainly qualified. Keeping my chin high, I walked forward, my sister at my side, down the aisle the courtiers had cleared. Overhead, the glowing flower shed light like golden pollen. It drifted softly down, dusting us with radiance.

All the light in the room couldn't brighten the figure waiting for me before the dais, however.

The Nightshade Lord wore an ornate silk and velvet tunic in a purple hue so deep it was nearly black. A dark silver cloak flowed from his shoulders, and tiny obsidian jewels winked from the elaborate braids framing his severe features.

I can't do this! I thought in a panic, all my resolve suddenly fleeing.

"Courage," Kian whispered from behind me.

With a steadying breath, I kept walking. The dais loomed ahead. The Nightshade Lord's throne had been moved to one side, and the three Oracles stood in the center of the platform, inscrutable in their white veils.

The skin of my left arm burned and itched beneath my elegant sleeve, and it was all I could do to keep from scratching viciously at it. My breath came faster, and from the corner of my eye, I saw Neeve shoot me a concerned look.

Then we arrived before the dais. The Nightshade Lord held his hand out to me, and I shivered at the thought of the claws hidden beneath his nails. What other inimical traits might he be hiding?

Thorne brushed his hand lightly across my back as he and Kian moved away. I tried to concentrate on that lingering sensation of warmth instead of the itch/burn/pain clawing at my arm.

"You are a princess," Neeve said softly to me. "Take this fate and make it your own."

I nodded mutely at her. Then she was gone, and I was left alone, facing the ruler of the Nightshade Court.

The middle Oracle moved forward, lifting their hands. Another soft chime shimmered through the air, although there was no need to summon the court's attention. Every gaze was fixed upon me and their ruler.

"Lord Mornithalarion Shadrift, Nightshade Lord and current Keeper of the Harvest, are you ready?" the Oracle asked.

The ruler nodded, his gaze snaring mine. "I am."

I knew his desire to wed me had everything to do with keeping his court in a position of power by securing the continued *nirwen* harvest, not to mention maintaining his connection to the Oracles and Thorne. But judging by the avaricious light in Lord Mornithalarion's eyes as he looked at me, those were not the *only* reasons.

"Princess Rosaline Valrois of Raine and Parnese," the Oracle intoned, "are you ready?"

No.

"Yes," I said unsteadily.

The Nightshade Lord extended his hands toward me. His skin was very white, his fingers long and elegant. I reached hesitantly to clasp them, wrist to wrist. My pulse raced, quicksilver. There was no turning back now.

The moment our skin touched, fire flared up my arms. Both of them, burning as though I'd thrust them into a smoldering hearth. I let out a whimper of pain and swayed. Only the hard, implacable grip of the Nightshade Lord kept me on my feet.

"Rose!" Neeve took a step forward, but the Oracle waved her back.

Flames spread through my chest and my breath came in short gasps, but I managed not to fall to the hard white floor. Yet.

"Speak the rune," the white-garbed figure said, their voice sharper than an Oracle's ought to be.

"No oaths?" The Dark Elf ruler gave them a curious look.

"There is no time." The Oracle twitched their robes in agitation. "Speak it. Now."

My belly was a bowl of fire, my head wreathed with invisible flames. Soon my tongue would be nothing but a cinder, my mouth full of ashes.

The Nightshade Lord turned back to me, something like fear moving across his expression. Nails pricking my skin, he leaned forward.

"We must speak it together," he said.

I nodded. Not because I thought I was capable of doing so, but to show that I understood.

Red flame flashed across my vision, the Dark Elf lord wavering with heat, the walls of the throne room curving strangely.

"Stop the ceremony," Thorne said urgently.

"*Galadhir*, you forget your place." Lord Mornithalarion said, as Thorne came to stand next to me.

"Don't you feel it?" Thorne asked, the edge of desperation in his voice. "Everything is about to—"

Fire ripped across the room, sorcerous red flames leaping and shimmering, hungrily questing for something, anything, to burn. The courtiers scrambled for the doors, screaming. The *nirwen* flower went up in a blaze of crimson.

The Oracles lifted their hands, and a blue dome of protection encased us. Just in time. Flames flung themselves against that barrier like ravenous wolves. Behind me, I heard Neeve cry out in elvish, and shards of ice began raining down from the ceiling.

It reminded me of the first Yule Feast, when flames had licked up the walls of Castle Raine and scorched the tapestries—except this fire was a thousand times more potent. It was the hot, hungry fire of the red priests, and I didn't understand how it could be here, in the land of the Dark Elves.

"Rose!"

Someone was calling my name. I blinked, fighting for breath, for consciousness, and realized Thorne was standing before me. He'd shouldered the Nightshade Lord aside and held me by the arms, his expression frantic.

"Rose," he said again. "You must control the flames."

I stared at him uncomprehendingly. "I have no magic."

His mouth twisted. "We were wrong—so very wrong. Somehow, this is *your* power. You must harness it."

I squeezed my eyes closed, hoping that when I opened them again, all of this would prove to be a strange illusion. But no. Neeve and Kian, Thorne and I, the Nightshade Lord, and the Oracles stood within a shield of azure light in the deserted throne room.

All around us, just outside that circle of protection, an inferno raged. The Nightshade throne was ablaze, the glimmering wall hangings blackened and curled. The acrid smell of smoke scraped my throat.

Wide-eyed, I stared at Thorne. How could this be my magic? Over and over, I'd been told I had no power.

And yet—this was the fire of human sorcery. Neeve could not wield it. Nor Kian.

Which meant that somehow, impossibly, I could.

CHAPTER 33

"*Esfera*," I whispered. The first word of the red priest's chant that I'd memorized from the hidden book in the library.

The flames dipped, and my breath squeezed from my lungs.

"Hurry." A bead of sweat trailed down Thorne's forehead, and I belatedly realized the heat was nearly intolerable. "We can't hold the ward much longer."

I nodded, then turned to face the fire.

"*Calma*," I said, lifting my hands, with no idea of where the word had come from. "*Calma to esfera*."

I smoothed the air, pressing the flames down, down. At first they didn't respond, and panic wrapped around my throat. We were all a heartbeat from perishing, devoured by the ferocious fire.

No.

"*Calma!*" I pushed my will into the word, as the Dark Elves did with their runes of power. Perhaps it wasn't the proper incantation, but I would make it so.

The flames lowered, no longer leaping to the ceiling and blackening the walls. I narrowed my eyes in concentration and repeated the word.

Then a third time, shoving the flames down with my hands, with my mind, smothering them against the hard marble floor of the Night-shade Court.

"*Calma.*"

The last bit of fire flickered out, taking the rest of my strength with it. My knees buckled. Someone caught me from behind, and I knew it was Thorne.

"Gently," the leader of the Oracles said. "The flames are only barely contained."

"What was that?" The Nightshade Lord rounded on the Oracles, his expression icy with anger. "How dare you play with fate in my court?"

The Oracles turned their veiled faces toward him, their voices sounding out in unison. "Fate plays as it will, Nightshade. Be thankful your court was not turned to ash."

The lord flinched slightly and narrowed his eyes. "What of this human girl? I cannot wed someone with untamed sorcery coursing through her blood."

"Nor will you." The leader of the Oracles shook their head. "It is too late to bind her to Elfhame. She must return to the mortal world before her rogue powers cause any more damage. Human sorcery can only be tamed in the human world."

"But..." I reluctantly stepped forward, out of Thorne's embrace. "What about the gateway? Won't it close forever if I do?"

The Oracles went very still, and Neeve and I exchanged a look. I noted that Kian had come to stand at her side. His fingers were wrapped tightly about the hilt of his sword, as though he'd meant to fight the flames however he could—even if a blade could do nothing against a raging, sorcerous fire.

"Everything has changed," the lead Oracle admitted, a rare note of uncertainty in their voice.

"I'll go back with you to the human world," Neeve said, meeting my gaze. "You sacrificed for me. It's only right that I do the same in return."

With a sharp shake of his head, Kian took her arm.

"It's too dangerous," he said in a low voice.

"He's right," I said. "You can't risk crossing over. Your life is at stake."

And mine wasn't. At least, I didn't think so. Who knew how my newfound power would react when I crossed between the worlds?

"The mortals are correct," the lead Oracle said. "Lady Neeve, you must remain in Elfhame. But it is possible that your sister, whom you have claimed by blood, may keep the gateway from closing entirely."

Thorne set his hand on my shoulder. "The forest has claimed her as well—both the Erynvorn and the Darkwood. Rose, show them."

I carefully parted the silken sleeve and held out my left arm. The leaf and vine inscribed on my skin glowed green, edged with gold. As one, the Oracles leaned forward. Their white veils fluttered, although the room was still. No breeze stirred the ashes of the throne or the black flakes of what had been tapestries scattered over the floor.

"Although our marriage is not to be," the Nightshade Lord said, his dark eyes intent on my face, "there is no doubt that you are bound to my court by fire and fate."

He slipped one pale hand into his robes and pulled out a ring. It was carved of deep red garnet and shone on his palm, reflecting the blue flicker of foxfire.

Thorne's grip on my shoulder tightened, as though he wished to pull me away from the Dark Elf lord, and the ruler gave him a tight smile.

"Fear not," Lord Mornithalarion said. "There are no oaths of binding upon this ring, no promises woven into the stone. It is a symbol of what might have been."

"Symbols have power, even so," Thorne said.

"Indeed." The lead Oracle reached out and lightly touched the ring on the Nightshade Lord's palm.

It flared a moment with white light. When the glow faded, the ring sparkled, tiny lights dancing in the depths of the translucent stone as though it had been imbued with stars.

"Hold out your hand," the Nightshade Lord said.

Despite his assurances, I was reluctant to do so. The memory of fire stirred in the pit of my belly.

"Leash your flame," the Oracle told me, with a sharp look.

Calma, I thought, and the heat subsided.

I could feel it there, though, waiting, like a wild creature that had exhausted itself for the time being. Once it regained its strength, it would be all too ready to leap forth again, intent on destruction. I'd tamed feral animals before, but this was different. This could kill at a moment's notice, and I had no idea how to keep it contained.

The Oracles were right—I must return to the mortal world. And I must carry everything with me possible to help maintain the doorway between the worlds.

Slowly, I held out my hand. My *right* hand, as my left was already overburdened with magical sigils.

Lord Mornithalarion took my fingers in his cool grasp. His eyes met mine, and while he still was fearsome and powerful, I found that my terror of him was gone.

"Rose," he said softly. "I am sorry I will not get to see what you would have become as the Nightshade Lady. I suspect you have a formidable future ahead—and I regret that it will not be at my side."

He sounded sincere, as though now that I had power of my own, I was worthy of his regard.

My eyes narrowed, but I nodded. "Thank you. I wish you all success in finding another bride."

Kian let out a faint snort, and bitter amusement flickered in the Nightshade Lord's eyes.

"Remember Elfhame," he said, and slid the ring onto my finger.

It fit as though made for me—which, of course, it had been, by whatever magical means.

"I will," I said. "Take good care of my sister."

He clasped my hand in his, and I briefly felt the prick of his hidden claws.

"*Namarie,*" he murmured, then let me go.

I took a half step back, glad of Thorne's warm presence behind me.

"Here." Neeve's hands went to her neck, and a moment later she held out the silver and ruby necklace Thorne had given her so many years ago. "Trade with me."

"A good thought," the *Galadhir* said softly.

I quickly unclasped my own and handed it to Neeve, the tiny

sapphires sparkling in the light. Solemnly, we each donned the other's necklace. I rested my hand over hers, where it lay just below my collarbone. My pulse fluttered quickly in my throat.

"I'll miss you," I said, holding her gaze. "Be careful. Be well."

"You too, Rose." Brightness glinted in her eyes, looking suspiciously like tears, though I'd never seen Neeve cry. I wondered briefly if Dark Elves were even capable of doing so.

"The bonds have been strengthened," the lead Oracle said. "Let us hope they are enough. Lady Rose, are you ready to depart for the human world?"

"Right now?" I swallowed. "Don't we have to travel into the forest?"

"The tides of fate are in flux," the Oracle said, a sudden resonance in their voice. "At this very moment, our power combined with the *Galadhir's* will be enough to transport you and Prince Kian between the worlds. But it must be now."

Neeve made a sound of distress and whirled to Kian. With a stricken look, he folded her into his arms.

"Don't worry," he said softly against her hair. "I'll wait for you. No matter how long it takes."

"I can't—" Her voice broke.

"You can, Neeve." I stepped to her side and laid my hand on her arm. "You're the strongest person I know. Besides, if I can truly serve as an anchor from the mortal world, then Kian can come and go as he likes."

I certainly had no intention of ever returning to Elfhame, despite the aching enchantment of the Dark Elves' world.

"We have a war to stop first," he said grimly. "But Rose is right—if this works, I'll come back as soon as I can."

"Provided the *Galadhir* will reopen the gateway for you," the Nightshade Lord said dryly.

Kian glanced at Thorne, and I could see he regretted all the times he'd belittled the *Galadhir's* responsibilities.

"I'm sorry." The Fiorland prince let out a heavy breath. "At your convenience, of course, Thorne."

"It is time." The lead Oracle raised their arms, followed by the other two white-robed figures.

Kian let go of Neeve. Her cheeks were the color of scarlet roses against the pallor of her skin, but she'd regained her composure.

"You'll be all right," I said to her, hoping with all my heart that it was true, that the healers would be able to conquer the sickness lurking in her blood.

She nodded stiffly. "As will you."

Our gazes met once more, and I could see the desperate hope, and fear, in her eyes. It surely mirrored my own. We each had a difficult road to walk ahead, and I wondered when I'd see her again.

And if it would truly end in sword and flame. A shiver of fear went up my spine at the thought.

Thorne clasped my hand, then reached for Kian.

"Take hold," he said.

The moment Kian's grasp met his, the air rippled.

"Now!" the Oracles cried in unison, raising their voices in a lilting elvish chant.

Light flashed about us, and I felt the beast of fire within me lunge forward. Then we were falling, falling through the dark.

"Thorne!" I cried, but his name was ripped from my lips and I tasted nothing but frost.

PART IV

CHAPTER 34

A heartbeat—or an eternity—later, we landed with a jolt in the cobbled courtyard of Castle Raine.

I clung to Thorne's hand and breathed hungrily of the sun-warmed summer air. The day was bright and filled with the smells of stone and horse and metal—so different from the hushed realm we'd just departed that I nearly fell to my knees in gratitude.

"Intruders!" A guard dashed toward us from his post at the castle gate, hand at his sword.

I noted with surprise that the portcullis was lowered, the first time I'd ever seen it so. Another soldier clattered down the castle stairs, and Kian stepped forward, hands open before him.

"Peace," he said. "I must speak with King Tobin immediately."

"Prince Kian!" The first guard sheathed his half-drawn blade, his eyes widening. "You've returned! And just in time. The Fiorland army is only a few hours' march away."

I blew out my breath, trying not to think of how close we'd come to disaster. Another turn more in Elfhame, and we would've arrived in the midst of a bloody war.

"Fetch the king," the guard said, jerking his head at the other soldier. Then he turned to look at me and Thorne. "Where is Princess Neeve?"

"Safe," Thorne said. "But we thought it best to return Prince Kian above all else."

"A few months ago would've been better," the guard muttered.

"We came as soon as we could." Thorne's voice was cool.

As though belatedly realizing our hands were still clasped, he released his grasp. Reluctantly, I let him go. The circle of garnet wrapped about my ring finger gleamed like rich red wine in the sunlight, little stars sparkling deep within.

We had come from Elfhame—but could Neeve ever return? Could Kian step back into that world? I glanced at Thorne.

"The gateway?" I asked in a low voice.

"Open—for now."

The tension twining through me eased a bit. It seemed our gamble had paid off, and I had proven an acceptable anchor point between the worlds. I wasn't delighted by the fact, but it was better than the alternative.

You wanted to be important, my little voice pointed out.

Yes—but carrying the responsibility for two worlds was a burden I hadn't bargained for. The dreams of childhood, I was now realizing, came with a cost.

"Sir Durum!" Kian called, gladness in his voice as the gruff captain of the guard emerged from the soldier's barracks.

The older man halted in blunt surprise, then, after blinking once, hurried to where we stood.

"Prince." He and Kian clasped arms in a warrior's salute. "Barely avoiding catastrophe, I see."

Kian frowned. "We must ride out as soon as possible to meet my people. They cannot attack Castle Raine."

Sir Durum gave a curt nod. "Proof you're alive will go far in convincing them to stand down. I presume the king— Ah, there he is now."

We all turned as Lord Raine strode down the steps leading from the castle's main doors. When he reached the bottom, I dipped into a curtsey. My heart dipped, too, heavy with the news we bore. Neeve wasn't coming back.

Not immediately, at least. And maybe not ever.

"Where is my daughter?" the king asked the moment he reached us, then turned to Thorne, eyes narrowed. "*Galadhir*, what have you done?"

"Neeve is safe, your majesty," Thorne said. "She is at the Nightshade Court, where they are treating her with all honor."

"But?" Lord Raine's voice was cold.

Thorne met the king's gaze steadily. "When she crossed through the doorway into Elfhame, the hereditary Dark Elf sickness lodged in her blood. She cannot, as of yet, return to the mortal world."

The king's expression darkened with anger. "We will speak more of this, Windrift. As soon as this damnable army is turned aside."

"I'm ready to ride out," Kian said.

Lord Raine looked him up and down, clearly noting his elvish garb, then gave a tight nod. "Sir Durum, fetch my personal guards. Prince, see to the horses."

The arms master nodded and hastened back toward the barracks, and Kian made for the stables. Lord Raine turned his stern expression upon me and Thorne.

"Whatever transpired in the land of the Dark Elves," he said, "I'll expect a full accounting the moment I return. But for now, Rose, go see your mother. She has not been herself since you left."

"My lord." I bowed my head.

"*Galadhir*, I command you to remain near. I'd have you come with us, but that would raise more questions in our allies' minds than I currently want to answer. Our first priority is averting a bloody battle. After that, we will reveal your identity—and the existence of Elfhame. Await my return."

"As you say." Thorne's voice was mild, and I was glad he didn't try to argue with the king. "Lady Rose, I'll escort you to your rooms."

We left Lord Raine and, amid the whispers of soldiers and servants, entered the castle. The interior of the great hall was cool and clammy, laden with memories. Familiarity wrapped about me like a musty cloak as we walked the stone corridors. They might only be lit with flickering mortal candles, but at least I knew where every hallway led.

"How is your wellspring?" I asked Thorne in a low voice.

"Adequate," he answered, but his face was drawn.

I suspected he wouldn't be able to send Kian back to Elfhame right away, even if the prince insisted. And now that we were back in the mortal world, with the Fiorland army at the castle doorstep, it wasn't reasonable to think Kian could solve matters and then just slip away again without raising an outcry.

When we reached the landing at the top of the stairs, I paused and glanced toward the east wing of the castle.

"I suppose I should do as Lord Raine asked, and tell my mother I'm back," I said.

Though I'd far prefer to go to my own rooms, change out of the elaborate gown, and see if I could find Trisk. Still, it was never wise to disobey a king.

Thorne nodded gravely, and so I turned down the corridor toward the royal suites.

I hesitated briefly before knocking at her door. Had Mama even missed me?

After a moment she opened the door, her eyes going wide in her lovely face. She seemed as fragile and luminous as a vase of finest porcelain, her features somehow even more beautiful than I'd remembered,

"Rose, my darling!" she cried, stepping forward to enfold me in her perfumed embrace. "I was so worried."

I placed my arms around her. Her shoulder blades were sharp wings, and I was afraid to hold her too tightly, for fear of breaking her. After two heartbeats she let go then, with a sweep of her hand, gestured me and Thorne to come inside. My pinky stub gave a little twinge as we entered, but quickly subsided as I rubbed at my left hand.

"Are you well, Mama?" I asked as she led us to her sitting area.

"As well as one might expect, after fearing my daughter was lost forever in some dreadful dark land, among enemies." She glanced at Thorne. "Yourself excepted, of course."

"Your majesty." He inclined his head to her. Although his expression was calm, I could see the glitter of annoyance in the depths of his eyes. Not that he'd ever be so rude as to directly contradict the queen.

She settled, graceful as a wilting flower, upon one of the brocade-upholstered chairs, and nodded at me to sit. I shook my head.

"I just wanted to come tell you that I've returned," I said, a bit awkwardly.

"And your stepsister and the prince as well, I presume. What a terrible time the three of you must have endured."

Now was not a good moment to tell her I'd almost married the Nightshade Lord. The news would either cause her to faint or throw her into a fit of hysterics, neither of which I currently had the energy for.

"Kian is already riding out to meet the Fiorland army. But Neeve..." I swallowed back the bitter irony that my sister was once again trapped in one realm and forbidden the other. Although this time, the worlds were reversed.

My mother cocked her head. "Oh no. She refused to return? The king will be quite displeased."

"It's not that she wouldn't return," Thorne said. "She couldn't. At least, not immediately." He didn't explain further, and, unsurprisingly, my mother didn't seem interested in the details.

"At least you escaped." She gave me a wan smile.

"About that..." I folded my arms. "It seems that I possess fire sorcery."

One hand came to her throat and she swayed, all the color draining from her cheeks. For a moment I truly thought she was about to collapse. Thorne took a step forward, ever the courtier, but Mama managed to remain conscious.

She gasped out a breath, then looked at me, eyes wide with horror. "Rose, no! How could this be?"

"I thought maybe you could answer that question for me." I kept my voice hard, despite her show of theatrics.

What, if anything, did my mother know about my late-blooming powers?

"My darling—I know you had a dangerous interest in such things, but I never imagined it would come to this." Tears sheened her eyes, and she turned to Thorne. "Can your people remove this power from Rose?"

Remove it? I frowned. Yes, the fire sorcery was feral and perilous—but it was also the one thing I'd yearned for all my life.

Magic.

No one was going to take it away from me—and judging by the look on Thorne's face, doing so wasn't an option.

"No," he said tightly. "Removing someone's power is akin to lopping off a limb or taking their eyes. If such an abominable action didn't kill Rose, it would certainly cripple her. And in any case, my people don't have that ability."

Maybe the Oracles did, I thought privately, but after Thorne's grim explanation of the risks, I wasn't about to let anyone attempt to excise my newfound power.

Of course, I had the difficult task ahead of actually learning to *control* that power. I let out a weary breath at the thought, and Thorne glanced at me.

"Rose is tired," he said. "Forgive us, your majesty, but traveling between the realms is draining."

Mama made a little pout, but waved her hand at us. "Go, take your rest. But come visit me again soon, Rose. Now that you've returned, we must discuss your future."

Wonderful. I closed my eyes briefly, exhaustion making me sway.

Thorne was at my elbow in an instant, steadying me. I threw him a grateful look, then curtseyed to my mother.

"As you wish," I said stiffly.

I'd all but forgotten the web of political alliances awaiting me in the mortal world. Now here I was again, a moth trying to avoid the sticky strands, searching for the light.

The true light, of course, was at my side as we left the queen's suite. But Thorne was as out of reach as the double moons of Elfhame. After all, he'd confessed that the woman he loved was promised to another—and though he hadn't said her name, of course he meant Neeve. For me to dream of him was an impossibility.

But in the meantime, I would savor every moment I had in his company.

"Now what?" I asked once we gained the sanctuary of my rooms.

A plaintive meow sounded from the bedroom, and then a thump. I went to my knees as Trisk came galumphing into the sitting room, heading straight for me. She didn't quite let me scoop her into my arms, but her purr, as I stroked her soft back, vibrated my fingertips.

"I'm so glad to see you," I whispered, relieved she hadn't forgotten me.

Thorne stood watching, a half-smile on his lips, until Trisk decided she'd had enough of a reunion. She went to the door and then, to my surprise, nudged open a portion of the lower panel with her nose. A hinged accessway had been cut there, just the size to accommodate a small cat. She hopped through, and the panel swung closed behind her.

"How clever." I'd have to ask Sorche about it, and any other changes that had occurred in my absence. It was strange to think that I'd spent less than two weeks in Elfhame, while months had flown past in the human world.

I rose, then grabbed for the chair as an eddy of dizziness swirled through me.

"I was serious," Thorne said, setting a steadying hand on my shoulder. "You need to rest."

"Then you should too, *Galadhir*. It's been an eventful day." To put it mildly.

I couldn't believe that only a short time ago I'd been standing before the Nightshade Lord, about to marry him, with his court and the Oracles as witness. It seemed almost a dream, only the deep red band on my finger reminding me of how close I'd come to a completely different life.

"I will," he said, glancing at one of my sitting room chairs.

"I'm sorry I can't offer you anything better," I said. He deserved a soft bed and a long sleep, not a chair before my hearth.

"This will do." He gave me a rueful smile. "The king is right that I must stay near. Hopefully, he and Prince Kian will be able to stop the attack."

"How could they not? The whole reason the Fiorland army is marching on the castle is because they thought we'd stolen their prince —and now he's back." With not a moment to spare.

"There are, however, difficult explanations to be made." Exhaustion edged his voice.

"But not immediately. Sit down," I told him. "I'll fetch you an extra pillow."

My bed looked most enticing, I had to admit, as I grabbed two pillows from it and returned to the sitting room. After Thorne was settled as comfortably as possible, I retreated back into the bedroom. I took off my cloak and shoes, removed the opulent elvish dress and the crown I'd all but forgotten I was wearing, and gratefully crawled beneath the covers.

CHAPTER 35

A great cheer and the babble of excited voices rising from the courtyard woke me. Groggily, I got out of bed, pulled a blanket about my shoulders, and went to the window. Peeking out, I could see sunlight glinting off armor, and the blue-and-white banners of Fiorland mixed with the gold pennants of Raine.

It seemed war had been averted.

Relief rose like a bubble in my chest. Then popped when I remembered that the king would be sending for us soon. With a sigh, I went to stand before my wardrobe. I had no intention of re-donning the elvish gown, but I could scarcely appear wearing my nightdress. No matter how much I wished to creep back into bed.

I chose a misty blue dress, grimacing as I struggled to lace it. The arms were constricting, the bodice felt too tight, and for a moment I sorely missed the elegant, comfortable clothing of the Nightshade Court.

But only for a moment.

Luckily, Sorche arrived at my bedroom door. After we exchanged warm greetings, she helped me finish dressing, then sat me before my mirror and began combing my hair.

"Thorne is in your sitting room," she said softly.

"I know—is he still asleep?"

"He was when I came in. As soon as I saw him, I tried to be quiet. Oh, Lady Rose, everyone was so worried about you. I wasn't sure if you were ever coming back. And it's so dreadful about the princess." She shook her head sadly, even as her nimble fingers wove my hair into a neat coiffure.

"We'll see Neeve again," I said staunchly—for my own sake as much as Sorche's.

I was tempted to tell the maid some of what had happened in Elfhame, but then she'd talk to the other servants. And though everyone would eventually know the tale, I owed it to the king to hold my tongue. He should be the first to hear of all that had transpired in the Nightshade Court.

Kian had perhaps told him some of it—although they'd had a war to avert, so maybe not.

After my hair was suitably tamed, Sorche fetched the crown from my bedside table. She placed it on my head with a satisfied nod.

"You look every inch the princess, Lady Rose."

I glanced up at her. "There's no need to be so formal. When did I stop being just Rose?"

The maid gave me a look. "You're all grown up now, with suitors arriving for your hand. It's only respectful to address you properly."

"Suitors arriving?" I stared at her, comprehension slowly uncurling through me.

Surely the Athraig prince wasn't in Raine. Which left—

"Prince Jenson came with the Fiorlanders," Sorche said, confirming my suspicions. "The squires told me that after being reunited with his brother, he said he was very interested in meeting you."

Oh no. I'd leaped from one potential arranged marriage to the next, with no respite between. No wonder Mama had wanted to speak with me about my future.

This time, though, I refused to meekly bow to the dictates of any king. I'd made my own choices in the Nightshade Court and would continue to do so here in the human world, no matter how difficult that path might be. As I'd told Neeve, perhaps I wouldn't marry at all —and we'd had that conversation *before* I'd learned I possessed fire sorcery.

Mastering that power was my first, and perhaps only, responsibility. If Lord Raine didn't like it, he would just have to accept it. I nodded at myself in the mirror. The young woman looking back at me had a determined lift to her chin, a resolute look in her eyes.

And magic. The knowledge made almost anything possible.

"Here." Sorche rummaged about in my dressing table and emerged with a few of the cosmetics my mother had sent over, after that long-ago day in her rooms. "A bit of color on your lips and cheeks will be just the thing."

The maid was so enthusiastic at the idea that I couldn't disappoint her. Once she'd left, I could wash it off, I reminded myself. I didn't want to give certain visiting princes the idea that I was trying to catch their eye, after all.

A knock came at the outer door as Sorche was finishing up. She went to answer, and I followed, surreptitiously rubbing some of the pigment off my mouth. In the sitting room, Thorne was awake, leaning back in one of the chairs with his legs stretched out before him. The long strands of his dark hair were tangled, as though he'd slept restlessly. Our eyes met, and I gave him a small smile.

Sorche opened the door, to reveal another castle servant.

"Lady Rose's presence is requested in the council chamber," the man said. "As is that of her escort."

"They'll be there shortly," Sorche said, then shut the door and turned to Thorne. "You'd best let me comb your hair, too."

"If you insist." There was a wry twist to his lips as he sat up and pushed his hair off his shoulders.

Once Sorche declared us both ready, Thorne and I made our way through the castle's hallways to the council chamber.

"Will you hide your appearance?" I asked, giving him a sidelong glance.

I was used to the sharp planes of his face, his odd eyes and pointed ears. But, with the exception of Kian, the Fiorlanders had never seen a

Dark Elf. Thorne generally kept up an illusion of humanity whenever he was within the castle walls. And even in the forest with Kian, when the prince had accompanied us to and from Mistress Ainya's cottage— what now felt like decades ago.

To my knowledge, the first time Kian had seen the Dark Elves' true appearance was when Neeve smuggled him along to the *nirwen* harvest.

"Well, Prince Kian knows what I am," Thorne said dryly. "And the Fiorlanders deserve the truth. At least the ones we're going to meet with—though I don't imagine their entire populace needs to learn about the existence of Elfhame."

I nodded. In my opinion, it was high time Raine's allies were made aware of the Dark Elves. Fewer secrets between the kingdoms might have averted the chain of events that had left Neeve stranded in Elfhame.

"It will be Kian and his brother at the council," I said, inwardly wincing at the thought of meeting the illustrious Jenson. "And Jarl Eiric."

"And whoever, besides Kian's brother, is in charge of leading the Fiorland army."

And the king and his advisors, of course, including Sir Durum.

We arrived at the door of the council chambers, where two of the castle guard stood watch. They allowed us to enter, and the conversation rising from the table in the center of the room stilled. The quality of the silence deepened as the participants looked first at me, then at Thorne. Everyone I'd guessed at was present, including two more of the king's advisors, and a blonde-haired woman with smile lines about her eyes, sitting beside a young man who could only be Kian's brother.

Kian met my gaze and gave me a commiserating half-smile. Then he nodded to his brother and raised his brows, and my own smile flattened. I'd need to tell him soon that, having just escaped one marriage, I had no intention of being yoked into another.

But not in front of the entire council. I did retain some sense of diplomacy, after all. And despite my belief that there had been too much withheld concerning the Dark Elves, I wasn't planning to reveal my own sudden acquisition of sorcerous powers.

Honesty was good, but they didn't need to know *everything*.

The scrape of Lord Raine's chair was loud in the stillness as he stood. "Council, this is Princess Rose Valrois," he said. "And Thorne Windrift, the guardian of the forest."

Lord Thornelithiel Windrift, *Galadhir* of the Erynvorn, more like. I wondered if the king was referring to him so plainly in order to ease the shock of his decidedly nonhuman appearance—or if Lord Raine truly didn't know that Thorne was a lord in his own land.

The silence stretched out. Thorne stepped forward, gently gesturing me to remain beside the door. This was his test to face alone.

"Well met," he said, his voice steady. "I trust Prince Kian has told you that he's been among my people, in the land of Elfhame."

"The Dark Elves," Jarl Eiric said, his narrowed gaze fixed upon Thorne. "And you've been concealing your true nature from us all this time."

Thorne dipped his head in agreement, and perhaps apology—though everyone knew the true responsibility for that decision lay with the King of Raine.

"Elfhame," Kian's brother said thoughtfully. "Where time, apparently, runs along a different course?"

"Yes," Thorne said.

"Honestly, Jens." Kian frowned at his brother. "Do you really think I'd stay away for months without a word, risking the alliance between Raine and Fiorland?"

"It just seems so strange," Prince Jenson said.

"No stranger than a magical doorway in the middle of the forest, leading to an entirely different world?" Kian pressed. "You accepted that well enough."

"Because we had spies searching and you obviously hadn't left the country," his brother retorted. "If your body wasn't lying murdered in the depths of the forest, then you had to have been *somewhere*. And I doubt the local villages have such an elaborate manner of dressing."

I looked at Kian, belatedly realizing he still wore the ornate tunic and silken half cloak from the Nightshade Court. The garments seemed normal to my eye—until I compared them with the far simpler clothes the rest of the room wore. Of course, they'd all been riding to battle, while Kian was dressed to attend a royal wedding.

"Claiming that time passes differently certainly makes a handy excuse," the jarl said, giving Thorne another suspicious glance.

"Magic is inexplicable," Thorne said mildly, though there was a layer of steel in his voice. "If you'd like to step through the gateway to see for yourself, that can be arranged."

Jarl Eiric scowled, then smoothed the expression from his face. He would do well in the Nightshade Court, I thought—though I had no wish to foist him upon the Dark Elves.

"Come, sit." Lord Raine gestured to where I hovered at the doorway, and then to Thorne. "We can discuss this around the table, like civilized folk."

Kian beckoned me to the empty seat beside him, while Thorne took a chair near the end of the table. I wished I could stay beside him. Indeed, I wished we weren't even in the room at all, but back in the peaceful shadows of the Darkwood.

"Lady Rose," Prince Jenson said, rising to greet me. I liked him an infinitesimal amount better for not calling me a princess. "As you may have guessed, I am Kian's brother, Jenson. And this is our commander of the army, Merkis Inga Strond." He indicated the woman beside him.

I curtseyed, recalling from my studies with Miss Groves that *merkis* was the title of the monarchs of Fiorland's handpicked commander.

"Well met," Merkis Strond said. Her voice was low and throaty, with a warmth to it that made me think she laughed easily and often.

"It is an honor, Prince Jenson," I said, "and Merkis Strond. Welcome to Raine."

It was not as smoothly managed as my mother would have done, but since I hadn't actually been in the kingdom when the Fiorlanders were marching on Castle Raine, I could speak the words without irony.

A smile flitted across Prince Jenson's face, and the commander lifted one eyebrow in amusement, dimples showing in her cheeks. She seemed rather good-humored to be the hardened leader of the Fiorland army—but then again, perhaps I only thought that because I was used to Sir Durum's dour nature. Not all warriors were glum creatures, after all. Just look at Kian. Maybe Fiorland bred cheerful soldiers as a matter of course.

As soon as I was settled in my chair, the king turned to me. "Rose, please tell the council how it is that you are here, while my daughter is not." Though his voice was mild, his eyes were like granite.

I swallowed, thinking of how to explain in the simplest terms possible.

"The gateway must have an anchor between the worlds," Kian said softly to the Fiorlanders. "Neeve used to be that point."

"I was judged by the Dark Elf Oracles," I said, raising my voice for the entire table to hear. "They determined I could return with Prince Kian and keep the gateway from closing while Neeve—" The words caught in my throat. Nobody liked to remind a king that his daughter was sick.

"Continue." Lord Raine's voice was cold.

"My people are subject to a particular illness," Thorne said, saving me from having to answer. "Unfortunately, when Princess Neeve crossed between the worlds, the malady settled in her blood."

The king's hand clenched into a fist. "Is this illness fatal?"

"Without treatment, yes," Thorne said. "However, she is being well tended to by our healers."

"But for that, she must stay in Elfhame," Kian added, helping deflect the rising fury in Lord Raine's eyes. "At least for now."

"And will my daughter ever be able to return to Raine?" the king asked tightly.

"She will," Thorne said.

"She must," Kian echoed. "For I've asked for her hand in marriage, and she has accepted. As soon as she's able to reenter the mortal world, we'll be wed."

His blunt words were a stone flung into a pool, the ripples spreading. I expected the king to explode with rage. Instead, Kian's announcement seemed to defuse his anger.

"Rascal," Prince Jenson said, clapping his brother on the shoulder. "You were supposed to wait for our parents' approval."

Not to mention Lord Raine's. I shot the king a quick glance. For a moment, he looked aged and weary, like a man who had carried a heavy burden for long decades.

He loves Neeve, I realized. Though he almost never showed it. But he clearly wanted the best for his daughter, even though their ideas on what that might be had differed strongly over the years.

"If Neeve has said yes, then you have my blessing," Lord Raine finally said, nodding to Kian.

"Perhaps it can be a double wedding," Prince Jenson said quietly to his brother, a sly look in his eyes.

I squirmed in my chair. Prince Jenson seemed nice enough, but I wasn't going to marry him. Oh, but I was weary of princessing. I wished I could take off my crown and fling it upon the flagstones with a satisfying clang.

The flames within me stirred, half waking, and I concentrated on breathing slowly, lulling them back into quiescence.

Thorne gave me a look from down the table, concern in his dark eyes. Of everyone there, he was the only one who could sense my sorcerous power—but that didn't mean it could be ignored.

I shoved away the memory of the Nightshade throne room consumed by flames.

Any alliance I made, if I even chose to take that path, would have to come after I'd mastered my dangerous new magic. And who knew how long that might take?

※

THE COUNCIL MEETING FINALLY ENDED, and Thorne accompanied me back to my rooms.

"Now what?" I asked, pulling the crown from my head and flopping down into one of the chairs before the unlit hearth.

While I was gone, Sorche had made my bed and opened the windows, letting the warmth of the summer afternoon waft in. I pulled in a breath, smelling faint wood smoke from the kitchens and the distant scent of the Darkwood's cedar trees.

"I must return to the Nightshade Court soon," Thorne said, remaining standing.

"To tend to Neeve," I said, hating the edge in my voice.

He gave me a sharp look. "And to assure the Nightshade Lord that all is well in the mortal world, and Raine has not been invaded by a hostile army."

I nodded. The Fiorlanders would be departing the next day—including Kian, who I was sorry to see go, and his brother, whom I was not. Once Kian had reassured his parents, the King and Queen of Fiorland, of his continued good health, he'd return to Raine. And hopefully to Neeve, though it was impossible to say when she'd be able to step through the doorway between the worlds.

"Before I go," Thorne said, "I'll accompany you to Mistress Ainya's. We'll have to determine how best to go about your training."

I glanced up at him, gladness leaping through me. "You'll help me master my powers?"

"In whatever way I can." He gave me a rueful smile. "Do understand that I might be of very little help."

"Still, you know more about magic than anyone else here." I gestured to the castle and, by extension, all of Raine.

The only place that understood the fire sorcery better was Parnese —and I wanted nothing to do with the red priests. No, I'd stay here, and spend my time diligently working with Mistress Ainya. And Thorne, whenever he was in the mortal world. I smiled inwardly at the thought.

Then sobered, as I considered how strange it would feel to be alone in Castle Raine. No Neeve to accompany me into the forest. No Kian to tease me at weapons practice.

And when winter came, no dark-eyed *Galadhir* waiting for me beneath the cedar trees.

"I hope you won't spend too much time in Elfhame," I said, glancing at Thorne. "Doesn't the Darkwood need your protection?"

He tilted his head, as if listening to some distant music. "It's a strange thing, but the wards about the forest are quiet. Whatever was previously threatening the Darkwood has not returned."

My eyes widened with possibility. "Does that mean the forest is safe again?"

"As safe as ever—which, as you know, means plenty of hazards still abound."

I waved his words away. "But surely if I stay at the edges of the wood, all will be well."

"Rose." Mild exasperation shone in his eyes. "Please don't roam about the Darkwood when I'm not present."

"It won't be any fun without Neeve, anyway." I made an exaggerated pout.

"I'll tell her you miss her already." A smile flitted over his expression.

I nodded. It was true, and we both knew it. "I do."

But please don't go. I bit my tongue on the words. Thorne would do what he must.

"Tomorrow afternoon, we'll go see Mistress Ainya," he said.

After the Fiorlanders departed. I drew in a deep breath, suddenly weary at what the morrow would bring.

"Rest." He gave me a stern look, though his eyes were warm.

"What about you?" I nodded at the chair across from me. "I can bring you more pillows."

"I will spend the night in the Darkwood," he said. "Sleep well, Rose."

Before I could rise to wish him farewell—or do anything foolish, like try to embrace him—he slipped out the door.

It was still afternoon, though shadows were slanting low across the trees. If I went to bed now, I'd miss dinner. Which, frankly, wasn't a bad thing, for then I wouldn't have to politely deflect Prince Jenson's pointed attentions.

But I'd also miss my last chance to spend time with Kian, for who knew how many months? Certainly he wouldn't be able to return until spring, when the seas calmed. A little nap, I decided, and then I'd rise and put on my crown and try to behave as a princess ought, and not a confused girl full of untamed fire.

DINNER WAS A STRAINED AFFAIR. Everyone was on their best behavior, which resulted in stiff conversation and awkward silences. Even my mother's talents weren't enough to keep things convivial, though Merkis Strond, with her jovial manner, did manage to help. But the fact that the Fiorlanders were there because they'd landed their ships and marched their army into Raine was lost on no one. The king, of course, had forbidden anyone to oppose them, so there had been no bloodshed. But still, it made for an uncomfortable meal.

Someone—probably my mother—had arranged the seating so that the Fiorlanders were mingled with the courtiers of Raine instead of together in a block. Unfortunately, that put me between Kian and his brother, with Merkis Strond across the table from me.

She watched me interact with the princes, brows lifting with amusement whenever I turned the conversation away from myself or ignored Prince Jenson's compliments. Kian's brother certainly did his best to be charming, and under other circumstances I might have found him so. But Thorne took up all my heart, and so I was pleasant to the prince, but not overly encouraging.

"Rose," Kian said quietly to me, when his brother turned to converse with Sir Durum, "give Jens a chance. The two of you might suit, you know."

I knew otherwise, but out of consideration for our friendship, I gave him a smile.

"I'll try," I said.

And truly I did, but though Prince Jenson was well spoken and seemed sweet, I could not muster a shred of romantic interest toward him.

You deserve better, my little voice said, and I couldn't disagree. Even though Kian's brother might seem the obvious political choice for my future.

Finally, the meal ended. Everyone breathed a sigh of relief as the king and queen rose, dismissing the diners. Kian sent me a crooked smile.

"Are you entertaining visitors this evening, Princess Rose?" he asked.

I frowned at him. While I'd be happy to share a final evening in his company, I most emphatically did not want his brother to join us—which was certainly his intent.

"I believe I'll retire early," I said.

His expression fell. "Very well—if you insist."

"I do." I set my hand on his arm. "But I'll see you tomorrow morning, before you go. Come have a scone with me."

And if he dragged his brother along, I resolved not to complain.

CHAPTER 36

To my relief, Kian appeared alone at my door the next morning. I was somewhat presentable, as Sorche had roused me in time to don a pale gray gown and tie back my hair. She'd also arranged for the kitchens to send up a tray of pastries, along with a pot of strong tea, and I thanked her profusely for looking after me so well.

"We missed you, milady," she said, then took her leave with a conspiratorial smile.

I wondered if the servants still believed Kian and I were in love. Well, his marriage to Neeve would disabuse them of that notion. Provided my stepsister ever returned.

With a sigh, I leaned against my bed. Trisk mewed sleepily at me from the nest of covers, and I absently stroked her soft fur. She'd climbed up onto the bed sometime in the night, and I'd woken with her heavy warmth nestled against my legs.

"Thank you," I said softly to her.

My only answer was a sleepy purr.

Then Kian knocked on my door, and I went to let him in.

"Good morning," I said, stepping back. "I'm glad you didn't bring your brother."

"You're becoming as direct as Neeve," he said, shaking his head at me.

"Since she's not here, someone has to take up that role," I said, refusing to apologize, even as a pang for my sister went through me. "And really, Kian, I hardly know Jenson. Give it time."

Not that I was planning to change my mind, but I could humor him for the moment.

"We don't have time." He frowned at me and went to one of the chairs, pausing to pour a cup of tea and grab a scone from the tray.

"Certainly we do," I retorted, settling across from him and procuring my own cup. "We have months, if not years."

He gave me a sorrowful look. "Do you really think it will take that long for Neeve to return from Elfhame?"

"I don't know." I sighed, then took a sip of tea, trying to breathe its warmth into my body. "But you'll be back next summer."

"What will you do in the meantime?"

"Work on mastering my sorcerous powers, obviously." And hope they wouldn't prove to be too unruly. "Then the usual, I suppose. Study with Miss Groves. Train with Sir Durum. It will be strange here, with you and Neeve gone."

I hated to think of how empty the castle would feel. And cold. And dark.

"At least you'll have Thorne—until he returns to Elfhame for the winter." Kian sobered, leaning forward. "I can see that you want nothing to do with my brother, and I understand why. But you and Thorne really need to have a talk."

"About what? I can't ask him to take me back to the Nightshade Court, if that's what you mean."

Kian let out an impatient breath. "About your feelings for one another. Stars, Rose, you can be so blind sometimes."

I swallowed back my sharp reply, unwilling to argue with him on the verge of his departure.

"Did you and my sister have such a conversation?" I asked sweetly, instead. "It's not like Neeve to discuss her feelings."

"Which makes any admission on her part all the stronger," he said, a touch smugly.

"Wait." I blinked at him. "Did she really tell you she loves you?"

He took a sip of tea, then grinned at me. "Almost."

"Almost?" I shook my head. "You're a fine one to encourage me to bare my heart to Thorne, when your own fiancée won't admit her true feelings."

He held up one finger. "Ah! But she has them—and that's the most important step."

"Then by that reasoning, words are unnecessary."

I had no intention of confessing my feelings to the *Galadhir*. The last thing Thorne needed to contend with was a lovesick girl pining after him when he thought of her only as a friend. Such an admission would only make things unbearably awkward between us. Better to keep things as they were.

Kian tossed back the last of his tea, then stood.

"I need to finish packing. Take care of yourself, Rose."

I set my cup aside and got to my feet. "I'm going to miss you." I tried not to let my voice crack on the words.

He wrapped me in a brief, bittersweet embrace. "Come wave us off."

I nodded, then let him go. His footsteps echoed hollowly down the hall. I stood watching from my doorway, too aware of Neeve's empty rooms across the corridor. They were like a stone in my soul, an ache of absence I couldn't ignore.

For a moment I recalled the heartbreak of leaving behind my child-hood friends in Parnese. Paulette and Marco. I hadn't thought of them in years: their bright laughter faded from memory, the golden days we'd used to spend chasing about the sunlit marketplaces all but forgotten.

I'd survived that parting. I'd survive this one too, though it cut far deeper.

But, as Kian had said, I still had Thorne. At least somewhat, though he'd made it clear he'd be leaving soon to see how Neeve's healing was progressing.

I could write to her, I supposed, and Kian too. For my own sake more than theirs, as I suspected neither of them would be particularly good correspondents. But I could share my days with them in some small way, evoke their presences in my mind, even if I couldn't speak with them.

Slightly comforted by the thought, I stepped back into my rooms to finish my breakfast.

⚜

THE MORNING HAD TURNED CHILLY, clouds covering the sun in a perfect reflection of my mood as I stood on the steps of Castle Raine. In the courtyard below, the last of the Fiorlanders assembled. The bulk of the army, I gathered, had decamped from the meadows outside the castle and marched away at dawn. I could smell the char of their doused campfires in the breeze.

Kian and his brother stood beside their mounts, in quiet discussion with Lord Raine. Jarl Eiric hovered beside them, clearly anxious to depart, as Merkis Strond mustered out her final cohort of officers.

The king nodded, then turned and strode up the steps to where I waited beside Mama. I caught myself looking for Neeve, and once again her absence was a needle to my heart.

"Farewell!" Kian called, swinging up onto his horse.

His brother lifted his hand, clearly trying to catch my gaze. I waved in his general direction and kept my eyes on the middle distance. Jarl Eiric narrowed his eyes, and the commander of the army, with a quick grin, wheeled her mount and gestured for her fighters to ride out.

A flurry of motion, the clatter of hooves over cobblestones, cloaks flapping in the wind, and then they were gone. Off to Portknowe, where their ships waited, and then across the stretch of sea to Fiorland.

The breeze pulled at the edges of my cloak and teased my hair free to tickle my face. Mama declared with an exaggerated shiver that she was going inside. Lord Raine offered his arm, gave me an inscrutable look, then escorted his wife back into the castle.

I remained alone at the top of the steps. Beyond the castle walls, the Darkwood stretched—the shadows beneath the evergreens deep with magic and mystery. Thorne lay somewhere in that black reach of trees, holding a part of my heart, whether he knew it or not.

Beyond that, in the very center of the forest, the gateway waited. Two upright granite stones inscribed with glowing runes. Quiet, but not closed forever. I almost imagined I could feel its waiting presence, hooked into my soul.

Anchor point, the trees whispered as the breeze rustled the branches.

Not always, I thought back at the Darkwood. Only until Neeve was healed, and she could return to Raine and take up her rightful place as the heir to the throne, Kian at her side.

Meanwhile, I was back in the familiar world, where the sun shone, time unspooled at its proper pace, and no jewel-hard Dark Elf lords were waiting to pounce upon me and wrest promises I couldn't give. I had the solace of the Darkwood, and, for now, I had Thorne.

And most of all, I had my newfound magic, the fire sorcery that had at last claimed me on my eighteenth birthday.

Even now I could feel the flames stirring restlessly, like a wild creature on the edge of waking. I'd best have a leash at the ready when it woke, I thought with a faint shudder, recalling the fire raging uncontrolled through the throne room in the Nightshade Court.

I thought of the book I'd discovered concealed in Castle Raine's library—strange recipes hiding a spy's account of infiltrating the Temple of the Twin Gods in Parnese. Neeve had confiscated the book and given it to her father, who'd shared it with Thorne. I wondered if the *Galadhir* still had it. Surely it could be of use in my new training.

Stars knew, I'd need all the help I could get.

CHAPTER 37

After lunch, I waited for Thorne to come fetch me for Mistress Ainya's. He was late, and I soon grew impatient at his absence. Perhaps I'd misunderstood, and he planned to meet me at the edge of the Darkwood. I donned my favorite blue cloak—mended and laundered by the servants, though I'd scarcely been back a day—and headed for the small door in the castle walls.

The stretch of grassy meadow between Castle Raine and the Darkwood was studded with daisies. The afternoon had warmed, though the sky was still skimmed with silver clouds. I pushed back my hood and breathed deeply, welcoming the scent of moist loam, the tang of the evergreens.

To my disappointment, Thorne was not waiting for me in the shadows beneath our customary cedar tree. I scuffed at the needles under my feet, thinking of the night I'd spent in the Erynvorn. Though that forest had been awe-inspiring, I preferred the normal-sized trees of the human world. Most of all I was happy to know that, even hidden behind the clouds, the sun whirled across the sky on a daily basis.

A rustle in the undergrowth made me turn, a greeting for Thorne on my lips. I blinked, my welcome dying when I saw no one was there.

Then, as if kicked up by a flurry of wind, a pile of sticks and leaves hurtled toward me. I glimpsed beady black eyes and pointed mouths filled with serrated teeth.

Boglins.

It had been years since they'd first attacked me in the forest. Thorne had dealt with them then, and the sticklike little creatures hadn't bothered me since—until now.

"Shoo!" I yelled, keeping my voice strong. I recalled that they fed on fear, and tried to tamp down the sudden worry prickling the back of my neck.

They kept coming, clinging to my cloak, diving for my ankles. I felt the first bite, just above my boot, and gritted my teeth to keep from crying out.

"Get off!" I kicked and whirled, trying to shake off the ferocious little things. The beginnings of panic ignited in my chest. Where was the *Galadhir?*

Another bite, this time on my wrist. They were climbing higher. What if they reached my face?

Think, Rose.

My single short blade would be useless against so many of the creatures. I couldn't run or they'd swarm me in an instant. All I had to defend myself was my newly awakened power. I wasn't certain I could call on it, but I must try.

"*Esfera,*" I gritted out, afraid to speak the entire chant.

I felt a flicker move through me, the power responding like a wayward child who hears their name called but refuses to acknowledge the summons.

"*Esfera.*" This time more forcefully, even as I swatted a boglin away from my neck.

My palms grew suddenly hot, and I held them out, willing fire to materialize in my hands. The boglins clinging to my sleeves let go and skittered away, but a dozen were still attached to my cloak, my skirts. They made a dry rustling noise as they clambered up my clothing.

My inner flames were tantalizingly close. If I just reached a little further, I knew I could touch them. I stretched my hands out and *pulled.*

Something twisted inside me, and with a whoosh, my hands

ignited. I bit back a yelp, staring at the red and yellow flames engulfing my fingers. Miraculously, I was unburned. The fire felt no warmer than sunlight upon my skin.

The rest of the boglins fell away like old leaves, leaving a few rips in my cloak, and whisked back into the shadows.

"Rose! What are you doing?"

I glanced up to see Thorne striding toward me from beneath the trees, his eyes filled with shock. The flames around my hands went out like a snuffed candle.

"I... The boglins..." I tried to form a coherent sentence, but he kept coming until he reached me and grabbed me by the shoulders.

"I thought you'd set yourself ablaze." His voice was stark with fear.

"No." I stared at him. "I was just trying to drive off the boglins. The fire didn't hurt me."

"Thank the moons." He pulled me against him, holding me closely for a heartbeat.

I was just beginning to let myself relax into his embrace when he set me back at arm's length, his expression hard. "Don't summon fire in the Darkwood again."

I stared at him, beginning to tremble with the awful realization that I could have easily caught the trees on fire, if the flames had chosen to slip from my hands. For a moment, I had a horrible vision of the evergreens burning, black smoke billowing through the air as the Darkwood blazed with sorcerous fury.

"I'm a danger to the forest," I said softly. "Oh, Thorne, no wonder..."

My legs could no longer hold me, and I sank down onto the needle-strewn moss. After a moment I realized my left arm was itching terribly, with a sensation bordering on pain. I pushed my sleeve up, to see that the skin of my inner elbow was red and blistered with small bumps. The leaf etched there glowed with a flat green light that faded as I watched.

"That day I first arrived in Raine," I said shakily, "the forest tried to strangle me. How did the Darkwood know that I'd have fire sorcery? I was scarcely more than a child at the time." I looked up at him. "You said I'd triggered the wards. Is this why?"

"It must be," he said softly, going to his knees before me. "The trees are not fond of fire, though it is a vital element." Our gazes met, held. "And it burns so brightly in the dark."

I caught my breath at the look in his eyes. Kian's admonition that Thorne and I must talk rang in my ears, and Neeve's accusation that I was breaking the *Galadhir's* heart...

"Thorne—"

"Hold still."

He set his cool fingers to my arm, murmuring a phrase in elvish. The blisters faded and the irritation eased, though my skin still buzzed softly with discomfort.

"You didn't have that reaction when your fire came in Elfhame, did you?" he asked.

I pressed my lips together and shook my head. "Will this happen every time I try to use my power in the mortal world?"

It was a dreadful possibility, and I shoved the thought away. *No.* I could not have come so close to having magic of my own, only to be unable to use it without hurting myself.

"I don't know," he said. "Perhaps it was a combination of summoning flame here, in the Darkwood, and my presence. Mistress Ainya can tell us more. I hope."

"Me too." And if the herbwife had no answers, I'd just have to keep searching.

He rose, then held out a hand to help me to my feet. We stood a moment, hands clasped. The trees about us hushed in a soft breeze, and birds chirped from a nearby thicket of berry briars.

I love you, Thorne.

The breath caught in my throat, my pulse sparking as the words burned in my mouth. Something moved across his expression, a combination of yearning and despair.

"Thorne," I began again, but he released my hand and took a step back.

"The *cailleach* is waiting," he said abruptly. "Lead the way. I want to make sure the forest lets you pass freely."

I frowned at him—but he was right; we needed to continue to

Mistress Ainya's. Now was not the time to confess the depth of my emotion for him. Though I couldn't wait much longer.

It seemed I'd decided to tell him how I felt.

I couldn't remember consciously arriving at that point, but now that I'd reached it, there was no going back. No matter the consequences.

He gestured me forward, and I set out on the trail leading to the *cailleach's* cottage. I understood his concern, after what had just happened. If the Darkwood decided to impede my passage, it would be maddeningly difficult to pass through—sharp briars tangling about my feet and snagging my hair, the trail obstructed with roots and rocks, and a multitude of swarming insects swarming to deliver painful little stings.

I'd experienced it before and had no desire to do so again.

"Why didn't my flames trigger the wards when I called fire to fight the boglins?" I asked as we wove between the rough-barked cedars. Whatever the reason, though, I was glad the Darkwood hadn't decided to strangle me.

"Your binding, I think. Either it restricted your flames, or the link between you was strong enough that the forest trusted you not to harm it. Perhaps both."

I thought of the blistering on my arm. I hadn't come away unscathed, and clearly the binding hadn't protected me from a boglin attack. The Darkwood wasn't a monolithic entity, though, as I'd come to learn over the years. Parts of it would let me pass unharmed, while other parts would, for instance, attempt to drown me.

"Is it safe for me to come into the forest?" I glanced up at the feathery branches of the evergreens overhead.

Thorne was silent a long moment, until I finally shot a questioning look at him over my shoulder.

"I'm not sure," he said slowly. "I would like to say yes—but only in my company."

I let out an impatient breath. "How am I supposed to go to and from Mistress Ainya's when you're not here to escort me? What about the hobnies? Don't they owe me a few favors?"

"I'm afraid Neeve has called in most of their debts already," Thorne said.

"That's not fair." I halted, pivoting to face him. "We both saved them."

In fact, I'd done most of the rescuing, with the aid of the small scissors I still kept in my belt pouch. The grumpy little creatures had the habit of getting their beards caught in the most unlikely, and often perilous, situations.

"It was necessary," Thorne said calmly. "They know more secret ways through the forest than even I, as *Galadhir*, am aware of. And it was essential for Neeve to meet with me to finish her magical training."

So that was how my sister had managed to slip away. Drat her.

I folded my arms, but my irritation couldn't mask how much I missed Neeve—her sharp silences, her unapologetic opinions. The forest seemed smaller with her gone, the shadows less mysterious, the air emptied of adventure.

"You'll have to take the long way," Thorne said. "Through the village."

I sighed. Little Hazel was a pleasant enough place, but quite ordinary, for all that it abutted an enchanted forest. They had a spring festival that Neeve and I had attended once, and there was an alehouse that I believed Kian used to sneak out to from time to time. Mostly, the village provided food and goods to the castle, and many of the servants of Castle Raine dwelt there.

I turned and continued down the pathway. "How often will you be away in Elfhame?" I tried not to sound too mournful about the prospect.

"It depends. I must see how Neeve's healing is progressing, and balance that with how much the Darkwood has need of me."

"The forest isn't the only thing in Raine that needs you," I said, a bit tartly.

"As I said, I'll be of little help to you in mastering your powers." There was a hollow note in his voice. "I'm sure you and Mistress Ainya will make fine progress without me."

At that, I looked over my shoulder at him once more. "I don't want you to leave."

"I know." He summoned a crooked smile for me, though his eyes were sad.

What are you thinking, Thorne? I wanted to take him by the shoulders and shake him, demand he tell me honestly who it was that he loved. Was it me? If so, then why did he persist in looking so unhappy?

Maybe my hopeful heart was wrong. Maybe it truly had been Neeve all along. My mood dimmed even as the sky overhead cleared, sunlight slanting warmly through the trees.

The path branched at a mossy stump crowned by a graceful sapling, which had grown taller since the last time I walked that trail. I took the turning toward Mistress Ainya's cottage, and a short time later, we came to her clearing. The air was fragrant with the profusion of flowers and herbs growing about her home. Vibrant orange and cool purple blooms nodded in the breeze, set off against the whitewashed walls.

I lifted the gate latch and stepped through into her garden. Bees hummed contentedly among the rosemary and mint. A bi-colored rose I didn't remember seeing before trailed up the arbor beside the cottage door. The petals—red as blood, white as snow—shone lushly against the deep green leaves.

Before I could knock, the door swung open.

"Come in, come in!" Mistress Ainya said, a smile beaming from her wizened face. "I'm so glad to see you."

Unlike the sapling in the forest, she'd grown even smaller since the last time I saw her. I wondered, in a moment of whimsy, if she'd shrink away year by year until she was no bigger than my thumb, and then transform herself into a butterfly and float away into the forest.

Thorne and I entered her cottage. It was as neat as ever, the flag-stones swept, bunches of herbs hanging to dry from the ceiling. The herbwife bustled to the hearth and swung the blackened kettle off the fire. Whenever anyone arrived, it was her custom to make tea, and I smiled at the familiar sight of her strewing handfuls of herbs into her glazed brown teapot.

"The *Galadhir* tells me you've suddenly come into sorcerous power," Mistress Ainya said, bringing the teapot and three cups to the table where Thorne and I had seated ourselves.

I looked at him. "You visited already?"

"Yesterday evening," the herbwife confirmed. "This late onset of power is fascinating, I must admit."

"And concerning," Thorne said.

I folded my arms, frowning. "Both of you told me I had no magic." And I'd suffered for it, for years.

"None that I could sense," Mistress Ainya said amiably. "Fate has always been woven thick about you, Rose. Perhaps we weren't meant to know of your sorcery until it was time."

"Or her power was deliberately hidden." Thorne didn't seem nearly as cheerful about it. Then again, I'd just avoided burning his forest down.

"Isn't that what I said?" The herbwife turned her piercing blue eyes on him. "But however it happened, Rose has power now, and we must do our best to help her master it."

"Yes." I nodded fervently. "The sooner the better."

"After tea." Mistress Ainya swirled the teapot a moment. "First things first."

She poured out three mugs of the herbal brew. I held mine under my nose, inhaling. The scent of mint and sage made me think of the tonic she'd had me take, and for the first time I wondered if it had played a part in the emergence of my powers.

"Do you think Rose's presence in your world triggered her latent sorcery?" Mistress Ainya asked, handing Thorne his tea.

"Perhaps." He sent me a look, his dark eyes serious.

"Does every human who enters Elfhame develop magic?" I pondered aloud, then shook my head at the obvious answer. "No. Kian was entirely unaffected."

"You are special, Rose," Thorne said.

I'd always wanted to hear him say those words, but never so somberly, with a hint of wariness in his gaze. Glumly, I took a sip of my tea and tried not to burn my tongue.

"There are instances of power coming late," Mistress Ainya said, settling across from me. "Though generally it is a sign of weak ability."

"Rose's ability is far from weak," Thorne said flatly.

"I'll be curious to see for myself." The herbwife smiled at him. "No need to be so concerned, *Galadhir*. Between the two of us, we'll be able to school Rose just as well as we did Neeve."

I glanced at her. "I've wondered—you have human magic. How were you able to teach my sister? I thought most of her tutoring came from Thorne."

"Oh, it did," the herbwife agreed. "But certain elements of magic wielding are the same. The concepts of control, of balance, of transformation and replenishment, of intent—those can be taught to anyone, regardless of the type of power."

"So, the theories of magic," I said. "I'm willing to learn those, of course."

Mistress Ainya let out a cackle of laughter. "Child, what do you think you've been doing here all these years?"

I narrowed my eyes at her. "Sweeping the floor. Sorting herbs. Picking through lentils and peas."

"Balance. Intent. Control." She nodded at me, mirth bright in her eyes. "You've learned more than you know."

Lips twisted, I considered her words. Considered that, despite my lack of formal training, I'd been able to exercise *some* command over my newfound power.

I shot her a look. "Does that mean you thought I'd gain magic after all?"

"It's best to be prepared for any eventuality," she said. "And at the very least, I had a clean floor and nicely sorted legumes." She laughed again, and even Thorne's expression eased.

I finished my tea, setting the empty mug down on the wooden table with a thump. "I'm ready."

The herbwife's expression grew serious as she pushed her chair back and stood.

"I presume you have cast wards of protection over your cottage?" Thorne asked, moving his tea aside.

"What kind of *cailleach* would I be otherwise?" Mistress Ainya shook her head at him. "But I will invoke a second circle about us, to be safe."

"I recommend it," Thorne said.

I bit my lip. It certainly wasn't my intent to set the herbwife's cottage on fire, but precautions seemed like a good idea.

"Stay there," Mistress Ainya told me when I started to rise.

She selected a few herbs and crumbled them on the floor around the table, encircling me and Thorne. While she did so, she chanted softly beneath her breath. At the end, she clapped her hands together, making me jump.

"Good," Thorne said, though I couldn't sense any difference in our surroundings.

"Ready, Rose?" Mistress Ainya asked.

I nodded, pulse notching up.

She came behind me and set her hands on my shoulders. "Just breathe normally."

I tried to, but it was difficult to keep my breath easy. What if my power come roaring back? What if it didn't?

"Now," the herbwife said, her voice calm. "See if you can summon your magic."

Fire, I thought. *Come.*

It didn't, of course. I narrowed my eyes and balled my hands into fists. *Flame! Esfera!*

A sluggish stirring, the barest glow of embers.

"Rose." Thorne leaned forward across the table. "Give me your left hand."

Slowly, I reached for him. "Why?"

"The Darkwood's binding might be interfering with your ability." He clasped my fingers. "Let me see if I—"

As if it had only been waiting for his touch, fire roared up inside me. Blue flame and red ignited on the tabletop, reaching for the dried herbs overhead. The circle scattered on the floor flared, the smell of scorched fennel stinging my nose.

"Let go!" Mistress Ainya cried, even as she hauled my chair back from the table with surprising strength.

The moment our hands parted, the fire died. Thorne looked paler than ever, and my chest was tight with exertion, as though I'd just raced heedlessly through the woods.

"What..." I swallowed, then turned to look at the *cailleach*. "What was that?"

Expression grim, she shook her head slowly. "Ah, Rose. It's worse than I feared."

CHAPTER 38

"Worse?" I stared at Mistress Ainya, the back of my neck prickling with anxiety.

She nodded gravely. "Not only is your sorcery untamed, it's drawing power from those around you. *Galadhir*, did you not notice the siphoning of your wellspring?"

Thorne, looking surprisingly vulnerable, glanced at the herbwife. "I thought... I assumed my wellspring was still depleted."

"If it is, then you have Rose to thank," she said tartly. "I've no idea how, as such a thing is supposed to be impossible, but it seems she's pulling magic from sources outside herself."

"How do I stop that from happening?" I asked, a touch desperately. No wonder the Oracles had wanted me gone from Elfhame immediately.

"Ah, that's a tangle." Mistress Ainya folded her arms over her belly and regarded me intently.

I met her gaze, hoping she might read some kind of answer in my eyes. By the bright seas, I had no idea how to go about controlling this so-called siphoning.

"Training, and lots of it," the *cailleach* said.

"Internal warding, perhaps?" Thorne looked at her. "Rose could learn how to mirror shield."

Mistress Ainya nodded thoughtfully. "Something of the sort might do. Though retraining her magic to draw on her own internal power instead of external sources won't be as easy as learning a simple shield."

"I'll try my hardest," I said. "I haven't waited my whole life for this just to fail."

I'd done hard things before, thrown myself upon difficulties that cut me to the bone, and kept going. To control fire sorcery of my own, I'd do almost anything.

Thorne turned his amber-flecked gaze upon me. "You'll be fighting against yourself, I fear. If Mistress Ainya is correct, then you must learn to harness your power tightly to keep it from running wild—yet at the same time, if you control it too strictly, it will not respond at all."

Some of my dismay must have shown on my face, for his expression softened.

"Small steps," the herbwife said. "Keep your wards up, Thorne, so that Rose cannot access your power. Now, try again. Call your fire."

I narrowed my eyes, reaching deep into myself for the restless flames.

"*Esfera,*" I whispered, cupping my hand and imagining flickers of fire springing up in my palm.

Something inside me stretched. *Reached.* For a moment, I felt embers, warm against my skin.

I leaned forward, focusing my will on summoning the flame. Surely there was a shimmer of heat pooling in my palm. *Come,* I told it.

There was a sudden wrench, a feeling of darkness. The beginnings of fire in my hand extinguished, like a candle doused with water.

Mistress Ainya gave Thorne a sharp look. "Did you sense it?"

He nodded, expression unhappy. "That's a powerful seeking spell. And you believe Rose is calling upon it unconsciously?"

"I've no idea what you're even talking about," I said irritably. "So how could I be doing it on purpose?"

"Of course you're not channeling it deliberately," the herbwife said, scooping up the teapot to refill with hot water. "Rose, you must come back every other day. It's a difficult problem, but we'll find a way through."

"What about the book?" I looked at Thorne. "The one with the red priests' incantations—could that help me? Do you still have it?"

"I returned it to the king," he said. "But I've no doubt he will lend it to you. We all want you to succeed."

Before I steal every shred of magic in the kingdom and then burn it all down, I thought grimly.

Mistress Ainya poured us all fresh cups of tea, and then she and Thorne became engrossed in trading magical theories. I slumped back in my chair, listening. Even though the conversation was all about me, I had nothing to contribute. I'd no idea how to cast wards of protection, or invoke containment spells, and the only binding I'd ever been part of had marked me indelibly.

And almost killed me.

Perhaps that incident had been some kind of backlash, for trying to tap the Darkwood's magic—if such a thing were even possible. I sighed, my thoughts whirling. My left hand ached as though my pinky had been sheared off recently, instead of eleven years ago.

"Once I return to Elfhame, I'll consult the Oracles," Thorne said. "And speak with Neeve."

Neeve. I thought back to the strange incidents that had befallen us over the years: the Yule Feast, the battles against drakes and basilisks. The way she seemed to sense magic around me—even if, perhaps, it wasn't my own.

"She's always thought I was responsible for calamities, like setting the tapestries on fire at the feast," I said. "Though she could never explain why. Is it possible I was accessing her power?"

Mistress Ainya pursed her lips. "Very possible. I'd be curious to know her thoughts on this."

Thorne rubbed his forehead with one pale hand. "I'll ask."

"Finish your tea," the herbwife said. "It's quite restorative. I'll show Rose the rudiments of mirror shielding."

He nodded, and Mistress Ainya settled across from me.

"Calm your mind," she said, as if she knew how my thoughts were swirling. "Then imagine a large sphere, mirrored on the outside, so that anything outside it is reflected back. Do you see it?"

I nodded, holding the image in my thoughts.

"Place the sphere around you," she continued. "It encloses and protects you."

I did as she said, imagining myself inside a shiny, safe bubble. A faint tickling sensation made me shift in my chair.

The herbwife leaned forward. "Don't lose focus. I'm testing your shield."

I tried to hold still, ignoring the strange feeling even as it increased in intensity. It moved to an uncomfortable tingling, as though my arms and legs had fallen asleep, then a series of sharp prickles.

"Is it necessary to push her so hard?" Thorne asked, with a look at Mistress Ainya.

"The world will not go easy on her," the *cailleach* replied. "We must not either. Breathe, Rose."

I pulled in a breath, trying not to wince. It felt like I was standing under a hailstorm of small, pointed rocks. My left arm itched, my pinky stub throbbed in time with my heartbeat. It seemed as through the protective sphere around me was shrinking.

My fire woke, leaping up like a startled creature. It *reached*, and the shield popped like a soap bubble.

"Hold back your power," Mistress Ainya said sharply.

I squeezed my eyes shut and wrestled the flames back down. *Calma*, I told it. *Calma. You are my power, and you must obey.* Slowly, the heat inside me subsided. When I felt as though I had it back under control, I took a deep breath and opened my eyes.

Both Thorne and the herbwife were regarding me intently. The *Galadhir* looked concerned, but Mistress Ainya seemed merely thoughtful.

"How did I do?" I asked, my fingers worrying at the red ring on my right hand.

"Quite well, until the end," she said. "You are strong, Rose, and were able to deflect almost all of my seeking spells."

"The mirror shield offers little protection against a direct attack, however," Thorne said. "It might withstand a single blast of arcane power, but then it will shatter."

The *cailleach* gave him a reproving look. "That's not the point of this exercise. Rose isn't going to become embroiled in sorcerous fights."

I certainly hoped not, though I couldn't forget the vision of facing my stepsister in battle—fire at my hands, a sword in hers.

"I know," Thorne said. "I just wanted to make sure Rose was aware of the shield's limitations. Just in case."

I nodded slowly. He knew of the vision Neeve and I had shared, and no doubt had been thinking of it, even as I had.

"Do you feel strong enough to try a variation on the shield?" Mistress Ainya asked me.

"Yes," I said immediately.

"Don't overtax yourself," Thorne said, a furrow between his brows.

I frowned back at him. "This is important."

"So is your health."

"Settle yourself," Mistress Ainya told him. "Rose is wise enough to tell us if she's too drained to continue."

I shot him a superior look, as though the herbwife's confidence in me was warranted. In truth, I wasn't at all certain I understood the full strength of my power, or how I'd know if was overusing it.

Thorne's mouth twisted, and I knew he wasn't fooled—but at least he stopped arguing.

I turned back to the herbwife. "There's another way to shield?"

"Aye." She leaned forward, hands loosely clasped in her lap. "This time, imagine that the *inside* of the sphere is mirrored. Thorne and I both know how to protect ourselves, but this will keep your power from drawing upon unshielded external sources."

Like Neeve, I guessed. Or maybe even the Darkwood itself.

"Will it hurt, to have my power reflected back at me?" I asked.

"It shouldn't. But if it does, even the smallest amount, you must tell us right away."

Wonderful. With my luck, I'd probably blast myself with a terrible headache. But there was no way to find out except by doing.

Once again, I imagined the sphere, this time with the reflection turned inward. "I'm ready."

Mistress Ainya began poking me with light—there was no other way I could explain the sensation. It didn't tickle, nor did it hurt particularly. I felt like I was being prodded along, like an unruly sheep being herded away from a lush patch of clover.

Esfera, rise, I told my power.

It leaped up, as though it had only been pretending to sleep. Again, that sensation of reaching out—but this time with no success. The flames in my belly burned hotter, pulling, pulling...

Thorne winced. "Strengthen your shield, Rose."

I furrowed my brow in concentration and imagined the mirrors shining back at me, containing the fire. *Stay here,* I thought at it. *You are strong enough on your own.*

The heat faded, the flames receding sulkily. I tried to hold on to them, to shape them, but they slipped out of my grasp, withdrawing to simmer just below the surface. Scowling, I leaned forward, trying to reach the fire in my mind.

Esfera, I thought, *come to me.*

No response. Mistress Ainya and Thorne both watched me closely.

Come!

No response. It seemed my powers could be as sulky and stubborn as myself. After several more tries, I slumped back in my chair, defeated.

"Are you all right?" Thorne asked, rising to come to my side. "Did containing your power cause any pain?"

"No." I frowned. "It just...went away."

"Hmm." Mistress Ainya gave me a considering look. "That's something, at any rate."

I supposed she was right. If I could force my flames back on themselves, then at least I was in no danger of setting the world afire. But if my powers weren't seeking outward, it seemed they wouldn't respond at all. It wasn't fair.

Not that I had a right to expect fairness. I sighed, and Thorne set a hand on my shoulder.

"Enough for today," he said. "Are you ready to return to the castle?"

The cold, empty castle.

"I suppose." I forced myself to straighten, suddenly aware of the weariness fraying the edges of my thoughts.

"Learning magic is draining," Mistress Ainya said with a keen look. "Make sure you rest between sessions and give yourself time to recover." She turned to Thorne. "That goes for both of you. Come back in two days. In the meantime, Rose, practice the mirror shield."

"Which way?" I asked. "Reflecting in, or out?"

She nodded approvingly. "Both have their uses. Keeping your sorcery from drawing on external sources is a necessity. And one never knows when it might be a good idea to hide your power."

"I'll try both directions, then." Though I wasn't certain I'd be able to succeed at either without her magic nudging me along.

"I am returning to Elfhame," Thorne said gravely. "Rose will visit alone next time, by way of the village."

"By herself?" the herbwife said. "That doesn't seem wise."

"She will be accompanied by a castle guard."

I looked at Thorne. "Are you strong enough to open the door between the worlds?" Especially since I'd apparently been trying to draw power from his wellspring.

"I believe so. I spent the night in the gateway clearing, sleeping between the stones." He gave me a wry look. "It was nearly as restful as the healer's enclave. If I sleep there again tonight, I'll be able to open the doorway tomorrow when the sun rises."

Mistress Ainya nodded sagely. "An auspicious time. How long will you be gone?"

I was glad she asked the question burning on my tongue, so that I didn't have to.

"A week in the mortal world. Perhaps a little longer."

"Well." The herbwife clicked her tongue against her teeth. "Come back as soon as you may. Now off you go."

She made shooing motions with her hands. I stood and let Thorne escort me to the cottage door.

"Thank you," I said, pausing on the threshold.

"Don't thank me yet," she said. "You've a hard road ahead, and no mistake. But it can be traveled, one step at a time."

I nodded, then went out into her garden, rich with summer. The sun played tag with the clouds as I led the way from the herbwife's clearing into the sweetly scented shadows of the Darkwood, Thorne at my back. With every step, my heartbeat raced.

Tell him, tell him.

Finally, midway between Mistress Ainya's cottage and Castle Raine, I halted. The trees rose around us, branches moving softly in the wind. Sunshine dappled the lacy ferns edging the path, and little star-shaped flowers dotted the moss beneath our feet.

"What's the matter?" Thorne asked, quickly coming to my side.

He scanned the way ahead, then turned to look at me, his expression somber.

"Nothing. Everything." I met his eyes and forced my voice to steadiness. "There is something I must tell you."

CHAPTER 39

"What is it?" Thorne held my gaze, concern shining in his dark eyes. "Are you suffering aftereffects from practicing the mirror shield?"

"No." I pulled in a steadying breath.

Now that the moment was upon us, I nearly lost my courage. But he was returning to Elfhame, and I couldn't let him go without speaking the truth of my feelings.

"Thorne..." I squeezed my eyes closed a moment, then opened them.

He regarded me so patiently that I nearly burst into tears. He had always been there, I realized—at my side to lend a steadying hand or a kind word, to save me from drowning or to banish poison from my blood.

I swallowed back my fear, then said the words emblazoned upon my heart.

"I love you."

There. It was out in the open, like a tender bloom unfurling in the spring sun.

The forest went suddenly still, the birds quieting, even the ever-present breeze ceasing to stir and sigh among the branches.

The flower of my hope began to wither as Thorne stared at me with a stunned expression.

"I just wanted you to know," I said hurriedly. "You don't have to say—"

He took me by the arms, pulled me to him, and pressed his mouth to mine in a fervent kiss. Stars flew through me as our lips met. My hands went to his shoulders, and I gripped him fiercely in return. We were flying between the worlds together—nothing but sweetness and sparks and two souls soaring through the dark.

The kiss lasted forever—and no time at all. He lifted his head and stared down into my eyes with a conflicted expression.

"Rose. I should never have—"

"Stop it. Don't you dare apologize for kissing me, Thorne Windrift."

"But—"

"Shh." I set a finger across his mouth. "I have loved you since the moment I first saw you in the Darkwood. But I always thought Neeve held your heart. It's only recently that I've let myself hope that, maybe, there was a place there for me."

He smiled crookedly, and I let my hand drop.

"It has always been you," he said simply. "Neeve is my charge, and my friend. But your joy and determination have been the sun to my moon, ever since you stormed into the Darkwood and upended everything I thought I knew."

I stared at him. "Then why did you never tell me? Why did you let me believe you loved another?"

A shadow crossed his face. "I knew I must wait until you came of age—and then, before I could confess my feelings, I had a vision."

My hands tightened on his shoulders. "What vision?"

"Of you standing, wrists clasped with the Nightshade Lord, about to speak the Rune of Binding." His voice was bleak. "After that, I could say nothing to you of my feelings."

My heart was a lock, his words a thousand keys opening doors I never even knew had been closed. So much made sense now—his behavior at the Nightshade Court, his offer to help me escape into the

Erynvorn to escape the wedding that would surely break both our hearts.

"Now what?" I whispered, staring into the amber-flecked darkness of his eyes.

"I don't know." He sounded so vulnerable, as though the mantle of *Galadhir* had fallen away and he was just a young man grappling with feelings he could scarcely control.

I understood completely. The world had changed in a heartbeat, in a kiss.

"I know you must go to Elfhame," I said. "But when you return, we'll find some way forward."

His lips tightened. "I cannot claim your affections, Rose. You have a different future ahead. What about Kian's brother, and the expectations of the king—"

I gave a sharp shake of my head. "It's my life. My choice. And I choose you. If you'll have me."

He lifted his hand to cup my cheek, and the tenderness in his expression made me dizzy.

"If this is truly what you want," he said softly, "then yes. A thousand times over. But what about when I must cross between the worlds? What of the winters? I fear I would be a poor mate, leaving you so much alone."

I felt my smile tip, but stared resolutely into his eyes. "We'll figure out an answer. Maybe the Oracles will have some ideas." I wondered briefly if those white-garbed figures had foreseen this, too. "Neeve and Kian face the same problem, don't forget. Somehow, there must be a solution."

"Then we will look for it." The hopeful light in his eyes dimmed slightly.

I squeezed his shoulders. "Don't you dare give up on us."

"I won't." He gave me a rueful smile. "I wish things weren't so complicated. I wish we could stay here in the Darkwood forever, and not worry about rulers or kingdoms or boundaries between worlds."

"Now you sound like me." I went up on my toes and brushed my mouth against his.

I'd meant it to be a quick kiss, but he wrapped his arms about me again, pulling me close, and I was filled with brightness. A thrush lilted its liquid song from a far thicket. The forest stirred, the boughs hushing overhead as the breeze teased my hair free to tickle both our faces. It seemed the Darkwood approved.

At least for now.

Finally, Thorne stepped back. "Much as I want nothing more than to stay here and kiss you all afternoon, we must get you back to the castle."

"And then you have to go." I glanced down, trying to ignore the sting of tears pricking my eyes. "But before you do, let me write to Neeve."

I'd have to tell her she'd been right all along. Not only about my magic's role in our various perils and adventures, but also about Thorne's feeling for me. Drat her.

He nodded, and we continued through the forest. The mosses were soft underfoot, the sunshine filtering through the trees, the scent of loam and cedars perfuming the air. A poignant feeling settled over me—a mixture of delight and wonder that Thorne did, indeed, love me, tempered with the melancholy fact of his imminent departure. Not to mention the problems we would have to face.

But he'd be back soon, and I had to trust we'd be able to find a path through whatever thickets and brambles lay ahead.

We reached the moat of grasses separating the Darkwood from Castle Raine, and he stepped with me into the afternoon sunshine. The guards nodded to him in greeting as we passed through the courtyard and into the castle, and it gave me hope. He might be *Galadhir* and a Dark Elf, but he was accepted by the people of Raine.

At least the ones who dwelt near the edge of the forest.

In my sitting room, I grabbed a sheet of paper and pencil from my shelves, remainders of my short-lived artistic attempts, and sat down to write to my sister.

DEAR NEEVE,

Try not to be too smug when you read this, but you were right about some of the magic being my fault. And about me and Thorne. If I were there, I'd be glaring at you in affectionate annoyance, you know.

As it is, Thorne can explain it to you, and you can give him your superior smile. I'll just imagine it from over here.

Kian left this morning for Fiorland, and that was sad, but his brother went too, which I didn't mind at all. They're pushing for a match between me and Prince Jenson—but I won't accept it, of course. Especially not now that Thorne and I have finally confessed our feelings.

Oh, I know, it took far too long. I should have listened to you—but you know how stubborn I can be. I wish I could tell you all this in person, but I suppose this letter is better than nothing.

Mistress Ainya has assigned me to work on the mirror shield. I presume you know what that is and are perfectly accomplished at it. But I will practice. So far, my first attempts seemed to go well enough.

At any rate, I miss you a great deal. I hope the healing is going well, and quickly, so that you can come back to the mortal world as soon as possible.

I don't miss the Nightshade Lord, though you don't need to tell him that. It's good to be back in Raine, although without you here, the castle seems far too empty. Hurry home.

All my love.

Your sister, Rose

I FOLDED the paper and handed it to Thorne, who had been watching me write, a slight smile on his face.

"It's not sealed," I said, unnecessarily. "You can read it if you like."

"No need." He tucked it into his tunic pocket.

We stared at one another a moment, and then moved simultaneously into a fierce embrace. I tried not to cling to him, though I wanted nothing more than to hold him to me, forever.

But he was the guardian of the forest, and of Neeve, and his responsibilities called.

Still, I could feel his heartbeat where his chest pressed against mine. For the moment, our pulses beat in unison, our breaths mingled as our lips met in a final, starry kiss.

"Hurry back," I murmured, as I made myself let him go.

"I will." He regarded me solemnly, the flecks of light in his eyes as bright as polished gold. "Stay safe, *melethel*. My love."

I nodded, my throat thick with sorrow, with yearning.

He stared at me a moment longer, then turned and went out the door, quickly, as though otherwise he would be unable to leave.

I took three ragged breaths and squeezed my eyes shut on my tears.

You'll see him again soon, I told myself. A week, perhaps a little longer.

Then why did it feel like we were parting forever?

CHAPTER 40

T hat night after dinner, the king gave me back the little red recipe book, which he'd been keeping in his study. Along with the book, I received a very stern warning to do no harm to Castle Raine or its inhabitants.

I promised I'd only practice my sorcerous powers at Mistress Ainya's cottage, with her supervision, and that seemed to satisfy Lord Raine. It was an easy vow to make—nobody, myself included, wanted to see me accidentally burn the castle down.

The next morning, Miss Groves welcomed me with a quick embrace when I came into the classroom.

"Well, Rose," she said, once I was seated at my customary spot at the long table. "I suppose, since it's just you, we can study whatever you like."

I was all too aware of the empty places on my right and left where Neeve and Kian ought to be. With a pang, I realized we'd never all sit in that room together again. Their formal schooling was at an end, and I didn't imagine mine would last all that much longer. After all, the world outside the classroom held lessons aplenty.

"Could we start a bit later in the mornings?" I asked. "Since it's just the two of us."

I'd always hated leaving the warm cocoon of my bed to head through the castle's chilly corridors in time for breakfast in the classroom. It wasn't quite so bad in the summer, but when winter set in, it would be a struggle. Even more so without Neeve coming to collect me every morning.

Miss Groves cocked her head, the light slanting across her spectacles, and gave me a thoughtful look.

"I suppose we may delay by an hour," she said. "Especially if you'd like to wait until after your morning meal."

I smiled at her. "That would be grand. Thank you."

I'd have time to wake up, cuddle with Trisk, and have a relaxed breakfast in my rooms. Not to mention that changing the schedule would help mask the hollowness I felt at being the sole student.

As for the deep longing for Thorne that edged my every breath, there was no remedy.

"What would you like our first topic to be?" Miss Groves asked.

I set my fingers to my mouth, thinking. "Not mathematics."

Amusement shone in her gray eyes. "I guessed as much."

"You don't have any textbooks about sorcery, do you?" I asked hopefully.

"If such things exist, they are locked away. Most likely in Parnese."

"What about the religion of the Twin Gods?" I thought of the red book on the table beside my bed. "Perhaps we could study that."

She raised her brows, but didn't argue. "I can find something on the topic, certainly. Meanwhile, I'd like to hear your account of what happened in Elfhame. There are rumors aplenty, but those are no substitute for firsthand accounts."

So I told her the tale, from arriving in the Erynvorn to the moment I almost married the Nightshade Lord. The morning passed companionably, and a servant brought up lunch. Miss Groves joined me in the simple meal of cheese, bread, and apples. We parted ways feeling a bit more like friends than teacher and student—at least to my mind.

Since I wasn't expected at Mistress Ainya's that afternoon, I reluctantly decided to don my training clothes and present myself to Sir Durum. I could hide in my rooms and shirk my weapons practice, but eventually the dour captain of the guard would roust me out—and he would be a harder taskmaster because of it.

Trisk watched me change into my trousers and jerkin, blinking sleepily from the blanket she'd claimed at the bottom of my bed.

"Don't you want to come with me?" I asked her. "Maybe there's some mice you can chase."

She yawned in disdain and closed her eyes. I envied her. The life of a cat seemed a pleasant one, and not for the first time I wished I was a feline instead of a human girl. With a sigh, I tied back my hair and headed for the sawdust-floored arena.

It was empty, sunbeams slanting through the dusty air, but just outside I heard the cries and grunts of soldiers drilling. I went to the outer door and saw Sir Durum in the courtyard, overseeing a dozen of the castle guard as they practiced their blade work. Ever the alert warrior, he noticed me right away and, after a quick word with his second, strode over to where I stood.

"Didn't know you'd be ready to train again so soon," he said gruffly, though I thought I saw a glint of approval in his eyes.

"I am." Not really, but I was there, wasn't I?

Perhaps, if I drove myself hard enough, I'd forget my missing companions for a time. It was worth trying, at any rate.

Sir Durum led me back into the arena, and to my customary target dummy. After a few warmups, I took my stance and lunged. To my surprise, I was able to drive my knife cleanly through the target's heart on the first try. The arms master squinted at the knife handle protruding from the straw, then to me, and back again to the knife.

"Hmph," he said, removing the blade and handing it to me. "Try again."

I did, with the same result, three more times in a row. It was as though *finally* my body understood what I was asking of it. My hesitation and clumsiness were gone, and only a trace of unsteadiness remained, probably because my muscles weren't yet accustomed to the exercise.

"I always could throw true," I said, somewhat perplexed. "I suppose the rest was a matter of time."

The arms master drilled me in different strikes, and each time I succeeded far more often than I failed. Finally, when my limbs were trembling with effort and sweat plastered my hair to my forehead, he called a halt.

"Tomorrow we'll try you on swords again," he said. "See if this newfound ability extends beyond knife work."

"I'm going to study with Mistress Ainya tomorrow," I told him.

"Then the day after. You're dismissed."

I sheathed my blade, nodded to him, and gratefully took my leave. But though my body was weary, my mind was racing. How had I suddenly gained such proficiency? Could it have anything to do with the sudden unleashing of my sorcerous powers? Perhaps Mistress Ainya could tell me, for I certainly had no other explanation.

❦

THAT EVENING, dinner was a quiet affair. I was seated beside Mama, with Sir Durum across from her at the king's left hand. No other members of the king's council joined us that evening, and the absence of Neeve, Kian, and even Jarl Eiric made the table feel extremely long and empty.

Partway through the meal, there was a commotion at the door. After a moment, the guards admitted a weary-looking woman in a black cloak, her thick brown hair pulled back from nondescript features.

"Forgive the intrusion, your majesty," she said, bowing to the king. "I bring urgent news."

Lord Raine frowned, but beckoned her forward. "Report, Cally."

"Who is she?" I whispered to my mother as the woman approached.

"One of the king's spies recently sent to Parnese, I believe," Mama answered, a tightness about her eyes.

Ah. Of course Lord Raine would have put an intelligence network in place, especially given the rise of the red priests to power, though I'd known nothing of it until that moment. I had no doubt Neeve was well informed, however—as she should be.

"The red priests are coming to Raine," the woman said without preamble.

Beside me, Mama stiffened and drew in a quick breath.

"Attacking us?" Sir Durum stood, his chair scraping over the stone floor. "Summon the Fiorlanders back. Cally, did you see our allies leaving Portknowe?"

"Their ships were gone when I arrived," she answered. "But it is not war, Captain. Only one small vessel is coming from Parnese. I sailed out as soon as I was sure, to bring you word—but they will not be too far behind me."

"Sit," the king said to Sir Durum, though his gaze remained intent upon his informant. "What is it about this single ship that caused you to race to inform us?"

The woman inhaled, nostrils flaring. "It bears the leader of the Twin Gods' red priests. Warder Galtus Celcio."

My mother flinched at the name. Fear tightened my muscles, wrapped about my lungs. Galtus Celcio. The man who had burned Ser Pietro to a cinder, and who'd summoned a fireball to incinerate us as we fled Parnese. I'd naïvely thought we'd escaped the reach of the red priests.

But now they were coming here.

"How soon until they arrive?" the king asked.

"Three days. Perhaps four, if the wind blows against them."

Mama let out a little moan, then turned to her husband. "You must not let them land. Turn them away at the harbor."

"Unwise, your majesty," the spy said. "From all accounts, the warder can summon fire and fling it some distance. We don't want to risk them burning down Portknowe."

Summon fire. Her words resonated through me. Though I feared the red priests, they were adept at the sorcery I now possessed.

"This is because of me." I forced the words out. It couldn't be a coincidence that I'd manifested my powers, and less than a week later the red priests were on their way.

Lord Raine shot me a glance. "Possibly. We will see what they have to say when they arrive."

"Not here, my lord," Sir Durum said gruffly.

"No." The king's expression was hard as granite. "It would be unwise to let them come to the castle. We'll meet them in Portknowe."

"And if the warder manages to kill you?" Mama asked, her voice trembling. "Then what becomes of Raine?"

"Then Neeve will rule," he said implacably. "But since my heir will not be with us in Portknowe, the priests wouldn't do anything so foolish. At least not until they are certain they could control the throne completely—which includes making sure Neeve is under their power."

Or dead. He didn't say the words, but I saw them in his face, and shuddered.

At least my sister was safely out of reach in Elfhame, though whether she could return to take the throne eventually was another matter.

"We'll bring half the castle guard to Portknowe," Sir Durum said. "And I'll send word to the Meriton garrison to meet us."

None of us mentioned our other allies, the Dark Elves. If the castle came under attack from the red priests, however, I'd no doubt they would come to our defense. Was there any way to get word to Thorne about this dire new development? Surely there was some method of communicating between the worlds—though I feared it might be in the hands of the Oracles.

But surely the king would do his best to alert the *Galadhir*. Or perhaps the forest itself could speak to him via some kind of leafy communication between the Darkwood and the Erynvorn.

"The day after tomorrow, we will travel to Portknowe and make ready to meet with Galtus Celcio," the king declared. "Cally, thank you for your warning."

The spy bowed again, then departed, though I'd no doubt she would meet later that evening with the king and Sir Durum.

"Rose." Lord Raine looked at me, his eyes hard. "You will accompany us."

Me? I swallowed, my throat dry with panic, wishing I could protest. But though I might defy him in my choice of whom I'd marry, I could not say no to this. If I tried, he would drag me along unwillingly—I saw as much in his expression.

"Yes, your majesty." I bowed my head.

"No," my mother said softly. "Please, let her stay with me."

"She *will* be with you," he said. "Both of you are coming with me to Portknowe."

Mama paled, and I thought she might swoon across the table then and there, but after a moment, she pulled in a ragged breath, clawing back a semblance of composure. Despite her obvious reluctance, she didn't argue any further. At least not publicly.

As for myself, my appetite was completely gone. I pushed my plate aside and waited numbly for the meal to end, while my thoughts chased themselves around and around in my head.

Two days and we'd be in Portknowe. Thorne wouldn't return before then—and even if he did, surely he could not show himself to the red priests. Who knew whether they'd be able to sense his magic? It was a risk that Raine—and Elfhame—could not take.

Suddenly, I only had one more session with Mistress Ainya before coming into contact with the fearsome Galtus Celcio. I desperately hoped that last lesson would be enough to help harness and hide my sorcery. Clenching my hands, I vowed to stay up all night practicing the mirror shield.

Two days.

Everything was about to change, the world tipping, the stars overhead whirling into new patterns. I felt it, like the flames in my blood, like the unyielding proclamations of the Oracles. Fate had me by the wrist and was hauling me forward into a future I couldn't imagine.

This time I had no reserved stepsister at my side, no heroic prince to champion me, no dark-eyed elf to catch me when I fell.

Whatever came next, I must face it as bravely as possible.

And I must face it alone.

~ * ~

ACKNOWLEDGMENTS

I've always been inspired by fairytales and folklore, and want to acknowledge all the early collectors of such things, especially Andrew Lang and Katharine Briggs. But no tale is complete without a reader to bring their own experience to the pages, so thank you to all my readers! You are much appreciated.

Particular thanks to my early readers on this book: Laurie, Cathie, Kimberly, and especially to keen-eyed Nic. Your feedback is, as always, incredibly helpful and keeps me out of all kinds of authorial trouble. Thank you.

A sweeping bow to the copy editing of Arran - ever dependable - and Ginger the typo-catcher extraordinaire.

Finally, I'd like to acknowledge the work of Leonard and the wonderful folks who compiled Parf Edhellen, a free online dictionary of Tolkien's languages. The Dark Elf language is deeply inspired by Sindarin, with many thanks to this excellent resource. www.elfdict.com

ABOUT THE AUTHOR

-USA Today bestselling, award-winning author of fantasy-flavored
fiction -

Growing up on fairy tales and computer games, Anthea Sharp has
melded the two in her award-winning, bestselling Feyland series, which
has sold over 150k copies worldwide.

In addition to the fae fantasy/cyberpunk mashup of Feyland, she
also writes Victorian Spacepunk, and fantasy romance featuring Dark
Elves. Her books have won awards and topped bestseller lists, and
garnered over 1.2 million reads at Wattpad. Her short fiction has
appeared in Fiction River, DAW anthologies, The Future Chronicles,
and Beyond The Stars: At Galaxy's edge, as well as many other publi-
cations.

Anthea lives in Southern California, where she writes, hangs out in
virtual worlds, plays the fiddle with her Celtic band Fiddlehead, and
spends time with her small-but-good family.

Contact her at antheasharp@hotmail.com or visit her website –
www.antheasharp.com where you can sign up for her newsletter, Sharp
Tales, and be among the first to hear about new releases and reader
perks.

Anthea also writes historical romance under the pen name Anthea
Lawson. Find out about her acclaimed Victorian romantic adventure
novels at www.anthealawson.com.

OTHER WORKS

~ THE DARKWOOD TRILOGY ~

WHITE AS FROST

BLACK AS NIGHT

RED AS FLAME

~ THE FEYLAND SERIES ~

What if a high-tech game was a gateway to the treacherous Realm of Faerie?

THE FIRST ADVENTURE - Book 0 (prequel)

THE DARK REALM – Book 1

THE BRIGHT COURT – Book 2

THE TWILIGHT KINGDOM – Book 3

FAERIE SWAP - Book 3.5

TRINKET (short story)

SPARK - Book 4

BREA'S TALE - Book 4.5

ROYAL - Book 5

MARNY - Book 6

CHRONICLE WORLDS: FEYLAND

FEYLAND TALES: Volume 1

~ THE DARKWOOD CHRONICLES ~

Deep in the Darkwood, a magical doorway leads to the enchanted and dangerous land of the Dark Elves-

ELFHAME

HAWTHORNE

RAINE

HEART of the FOREST (A Novella)

~ VICTORIA ETERNAL ~

Steampunk meets Space Opera in a British Galactic Empire that never was...

PASSAGE OUT

STAR COMPASS

STARS & STEAM

COMETS & CORSETS

~ SHORT STORY COLLECTIONS ~

TALES OF FEYLAND & FAERIE

TALES OF MUSIC & MAGIC

THE FAERIE GIRL & OTHER TALES

THE PERFECT PERFUME & OTHER TALES

COFFEE & CHANGE

MERMAID SONG

CPSIA information can be obtained
at www.ICGtesting.com
Printed in the USA
LVHW111709240821
695997LV00011B/206/J